Rory's Proposal

A romantic comedy by
Lynda Renham

IT HAD TO BE *You*

A romantic COMEDY by

Lynda Renham

Coconuts and **WONDERBRAS**

a romantic comedy adventure

Lynda Renham

The Dog's *Bollocks*

a romantic comedy

by
Lynda
Renham

Rory's Proposal

a romantic comedy by

Lynda Renham

Pink Wellies and FLAT CAPS

Lynda Renham

LYNDA RENHAM

Croissants
and Jam

About the Author

Lynda lives in Oxford, UK. She has appeared on BBC radio discussion programmes and is a prolific blogger, Twitter and Facebook contributor. She is author of the best-selling romantic comedy novels including *Croissants and Jam*, *Coconuts and Wonderbras, Confessions of a Chocoholic, Pink Wellies and Flat Caps, It Had To be You* and *The Dog's Bollocks*.

Lynda Renham

The right of Lynda Renham to be identified as the author of the work has been asserted by her in accordance with the Copyright, Designs and Patents Act 1988.

ISBN 978-0-9927874-4-8

first edition

Cover Illustration by Gracie Klumpp
www.gracieklumpp.com

Printed for Raucous Publishing in Great Britain by
SRP (Exeter)

Copyright © Raucous Publishing 2014
www.raucouspublishing.co.uk

Chapter One

Don't you just hate exercise? Well, maybe you don't, you're probably one of those women who run 10k before breakfast and do three Zumba classes a week. Good for you. I'm one of those women who think scooting around Tesco Express is exercise. After all, I'm usually panting by the time I've lugged the bags up the stairs to our flat, so I figure that is exercise enough. Unfortunately, my boyfriend Luke, who is a keep-fit fanatic, disagrees and thanks to him I have spent the past two years trying to get fit. Don't get me wrong I've nothing against getting fit, as long as someone else is doing it. In fact, I met Luke at this very sports centre. It was his physique, good looks and charm that won me over. Of course then, he only worked out once a week and was still a carnivore. As time has gone on his addiction to fitness has gone totally overboard and he isn't happy with just himself being fit, he wants me to be too, which is easier said than done as I've something of an aversion to exercise. In the past two years I've gone through every fitness regime known to man and have, frankly, failed at all of them. The latest fad I've taken up is kettle bell classes. Now, as far as I'm concerned, the only thing a kettle should be used for is to make tea but here I am throwing it around for all I'm worth, and by the time the class is over I assure you I'm not worth much. Since starting kettle classes, *kettles* have taken on a whole new meaning. I can't even make a cup of coffee without thinking of hip thrusts and squats.

'Let's tone those glutes, butt and bootie ladies,' calls Martine, our instructor. 'That's it, get a good hip thrust going there.'

'Ooh thrusting away,' shouts Veronica from behind me, practically thrusting herself up my arse. Don't you hate women who go into exercise frenzy? Those pink cheeks always look far from healthy to me.

'Shouldn't you be on a heavier kettle by now?' she says between breaths.

'I want to get fit, not have a hernia,' I pant.

Mind you, at least a hernia would get me a break from hip thrusts and kettle chucking.

'You're fine with that weight,' says Devon, supportively.

'Keep going ladies. It's bikini weather in a few months. You want to show these toned bodies, no sarongs for my girls,' says Martine.

I quite like sarongs. In fact I would be quite happy to cover up the bulges and indulge in the chocolate. I wouldn't feel in the least ashamed.

'Get speed on your kettle bell Flora, come on thrust those hips.'

Yes, you heard her right, my name is *Flora*. I've never really forgiven Mum for that. If we'd lived in Surrey or St John's Wood it may have been decadent, but I was born in Islington and there aren't many Floras there I can assure you. The only *Flora* my friends knew was the margarine. They were not happy school days. Fortunately we moved to Chelsea when I was fourteen but even now I cannot look at margarine without shuddering. I much prefer to be called *Flo*.

'Now lock those knees and swing.'

'You're not swinging right,' says Veronica.

I'll swing for her in a minute if she doesn't shut up.

'And your knees aren't locked.'

She'll get hers kneecapped if she carries on like this.

'That's it, swing. Don't lose that kettle,' calls Martine.

Oh, what I wouldn't do to lose this bloody kettle, preferably in Veronica's direction.

'Don't forget to breathe.'

Now I forget a lot of things but breathing isn't one of them.

'I've got some news,' says Devon excitedly, swinging to the right as I swing to the left and almost colliding bells.

'You *are* swinging wrong,' says Martine.

'Sorry,' I pant.

'You'll never guess,' says Devon.

Oh please don't let it be what I think it is. Because if anything will make me forget to breathe, it's that. I don't believe it. Why does everyone have good news except me? I tell myself she's most likely been given a new Prada handbag by some grateful model and wants to know if I would like her old Marc Jacob. It will be nothing more than that, and I'm all poised to say *yes* as there is no way I could afford a designer handbag, and seeing as my Primark ten-pound one has seen better days the offer couldn't come at a more perfect time. Not to mention the fact that my exhaust is blowing something awful. Every time I start my little Clio I sound like a boy racer.

'Mark asked me to marry him last night.'

Oh no. She may as well have clouted me over the head with her kettle bell. In fact, it would have been better if she had. At least I wouldn't have to hear all the sickening details.

'What?' I gasp, feeling myself reel. 'What about the handbag?'

'Congratulations,' says Veronica. 'Welcome to the engaged club.'

I'll clout her over the head with the kettle bell in a minute and welcome her to the concussion club.

'What handbag?' Devon asks.

'Breathe Flora, don't forget to breathe.'

I would breathe if I could. I need chocolate, I so need chocolate. Bugger therapy, just give me a Crunchie bar and I'm sorted. I'm a closet chocoholic with a particular weakness for Crunchie bars. You'd be amazed at where I hide them. I have three in a Tampax box in the bathroom. I know Luke would never look in there. Apart from having sex, Luke considers a woman's vagina to be a mystery. Mind you, even during sex it seems to be a mystery to him as he has no idea what to do with it apart from the obvious, and even then he's so quick that even if I wanted to plan a shopping list there isn't time. I know, I shouldn't; eat chocolate that is, not plan a shopping list. I know I would be at least a stone lighter if I stopped my Crunchie eating but my life is one hurdle after another which can only be climbed with chocolate as fuel. My head spins and my breath comes in short sharp gasps. Mind you, this is how I normally am after thirty minutes of hip thrusting. God, I hate exercise. I only suffer it because Luke insists he can't be with an unfit woman, not that I am unfit as such. Chance would be a fine thing. *A woman who lets herself go is a weak woman*, is his favourite quote. Personally I think a woman who lets herself go is a happy, relaxed and contented woman.

'But how?' I say, between gasps.

'He just took my hand and slid this on my finger.' she says, pulling off her glove and flashing a huge solitaire in my face. 'It was so romantic.'

'Oh no,' I pant.

'Don't flag Flora,' says Martine, while swinging for sodding England.

I'm not flagging, I'm bloody dying. Oh God, I'm going to have a heart attack. I yank an inhaler from Devon's pocket and pump madly at it.

'What are you doing, you don't have asthma?' Devon says, worriedly.

'I do now,' I gasp.

'Are you okay Flora?' she asks anxiously.

No, I'm not and what's worse I'm not even getting a Marc Jacob handbag out of it. Let's face it, that would have lessened the pain a bit.

'Oh what a beautiful ring,' says Veronica gleefully. 'When is it going to be your turn?' she asks. 'You can't leave it much longer.'

I make a concerted effort to take a breath. If this is being fit then you can stuff it. I need an oxygen canister, not a sodding asthma inhaler. Why is it that everyone is getting engaged, married or pushing out babies, except me? I mean, Devon's only twenty-seven for God's sake. I'm hitting the big '0' in a few weeks. Don't think about it. Don't think about it. Oh God, how can I not think about it?

'Just breathe,' says Devon. 'Are you having a panic attack?'

Why does everyone keep telling me to breathe like I have no idea how to do it without instruction? I've been doing it for thirty years for goodness sake, no, correction: twenty-nine. I'm not thirty yet.

'Take a break Flora,' instructs Martine.

I pant and stumble to the seating area at the back with Devon following me. I don't believe it. Devon has only been going out with Mark for ten months. Luke and I introduced them to each other for heaven's sake. I stop, rest my hands on my knees and pant in shock. I've been with Luke for two years. I'll be thirty soon.

4

My ovaries will wither up and if I don't marry this year I'll have to pop out a baby every year just to catch up with everyone else. Why doesn't he ask me? What's wrong with me that I can't get a man to propose? I mean, two years, that's long enough isn't it?

'I was hoping you'd be my maid of honour,' Devon says.

This will be my third time as bridesmaid. Isn't there a saying three times a bridesmaid never a bride? This is unbelievable. I'm becoming everything except a wife. I'm to be Rosalind's birth partner. I've been practising the panting and everything, and at the rate I'm going that will be the only panting I do, apart from my faking orgasm pants. I know, one shouldn't fake it, but Luke is like streaked lightning. I've not even reached the thunder rumble stage by the time he's finished. I'm sure he is a wonderful lover. I'm just not very responsive. Don't get me wrong; I don't fake it every time. That would be awful. It's just that Luke is so nice and polite in bed as well as quick. Everyone tells me how lucky I am to have Luke for a boyfriend and I can't disagree. But it's very hard to get sexually excited by a man wearing Marks and Sparks pyjamas and who says things like 'fancy a cuddle?' when what he really means is 'fancy sex?' Not to mention his bedside ritual of cutting his toenails. Writhing in passion with the odd nail clipping sticking in your arse is not the greatest turn on. As you can imagine, all these things have had a detrimental effect on my libido. I did try to spice things up with a sexy film once but Luke was so horrified that you'd think I had suggested a foursome. In fact Luke is the only man I know who has tea and biscuits after sex, Rich Tea biscuits to be exact. I can't stand the things myself. But apart from that he's everything a woman could want. At least that's what my friends tell me. Good-looking, successful and enterprising, and most importantly he's dependable, smart and reliable. Sometimes I think we could be talking about a car. He's also a top golf player, not that I'm into golf, but he is good at everything he does, well, apart from sex. I really feel that could be improved upon. Sometimes I wonder if I'm good enough for him. After all, what is a good-looking successful solicitor doing with a simple hairdresser like me? No, don't think about it, don't think about it but how can I not think about it? The truth is my whole adult life I have dated nothing but total cock bags and now here I am with a man who is as far from a fuckwit as any man could be.

I pull a Crunchie from my bag and Devon gasps.

'Is that allowed? I thought you and Luke were doing that colonic clean out diet?'

Ah yes, well that was before the colonic clean out diet totally cleared me out. I've had to take shares in Windeze. I've been swallowing the things like no tomorrow. Three days in to the colonic clean out and I have more air in me than a hot air balloon. It's embarrassing. I'm glad I escaped the squat or the whole place would have been evacuated. I swear in the past three days I have popped out more air than I have in my entire life. I've used up most of my Womanity perfume covering the so-called colonic clean out. Of course, Luke doesn't release wind at all does he? He says it is rude. I often wonder where the hell it must go. If I held it in like him I'd explode. But he seriously doesn't do it, he really doesn't. I'm going out with superman, this is becoming very clear. It's also becoming very evident that I am far from being his superwoman.

Devon looks at me longingly. How can I not be her maid of honour? The truth is all I want is to be someone's bride, obviously not just anyone's; I prefer to be Luke's bride if that is at all possible and preferably before I'm thirty-one. I'm starting to feel that Luke doesn't think I'm good enough to be his wife. He's not said that of course but I sometimes think I'm not good enough for him. No that's not true; I'm *always* thinking I'm not good enough for him.

'Will you?' asks Devon, wiping the perspiration from her forehead. She pulls her blonde bob into a bun at the nape of her neck and looks at me pleadingly. I nod. Well, how can I not be Devon's maid of honour? Devon is my closest friend. We've known each other since college where she studied fashion and I did hairdressing. I always imagined she'd be my maid of honour first, not the other way around.

I blow a puff of air up to my sweaty fringe and say,

'I'd love to.'

'Oh great,' she cries gleefully, throwing her arms around me. 'I'm having the dress specially made. Well, I'm a buyer for a top fashion house so if I can't get a designer dress, no one can,' she laughs.

I'll probably end up with an off-the-peg dress from Pronuptia, that's if I ever buy a dress of course. Don't think about it, don't think about it but how can I not think about it? I don't work for a top fashion house. In fact, the closest I've come to a top fashion house is Devon. I'm a hairdresser. I have my own little hairdressing salon, it's not much but at least it is mine, well the mortgage is mine which is the same thing I suppose. I only wish I could get my own wiry mop into some kind of shape. It won't even stay in a bun like Devon's. I can feel bits of hair sticking to my neck. I'd love to be a natural blonde, but I am a brunette with a small snub nose and wide brown eyes. No matter how much I watch what I eat, not counting my Crunchies, of course, I always seem to be curvy. Mind you, I don't watch what I eat very often; I tend to leave that to Luke these days, whereas Devon has an enviable figure and lovely shiny hair. She does two kettle bell classes each week, which I suppose is why she got engaged and I didn't, not because she throws a kettle around, obviously, but because she is slim and appealing. Well, there has to be a reason doesn't there? How did I get to be thirty and unmarried? How did I get to be bloody thirty is what I want to know. What happened to my twenties?

My stomach gurgles and I hurriedly pop another Windeze as Martine calls,

'Rest over ladies, let's do squats.'

Just when you thought it couldn't get any worse.

Chapter Two

I climb into my little Clio and turn the key in the ignition. I can't believe Devon is engaged. When I tell Luke perhaps he will also get down on one knee, but I don't think Luke is ever going to pop the question. Don't think about it, don't think about it but how can I not think about it? This is my life. My mother wants grandchildren, more importantly so do I, children that is, not grandchildren, although I will want those eventually. Mind you at the rate I'm going I'll probably run out of time. I'm going to die a spinster. I push my foot on the accelerator and reverse back. The exhaust roars and all I need to complete the image of a boy racer is loud booming music and a persistent bass. Seconds later there is an almighty crunch. I watch as my bag slides off the passenger seat and I make a stupid attempt to rescue it. I look in my rear-view mirror to see a black Audi coupé car has reversed into me. Great, a posh plonker no doubt and it will be just my luck that the little bugger is driving the car without his parents' permission. The little bugger climbs from his car and walks towards me. His dark hair is expertly cut, and I should know. I can see he goes to a good class of hairdresser. His bright blue eyes are surveying my car. Close up I can see he is not merely good looking but breathtakingly so. I now vaguely remember seeing him once at the club playing tennis. Devon had commented on his good looks.

'Now there's a dish. He's everything a woman could ever want isn't he? Handsome, stinking rich and most certainly fit. You'd need to be a socialite to get off with him.'

Obviously, you just have to be a hairdresser to get banged by him, with his car, of course. He's clean-shaven, fresh-faced and very appealing, more than very appealing in fact. I bet he doesn't wear Marks and Spencer pyjamas, if he wears any at all that is. I feel myself come over all hot. That's what happens when you hit thirty, your hormones dance all over the place. That's my excuse anyway. The truth is it is most likely two years of crap sex. No, don't think about it, don't think about it but how can I not think about it? I'd like to think it's my overwhelming sexuality that tips Luke over the edge after just fifteen seconds but even I'm not that naïve. Perhaps I'll discuss it with him tonight over some wine, organic of course.

'You should try that Masters and Johnsons grip. You know, where you grip the shaft and squeeze,' Rosalind had suggested. 'Personally though, I think you should be grateful. Anything over five minutes and I feel I deserve a medal.'

Considering just stroking K-Y Jelly on his penis has been known to have Luke coming all over the sheets I didn't think giving it a squeeze was such a great idea.

I pull my mind back to the present. Best not to be thinking about sex when facing the dish that just banged me up the arse. I glimpse the squash racquet and sports bag in the Audi. At least I can be sure that he will have insurance. Thank God. I look at my car and see a brake light is smashed. Oh, that's just great. Now I've got a faulty exhaust and a broken brake light, if the police don't do me now they never will.

'You reversed into me,' he says calmly.

What? I know for a fact that he reversed into me. I'm not letting him get away with that. That's typical of posh rich plonkers isn't it? They don't want to pay for anything.

'I think it was you who reversed into me,' I protest.

'I was partway out when you suddenly revved up and reversed,' he says, his bright blue eyes dancing mischievously.

'I didn't rev up, I have a hole in my exhaust,' I say and immediately regret it.

His raises his eyebrows and looks into my eyes.

'You do,' he says with a smile.

How does he manage to make a hole in an exhaust sound so sexy? I blush.

'My boyfriend's a solicitor,' I say stupidly and then immediately wish I could take it back.

'I'm surprised he didn't advise you about the exhaust then.'

Damn. My legs turn to jelly and I lean on my Clio for support.

'Are you okay? You look a bit shaken up. Why don't we sit down with a hot drink and we can sort out the car details? There's a place around the corner, Georgie's, do you know it?'

'No, really I'll be fine,' I insist.

'It's the least I can do after *you* reversed into me,' he says with a wide smile. 'It's only around the corner, you'll be quite safe.'

I hate to say that being shaken up is more to do with missing breakfast, kettle bell swinging and Devon's sparkling solitaire than the accident. Two minutes later we are sitting in Georgie's and I am surveying him over a steaming mug of tea. He's warm and friendly and not in the least bit stuck up as I had imagined he might be. He's deliciously attractive and I'm finding it hard to take my eyes off him.

'Do you want something to eat?' he asks. 'It's lunchtime.'

Ooh, the temptation. The only place Luke and I go to is Healthy Juice. I really shouldn't be eating here, not on our regime. Christ, I sound like I've escaped from rehab. The smell of frying bacon seduces me; I can have a couple of rashers can't I? It's not like I'm going to have a massive coronary is it? I've just worked through a kettle bell session after all and if anything was going to give me a coronary it would have been that. Anyway I'd just be replacing the calories wouldn't I? We head to the counter.

'Next,' calls the assistant.

'What would you like?' asks Mr Audi.

'I'll have a bacon butty,' I say feeling somehow liberated, 'but without butter.'

'You want Flora instead?' asks the assistant.

Oh, very funny.

'No butter or Flora.'

'You want a bacon butty without butter or margarine?' the assistant says in amazement.

Honestly, anyone would think I was asking for a bacon butty without the bacon.

'I'll have mayonnaise,' I say.

'You want mayonnaise on your bacon?'

I'm paying aren't I? Well, hopefully Mr Audi is but you know what I mean.

'Yes, what's wrong with that?'

'It's your stomach,' he says flippantly, pulling on gloves like a surgeon. He snaps them over his wrists and scoops up the bacon rashers.

'Make that two,' says my companion, 'one with butter and not mayonnaise. I'll leave that combination to you,' he smiles at me.

'Bap, ciabatta, flat bread, pitta?' asks the assistant.

'Ciabatta,' I say.

'Large or small?'

Christ, it's worse than Subway, not that I've been to Subway recently of course. Luke wouldn't be seen dead in there. He says all fast-food restaurants are a coronary on a plate. Oh well, I'm not likely to come in here again am I?

'Large please.'

Well, might as well make the most of it. A kettle bell session, a car accident, and an engagement have all made me ravenous.

'Both?'

Mr Audi nods.

'With or without salad cream?'

Obviously I don't want salad cream if I'm having mayonnaise do I? Anyway, who has salad cream on bacon?

'I've got mayonnaise,' I point out.

'No salad cream on the bacon,' says Mr Audi.

'I have to ask,' snaps the assistant.

'Just the bacon and mayonnaise is fine,' I say.

'So you don't want salad?'

'Well yes, I thought that was automatic,' I say grabbing serviettes.

'Not unless I can read your mind, and I wouldn't be here if I could.'

'But no lettuce in my salad and I don't want the salad in the butty and a separate dressing please, I don't like it on the salad.'

'You want a salad without lettuce?' he asks his eyes widening.

'Yes, I don't like lettuce.'

Mr Audi smiles and says.

'I'll have it as it comes.'

I give him a sideway glance. Yes, I bet he has it as it comes. He's very good looking, even better looking than Luke. At a guess I'd say he is about thirty, and like me, no ring. I wonder if he's having a hard time getting engaged. With his handsome face and obvious wealth I would think not. We squeeze our way into a corner to wait for our order. At that moment the door behind him swings open and he pushes himself towards me so the person can come out. I feel the heat of his body against me and his hand brushes my hip. The feelings that run through me are so powerful that for a second I can't breathe. I'm jostled from behind and have to reach out with my hand to steady myself. It lands on his chest and I feel his heart beating through his shirt. Our eyes meet and lock and for a few seconds I completely forget where I am. I've never experienced feelings like these in my life. Our faces are so close and I find myself leaning towards him, or is he leaning towards me? I pull my eyes from him and squeeze past to sit on a chair.

'Not the best place for a loo,' I say shakily as the assistant calls our order. Mr Audi excuses himself and comes back carrying a tray.

'Two bacon butties, two salads, one without lettuce and dressing on the side, plus two mugs of tea,' he says, placing two plates on the table.

I stare at the food and feel my mouth water. No one would believe I was on the colonic clean out diet would they?

'Tuck in,' he says with a smile. 'You've been working out.'

I won't let on it was only a twenty-five minute session and that I've done more panting than exercising. He watches me over a mug of tea. If Luke could see me now he'd have a dozen canary fits, because of all the food I'm eating not because I'm with another man. We eat in silence until he says,

'Come here often?'

I lift my eyes to look at him and we both laugh.

'It seemed a sensible question when I asked it,' he laughs.

'No, I don't actually. I usually go to Healthy Juice after my class.'

He lifts his eyebrows.

'Seriously?'

I look at him and nod. He is breathtakingly handsome and much more laid back than Luke. He has beautiful eyes and very kissable lips.

'I'm supposed to be on the colonic clean out diet,' I say confidentially before stuffing the last of the bacon butty into my mouth.

'I can tell,' he smiles.

'My boyfriend is into health fads, well I am too. I just ...'

'Lapse sometimes?' he laughs.

I nod.

'I have a bit of a sweet tooth.'

A bit? That must be the understatement of the year. I've more stash hidden away in the flat than the great train robbers. I so wish I was wearing something nicer and that my hair was down. Not that I fancy him or anything but it would have been nice if he had seen me with some make-up on and my hair looking decent rather than all damp with sweat. I really should offer to pay for his car. God, more money I don't have and I daren't ask Luke. He'll only say I was irresponsible which I suppose is the truth. I should be more mindful.

'We should sort these cars out,' he says, reading my mind. 'I'm really sorry about that. I'd like to settle it with cash if that's okay. The excess on the insurance will be more than the damage.'

Before I can speak, he has pulled out his wallet and is counting out ten-pound notes.

'It's just the brake light a hundred should do it, if it's more you must let me know.'

'Oh no, I should be ...' I begin, but he pushes the money across the table.

'Don't worry about it. I'm Tom by the way,' he says, holding out his hand. I look at it for a second and then place mine in his feeling that powerful surge of emotion again as I do so. He has a South London accent, similar to Luke's but softer and more cultivated.

'Flo,' I say, 'and thanks for the lunch, and there is really no need to pay for the car ...'

'I want to,' he says, looking into my eyes.

I blush and see that he is still holding my hand. I look down and he takes his hand away.

'I'm sorry I've got to go. I've got a meeting. Look, if you should find any other problem with the car email me. Send it here, it will get lost in the system if you send it to the business address.'

I take the card and glance down at it.

Email me
tomry@gmail.com

He grabs his jacket.

'Do you have an umbrella?' he asks. 'It's tipping it down.'

'I'll be fine,' I say in my martyr voice.

'I'll walk you back to your car, we can share my umbrella.'

Before I know it, he has his arm around my waist and we are running in the rain. I look at his profile and find myself wondering what his girlfriend is like. He escorts me gentlemanly to my car.

'Don't forget to email if there is a problem,' he calls as I start the engine. An overwhelming urge for a Crunchie consumes me and that's when I remember. Shit, I'd booked a home delivery with Rory's online. Oh shit, I'm late. I just hope they are not on time.

Chapter Three

'Eight kilos?' I ask. 'What am I supposed to do with them? I don't own a bloody horse.'

'You ordered them,' says a sour-faced Tony. 'I only deliver.'

I am sure the order was per item. What am I supposed to do with eight kilos of carrots? Even eight single carrots would have been too much. This is a flat, not a soup kitchen. God, I wish I was more organised. I also wish I was slimmer and gorgeous, and richer. I'd probably be married by now. All my chances of being married and with children by the time I'm thirty come down to the fact that I lack everything that makes me appealing. I can't even order eight carrots. I'm absolute shit. We'll be living off carrot soup for the next year. Honestly, who orders eight carrots and ends up with eight kilos?

'And what is that?'

Tony folds his arms as I point to a miniature tin of sweetcorn. That's the problem, I was sure the tin was normal size from the picture on the web page and not the size of an eggcup. I don't suppose I accidentally ordered a crate of wine rather than one bottle, or two kilos of Crunchies instead of two bars. That would be a good mistake.

'You have two substitutions,' he says, making it sound like the FA Cup final at Wembley. 'They didn't have the Quorn spicy sausages so you've got these.'

He hands me a pack of Bernard Matthew's pork sausages. How are they a substitute for Quorn?

'But we don't eat meat,' I say.

At least Luke doesn't and I'm not supposed to.

'I don't make the rules,' he says. 'If you don't want them I can take them back.'

'I'm just saying it's a strange substitute isn't it? It's like giving me soap because you don't have cheese.'

He looks at me.

'I just deliver, I don't do the substitutions,' he says earnestly and I begin to wonder if he is reciting a script that Rory's make them learn by heart.

'Right,' I say, pulling the ring on a diet Coke can.

'And the nut roast they didn't have so they've replaced that with ...'

He fumbles through the bags.

'Don't tell me, leg of horse?' I say at an attempt of humour. He looks sour faced at me.

'I just deliver,' he says. 'They've given you half a duck.'

'That makes sense,' I say.

'I only deliver,' he says again. 'You've got fifty loyalty points.'

No doubt they were for the carrots. I close the door and dump the bags in the kitchen. I retrieve a Crunchie bar from the Tampax box and grab two bags of carrots before leaving for the salon.

You know when you think things couldn't get any worse. Well in my case it seems they can. I enter the salon which smells comfortingly of hairspray, shampoo and Sandy's lavender oil. Ryan is backcombing Mrs Michael's hair into a bouffant frenzy and stops at the sight of me.

'You look more harassed than usual,' he quips.

'Thanks for the compliment. I brought you these,' I say dropping the carrots into the small kitchenette out the back.

'You're so kind sweetie. What's tomorrow's treat, sawdust on the floor? I'm reporting you to the RSPCA for the way you treat your staff,' says Ryan, displaying another piercing.

'Oh God, not your lip,' I say.

'Do you like it?'

'It's gross.'

'Oh thank God you're back,' says Sandy, her bottom lip quivering. 'Tell her Ryan,' she says, urgently.

Now what? I pull my long dangling earrings from my bag and pop them in.

'Decapitation alert, she's got the earrings in,' cries Ryan.

'They're not that big,' I protest.

'All your earrings are lethal darling and if you're not almost decapitating us with those, you're whipping us in the face with your shawls.'

'She can't help being weird,' says Sandy.

Weird, what a cheek! If anyone is weird it is Sandy with her oils and odd herbal remedies.

'Are you going to tell her Ryan?'

'Tell me what? You haven't both gone and got bloody engaged have you?' I say irritably.

'What us?' says Ryan with a giggle. 'I wouldn't marry this mad bitch if you paid me. Besides I sit on the other side of the fence sweetie, remember?'

'It's the salon,' says Sandy.

We turn to look at her as she composes herself as if to make an announcement. As she is about to speak the dryer over Mrs Willis bleeps, making us jump

'You're cooked darling and the colour looks divine,' says Ryan.

'Oh lovely,' smiles Mrs Willis. 'Do you think Sandy could do my feet if there's time?' she asks.

It's a hair salon not a reflexology clinic.

'What about the salon?' I ask nervously. 'Is it those cracks in the wall? Did the man come?'

'Oh yes he came, but it isn't substance,' says Sandy.

'It's probably all these bloody oils of yours. If they give me a headache God knows what they're doing to the poor walls and it's *subsidence* you mad bitch,' corrects Ryan.

'So, do we have substance or don't we?' I ask Ryan.

'No we don't have *substance*. I imagine you'd be buggered to find anyone who does. It's subsidence, the word is subsidence, but it's not subsidence,' he retorts.

Is he going for the *Guinness Book of Records* for the number of times one can say subsidence?

'It's not subsidence then?' I say.

'It's not subsidence.'

'But we have a problem?'

'Yes, but not subsidence.'

'They're going to pull down the salon,' blurts out Sandy, bursting into tears.

'Oh dear,' says Mrs Willis. 'Does this mean she won't be able to do my feet?'

What does she mean pull down the salon? Who's going to pull down the salon?

'What?' I say, confused. 'But if it isn't substance.'

Ryan rolls his eyes in frustration.

'I mean subsidence, why do they want to pull it down? It's not like we have tree roots underneath. It's Notting Hill after all.'

'Rory's are building a supermarket and I hate them,' Sandy says before running out to the loo in tears.

'Can someone explain what's going on?' I ask, looking at Ryan. 'What has Rory's building a supermarket got to do with the salon?'

'Rory's have made an offer to Patel's next door, and they're selling. They want the salon too.'

I flop into one of the chairs and look at my reflection in the mirror. Is that what I look like? My hair is hanging in tendrils around my neck and my face is flushed from coming into the heat straight from the cold and I look so, so, oh God, so plain. What must Tom have thought of me? No wonder Luke doesn't want to marry me, I wouldn't want to marry me either.

'But what about Mr Patel's sister in Bangladesh?' I ask.

'Bangladesh, are you sure?' says Sandy returning with camomile tea, valerian tablets and half a pack of chocolate digestives.

'I thought you might need these,' she says, tearfully.

I look longingly at the digestives. Sod the colonic clean out. This is a crisis and in a crisis food is essential.

'I wouldn't have thought they would have had the money to come here from Bangladesh,' she says thoughtfully before swallowing two valerian tablets and washing them down with my camomile tea.

'Bangladesh, no way,' says Ryan. 'They're from Dubai aren't they?'

'Surely with a name like Patel they are from Pakistan,' says Mrs Michaels.

Oh for God's sake. I reach for the valerian and throw three down with the tea.

'I'm not sure you should take three,' says Sandy uncertainly, moving the bottle out of reach. 'You don't want to overdose.'

On valerian and camomile tea, is that even possible?

'Does it matter if they're from Clapham,' I say. 'The thing is he can't sell, otherwise how can he send money to his sister who lives wherever and is obviously starving and dependent on Mr Patel?'

This can't be happening. How can my lovely hair salon be under threat?

'He's been offered a job managing the post office in the new store in Holland Park, so he'll still be able to send her money,' says Sandy, biting into a biscuit.

'Are you sure about this?' I ask.

'We have good intel,' says Ryan nudging Mrs Willis. 'Don't we dear?'

I wish he'd stop watching those crime programmes.

'Yes love,' says Mrs Willis. 'Mr Patel told me yesterday and I've heard on the grapevine,' she lowers her voice although I'm not sure why as no one else is in the salon. 'Terence is selling the video shop too.'

'Well I for one will be glad to see that pervert go,' says Ryan, tossing his hair out of his eyes.

'Yes, it's a bit seedy in there, stuffy and gloomy if you know what I mean,' Mrs Willis finishes, like that is good enough reason to sell if anything was.

'But if Mr Patel sells and Terence sells, then I'm stuck in the middle which means ...'

'Sandwiched dear, you're sandwiched and most likely to be toast,' says Ryan, combing through Mrs Willis's hair. 'This colour is super divine. Mr Willis won't be able to keep it in his pants when he sees you, love.'

'Well, won't that be something new,' laughs Mrs Willis.

'Ryan,' I say firmly.

'I'll make tea,' says Sandy.

'Ooh lovely,' says Mrs Willis. 'Don't worry Flora we can all go to that new place in the market that's opening.'

I exhale and pop another digestive into my mouth. No loyalty here then.

'They haven't contacted me. I don't think it's going to happen,' I say resolutely.

'You had a letter,' says Ryan.

'Yes,' says Sandy miserably. 'Here it is. It has Rory's in big letters on the envelope.'

'Probably waiting until you were the sandwich, the little creeps,' snarls Ryan.

I take the letter gingerly.

'It's not got anthrax on it,' says Ryan. 'That one comes when you refuse.'

'I do wish you'd stop watching those programmes.'

I stare at the letter, terrified to open it. There is a tinkle as the door opens.

'Your perm has arrived, lovely. Don't you think you should perhaps change,' whispers Ryan.

Oh God, I'm still sitting in my tracksuit. I dash out the back and into the loo where my leggings and shirt are hanging on the back of the door. I sit on the loo and study the envelope. I seriously don't believe this, the salon is the only thing that I can call mine. I don't even own our flat; Luke bought it four years ago before we met. I buy the food, if you call the healthy crap we eat food, and he is happy with that. If only he would ask me to marry him. Don't think about it, don't think about it. I rip open the envelope and scan the words.

Dear Miss Robson

Rory's Supermarkets Ltd would like to make a generous offer for the purchase of your hairdressing salon. Your shop and the adjoining premises have been selected for the site of a new Rory's supermarket as part of our community development and expansion plan. Our purchase offer will include a substantial relocation package, should you require this, and we have already found a number of suitable locations for your salon in a popular area in the East End of London. We will send our representative to see you on Wednesday at 1pm to discuss your options. If this time is not convenient for you please let us know so we can re-arrange.

Regards
Grant Richards

East End of London, are they insane? Why would I want a salon in the East End of bloody London? It's sodding gangland there isn't it? Isn't that where the Krays started? I can just picture Ryan telling some mobster's moll that Frankie won't be able to keep it in his pants when he sees her new hair. Christ, he'll be beaten to a pulp. I can't possibly have a salon in the East End; I'm far too snobbish for a start. I love telling people my salon is off Portobello Road.

'Hello. Mrs Carter is waiting,' calls Ryan.

I grab a bundle of towels and throw the letter into my handbag.

'Can you wash her hair please Ryan?' I call back.

'I'm in the middle of Mrs Willis's colour. I've one pair of hands love; God gave me only one pair of everything.'

'Okay, give me a sec. Sandy make the clients tea please.'

'I already have.'

I sigh and pull my mobile from my bag and phone my mother and get the call waiting service that she insists on having.

'The person you are calling knows you are waiting.'

If she knows I am waiting why doesn't she answer? I redial only to get the thing again. Why is my mother always on the phone? More importantly, why is she always on the phone when I need her? I hang up and am about to go into the salon when my phone rings.

'I just did 1-4-7-1 dear, did you call me?'

Obviously.

'Is Dad there?' I say.

'He's gone. I did try to phone you earlier but I just got your voicemail.'

Gone, what does she mean Dad's gone? Does she mean Dad's gone as in … Oh my God, it really is one of those Boomtown Rats Mondays isn't it?

'What do you mean *gone*?' I say with my heart jumping into my mouth. He hasn't finally left her has he? 'He's okay isn't he?'

'Of course he's okay. He's gone to Birmingham for the golf festival. Is Luke going to the tournament in Dublin?'

'I think so,' I say absently.

'Perm waiting,' Ryan taps on the door. 'You do want to keep your clients, don't you love? The salon hasn't gone yet.'

'I'm coming, I'm coming,' I whisper.

'Not literally I hope darling.'

'Rory's Supermarkets want my salon. I'm going to need a solicitor,' I say into the phone.

'Oh really dear, let me tell Maud.'

'What does Maud know? She spends her whole life in some doddery old home. She never goes anywhere apart from her knitting group. I suppose they're the hive of all knowledge are they?' I say irritably.

'I'll just turn off the hands-free shall I?'

Shit.

'Luke's a solicitor,' she says, like I don't know.

'But he's not interested in the salon. Can you ask Dad to call me when he gets back? He's the best solicitor I know.'

'Okay dear. But I think they'll make a good offer. You may get a few surprises,' she says.

'What kind of surprises?' I ask suspiciously.

'I'd better go, Aunt Maud isn't safe on her own with knitting needles.'

I hang up, take two painkillers from my handbag and sigh. It can't get any worse can it? But then again in my case maybe it can.

Chapter Four

I push my way through the throng of people in the wine bar all enjoying an after work drink, and look for Devon. It's not a bar we frequent often and all the women look very young, or maybe I'm getting old. After all I'll be thirty in a few weeks. Don't think about it, don't think about it but how can I not think about it? I weave my way to the bar where I spot Devon nursing a white wine spritzer. She flashes a bright smile on seeing me.

'I don't believe it,' she says, kissing me on the cheek. 'Have you spoken to the people at Rory's and what does Luke say?'

I order a large white wine and sigh.

'He says it's probably a good thing,' I say, pulling Rory's letter from my handbag and handing it to her. 'That I don't make that much money from the salon anyway, but we only discussed it on the phone. Someone from Rory's is coming on Wednesday. I really don't believe this is happening.'

'What sly buggers,' she says scanning the letter. 'But ...' she ominously holds up a finger. 'Maybe this is the time.' She lifts a bag that sits by her feet.

'The time?' I ask, trying to avoid the eyes of a man who is winking at me from the other side of the bar.

'You know, to get engaged, and start planning your wedding.'

'Yes, well Luke has to propose doesn't he?' I say, popping some peanuts into my mouth while hearing Luke's voice echo in my head: *never eat peanuts while drinking it's the quickest way to get drunk.*

'I got you some things, they were in the sale. Tonight could be the night.'

'Sure could be doll if you play your cards right,' says a voice behind us.

'Pillock,' mumbles Devon flashing her engagement ring for all she's worth. I'd flash mine if I had one. Don't think about it, don't think about it but how can I not think about it? I look up to meet the eyes of the winking man and find myself hoping he doesn't *flash* anything sometime soon.

'Hey gorgeous, do you fancy a good time?' he says, smiling at me in what I presume is a sexy manner, shame about the body odour and the pimple on the chin though.

'Sorry but I don't date outside my own species,' I say sweetly.

'Nice one,' congratulates Devon.

'Bitch,' he mumbles before wandering off.

Devon pushes the bag towards me.

'Ann Summers,' she whispers.

'Oh God, you are joking. You are bloody joking aren't you? You know what a prude Luke is,' I say pushing it back.

She sighs.

'Don't you think it's time to inject something into your relationship?'

'Yes, like a high dose of Viagra. Is that in the bag? Frankly that's what he needs. A good shot in the bum.'

She gestures to the bartender.

'Jesus, the bartender has Viagra?' I gasp.

'No. I want another white wine spritzer you silly mare, and if you ask me it's a shot of chill out meds he needs. Have a look,' she says excitedly.

I open the bag and pull out a silky red basque that has holes for nipples.

'Isn't it gorgeous? And it pops open here at the crotch. And there's a flogger too. Mark and I have one ...'

'Too much information Devon,' I say fingering the flogger. 'I'm sure you and Mark have a fab time,' I say, trying not to sound too envious. 'But I really don't want to hear about it. Jealousy is a terrible thing.'

She laughs.

'Give it a go and let me know. Go home shave your legs, light a Jo Malone candle ...'

I wrinkle my nose.

'Okay, some tea lights, open some champagne, put on some Michael Bublé ...'

I pull a face.

'I thought I was supposed to be having a good time.'

'Okay, whatever music turns you both on. Lay there sexily. You know,' she says draping herself seductively across the seats in a demonstration. 'And give him the best sex of his life.'

'I actually think I do give him the best sex of his life. I wouldn't mind a bit of the best sex of *my* life,' I say doubtfully.

'But that's the time to get him to propose. At the height of his, you know ...'

I raise my eyebrows.

'I'll have to be quick,' I say.

'While you're lying there wantonly, hint about giving up the salon and how Luke is all you need. Big masterful Luke with his ...'

'Yes, I get the picture Devon.'

'What I'm saying is you don't have to wait until he ...'

'I never have to wait Devon.'

'Honestly, they'll say yes to anything in heightened moments of passion.'

I knock back my drink and consider Devon's idea.

'Okay,' I say thoughtfully. 'He is at the gym tonight, let's just hope he doesn't put his shoulder out again or I'll be spending the evening rubbing Biofreeze into his aching muscles.'

'I love it when Mark comes home all sweaty and ...'

'Yes right. Okay, tea lights, basque, flogger, and organic champagne if that even exists,' I say standing up.

'Good luck,' she winks.

I check my BlackBerry. Just enough time to pop to the off-licence. I kiss her on the cheek.

'Right, I'm off to have the best sex of my life.'

Somehow with Luke I don't see that being a reality.

♥♥

Back home following a short shopping trip and I have tea lights lighting a trail to the bedroom. I've showered, douched and lightly covered myself with Womanity lotion. The hairy legs had to stay unfortunately. There just wasn't time. I'm hoping Luke won't notice. It's only about a millimetre of hair anyway. Not that I measured it or anything but I don't think men really notice the length of the hair on your legs when they're about to have sex with you do they? Anyway, the lighting is so dim I'll be surprised if he even sees *me*. If I'm not careful he'll end up fucking the gigantic teddy bear on our bed. Luke won it at some stupid golf charity ball and seems to think I love it. Personally, I think two's company and three's a crowd. I've draped my silk robe over the basque, turned the duvet back and opened a bottle of sparkling wine and placed two glasses on the bedside cabinet. I chose some soft background music and now wait patiently for Luke to come home. I've hidden the flogger under the bed for when things hot up. When I hear the key in the lock I place myself in the sexual pose I had been practising.

'In the bedroom,' I call.

'What?' he replies. There is a crash followed by a groan.

'Shit. Have we had a power cut? Have you checked the trip switch?'

I fight back a sigh and lean against the bedroom door in my best Mae West imitation.

'Have you blown something?' he asks.

'Not yet,' I say seductively. 'But there's still time,' I add pouting.

He looks at me.

'Is it an anniversary? Have I forgotten something?' he asks, tripping over his gym bag as he stumbles towards me.

'Can't I be romantic without it having to be an anniversary?' I say sexily, leaning a bit too far forward, except I haven't got my contact lenses in and he catches me as I veer to the left. He kisses me softly and I part the robe revealing the basque. He breathes in sharply.

'Christ Flo, where did you get that?' he says huskily, his fingers gently playing with my nipples.

'You like it?' I ask, grabbing him before he has time to remove his jacket.

We stumble awkwardly and fall on the bed, narrowly missing the bedside cabinet. He pushes me down and shoves one hand under the basque and un-pops the button. I fumble to reach the flogger but he is already pulling at his trousers.

'Do you need the K-Y?' he whispers, trailing kisses down my neck.

'If we take just a bit longer,' I say softly. 'We may not need it. You can flog me if you like. You can be my master.'

I pull the flogger out from under the bed. He stares at it in horror. I feel my initial excitement flag.

'You want me to abuse you,' he states flatly, not taking his eyes off the flogger.

I open my mouth to speak but nothing comes out. *Yes* doesn't seem quite the right answer to that does it? I hadn't exactly envisioned panting, 'Oh abuse me master, abuse me,' as such. I was thinking more along the lines of 'Oh yes, master punish me, punish your naughty slave.'

Well, you get my drift don't you? I lower the flogger as somehow holding it up seems rather aggressive.

'Well no, not abuse me as such, obviously. Just spank me, you know ...'

It's just sounding worse isn't it? It's only an Ann Summers flogger for goodness sake, not a horsewhip.

'Abuse you?' he says flatly.

'Well ...'

I suppose if you put it like that.

'That Fifteen Shades of Grey has a lot to answer for,' he snaps.

'Fifty,' I correct.

'What?'

'It's *Fifty Shades of Grey*, and Mark and Devon do it?' I say defensively, feeling tears prick my eyelids. I only wanted to make it sexy.

'I don't care if he handcuffs her and they do it from their kitchen rafters.'

Ooh that sounds like fun.

'Anyway what they do isn't our business,' he says sharply, taking the flogger from my hand and stroking my arm.

'Besides we don't need sex toys do we?' he whispers.

Not much.

I put my arms around him and kiss his earlobes. He shudders and strokes my thighs.

'Let's have some wine,' I say. 'It's organic.'

'Not before sleeping,' he whispers, 'and you've already been drinking.'

He sure knows how to dry up my juices doesn't he?

'I'll make us some Redbush tea after,' he whispers.

I feel a K-Y Jelly moment coming on.

'I need the ...' I mumble.

'Okay, quickly,' he groans, 'I can't wait much longer.'

I fumble in the bedside cabinet, throwing out undies, bras, vibrator, batteries, Ralgex and socks until my hands fall on the blue tube. He sighs heavily.

'I wish you'd be more organised,' he mumbles.

I wish you'd be a bit slower I think, but don't say.

'I've got it.'

I squeeze some onto my hand and gently stroke it onto his penis. He groans and pushes me back.

'Christ that's cold,' he mumbles.

I wrap my arms around him and moan gently as I feel him begin to enter me and then suddenly he groans loudly and I feel his once nice firm erection quickly dissipate to a shrivelled sausage. Not already? We'll be in the *Guinness Book of Records* next.

'Jesus, for the love of God, what the hell did you put on my cock? It's sodding freezing.'

I fumble for my glasses and grab the tube. Oh no. I wince. How do I tell him I've just Biofreezed his cock? Well, it's not my fault the tubes are the same colour is it?

'Biofreeze,' I say. 'I put Biofreeze on your penis.'

Oh well, that was easy enough to say wasn't it?

'What, Jesus Christ, what were you trying to do, cauterise it?'

'I rather think it needs more than Biofreeze to do that,' I say irritably.

'Jesus Christ Flo, is this your way of getting at me because I wouldn't use that damn flogger?'

'I didn't do it on purpose. I thought it was K-Y Jelly.'

'I hate that you're blind as a bat,' he says hurtfully.

He jumps up and rushes to the bathroom, scattering tea lights as he goes. I feel my vagina tingle. It feels quite nice actually, still best not to mention using Biofreeze in the future. I blow out the candles and listen to Luke's groaning.

'Christ, hot water is making it even worse. I'll probably never have children now.'

That makes two of us then. I throw back the duvet and slide into bed, the cool sheets making me shiver. Luke finally returns from the bathroom, holding onto his penis as though it may drop off any minute.

'Sorry if I said some hurtful things,' he says, climbing in beside me. 'But it was a shock. It's not every day I get Biofreeze on my cock is it?'

'Perhaps you should have the tube on your side of the bed,' I say, refusing to take the blame.

'Perhaps you should be more responsible.'

'Are you saying it's my fault?'

'I'm in too much pain to argue,' he says. 'By the way, have you gained some weight?'

'What?'

'Your stomach looks bigger in that thing.'

I lift the duvet and study my stomach.

'I don't think so.'

I pull my stomach in and watch as my breasts push out.

'Luke, about the salon ...'

'Do you have some painkillers, I'm in agony.'

I lean into my bag and pass him a foil.

'Can we talk about that tomorrow, that's done me in,' he says swallowing the pills and turning off the lamp.

'Fine,' I say, turning over.

I turn off the bedside lamp and find myself thinking of Tom and wonder how he would have reacted if I'd stroked Biofreeze on his penis and have to throw off the duvet as I come over all hot. Ten minutes later and Luke is snoring. I sigh, so much for Devon's great idea. I creep out of bed and lock the bathroom door behind me. I quietly remove the Tampax box and sit on the loo eating a Crunchie bar. Honestly what am I doing? This isn't right is it? Seriously who sits on the loo eating a Crunchie that they've hidden in a Tampax box? Something's wrong. If only Luke wasn't so fanatical about healthy eating and exercise. More importantly, if only he wasn't so fanatical about *my* healthy eating and exercise. I fold the Crunchie wrapper and hide it in my dressing gown pocket and slide back into bed.

Chapter Five

'Devon and Mark got engaged,' I say, mixing water to a Nescafe sachet.

'What's that?' Luke asks, pointing at my mug.

'*Nescafe Three in One*,' I say, adding extra milk.

'That stuff is so bad Flora, I'm always telling you,' he says in that tone that makes me feel like a child.

'The decaf doesn't hit the spot first thing in the morning and anyway, I'm out of it,' I lie.

The truth is the decaf doesn't hit the spot at any time of the day.

'That proves you're addicted to caffeine,' he says, shaking his head.

Oh well it could be worse, I could be a crackhead couldn't I? He stares disapprovingly as I sprinkle a spoonful of sugar on my cornflakes.

'It's just cornflakes Luke,' I say.

'Sugar is so bad for you only last week I read in …'

'I'm not going to shoot up half a ton of sugar Luke. It's a teaspoon on my cornflakes.'

He sighs.

'Luke, I said Devon …'

'Why have we got a duck in the fridge? When did we start eating duck, and Bernard Matthew's sausages? I mean for Christ's sake Flo. How can you expect your body to function if you feed it crap?'

For God's sake.

'They were substitutes,' I say.

'Substitutes for what?'

'Quorn,' I say indifferently.

'Don't you know that meat and Quorn are two different things? If you want to eat meat just say so.'

I exhale. Luke can be so patronising.

'Rory's substituted them,' I say. 'It wasn't me.'

He sips his herbal tea.

'Luke, did you hear me, Devon and Mark have got engaged?'

'Yes, I know. Mark mentioned it. You know he felt pressured?'

I shake my head.

'He did?'

He waves a hand dismissively.

'It's not our business any more than their sex life is our business. I sometimes think Devon is a bad influence.'

I sip my coffee.

'How is your ...?'

He waves a hand.

'Fortunately it is okay. I'd prefer you didn't share this with Devon.'

'Of course not.'

'By the way, I'm going to Dublin next Friday.'

'I thought you would be. I was thinking I could come too; it's my birthday. We could celebrate in Dublin,' I say hopefully.

'You hate golf. You'll be bored to death. We can have a big celebration for your birthday when I get back. After all, you're not thirty every day,' he smiles.

I wish I wasn't going to be thirty any day.

'I've never been to Dublin,' I say. 'It would be romantic.'

'It's Dublin Flora, not Venice. It's also extravagant and besides, it's connected to a conference so the trip is on expenses,' he says, always the practical one. 'And you need to be at the salon don't you?'

'Do you have to go away? I really need a legal mind.'

'I don't see as there is anything you can do legally. Either you agree to sell or you don't. Personally I think you should get rid of that place, it's nothing but a headache. If you can't make a success of it in three years, you never will. You can be a hairdresser anywhere can't you? Personally I would prefer it if you got a proper job.'

'I have a proper job.'

'You know what I mean. A job where people can see you're a success.'

Is he trying to say I'm not a success?

'But I like having my own business.'

He grabs his briefcase.

'A shame you don't make much money from it, anyway I've got to get going. And what happened to your car? The brake light's broken, did you know? You should get that fixed; you don't want to get pulled up. It won't look very good for me if you do.'

He pops a vitamin pill into his mouth and reaches for the glass of water on the kitchen counter.

'No,' I yell.

I wince.

'Shit Flora, how many times do I have to tell you not to leave your contact lenses in the kitchen? Why don't you have them by the bed like everyone else?

'Sorry, it's just easier. Did you swallow them?'

That's all I need. He studies the contents of the glass.

'Fortunately not,' he says, handing it to me. I sigh with relief. 'But I really don't need this kind of drama in the mornings. You need to be more responsible.'

Drama? Christ, if the only drama in our lives is Luke drinking my contact lens and getting Biofreeze on his cock maybe we should get out more.

'So, what happened to your car?'

'Someone reversed into me. I'm taking it to the garage this morning.'

I pop in the contacts, relieved they have not been swallowed.

'You haven't forgotten we're going to the Jacksons' fundraiser on Friday have you? There will be some prospective clients there.'

Shit, I had forgotten. I really don't care for the Jacksons and their posh legal set. But, you never know, there may be someone there who can give me some advice about this Rory business.

'Clients for hairdressing?' I say.

'Legal work, silly. Can you meet me there at seven? I know it's usually your late night at the salon but it won't look good if I go alone.'

'But ...' I begin

'I'll go straight from work. Wear something nice won't you. Right I'm off. Take your vitamins, you look peaky.'

He kisses me hurriedly on the cheek, scoops up his briefcase and marches out of the door.

'You could get a cab to the Jacksons,' he calls. 'Better that way. We can both drink, unsociable not to.'

Ooh lovely, permission to drink, maybe it will be worth going after all.

Chapter Six

I climb into my car, start it up, sound like a boy racer and zoom off. My exhaust bangs so much it sounds like I have a pneumatic drill bolted to the back of the car. I pull up outside Lois's teashop. I've a craving for something sweet. Maybe Luke is right, I'm a sugar addict. He'll be booking me in for rehab at The Priory if I'm not careful. I hurry in and buy half a dozen cupcakes.

'For the staff,' I say.

'Yeah right,' she smiles.

A chocolate cake in the window catches my eye.

'I'll take that too,' I say.

'Someone fell off the wagon?'

I don't think I was ever really on it to fall off, but hey. I climb back into my car and drill my way into the garage to the amused stares of the mechanics, all who seem to be on their tea break. One swaggers towards me as I open the car door.

'Could hear you coming miles away,' he says.

Yes, right. After last night I don't think anyone is going to hear me coming for a while. Mind you, it would be awful if you could hear me *coming* from miles away.

'Got the handbrake on love,' he asks through my open window. 'Don't want it rolling away now do we?'

Over your patronising foot might not be a bad idea.

'It doesn't sound too healthy does it?' he says.

Yes, well if it was healthy it wouldn't be in the garage would it? After all, the whole thing is going to cost me an arm and leg no doubt and by the look on his face most likely a few other body parts too.

'Sounds like your rear end's blowing,' he says bluntly, walking to the back of my car.

He must have heard about my colonic clean out diet.

'Rear end?' I say.

'Yeah, or as we say in the trade, your exhaust is knackered. Did that sound like the rear end to you Dan?' he asks the other mechanic who is stuffing a doughnut into his mouth.

That's a bit worrying if he has to ask Dan for confirmation isn't it?

'Could be her back end,' he replies with a snigger. 'Won't know without a good look.'

Blimey doesn't he know either? Either my rear end has gone or it hasn't. Whichever way it goes a rear end sounds worrying doesn't it? Honestly why is it when you bring your car in for one thing they find a hundred other things to repair?

Don't you just hate car mechanics? He bends down to study the brake light and I swing my handbag onto my shoulder deliberately walloping his rear end.

'Do you know you've got a hole in your exhaust darling?' he asks with a wink.

'That's why I've booked it in. I've got a broken brake light and a faulty exhaust.'

'Lucky you haven't been done darling,' the other mechanic sniggers.

I'll do him in a minute. The mechanic studying my rear end stands up and says.

'You want servicing?'

Now there's an offer I can easily refuse. Greasy haired, dirty fingernailed mechanics in dirty blue overalls surprisingly enough aren't a sexual turn on for me, odd as that may seem.

'Just the brake light and exhaust please.'

'Your tyres are illegal,' he says without looking at them. 'We can do you reconditioned for half the normal price.'

'Are you absolutely sure they need changing?'

'Only needs a wet road,' he says ominously with a click of his fingers, 'and it's all over.'

I sigh. I'll need to take out a mortgage at this rate. As it is the car isn't worth much.

'Your other back light looks a bit dodgy, best to change them both.'

I look at the brake light which looks perfectly fine to me.

'Okay,' I say. 'Will it be ready later today?'

They look at each other for what seems an eternity. The workshop radio pipes in the background.

'Did we say today?' asks the one called Dan through white sugar-dusted lips.

'I never asked.'

'Oh well, if you never asked,' says Dan, like that clinches it.

'We've a lot on,' says my mechanic kicking my tyre.

Yes, I can see that. Maybe if they stopped stuffing their faces with doughnuts and actually worked on the cars, maybe, just maybe, my car would be ready by this afternoon.

'When will it be ready?'

They both look thoughtful.

'Well we can't guarantee but we'll try and get it ready by tomorrow for you,' says sugar-lips Dan in the manner of a superhero.

'Right, thank you,' I say.

'You want a courtesy car?'

At an exorbitant price, I don't think so. I pull the baker's bags from the car and hail a cab. Before entering the salon I drop into Mr Patel's. Mr Patel is serving a customer so I hover around the *Hello* magazine and stare enviously at the celebs' perfect figures.

'Hi Flora.'

I turn and hand him the chocolate cake.

'For the boys,' I say.

'That's nice of you,' he says cautiously.

'I came to erm ...' I grab the *Hello* magazine, 'to buy this for the salon.'

He nods.

'You know you don't have to sell to Rory's,' I blurt out.

He smiles.

'No it's fine. Don't feel bad about it. I will be fine. No more worry about cracks in the wall now.'

Oh well, if that's all it is.

'You don't have to worry about those, it isn't substance. I was worried about that too. I had a guy come and everything,' I say eagerly, seeing an opportunity to get him to change his mind.

He looks at me curiously.

'I don't know about your guy but Mr Grant Richards, very nice man from Rory's looked at the cracks and said he would send their own surveyor, no charge and he confirmed subsidence. I'm relieved to sell and they give me good job in the store in Holland Park.'

'They said the cracks were subsidence?' I say puzzled.

He nods.

'Nice people the Rory family.'

Nice people my arse. Well, I've made my mind up; I'm not going to sell. I've done some research on Rory's, and Mr Rory in particular. It's not been easy. He was harder to find than Saddam Hussein with his weapons of mass destruction and in the same category as far as I'm concerned. He certainly keeps everything close to his chest. John Rory started with a little market stall in 1964 and slowly grew his supermarket empire, shop by shop and town by town. He is probably aiming to take over the world. Well, this is how it starts right? After all, Hitler started small didn't he? A country here, a country there and then the whole world, I'm right aren't I? I detest the old man even though I've never met him, but you didn't have to meet Hitler to hate him did you? I take the *Hello* magazine and fumble in my purse for some money.

'On the house,' Mr Patel smiles, 'for the punters.'

I force a smile and make my way to the salon. Ryan is waiting outside.

'You're keen,' I say.

'I want to leave early, I've got a date with the most gorgeous man and I'll need plenty of time to get ready. I bought a new silk shirt, salmon pink, it's divine.'

'You're such a poof,' I say, unlocking the door. 'In my next life I'm going to come back as a gay man so I can eat whatever I like and not have to worry about getting married.'

'Yes darling, like that's all being gay means. You don't want to take into account queer bashing do you or the agonies of coming out to everyone and ...'

'Alright, keep your hair on. By the way the guy who came to look at the cracks wasn't a cowboy by any chance was he?'

'I wouldn't have thought so love. Mrs Willis recommended him. He's a retired cousin of hers, remember. That's why we got him cheap.'

'Rory's told Mr Patel he had substance.'

'Subsidence, it's subsidence.'

'Do you think he does?'

'What?'

'Have subsidence?'

'I don't know, but we certainly don't.'

I don't believe it. Rory's scared Mr Patel into selling. I wonder if I should go to the newspapers. But then Mr Patel seemed so happy about his new job. Oh, sod Rory's. They can't even get a bloody carrot order right. I turn on the lights and Ryan fills the kettle. I throw a Nescafe sachet at him and place the cakes on the table by our reception desk as a breathless Sandy walks in.

'I've been thinking,' she says.

'Christ, I'm surprised you didn't need to take a week off work,' quips Ryan.

'We could get the oldies prescriptions for them. Have them here for them to collect. It's much nearer than the doctor isn't it? Rory's don't offer that do they? It will strengthen our case. What do you think?' she looks at us both hopefully.

'She's a genius,' smiles Ryan.

'Play dirty with dirty,' I say feeling myself getting excited. 'It's a brilliant idea.'

'I'll pop to Heroes shall I? Cappuccinos all round to celebrate,' smiles Ryan

I throw him some money before dashing out the back to phone Devon.

'Well, are congratulations in order?' she asks excitedly.

'Sandy came up with a great plan.'

'Better than my flogger and basque?' she asks surprised.

'I mean about the salon.'

'Sod the salon; I'm talking about your love life. So … are you getting engaged?'

'No, I Biofreezed his cock. I mistook it for K-Y Jelly.'

There is a short silence.

'You did what?' she asks finally.

'It was an accident. But it rather threw a chill over everything to say the least.'

'God Flo, only you.'

She's quite right of course. Do you know anyone else who has Biofreezed their future fiancé's cock? I rest my case.

'What now?' I ask, hopefully.

'I'm afraid to suggest anything.'

I exhale.

'I might phone him. You know have a bit of phone sex. Warm him up for later.'

She chuckles.

'Good idea.'

'Oh, and I haven't told you okay? He was mortified about the flogger and he doesn't want you knowing about the Biofreeze.'

'Who am I going to tell?' she asks, fighting back a giggle.

'It's not funny,' I admonish.

'I'm just picturing Luke with Biofreeze on his whatsit.'

I hang up after making her promise that she wouldn't mention anything to Mark. I've just put the towels out when Chloe walks in for her eight-thirty appointment.

'I hear Rory's are buying you out?' she says before taking off her coat.

Oh great.

'Where did you hear that?' I ask, throwing a wrap around her.

'It's in the local paper. Everyone has seen it.'

How dare they? My God, these people are devious.

'Will you be doing hair at home?'

Hair at home? I can just see Luke agreeing to that. A flat full of chattering women with shampoo and hair dye all over the place is not his idea of heaven. He'll be telling me it's a health hazard.

'Creeps,' says Sandy her lip starting to quiver.

'Not today Sandy, have a cupcake,' I say, 'and you can do Chloe's nails if there is time.'

'I'm not selling,' I repeat.

'But you're sandwiched darling ... hello,' says Ryan. 'It might be good to be sandwiched but not in this case.'

'No, I'm not going to give in,' I say sipping from my cappuccino.

'But you have to,' says Chloe, almost gagging as Sandy ties the robe around her throat.

I don't have to do anything the way I see it. Not unless Mr Rory is also the Godfather and is making me an offer I can't refuse.

'I don't have to,' I reply.

'I think it's nice what they did for Terence in the video shop. When they found out his mum was poorly they offered to pay for her treatment, you know, private and everything.'

I don't bloody believe this. The way she talks you'd think Rory's was a sodding charity instead of a giant corporation bent on putting hard-working honest people out of business and destroying the community. Chloe leans her head back into the basin and Sandy stands over her menacingly with the shower head. For a second she hesitates with the water jet. Christ, she's not thinking of drowning her is she?

'My job is on the line,' says Sandy in a strangled voice.

'Yes they're putting people out of work,' I argue.

'I was hoping to put an offer in on the video shop,' sniffs Sandy. 'I thought I had a year to save. That's what Terence said wasn't it, that he would sell up in a year and then I could have had my own beauty salon right next door to the hairdressers.'

I hand her a tissue.

'At least I wouldn't have to get headaches from your awful oils and earache from frigging Enya,' moans Ryan. 'Talking of which, she isn't being very helpful today, is she darling? Some Black Eyed Peas, maybe?'

'Perhaps you should start a petition,' he suggests, changing the music.

'Good idea,' says Sandy, turning the shower head on full blast. I wince and discreetly make an exit. When I return a man is waiting by the reception desk and Sandy looks like she has seen a ghost. Chloe looks like a drowned rat and as for Ryan, well he is just swooning. Honestly, there is no controlling him.

'Hello,' I say pleasantly. 'Can I help?'

'Flora Robson?' he asks smiling.

I nod.

'Grant Richards, I represent Rory's Supermarkets.'

He may as well have said he represented terrorism. So this is Grant Richards, sender of surveyors.

'I'm not selling,' I say firmly, 'and no Nazi representative will make me change my mind.'

'You tell him darling,' says Ryan.

'That's right, we're not selling,' reiterates Sandy.

Hello, when did Sandy have a say? My cheeks are hot and I feel myself tremble. He smiles pleasantly at me, not in the least ruffled by my outburst. The doorbell dings and two of my regulars walk in.

'Hello Mrs Ceylon, how are you?' I say ignoring Grant Richards.

'I'm fine dear. I heard you were ...'

'Ryan is all ready for you,' I say, pulling her by the arm.

'Ready and willing,' laughs Ryan.

'Oh you're such a queen,' says Mrs Ceylon.

'I'm going to shag you today aren't I darling,' grins Ryan.

Grant Richards raises his eyebrows and I give him a sultry smile and am rewarded when I see him squirm in his seat.

'Not too much though,' says Mrs Ceylon. 'Too many layers and Mr Ceylon says I resemble an old dog. Just a nice shaggy look please.'

'Well, that could be a compliment, you never know sweetie,' laughs Ryan, propping a hand onto his hip.

I turn to Mr Richards.

'I really don't see the point in you staying because there is nothing for us to discuss. If you'll excuse me I have a client waiting,' I say.

He reaches into his briefcase and produces a small box.

'Before I go, I hope you will accept our little gift. We do realise that we are asking a lot of you. *Charlie Red,'* he smiles handing me the box. 'A little bird told us that you're a fan.'

Sandy gasps, I'm not sure if it is with pleasure or shock. I don't believe this; they're trying to bribe me with perfume. Who's the little bird, that's what I want to know? I'll clip their bloody wings before the day is out. It has to be my mother who has no idea what I like because if she did she would stop buying me that *Charlie Red* stuff, which I absolutely hate. I've had everything in Charlie-bloody-Red from talcum powder to body spray. Fortunately Sandy loves it so she has been the benefactor of all my mother's gifts. I'm about to tell him where to stick his *Charlie Red* when he lifts a hand to stop me.

'Oh,' he says as though it is an afterthought, 'I almost forgot the chocolates.'

Well that wasn't my mother. She would have told him to bring a crate of Crunchies. Honestly it's laughable, as though chocolates and perfume would make any difference.

'You got to my mother,' I say.

'It's not gangland New York,' mumbles Ryan.

'Let's just say a little bird ...'

'A little bird my arse,' I snap.

He smiles, and I have to admit he is attractive but I imagine Jack the Ripper was attractive when he smiled too.

'Chocolates, perfume, you'll be asking me out on a date next,' I say, trying to hide the scorn from my voice.

'If you're free for dinner,' he says in a heartbeat, 'we could discuss things in a more relaxed environment.'

Un-bloody-believable. I can see the charm and why everyone falls for it. Well not Flora Robson.

'I thought you weren't coming until one o'clock, or did you think taking me by surprise may mean I'm more likely to say *yes*?'

He scratches his nose and smiles.

'I can see you're busy. I can sit and wait until it's quieter.'

'Only if you want a Sweeney Todd mate,' says Ryan in his best macho voice.

'And how dare you print a story in the local paper saying you have bought the salon,' I say angrily. 'I'm not selling and you can tell Mr Rory that and you can also tell him that he can stick Charlie Red up his arse, along with the chocolates and anything else he wants to offer me. I can't be bought and I'm not easily intimidated.'

There is silence. All that can be heard is our breathing. This is probably the moment he locks the door and pulls out a gun and shoves the contract under my nose, assuring me that either my signature or my brains will be on it before the end of the day. I so wish I didn't have such a vivid imagination. I wonder if that is how they got Mr Patel. What if they threatened to deport him? His hand hovers on the back of the chair and we stare at each other. I don't move and neither does he, like a scene from a cheesy western. I almost expect him to say something along the lines of *this town ain't big enough for the both of us* but he zips up the case and sighs.

'Right, I'll get back to the office and report to Mr Rory. Is there any offer you would like us to consider?'

I shake my head.

'Nothing you would like me to pass on to Mr Rory, aside from sticking his gifts up his arse?' he smiles and I almost smile with him.

'No that's about it. I'm not for sale.'

'And neither is the salon,' he says with a wink.

Dirty sod.

'Let me know if you change your mind about dinner. Here's my card.'

I keep my hands by my side. Well you don't know do you. Just taking his card may make me guilty of something. Or I'll touch it and he'll make an excuse to give me another one. That way they'll have my prints and who knows what they'll do with them. Plant them at a murder scene no doubt and then, when I'm arrested they'll be there to get me out, for a price of course. I look at Ryan and he rushes forward.

'I'll relieve you shall I?'

'I beg your pardon?' says Grant, looking decidedly uncomfortable.

'Of the card love, don't worry; we don't offer extra services here but if you're interested I could give you my details ...'

'Ryan,' I snap. 'Just take the card.'

Grant quickly places it onto the reception desk.

'We're starting a petition,' says Ryan. 'Save our small businesses from Rory's.'

We are?

'Yes, and we're having a protest, isn't that right Flora?' adds Sandy, nodding enthusiastically. 'And we're going to have stickers for all the signatories.'

A protest and stickers? Where did that come from? Holy shit. I'm not so sure Luke would be happy if I did that. But then again it's not his salon is it?

'Right, I'll get the news to Mr Rory. Thank you for your time.'

'And you can tell Mr Rory that we hold the prescriptions here for the elderly, save them going to the doctor's surgery,' says Sandy. 'That's more than Rory's do.'

Ryan sucks in his breath.

'It's also more than we do at the moment,' he whispers into my ear. 'Peaked a bit too soon there didn't she?'

'The papers may like that story,' continues Sandy, who is now on a roll. Ryan gives her a gentle nudge and she grimaces.

I step in front of her.

'And don't pull the flowers thing on me either, just in case that was your next plan. It won't work. Mr Rory can bog off,' I add as he closes the door.

'Well done,' says Ryan.

'Shame about the Charlie Red,' mumbles Sandy.

'Shame about your mouth as well,' says Ryan.

'Still, we won the first round didn't we?' I say.

Chapter Seven

'Church Lane is becoming a bit of a ball ache,' says Grant pushing a folder across the table to Thomas Rory.

'I thought that Florence woman was happy to sell,' says Thomas as he flicks through the file.

'Flora, her name is Flora,' corrects Grant.

'Oh right, like the margarine. What do you mean *becoming a bit of a ball ache*? Has she died or something?'

'Not exactly,' says Grant hesitantly.

'What do you mean *not exactly*? Either she's dead or she's not.'

Thomas glances at the papers.

'Well no, she hasn't died exactly,' says Grant.

Thomas rolls his eyes.

'We are making a good offer after all. She's smack in the middle so obviously I made it worth her while. I didn't for one minute think she would be a problem but suddenly she's saying she's not selling.' says Grant, pouring himself a coffee.

Thomas Rory lifts his hands palms up.

'Just make her a bigger offer if that's what she wants. Right, what's next on the agenda? I want to ...'

'She's starting a petition,' says Grant.

Thomas smiles.

'What kind of petition?'

'Save our small businesses from Rory's. She's got stickers apparently.'

'Stickers? Now I feel very afraid.'

'She won't sell,' says Grant, sipping his coffee. 'She's out to make trouble.'

'A petition and stickers aren't exactly trouble.'

'Right,' says Grant, seeming unconvinced.

'Everyone has a price Grant. Just find out what hers is.'

'She isn't going to sign.'

'I pay you to get people to sign. Just make her a better offer. Ask her what she would be happy with and negotiate down from that. I'm sure Florence will sign eventually.'

'Flora,' corrects Grant.

'Flora,' says Thomas Rory. 'Right, I'm off unless there is anything else?'

'I've just been there. She basically told us to stick our offers where the sun doesn't shine and to tell Mr Rory that any offer of his can go back where it came from and be shoved up his arse.'

Thomas bites back a grin. He runs a hand through his hair and then rubs at his tired eyes. He feels ancient and wonders idly if he looks it. Beth comes in to collect the coffee cups and gives him an appraising smile. Oh well, maybe he doesn't look so bad after all. Beth moves closer to him and leans over him to fetch the cups.

'Are you finished Mr Rory or can I get you something else?'

'That's fine, we're finished, thank you Beth.'

He hands her a cup and his hand accidentally brushes hers. She blushes and he sighs inwardly. He doesn't have time for women. Not after Caroline. He'd rather focus on work.

'So she's playing hardball?' he says.

Grant nods.

'Yep, in a nutshell'

Thomas gives an impressed nod.

'Have you tried softening her up with the usual, chocolates and flowers?'

'Chocolates and perfume, and I was thinking of sending a bouquet until she said don't pull the flowers thing with me either. She's not budging.'

'Right, so let's clarify the situation here. Both shops either side we're in the process of purchasing, is that right?'

Grant nods.

'Florence was happy to sell but suddenly has changed her mind?'

Grant nods, his eyes focused on his coffee mug.

'Excellent, so just this salon which stands smack in the middle is the problem and Florence ...'

'Flora,' interrupts Grant.

'Yes, Flora is planning to stay even with the other two shops now owned by us? Is that it?'

'She's planning a protest. I don't think she will budge. I made an attempt to take her for dinner but she wasn't having it.'

Thomas raises his eyebrows.

'Putting that on expenses were you?' he laughs.

'Well ...' stammers Grant.

'No, it's fine if it gets the contract. If she *was* willing to sell then it's obviously about money.'

Thomas looks thoughtful for a second.

'Right,' he says with finality. 'If that's all, I have to go. I have a meeting with the town planners and I'll see Flora myself after that. Get me the biggest box of chocolates you can find and I'll see if I can make her an offer that I won't have to stick back up my arse. Any advice before I go?'

'She's a bit deceptive,' warns Grant. 'I wouldn't believe everything she says'.

'I think I can handle that,' Thomas smiles.

'Just one thing,' says Grant. 'I was thinking. Some of the elderly people have a long way to travel to get their prescriptions from the doctor's surgery. We could look into offering a home delivery service. Good publicity for us, giving someone a job on top of helping the aged, that kind of thing.

Thomas Rory pats him on the back.

'Serving the community, that's a great idea. I knew there was a reason I paid you an obscene salary. Look into that one. If we can announce that as soon as possible that would be great. Try and get it sorted before the Jacksons' charity event.'

He stands up and dons his jacket. He waves to Beth before leaving the office block. Grant watches his boss climb into his Audi. Good luck with Flora Robson, he thinks. Let's hope you have more success than I did.

Chapter Eight

I throw the towels into the washing machine and sigh.

'Will you be okay?' Sandy asks, her brow creasing.

'Of course I will. I'm not going to electrocute myself under the dryer if that's what you're thinking.'

'I hate Rory's,' she says with venom.

'I'm sure it will be fine,' I say, not feeling it will be fine at all. After all, they are a massive corporation while I'm just a little hairdresser. I've spent three years of my life trying to build up my business and Rory's think they can push me out. I wish I'd never shopped at Rory's. I can't believe I've given the sods my custom.

'The petition is great though isn't it?' Sandy says proudly, studying the names. 'We've got over thirty already, and that's just one afternoon.'

Ryan had drawn up the petition and a quick phone call to the printers around the corner had produced our stickers with the salon's logo and *Save Our Small Businesses from Rory's* printed on them. Sandy sticks one onto her handbag and admires it for a few moments.

'The prescription idea is a good one too isn't it?'

I nod and make a mental note to book a meeting with the surgery practice manager. The doorbell tinkles and Sandy's face lights up.

'That will be Jethro. I'll just get my coat and go to the loo,' she says.

My heart sinks at the thought of a conversation with Sandy's boyfriend, Jethro. How Sandy communicates with him is beyond me. Sign language would be easier. When I enter the salon I see him looking at the products on the display shelf.

'Hi Jethro, Sandy will be out in a sec, she's just getting her coat.'

He turns, his head cocooned in a bobbly hat.

'Hey, how you cats doing?'

Seeing as we don't have cats in the salon one has to presume he means us.

'Yes, we're fine. How about you?'

'Great chick, we're going to Marty's tonight; flip it up a bit, it should be dope.'

'Great,' I say, translating *flip it up a bit* to mean they are going to eat and listen to a band. I could be completely wrong of course. They could be going to Marty's to turn the joint over as in *flip it up* and then smoke some dope but I somehow think my interpretation is right.

'You okay? Sandy said you're all assed out.'

I'm assed out alright. The colonic clean out diet has nearly finished off my poor arse. If it wasn't for the Windeze I'd be totally assed out for sure. But somehow I don't think Jethro is talking about my gas problem, or the state of my arse.

'I'm sure it will all be okay,' I say, thinking of my wind problem and how I can't stay on Windeze forever.

'You want me to get someone to give these Rory cats a chin check?' He says, pulling out a chair. Oh no, please step away from the chair. I really could not stand more than five minutes of Jethro tonight.

'A chin check,' I repeat.

It sounds harmless enough when you say it but I'm sure it isn't. I sigh with relief as Sandy comes into the salon with her coat on.

'Hey Jeth, I'm ready.'

'I was just sayin' to Flo, she should give those Rory cats a chin check. Or I could get someone to come round with a banger.'

I'm so hoping he means a firework.

'No it's fine Jeth. But I'm sure Flora is grateful.'

'Oh yes, dead grateful thank you. But I don't think it has reached the banger stage yet.'

What am I saying? It sounds like I'm considering it.

'You wanna come with us to Marty's, flip it up a bit?' he asks.

'Oh no, I'm really not in the mood for flipping it,' I say.

'You sure, it's going to be dope.'

I shake my head.

'You getting afro products?' he asks.

'Yes, I have a feeling I may well be,' I say. Well, let's face it if I end up with a salon in the East End of London I most certainly will be. I've got to make a living after all and the thought of working for someone else now sends me into despair. I see them out and decide now is as good as time as any to phone Luke. I dial his direct line and he picks up immediately.

'Hello, Luke Wright's phone.'

'Hello gorgeous, how's that little cold cock of yours after its Biofreezing? I was thinking we could warm it up later. I could lather it in a nice hot bath and then give you the best shag of your life.'

There is an intake of breath. Maybe Devon is right and this is the right tactic.

'Well, that sounds great. And do you have a message for Luke? He's in a meeting at the moment, shall I get him to call you.'

Buggery fuck.

'Sorry wrong number,' I mumble before slamming the phone down. Shit, shit, and I mentioned the Biofreeze. I didn't mention Luke's name though did I? So hopefully they'll think it was an obscene caller. I suppose I was in a way. With a red face I blow out the candle under Sandy's oil burner and go to lock up when I see the basin is overflowing.

'Oh bugger,' I curse. Not again. This basin is always getting blocked. I quickly turn the water off at the stopcock and search for the mop and wrench. I struggle for five minutes trying to unblock the pipe and finally phone Tim the plumber, and get his voicemail. I go back and try again without success. I phone Tim a second time and leave a message before returning to the wrench and struggling with the pipe.

'Piss it, stupid wrench.'

I kick the wrench angrily. The knees of my leggings are completely soaked. My phone rings and I dive across the room, slipping on the wet as I do so and almost landing on my bottom.

'Christ,' I moan clicking on the phone. 'Hello, is that the plumber?'

'Miss Robson?'

'Yes,' I say breathlessly.

'It's Tim, the plumber. You left a message.'

I've left hundreds of messages over the past six months. This basin leaks on a fortnightly basis.

'Can you come?' I ask desperation in my voice.

'I've got no one available at this moment in time but I should have in about an hour or so,' he says. 'Is it the leaky basin again?'

'An hour or so, I'd have drowned by then,' I say dramatically. 'Don't you have anyone at all?'

'Not at this moment in time,' he says again, 'but I can send someone directly.'

I try to get my head around this.

'What moment in time do you think you will have someone?' I ask quizzically, 'and how directly will that be?'

Christ, I'm speaking his language and I don't even understand it.

'I'm sorry?'

I sigh. It seems he doesn't understand it either.

'Just send someone when you can please.'

I hang up and look at the basin, trying to give it my best menacing stare. I imagine the basin is turning into some kind of alien as it seems to hiss at me every time I get close. I turn when I hear the bell above the door tinkle and see him.

'Oh,' I say, wondering why Tom is standing in my salon.

I'm thrilled he is of course, but it does seem odd. He is staring at me like I'm the alien. He looks very smart in a white shirt, grey waistcoat, maroon tie and grey trousers. He must be on his way to somewhere posh. He looks good enough to eat, and smells fabulous. In the words of Jethro, he really is one *peng* man.

'*You're* Flora Robson,' he says in a disbelieving tone.

I'm not quite sure how to take that. I don't think my perms are that famous yet but you never know.

'Yes, the one and only infamous Flora Robson.'

He seems to quickly recover and smiles at me. My legs go weak and I lean my hand out to grasp the back of a chair.

'This is your salon?' he says looking around.

I nod.

'Right,' he says looking behind me. 'Looks like you've got a bit of a problem.'

A bit of a problem is, I rather think, an understatement considering I've got a mega corporation trying to take over my salon. He's holding an enormous box of chocolates. Heavens, I've never seen one that big before, box of chocolates that is. Even Grant Richards from Rory's didn't bring one that size. Just as well because they will go straight in the bin if he does. I won't be bribed by that Rory corporate piece of scum.

'Oh yes, the leak, the basin's blocked. It does this on and off. I need new pipes or new basins one or the other. It's just there is never enough time or more importantly, never enough money and ...'

Jesus, I'm rambling. I wander back into the salon, careful not to slip again. I don't want to fall arse over tit in front of him do I? I must look a sight. Why is it every time I see him I look like Dot Cotton? I fumble with my hair nervously and lower my eyes to the chocolates and hear myself say,

'They're big,' and could have died from embarrassment. 'I'm sorry, it's just I thought the chocolates that Rory's tried to bribe me with were big', I add. 'A bit of an insult to my intelligence really, thinking just because I am a woman I can be bribed with chocolate.'

He looks at the chocolates and then hands them to me.

'Yes, I nearly forgot. It's an apology ... for the car accident. You said you had a sweet tooth,' he smiles.

But I thought he said the accident was my fault. Surely I haven't pulled someone like him? No, that's impossible. He can't for one minute fancy me. I'm slightly overweight for a start. Not obese, but certainly overweight compared to the type of model girlfriend he must surely go out with. I'm not in the least glamorous and I'm rubbish with make-up. I always smudge mascara and end up chewing off lipstick in minutes. No, there must be more to this, but what? I feel my mouth water at the thought of the chocolates.

'Wow, thank you,' I say, taking the box.

I lift the lid and look inside. Belgian chocolates, ooh my favourites. I'm already thinking of where to stash them.

'Let me help with the blocked basin,' he says as he takes off his jacket.

I hand him the wrench.

'It's all I've got to offer I'm afraid,' I say apologetically.

He grins mischievously.

'Oh, I think you've got a lot more to offer. I'll get my toolbox from the car,' he says.

I feel my face grow hot and I swallow.

'Right,' I say. 'Just give me a shout when you're back. I need to get my leggings off ...'

Oh what am I saying? You see what I mean? That sounded awful didn't it? He'll think I'm anyone's for a box of chocolates. He looks at me.

'What I mean is ...'

He smiles and turns to the door. I dive into the loo and check my face in the mirror. I look flushed and wild. My hair is sticking up where I ran my hands through it. God, I look like a witch, and the smock makes me look like a mad artist. I pull the smock and leggings off and grab a spare pair. I tidy my top and splash my face with water and look despairingly at my hair before heading back to the salon. He has the pipes off when I reach him.

'Would you like a coffee or something else?'

Christ, what's wrong with me, what is the *something else*? He raises his eyebrows and as though reading my mind, says with a smile,

'What is the something else?'

I come over all hot at the thought.

'I have some lemonade in the fridge.'

'That sounds good, and one of those cupcakes would be nice.'

Cheeky bugger, he's lucky there are any left. I place the cupcake onto a plate.

'I'll put them on the counter here,' I shout over his banging.

'Great thanks. This is unblocked. Do you have a mop or something?'

I fetch the mop and bucket and hand them to him. He smiles and looks at the lemonade.

'Looks good,' he comments.

God, he is good looking.

'Do you want to try it?' he asks.

Try what? He's a bit pushy. He nods to the sink. He's got my head in a spin.

'Thank you so much, you're a good plumber.'

'Not really,' he smiles. 'Anyone can unblock a sink.'

'What do you do?'

He looks taken aback.

'I'm a director of a company. It's a family business.'

'Sounds grand,' I say.

'I heard somewhere that this parade of shops had been sold,' he says pulling out a chair and sitting down. I feel the hairs on the back of my neck bristle.

'No, we're not selling. Everyone else can, but not us. I'm having a rally to show Mr Rory that we won't be bought. Sodding Rory's can go and ...'

He raises his eyebrows.

'He wants to buy the salon to build a supermarket would you believe. Well, not while my name is Flora Robson. It's about time someone stopped these people. There are plenty of supermarkets. We don't need another one. I've started a petition. I can't believe they tried to bribe me with perfume and chocolates, talk about insulting my intelligence ...'

He glances at the chocolates on the counter.

'Oh no, it wasn't a nice gesture like yours,' I say quickly, not wanting to offend him. 'Mr Rory is a scumbag. He's putting local people out of business,' I add hotly. 'People like him are just money crazy.'

I stop when I realise he is smiling at me.

'I'm a bit passionate about my salon,' I say, blushing.

'Yes, I can tell, your eyes go a bit wild.'

Oh no, do they? Now he will think I'm totally nuts. He knocks back the last of his lemonade and stands up.

'Right, I'd better be getting off.'

'Oh Tom,' I say quickly, grabbing the petition from one of the tables. 'Would you sign the petition? Every name helps.'

He looks unsure for a second and then takes the pen and scribbles his name. I look down at it, trying to discern his name but it's barely legible.

'Thanks so much,' I say pushing a sticker on his shirt and liking the feel of his warm chest against my hand.

'There, now everyone will know you support us,' I say.

'Great,' he responds with a wry smile.

I look at the sticker with satisfaction.

'Thank you so much,' I say, aware my hand is still on his chest. 'I hope you'll come to our protest.'

He smiles.

'I'm pretty busy most days.'

'Well if you're free. I could let you know when we have a date.'

He has a lovely voice, crystal clear but soft. He looks thoughtful and then with a wink says,

'Do you fancy a hot chocolate?'

'A hot chocolate?' I repeat stupidly.

'Heroes, in Portobello Market. Do you know it?'

I nod.

'They do the best hot chocolate.'

I hesitate. Luke will be expecting me. He is my boyfriend after all. What's wrong with me? The guy's inviting me for hot chocolate, not a quickie in the back of his Audi. I'm not sure which is the most enticing. It's no good I've got to get this sex thing sorted with Luke or I'll be ripping the clothes off the nearest man and that could well be Ryan. Heavens, that really doesn't bear thinking about does it?

'You've probably got something else on,' he says.

'I thought you had something else on,' I say, appraising his suit.

'Oh this,' he says looking down at the waistcoat. 'I had a business meeting in town earlier.'

I bite my lip. Luke will be expecting me home. I don't suppose a few extra minutes will matter. I'm already late because of the leaky basin anyway and he did fix my blocked pipe, so to speak. It's the least I can to do to have a hot chocolate with him. Yes right Flora, like it's some kind of sacrifice.

'Won't ...' I say and hesitate, 'someone be expecting you?' I finish boldly.

He shakes his head.

'I suppose they would, if there was a someone.'

'I'd love a hot chocolate,' I say. 'I'll just get my jacket.'

I text Luke to say I'm running late. After all, he is always running late so it makes a change for it to be me for once. I grab my jacket and meet Tom by the door. It is chilly and I wrap my pashmina around my neck.

'We can take my car,' he says.

I attempt to get into the car as elegantly as I can. He climbs in beside me and starts the engine which I have to admit sounds much healthier than mine.

'It's a nice car,' I say.

'A car's a car,' he says with a shrug.

Oh really? He should have mine.

'How is yours?' he asks, reading my mind.

'Sick, very sick,' I laugh.

The car pulls away smoothly from the kerb. His hand brushes my knee as he changes gear. The multitude of emotions I am feeling just from his touch has practically knocked the breath out of me. A few minutes later he parks outside Heroes in a parking bay. I rummage in my over full handbag and produce a crumpled pass which I stick on the windscreen. My phone is flashing and I push it underneath my make-up bag.

'Great,' he says, climbing from the car. He opens the door before I have time to grasp the handle. He takes my hand and I feel that familiar jolt. It is warm in the coffee shop and I feel my face grow hot. Tom helps me out of my jacket and leads me to a table at the back. The smell of coffee and warm waffles seduces me. The milkshake blender drowns out the music from the juke box. I love Heroes but Luke refuses to come here, saying it is a heart attack waiting to happen. Tom looks up from the menu as the waitress approaches.

'Two Belgian hot chocolates,' he says.

'With cream and marshmallows?' asks the waitress. God, is she fluttering her eyelashes?

'Do you have soya milk?' I ask.

'Seriously?' says Tom. 'You'll be murdering it.'

He's quite right of course.

'Okay, can I have my marshmallows on the side and not on the cream?' I ask. 'And only the white ones please.'

Tom smiles.

'Sure. Anything else?' she asks.

I shake my head. She walks away and I look shyly at Tom. He looks so sexy in his shirt and tie.

'So, why aren't you selling to Rory's? I imagine they made you a good offer. It's a good location for a supermarket,' he says leaning back in his chair. 'What made you change your mind?'

What makes him think I changed my mind? Do I look the indecisive type?

'Because it's all I have,' I say simply. 'Luke, that's my boyfriend, is very successful and the salon is my success ...' I break off realising I have never shared this before, not even with Devon.

'Luke doesn't see it as a success. If I sell the salon I've proved him right and I would have failed at the one thing I can do,' I finish.

I'm relieved the hot chocolate arrives and I can hide my red face behind the mug. I pop a marshmallow into my mouth and savour it.

'What does he do, this Luke?'

'He's a solicitor,' I say proudly. 'He's very successful. He's going to Dublin next week for a golf tournament. He's playing, he's very good.'

'Ah, yes, I remember now. Maybe I'll see him in Dublin,' he says casually.

'You're going to Dublin too?' I say widening my eyes.

That's about right. I suppose Devon will say she and Mark are going to Dublin next. You know, to celebrate the engagement. I'll be the only one not going I suppose. Typical.

'My father is also in the tournament,' he smiles.

There is silence as we drink our chocolate.

'Owning your own business is being successful,' he says suddenly, looking up at me. 'You could make another salon just as successful, maybe even more so. I think they would help with the relocation'.

I scoff.

'Do you know where they're offering to relocate me? In the East End of London, I mean, can you imagine?' I say hotly, pushing loose strands of hair back into my messy bun. 'Besides it's ridiculous, that Rory guy is money mad. I hope he pops his clogs before he gets the salon.'

He widens his eyes.

'That's a bit harsh,' he says, his handsome face creasing into a grin.

'Well he's ancient apparently.'

'Right.'

'Jethro was all up to give Mr Rory a chin check or to go around with a banger.'

'That's an old car is it?' he laughs.

'I've no idea. I was too scared to ask. But I can understand he's upset for Sandy. She hoped to one day buy the video rental shop. Open a beauty salon. We were going to work together,' I say miserably, feeling for Sandy and knowing how it feels to have a dream.

He nods and gestures to the waitress.

'Do you have those wonderful Bakewell tarts?'

'We have just the one,' she smiles. 'I was saving it for you.'

'You're my girl,' he says winking at her. 'Would you like something?' he asks, turning to me.

I shake my head and stir the cream into my chocolate.

'It's not failing at all if you sell your salon. Is that what your boyfriend Luke tells you?'

'Luke's very supportive,' I say.

Yeah right, if only.

'We're going to fight,' I say.

'We shall fight on the beaches, we shall fight on the landing grounds,' he says, laughing.

'We shall fight in fields and in the streets,' I say.

'Inside and outside of the salon,' he adds.

'And along Portobello Road,' I say with a giggle.

'In front of the basins and under the dryers, we shall fight with combs and pliers.'

'Pliers?' I say.

'It rhymes,' he laughs.

I carefully put my mug down so as not to spill it. I find myself thinking how it has been a long time since I laughed with Luke. Don't think about it, don't think about it.

'Do you think I shouldn't fight?' I ask.

'It's a lot of energy, especially if they're offering another salon. Look Flo, I came to the ...'

He stops as the waitress approaches with his Bakewell tart.

'You want to share?' he asks.

Oh God, I really shouldn't, but then again I have lapsed so badly since hearing of Devon's engagement that I guess one more won't hurt.

'Get your energy up for your fight.'

'You're a bad influence,' I say.

He places half on my saucer.

'The thing is Flo ...' he begins.

My mobile trills and I give an apologetic look.

'It's probably Luke, wondering where I am.'

I pull it from my bag and answer the call.

'I had a flood at the salon, so I'm running late,' I tell Luke.

'Again? You need to get that fixed properly. I'm also running late. I'm on my way home now. I'll get two carrot and chickpea salads from Healthy Juice. I'll see you in a bit.'

Great, just what I fancied, *not*. I wait for him to say I love you but he doesn't. He never does unless I say it first. I'm not going to say it in front of Tom am I? I'd then need to say I love you too so Tom thinks Luke did say I love you but seeing as Luke never said I love you in the first place, it will seem odd saying I love you too, and then Luke is bound to think I'm being funny. My head is spinning. All I know is I really shouldn't be having hot chocolate with Tom.

'I have to go,' I say rummaging in my bag for my purse.

'How much was it?' I ask the waitress.

'No, it's on me. Flo, about Rory's ...'

'It's kind of you to advise me but I really have to go.'

He bites his lip.

'I was just going to say, why don't you tell them what you want, name your price, or ask for a salon in a nice area? I think, from what I've heard, Mr Rory is not so bad and ...'

I scoff.

'Even you believe the propaganda,' I say, fanning out my pashmina and wrapping it around my shoulders.

'I'm a business man Flo. Some things make good business sense.'

'Well it doesn't make good business sense for me to throw in the towel on the one thing I've started to make a success of. Luke won't want to marry a failure and I really want to marry Luke.'

'I can't think why, if he makes you feel so bad,' he says scathingly.

I stare at him.

'How dare you, you don't even know Luke. Thank you for the chocolates, and the hot chocolate but I must go now.'

Before he has time to speak I am out in the street hailing a cab. How dare he say that about Luke? I feel like crying but the truth is he is right. I don't think I'm good enough for Luke, and Luke makes me feel that way with his dismissive attitude towards the salon. I know he loves me, I just know he does, but why doesn't he ask me to marry him? No, don't think about it, don't think about it but how can I not think about it?

'I can give you a lift Flo,' Tom calls from the doorway.

I decline his offer. *Good business sense* my arse. I'll show Rory's. It's not until I'm halfway home that I realise Tom knew my full name. A little tingle of pleasure runs through me. Why would he go to all that trouble if he didn't like me? I quickly dismiss the idea as stupid. Someone as successful as Tom wouldn't give me a second glance would he?

Chapter Nine

Tom, one hour earlier.

I drive slowly towards Portobello Road, checking the directions Grant had given me. I remember Grant's words and repeat *Flora* in my head a few times. A dotty spinster. I can't understand why Grant is making such a big deal over this. She should jump at the chance to get well over the market value for her little salon. It shouldn't take long to sweeten her up. Grant must be losing his touch, everyone has their price and Flora Robson would have hers. She's smart though, I'll give her that. Pulling out at the last minute, and after the two shops either side have signed. She's got us over a barrel and she knows it, but it will all be down to money at the end of the day. I go over the agenda for tomorrow's board meeting and by the time I turn the corner into Church Lane I'm singing along to James Blunt. I grab the chocolates and tap on the door. I try the handle and the door swings open, a little bell announcing my arrival. She turns at the sound and I recognise her immediately. It's Flo, the girl who reversed into me. Flo, Flora, this has to be a joke. She turns to look at me. Her warm brown eyes sparkle with recognition. Her mouth turns up at the edges and she smiles. Her face is open and expressive, the kind that you can read like a book. I was not expecting this. She is wearing leggings that show off her slim legs and sexy backside and I make a conscious effort to make eye contact. Her dark hair is tied back and she runs her hands over the back of her neck.

'Oh,' she says.

'You're Flora Robson,' I say and could kick myself.

She smiles.

'Yes, the one and only infamous Flora Robson.'

Her leggings are wet and she looks harassed. I smile back and glance around her salon. It's nicer than I imagined it would be. I could kill Grant for giving me the impression she was some old spinster. Still, on reflection, I suppose I should have realised she wasn't, else why would he want to take her to dinner? I feel a pang of irritation at the thought of Grant coming on to her.

'This is your salon?' I say.

She nods proudly.

'Right,' I say and it is then I spot the water behind her. She's got a leak. This is good. I if I can help her out she will think I have her interests at heart. Best to help first and talk later.

'Looks like you've got a bit of a problem,' I say, pointing to the wet floor.

'Oh yes, the basin, it's blocked. It does this on and off. I need new pipes or new basins, one or the other. It's just there is never enough time or more importantly never enough money and ...' she trails off and looks embarrassed.

Perhaps best not to say who I am until I have helped her with the flood. I follow her into the salon, the smell of her perfume enticing me in. She turns and fiddles with her hair nervously. Her eyes lower to the box of chocolates under my arm. Damn I'd forgotten all about them.

'They're big,' she says and blushes like a schoolgirl. 'I'm sorry, it's just I thought the chocolates that Rory's tried to bribe me with were big,' she adds. 'A bit of an insult to my intelligence really, thinking just because I am a woman I can be bribed with chocolate.'

I can't really hand her the chocolates now can I and say, 'Hi I'm Thomas Rory and I'm here to insult your intelligence by bribing you with chocolate.' I'll be bashed over the head with the mop, no doubt. I sigh. The stupid thing is I don't want to tell her. I like the way she looks at me and I feel quite certain Thomas Rory would not get that look. How the hell do I explain the chocolates? The box is ridiculously huge. I feel a right plonker holding them.

'Yes, I nearly forgot. It's an apology ... for the car accident. You said you had a sweet tooth,' I say smiling at her.

'Wow, thank you,' she says lifting the lid and looking longingly at the chocolates.

'Let me help with the blocked basin.'

She hands me the wrench.

'It's all I've got to offer I'm afraid,' she says apologetically.

Well that wrench is pretty useless. No wonder she didn't get anywhere with that. I grin at her. She is so appealing that the temptation to tease her is overwhelming.

'Oh, I think you've got a lot more to offer. I'll get my toolbox from the car,' I say and am rewarded with another blush. I'm sounding more like a plumber by the minute.

'Right, she says. 'Just give me a shout when you're back. I need to get my leggings off ...'

She blushes again and looks delightful.

'What I mean is ...'

I smile and walk out to my car. What am I doing? I've got to tell her. This is ridiculous. I've got to say something positive at the board meeting tomorrow. We need to get moving on this site and the board are expecting some news. I'll fix the leak and then introduce myself properly. I'll make the offer. Tell her she can keep the chocolates. If the offer isn't enough I'll ask her to name her price and that will be it. I undo the pipes and clear out the muck. She comes back into the salon wearing new leggings.

'Would you like a coffee or something else?' she asks, blushing for the umpteenth time.

'What is the something else?' I ask teasing her again.

'I have some lemonade in the fridge,' she says shyly.

'That sounds good and one of those cupcakes would be nice,' I say.

She smiles and I feel captivated by her as I watch her take the lemonade from the fridge.

'Great, thanks. This is unblocked. Do you have a mop or something?' I ask, wondering if now is a good time to tell her. I glance at the cupcake and lemonade and feel my mouth water.

'Looks good,' I say. I want to add *and so do you*, but of course I don't. I don't seem to be saying half of what I should be.

I feel I am digging myself into a hole. How can I now say *I'm Thomas Rory and I'm here to talk you into selling the salon?* As it is the chocolates must seem a bit excessive for a car accident that was, after all, her fault.

'Thank you so much, you're a good plumber,' she says.

Blimey, she's easy to please. Surely her boyfriend can unblock a sink.

'Not really,' I smile. 'Anyone can unblock a sink.'

'What do you do?'

Right, this is the time to tell her. I really should. What's the worst that can happen? She'll wallop me with the mop? She seems controlled. Yes, well, all women seem controlled don't they? Until you upset them and then all hell breaks loose. But if I tell her now, she'll think I am either a fraud or an idiot, and either way that does not put me in a good position to start negotiations.

'I'm a director of a company,' I say. 'It's a family business.'

At least that's the truth. If only I could get past this stupid stumbling block and tell her who I am. If only she weren't so damn appealing and nice, because basically, that's what she is, just plain nice.

'Sounds grand,' she says.

'I heard somewhere that this parade of shops had been sold,' I say casually, pulling out a chair.

'No, we're not selling. Everyone else can but not us. I'm having a rally to show Rory's that we won't be bought. Sodding Rory's can go and ...' she says passionately.

I raise my eyebrows. Perhaps now is not the right time. I sip the lemonade. She obviously has me down as one big scumbag.

'He wants to buy the salon to build a supermarket would you believe. Well, not while my name is Flora Robson. It's about time someone stopped these people. There are plenty of supermarkets. We don't need another one. I've started a petition. I can't believe they tried to bribe me with perfume and chocolates.'

Oh dear. I glance sideways at the chocolates on the counter, she follows my eyes.

'Oh no, it wasn't a nice gesture like yours,' she says quickly, seeing me look at the chocolates. 'Rory's are scumbags. He's putting local people out of business,' she adds, her face turning red with emotion.

She sure hates me. I finish the cupcake and consider asking for another but change my mind.

'People like Rory's are just money crazy.'

Money crazy? No one has ever called me that before. I smile.

'I'm a bit passionate about my salon,' she says.

Yes, and you look beautiful when you are, I want to say.

'Yes, I can tell, your eyes go a bit wild,' I say instead. There is something captivating about her. For a moment I forget who I am and why I am here, and sit looking at her, and then I remember. I've made a right pig's ear of this meeting and feel a bit of a fool. I stand up abruptly.

'Right, I'd better be getting off,' I say more sharply than I mean to.

I need to suss her out a bit more. Find out what her dreams are, apart from owning a salon that is. Obviously chocolates aren't going to do much for her. Grant will have to visit in future. She looks uncomfortable and then says,

'Oh Tom, would you sign the petition? Every name helps.'

I look down at the petition. *Say NO to Rory's and Save our Small Businesses.* She wants me to sign a petition against myself. This is just getting worse by the second. I pick up the pen and quickly scribble my name making it as illegible as I can. If Grant hears about this I'll never live it down.

'Thanks so much,' she says, pushing a sticker onto my shirt, her hand warm against my chest.

'There, now everyone will know you support us,' she says cheerfully.

Wonderful, it couldn't get any worse. I'm petitioning against myself and wearing a sticker to prove it.

'Great,' I respond.

'Thank you so much. I hope you'll come to our protest.'

And get lynched, I don't think so.

'I'm pretty busy most days.'

'Well, if you're free. I could let you know when we have a date.'

She removes her hand from my chest and it is then that I realise I don't want to part from her just yet. I can't leave the business unfinished. I have to tell her who I am.

'Do you fancy a hot chocolate?' I ask.

It is after some deliberation that she agrees. Thirty minutes later and I still haven't told her. What the hell happened? I'd set off with the chocolates determined to wrap the whole thing up with this Flora woman. I had the offer ready and everything, it should have gone as smooth as silk. Instead, I'm back in the car, minus a box of chocolates and a signature on a contract. I was close until she mentioned all the stuff about not being successful enough to be with her solicitor boyfriend. I sigh. The last thing I need is complications with a woman, and especially this woman. Grant might have warned me. She was far from the image of a batty spinster that Grant had painted. Worst of all, I could tell the attraction was mutual. I'll have to avoid her that's all. I'll get Brent to go round in a few days. Try to talk her round before the protest. Hopefully she'll have her price. We'll pay her off and she'll move on. I put the car into gear and start wondering what the hell I am going to tell Grant when I get back.

Chapter Ten

Tom

I check my watch as I enter the office. I'm still wondering how I managed to blow the whole thing with Flora Robson. The office is quiet and I dump my briefcase and jacket on a chair and make my way to the conference room.

'Evening gentlemen,' I smile.

'Everything okay Tom?' Brent Galway asks, looking at me intently.

'Yes, great,' I reply.

'Good,' he says, looking at me oddly.

'How did it go?' Grant asks.

'I'll tell you later,' I say.

He leans towards me.

'Why are you wearing that sticker?'

'What sticker?'

'Why are you wearing a sticker that says *Say NO to Rory's and Save our Small Businesses*?' he whispers. 'Is there something we should know? You're not dropping a bombshell or anything are you?'

Damn. I'd totally forgotten about that.

'Shit,' I mumble.

'Go well with Robson did it?'

'You could have warned me. She's not exactly unattractive. You gave me the impression she was an old spinster,' I say under my breath.

I exhale and peel the thing off. Grant raises his eyebrows.

'At least I didn't come back with an anti-Rory sticker,' Grant says with a grin.

'Okay okay,' I mumble. 'Do you want to keep your job?'

'Did you tell her who you were?'

'Not exactly, it all got a bit complicated. I'd be here with a black eye and a broken arm if I had,' I grin.

'So you didn't close the deal then?' he grumbles.

'I was thinking you could go to this protest, whenever it is. Be the Rory representative.'

'Yeah right ...'

I pour myself some coffee and sip at it slowly. I can still smell her intoxicating perfume.

'Right, let's get this meeting on the road shall we?' I say, forcing Flora Robson from my mind. 'How about ordering some pizza Grant? I don't know about you gentlemen but I'm starving.'

Two hours later, I lean back tiredly in my chair and watch Grant collect up the folders.

'You do realise we paid over the odds for the video shop in Church Lane don't you?' says Grant.

'I know, I know.'

'The plans are done. The contract signed with the builders, I mean we've tied up a lot of people with this deal. You can't let one woman get the better of us. I wouldn't want to be in your shoes at the shareholder's meeting.'

'It was awkward. She had water everywhere. One of the basins was leaking.'

He gives me a cynical look.

'And when did you become Mr Softie? I've never known you come back without closing a deal.

'Everyone has a price. See if there are other salon sites we can offer but not in the East End, I can't understand why she asked for that site in the first place.'

'Do you have any idea of the prices in upmarket London? It won't be worth buying her salon if we're going to offer a place in Notting Hill. It'll be the most expensive site we ever buy at this rate.'

'Just look and come back to me with them okay?'

'By the way, we had a meeting with the senior partner at the surgery.'

'You didn't waste any time.'

'That's why you pay me an obscene salary. They'll train one of our drivers and we will be okay to take it on. He loved the idea.'

I slap him on the back.

'Great work.'

'Of course, this Flora Robson issue could easily be settled. We just make sure her hairdresser business goes downhill,' he says, avoiding my eyes.

'We don't work that way Grant, and you know it,' I say firmly. 'This is my company, my reputation. My father built this company on honesty and integrity and now I am CEO nothing is going to change. We don't do anything underhand. Anyone who does is out, no matter who they are. We're clear on that aren't we?'

Grant pulls at his tie uncomfortably.

'Just a suggestion,' he says casually.

'It's not a suggestion I'm interested in.'

He nods.

'I'll start my research on Flora Robson then. I think I'll rather enjoy it,' he grins.

'Just don't get personal with her,' I say firmly.

The last thing she needs is Grant hassling her.

'Spoilsport,' he laughs.

'Go home. You work too late.'

I watch him walk from the boardroom and find myself thinking of Flora. I sigh. The last thing I need is a woman on my mind again.

Chapter Eleven

Flora

I park outside my parents' bungalow and stare suspiciously at the Ford Mondeo parked in the driveway. She's not invited someone has she? I really want to talk to Mum and Dad about Rory's and the salon, and preferably without one of Mum's friends giving her two-penny worth. The door is flung open and my mother stands there decked out in country casuals and Marks and Spencer pearls, and smelling of Jo Malone's Grapefruit. She's a cross between the Queen and Joan Collins, and that's hard to accomplish let me tell you. In fact the whole house smells of Jo Malone's Grapefruit with a candle in the lounge and a diffuser in the hallway. Grapefruit overkill or what? She hugs me stiffly, careful not to dislodge her newly sprayed hair.

'Gordon did it yesterday. What do you think?'

My opinion on Gordon's hairdressing should never be voiced. I sometimes think Gordon's full name should be *Gordon Bennett* for the reaction it gets from me. She does a little turn and I see a blue streak running through her white bob.

'What was he aiming for exactly?'

That is, aside from making my mother look ridiculous.

'I wanted to be more *with it*. I don't want to end up like your father with salt and pepper hair. Very *with it* don't you think? Your dad doesn't like it, but he'll get used to it.'

I feel myself sympathise with my dad. Her nails are a dark blue too and I cringe. She sniffs around me.

'Is that *Charlie Red* you're wearing?'

No it bloody isn't. I haven't worn that since I was nineteen.

'No, I've gone off that a bit,' I say delicately.

'Oh have you? Oh dear, that's a shame.'

That means she has got a carrier bag full of the stuff for me to take home. That will be a nice surprise for Sandy.

'Yvonne's here. I thought we'd have a treat.'

Oh God no. Yvonne conjures up anything but a treat. Chinese torture yes, a treat no. A treat is a Crunchie bar with a glass of wine right?

'She's going to thread our eyebrows and wax our legs. It's my treat. I know how you hate spending money on pampering.'

Pampering? Is she insane? Pampering is holding hands with a stranger while they file and paint your nails. Eyebrow threading is masochistic torture that should be used to make terrorists talk. Forget the waterboarding, just hold up the eyebrow threading equipment. That should do it. I don't know how many Saturdays I have spent avoiding eyebrow threading in Portobello Market because Devon has always been keen. Personally I don't do pain, at least not voluntarily.

'Mum, I really don't …'

'It's on me darling.'

That somehow doesn't make it any more bearable. Hopefully the morphine will be on her too. Being as I'm driving I can't even have a glass of wine to deaden the pain. Still, I suppose there is some comfort in not paying for my own torture.

'I'm driving,' I say. 'Don't you need some kind of anaesthetic for eyebrow threading?'

I feel quite certain I will. I need two glasses of wine just to get my legs waxed.

'Don't be silly dear, you'll be fine and Luke will be amazed when he sees you.'

I don't imagine Luke will even notice. He's still bemoaning the state of his penis although it looks fine to me. Any hopes I had of getting him to say yes during a mind-blowing orgasm is pretty unlikely now. Anyone would think I'd taken a blow torch to his cock instead of rubbing a little bit of Biofreeze on it.

I follow Mum into the lounge.

'Hi,' waves Yvonne holding a glass of wine.

Shit, she's been drinking too. How many has she had? I'll end up getting my nose threaded. I certainly won't be having a bikini wax that's for sure. I'd like to keep my clitoris. It may not see much action but that's no reason to let it go is it?

Dad strolls from the kitchen carrying a tray of glasses and a bottle of ginger wine. He kisses me on the cheek.

'Ooh ginger wine,' I say, 'my favourite.'

'Did you see the hair?' he whispers.

I nod.

'Your mother thinks she's Lady Gaga. I wish we'd never watched that programme on the woman. Your mother has never been the same since. I worry she'll think Boden is too tame soon.'

I laugh.

'How are you Flora?' he asks.

'Well, I've been better,' I say. 'It seems I'm to have my eyebrows threaded.'

'Yes, good Lord. I imagine that's going to be painful.'

'Thanks Dad.'

'Just knock back the ginger wine. Your mother will be knocking back the red. I'll run you home if you're over the limit. You can pick up the old jalopy tomorrow.'

'I wish you two would not talk about me as though I'm not here,' grumbles Mum.

'So what's happening to the salon?' asks Mum, helping Yvonne to set up her bed between the coffee table and the small bookcase that houses Mum's treasured Barbara Cartland novels. I've decided if my mum ever attempts to look like her heroine I am divorcing her. Lady Gaga is one thing but Barbara Cartland, that's surely grounds for matricide isn't it?

'I'm not selling,' I say. 'They came round with perfume and chocolates and ... that reminds me did anyone come to see you and ask what perfume I liked?'

Mum looks thoughtful and lifts her eyes to the ceiling and Dad starts humming.

'Did they bring your favourite *Charlie Red*?' asks Yvonne.

When will everyone realise *Charlie Red* has, in fact, never been my favourite?

'You're both as guilty as hell aren't you? What did they bribe you with? Don't tell me, it was Boden wasn't it? Or was it Jo Malone?'

Mum looks at Dad.

'It was two tickets to the opera at the Royal Opera House.' She turns to Yvonne and adds, 'In a box.'

'A box,' says Yvonne, awe stricken.

'I'll put *you* in a box,' I say angrily turning on my mother.

'Oh dear Flora, don't be like that. They said they were going to give you a nice selection of *Charlie Red* as well as chocolates. I said you had a sweet tooth.'

'But you don't even like the bloody opera. You complain that Andrea Bocelli gets on your nerves.'

'But a box at the Royal Opera House, well it's something isn't it?'

I shake my head.

'You'd sell out your daughter just to get a box at the Royal Opera House. I don't believe it.'

'I really feel that salon is what's holding Luke back from proposing,' she says petulantly. 'Besides, Mr Richards was very sweet. He went out of his way to check what you liked.'

'I bet he did.'

'Who's first?' asks Yvonne.

'Her,' Mum and I say in unison.

'You're younger,' says Mum.

'What's age got to do with it? It's eyebrow threading not open heart surgery.'

I climb onto the bed, might as well get the torture over with quickly. My legs could do with a wax.

'Heavens, you're turning into an ape,' says Yvonne as I pull my leggings off. 'When did you last wax?'

'I've been shaving,' I say, thinking I really shouldn't feel this guilty about hairy legs.

I hold my glass out to Dad.

'A refill darling?' he asks, reaching for the ginger wine.

'Anyway that's not true about the salon,' I say. 'Luke likes a successful woman.'

'Well, he obviously doesn't want to marry one.'

'Legs or eyebrows first?' asks Yvonne.

'Neither actually, but if I'm being treated,' I glare at Mum, 'then legs.'

I knock back the wine and hold the glass out again.

'Rory's Supermarkets are taking over everywhere,' Yvonne says, applying warm wax to my calf. 'Just a half leg is it?'

She sounds like a butcher. Still, she's not far off being one. I wish she'd stop drinking. She'll be paralytic by the time she gets to Mum.

'I don't show off the top half.' I say in a strangled voice.

'They're building one near us too. A small one, but hell it's progress and I hear Burt at the shoe shop was made a good offer so they'll be off like a bride's nightie,' she says, whipping off the wax so fast I don't have time to breathe let alone scream.

'But I can't sell up,' I say, pulling out my soapbox. 'These big corporations are ruining small businesses.'

'They even bought Mary, Burt's wife, chocolates when they last came round,' she adds, tearing at my skin for the second time. I fight back a scream.

'Yes, well I got offered those too, I told them to take them back and stick them up Mr Rory's arse.'

'What about the perfume?' asks Mum.

'Up his arse.'

'Oh dear.'

'I said he could forget sending flowers too because they'll end up his arse as well.'

'I reckon he'll be running out of room up there,' says Yvonne, pouring wax onto my toes.

Dad coughs.

'It's a damn shame that,' he says, glancing through the *Radio Times*.

'You're worried about Rory's arse?' I ask.

'Roger,' snaps Mum. 'Don't be coarse.'

'I like Rory's,' says Dad. 'It's a good little supermarket. It could be worse.'

'Dad,' I gasp.

'I'm just saying. They're a decent company.'

I harrumph loudly.

'Decent company my backside.'

'I know their solicitors, and from what I've heard Rory's are not underhand. Everything is always above board with them, and they are very generous.'

'I don't believe this. The bastards have got to you too.'

'It's not quite like that,' says Mum.

'Oh no, a box at the Royal Opera House?' I remind her.

'Yes well ...' she stutters.

'I'm not selling,' I say, feeling like I'll be saying that in my sleep soon. 'Is there anything legal I can do Dad?'

'Don't be silly Flora. You should be looking for a husband not having airy-fairy ideas about taking on a corporation,' says Mum.

'No, there isn't. You can refuse to sell but with everyone selling around you ...' he trails off.

I turn onto my stomach and accept an After Eight from a box Dad is handing around.

'I met someone, really nice actually. His name's Tom.'

'Ooh,' says Yvonne excitedly, throwing back her wine and nodding at my dad to pour more. Christ, she won't be able to see straight soon. I'll end up with threaded eyelids. I've not got great eyelashes as it is. I really can't afford to lose any more.

'Is that sensible dear?' says Mum worriedly.

For a second I think she is talking to Yvonne about the wine and then realise she is actually talking to me.

'I only had lunch with him. He banged me in the car park.'

'Good Lord,' says Dad.

'No, my car not me.'

'I was about to say, that was daring of you,' says Yvonne excitedly.

'He's very nice, rich and good looking. I have his email address. I just think Luke is never going to propose and now this thing with the salon. I don't know what to do. Devon got engaged too. I feel like I'm on the shelf ...'

'You are on the shelf,' agrees Mum.

I sigh. Maybe she's right. Two years is stretching things a bit isn't it? Luke probably has no intention of proposing. We'll drift along for years like this if I leave it to him. I had this thing about getting married in my thirtieth year but I don't think he is going to take the initiative. I pop another After Eight into my mouth and as the minty flavour melts on my tongue it comes to me. How stupid, why didn't I think of it before?

'I'll propose to him,' I say.

Yvonne turns me onto my back.

'What if he says no?' she asks, lurching towards me with her thread.

I feel a prick above my left eye and gasp. That's a point, what if he says no? He won't, surely. After all, we've been together for two years. We've just got into a routine that's all. I feel a tremor of excitement at the thought. This time next month I could also have an engagement ring on my finger, if I could just get engaged in time for my birthday. In fact …

'I'll propose on my birthday. Ouch, Christ Yvonne, you're scalping me of eyelashes.'

'But won't Luke be in Dublin on your birthday?' says Mum gently.

'It's the tournament, he can't miss that, he's the best in the club,' says Dad, looking concerned.

Oh, well that's that then. God forbid I should come before the sodding golf.

'Go to Dublin,' says Yvonne, taking a break to top up her glass. I gingerly feel my eyebrow, just to check it's still there. Ooh, it feels rather good. I take a sip from my glass and it hits me, not the wine obviously, but my great idea.

'Yes, that's it. I'll surprise him in Dublin, on my birthday. It'll be a double surprise.'

There's no stopping me now. I picture the scenario. I'll have to get a ring for Luke, or something that represents my love for him. It will be great.

'The flights are going to get booked. It's a big tournament,' says Dad.

I wave a hand airily.

'I'll get there, but don't say a word about it to anyone. What do you think?'

I'll be engaged by thirty. After all, we have equal rights don't we, and it's not that unusual for a woman to propose is it? I'll have to plan it properly. I feel myself tremble with the excitement. I'm sure I'll have more confidence to take on Rory's if I'm an engaged woman.

'You should have your eyebrows done more often,' says Mum. 'It makes you very positive.'

The ginger wine has a lot to do with it of course.

'Oh, and about Rory's, I've started a petition and we have stickers. I'm having a protest in a few weeks. I want you to come and support me. You too Yvonne,' I say. After all every body counts doesn't it?

'You sound like Jane Fonda,' says Mum.

'I'd love to,' says Yvonne, playing with the thread and making my eyes water.

'Well I suppose we could,' says Mum.

'I think it's wonderful what you're doing,' says Yvonne dabbing at my eye.

'So, you'll come?' I say, helping myself to wine.

Mum sighs resignedly.

'I suppose so. Will it be in the papers?'

'I don't know, why?'

'I'll dress like a proper activist if it is,' she says.

Dad rolls his eyes.

'I dread to think what one of them looks like,' he groans.

As long as she doesn't turn up with pink hair and wearing something outrageous I don't care. I glance at Dad.

'I'll keep her on a short leash,' he smiles.

'We have three weeks to prepare,' I say.

'I so wish you'd just find a husband,' says Mum, 'instead of gallivanting around activating like this.'

'I think it's very commendable,' says Yvonne, lifting her wine glass. 'Here's to you and your fight against Rory's.' She clinks her glass against mine.

Great, that's eight people. I need to get more. I wonder if you can rent a crowd. I'll ask Devon.

'Wonderful,' I say.

Chapter Twelve

I'd decided to wear my slinky black dress after scattering my whole wardrobe across the bed. I'd bought it two years ago in Zara and I think it enhances my figure. I'd used large heated rollers to add some bounce to my unmanageable hair and attached some sparkly drop earrings that Devon and I had found at Camden Market. I'd been pleased with my appearance until I had entered the Jacksons' hall and seen all the other women in their designer outfits. I would have turned around and gone home if Luke hadn't spotted me. He pushed passed the guests and wrapped his arm around my waist.

'You look gorgeous Flora. Did you get the car sorted?'

Now is the time to tell him about Tom, but before I can say anything he whisks me into the hall.

'Okay if I mingle? There are some good contacts here. I promise not to be too long,' he says, and then whispers in my ear, 'and then we can go home and check out that basque.'

He squeezes my bum and I suppress a squeal. Ooh maybe there is still time for Luke to propose. I kiss him on the cheek.

'It's fine, mingle as much as you like. I'll check out the buffet.'

'They have a nice spinach quiche, and the vegetarian spring rolls are delicious. I've had two,' he smiles.

I grimace. They also have some lovely sausages on sticks, an enormous cheeseboard and nice ham from what I've seen on people's plates, not to mention pizza. The Jacksons' house, or I should say mansion, is heaving with people and a live band is playing *If Not for Me.* It's all very decadent and snobbish. There is more food going spare than at a rehearsal for the Great British Bake Off. Seriously, the place is bursting with it. A large banner hangs above the table.

Fundraising for those starving in Africa tonight.

Not the best place for the banner. I try to work out if we are fundraising for those who are starving *tonight*. Or if *tonight* we are fundraising for the starving. You have to admit it is confusing. It seems a bit unfair to only fundraise for those starving tonight, don't you think? What about those starving tomorrow? Or come to that those who starved yesterday.

'An unusual sign,' says a familiar voice behind me. I turn sharply, my heart fluttering. It's him again. In the last few days I seem to be bumping into Tom everywhere.

'If I didn't know better I'd think you were stalking me,' I say with a smile.

'Maybe I am,' he says, his eyes mischievous. He is so gorgeous that I'm surprised every woman in the room isn't looking at him. His hair falls beautifully across his forehead and he brushes it back. His eyes are sharp and keen. He is wearing an open-necked shirt and I glimpse a few hairs on his chest. The feelings that run through me seem so unfamiliar. This man is sex on legs. I wish Devon were here. She would love to be this close to him. Then again, maybe not, because whenever Devon is around she always gets the attention. Not that I'm interested in Tom. I'll be engaged soon and I'm so excited about it that it is all I can do not to ask Luke right away.

'I could smell your perfume as I came in from the patio, I knew you were here.'

'Oh really, is it that strong?'

I sniff my wrist. I wish Luke had said something.

'No, it has a real pheromone effect,' he says pretending to sway in ecstasy. 'What is it?'

I blush. My scent is turning him on, is what he's saying. Wait till I tell Devon, I can barely speak, I'm feeling so breathless.

'Mugler, Womanity.'

'Ah, it suits you. Are you here with Luke?' he asks looking around.

'Yes, he's mingling.'

'Are you allowed a drink?' he asks.

'Yes, why wouldn't I be?' I laugh.

'I don't know, maybe you have to drink healthy juice or something. They've got champagne on the patio, and desserts. I think you'll like them.'

I look for Luke but can't see him anywhere and then I spot Grant Richards and feel myself fume. The further away from him I get the better. I follow Tom. I tell you, I'm anyone's for a profiterole. The fresh air hits me and I breathe in gratefully. Heaters are at each end of the patio and under a canopy are desserts and champagne. Another banner hangs above the food and I find myself tutting.

'It's a bit of a contradiction isn't it?' he says his eyes following mine. A small group pass us and acknowledge Tom. My eyes feast on the desserts and I look behind to see if there is any sign of Luke.

'What would you like?' Tom asks, holding a plate.

My eyes scan the desserts in a second. Eating dessert at functions when Luke is around has become quite a skill for me. I memorise everything and make a choice in my head.

'I'll have a small slice of the lemon meringue, but only if it has a biscuit base. Two profiteroles, a small dollop of cream, on the side not on the profiteroles, a spoonful of chocolate mousse, and a tiny piece of cheesecake but only if it has a biscuit base, I don't like pastry.'

He stares at me.

'Cheese and biscuits?' he asks after a few seconds.

'Yes please as long as it's not Gorgonzola. That smells like a pig farmer's bunions. I hate it.'

He laughs.

'I'll be right back.'

I watch as he approaches the table, slapping a few people on the back as he does so. He returns with two plates and we sit on a bench overlooking the lawn. Food somehow tastes better when it's forbidden. He dips a strawberry into the champagne and pops it into his mouth.

'How are things with your salon?' he asks.

I look lovingly at the cheesecake in my dish.

'Good actually, I'm organising a protest. My mum and her friends are coming, and loads of other people.'

'I'd like to talk to you about your salon ...' he begins when Henrietta Jackson wanders towards us.

'Hi guys, what do you think of our little fundraiser? Brilliant isn't it? I can't tell you how much work has gone into it. I'm absolutely exhausted. And Tom, I can't thank you enough.'

He shrugs and I wonder what she's thanking him for. Her black shiny hair hangs beautifully around her shoulders and she has on the most stunning dress. Her make-up is immaculate and diamond stud earrings sparkle at her earlobes. I openly admire the chiffon of her dress.

'That's a lovely dress,' I say.

'Paris darling, where else?' she says flicking back a stray hair.

Where else indeed. A string of pearls adorn her neck and on her wedding finger is the hugest bling I have ever seen. I could gladly murder her. Her smoky grey eyes survey me. I'm wondering how much organising she had to do for the party aside from go through her address book of course. I can't imagine that exhausted her that much, especially when she is overrun with hired help. Seriously, her house is something out of *Downton Abbey*.

'It's very nice,' I say.

'Aw, thank you, you're so sweet. That's a pretty little dress you have on too. Where is that from?'

'Good old London,' I say, forcing a laugh. 'Oxford Street, Zara to be exact.'

'Oh, how quaint,' she says, but *how common*, is what she means. The wrinkling of her nose says it all.

The way she said *pretty little dress* deflates me. I feel like the poor relation. My little black dress suddenly feels too tight, too cheap, and exceptionally unfashionable. I finger my cheap drop earrings and stare jealously at the bling on her finger. Christ, that alone would feed the whole of Africa, not just those starving tonight. It is new, I'm certain of it. I'm sure the last one she wore was a sapphire. I wouldn't mind a sapphire. To be absolutely honest I wouldn't even mind a zirconia as long as it sits on my marriage finger. I don't believe it. I can't even get one little single solitaire on my finger and she has two. Does everyone have a ring on their finger except me? I bet everyone is talking about me, how I can't get a man to marry me. Still, by the time we get back from Dublin I'll be engaged. Thirty and engaged, I couldn't ask for a better birthday present.

'Is that new?' I say, pointing to the bling.

'Oh this little thing?' she says, flashing the little thing in my face. I hate the bitch, I really do. I swear she is looking at my wedding finger.

'I've had this for yonks. Martin bought it for me on our third anniversary.'

Well, that was only last year, wasn't it?

'It's lovely,' I say.

'When are you and Luke going to tie the knot? Isn't it time the bugger asked you? He's such a cock making you wait.'

'Oh, I'm in no hurry,' I say, wishing she wouldn't mention Luke and *cock* in the same breath. It's clearly evident where her brain is going isn't it? She has always fancied Luke. I bet she would never mistake Biofreeze for K-Y Jelly.

'Where is the handsome bugger?' she asks, looking around. 'I want to thank him for his donation.'

My reflection in the patio doors catches my eye. From this angle I can see my bum, and it really does look big in this. Oh my God, all of me looks big. Let's face it, I imagine it looks big in anything not just this. I must lose some weight, I tell myself as I reach for my dessert dish. Oh no, is that a split under my armpit. I really must lose some weight, I really must.

A man in a colourful waistcoat and long scarf joins us. He is holding an electronic cigarette in one hand and a glass of champagne in the other.

'Divine Hen, just divine darling, I cannot believe what you do. It's fantastic. So much giving.'

He makes her sound like Mother Teresa in Prada.

'Thank you Basil,' says Henrietta basking in the glory.

'Don't you think it's marvellous,' he says turning to me.

'Well, I ...'

A loud booming noise quietens the hall as the Master of Ceremonies takes the stage and I step inside to see what is happening.

'Champagne for the toast,' says a waitress offering me a glass from a silver platter. I take it and look for Luke, but he is nowhere to be seen. For a second I think my ears are deceiving me when the host calls Grant Richards to the stage.

'Ladies and Gentlemen, as you know Rory's are sponsoring our fundraiser tonight. So please give a big hand to their representative for the evening, Mr Grant Richards.'

I follow everyone's eyes to see Grant Richards strolling towards the stage. I seriously can't believe this. I catch a glimpse of his smug face.

'Good evening everyone. I hope you're having a marvellous time. I must first thank Henrietta Jackson, for all her hard work ...'

There are lots of 'hear hears' echoed around the room and Grant smiles like the bloody Cheshire cat.

'As you know there will soon be a new Rory's supermarket in this locale and as part of our community support programme, both local and worldwide, may I, on behalf of Rory's, present a cheque for ten thousand pounds towards this wonderful cause.'

He waves a hand and two people walk forward with a huge cheque. I should have brought a larger handbag to throw up into.

'Fantastic,' the MC shouts. 'The children of Africa thank you.'

Obviously doesn't take much to get this guy excited.

'Rory's pleasure,' says a smug Grant Richards. I think I hate the bugger more than Mr Rory himself.

'And before I step down, as I'm sure I'm overstaying my welcome up here,' he laughs.

Too right.

'Not at all,' the MC laughs and everyone cheers in agreement.

'Rory's have some good news for the community. We've just launched a new programme to help the elderly and busy families.'

'Well, that's marvellous news isn't it folks?'

Grant Richards smiles smugly.

'From next month those who struggle to get their prescriptions from the surgery can ask to have them delivered by Rory's, direct to their homes and free of charge.'

I choke on my champagne. I see Grant Richards look at me and smile. The bastard, the conniving deceitful lying and idea-thieving little prick. I could kill him. I wish I was skilled in knife throwing. So help me God, I'd aim a cheese knife in his direction. Someone knocks into me while clapping overenthusiastically, spilling champagne down my dress. By the time I've wiped it with a tissue and dabbed my watery eyes, Grant Richards has gone and I can't spot his smug face anywhere. It's all I can do not to cry.

'I don't believe it,' I say to Tom. 'That's the guy who came to the salon. I can't believe he stole ...' I break off as tears threaten.

I feel the comforting touch of Tom's hand on my arm.

'And who might you be?' Luke says rudely, appearing out of nowhere. 'And what have you done to your dress? You've spilt something down it'.

'Luke,' I say softly, 'this is Tom, he reversed into my car, you remember, the broken brake light?'

Luke surveys Tom.

'I hope you paid for it,' he says.

'It was my fault, Luke,' I whisper.

Tom grins.

'Yes, of course,' he says without taking his eyes off Luke.

Luke lowers his eyes to my dish.

'Have you eaten that?' he says in his accusing voice. 'It's full of sugar.'

God, it's just a bit of cheesecake. It's not like I've just fallen out of the loo after shooting up is it? That's what I'll be doing next. Hiding in the loo and shooting up sugar. I'll be like a diabetic but in reverse.

'My fault,' says Tom. 'I tempted her. I hear you'll be playing at the tournament in Dublin. My father is competing too.' He offers Luke a glass of champagne, 'I didn't catch your last name?'

'Really, it should be good,' says Luke. The mere mention of golf seems to transform Tom into Luke's best friend. 'Wright, Luke Wright,' he adds, offering Tom his hand.

'Ah, you're Flo's Mr Right are you?' says Tom, with a cynical grin.

'Yes I suppose I am, and it's Flora actually.'

'Are you flying?' Tom asks.

'Yes, from Stansted.'

'Well, if you have any problems just give me a bell. I'm travelling there for the final. I've got a few spare seats on the train so I'm happy to help out.'

'I've got a headache, I think I'll go home,' I say.

'Already? But we haven't been here long. I would really like to stay a bit longer.'

He's changed his tune. I thought he was keen to check out my basque.

'I'm leaving. I can take Flora home,' Tom says, a bit too quickly for my liking.

I notice he called me Flora. I presume it was for Luke's benefit.

'Well ...' considers Luke.

'Here's my number,' says Tom, jotting it down onto a serviette. 'Give me a bell if you need a seat on the train. Good luck at the tournament,' he smiles. 'Sure I can't give you a lift Flora?'

'Are you sure you don't mind?' I ask Luke.

'Well, I'd prefer you to stay but I expect you feel a bit stupid in that dress now,' he says carelessly.

I fight the urge to cry. Bugger Luke, Grant Richards and Rory. I hate them all. Men, they're all more trouble than they're worth.

Chapter Thirteen

Tom

As soon as I'd offered I was regretting it. What was I thinking? I just felt the need to get her away from that *up his own arse* Luke Wright. What does she see in him? And why she's so desperate to get engaged to the little prick I'll never know. She can do better than him.

'Are you sure it's not out of your way?' she asks, climbing into the Audi.

'Of course not,' I say foolishly, as I haven't got the faintest idea where she lives, and it probably is well out of my way.

'You don't know where I live do you?' she smiles.

'This is true.'

We laugh. It's like she can read my mind. I've got to get a grip and tell her who I am and get this whole salon thing sorted. It would be so much easier if she wasn't so nice. If only she didn't come over as so damn vulnerable. Every time I go to say something the moment is lost and all I can think about is how I don't want to hurt her. This is ridiculous; I'm supposed to be running a business. Her soft fragrance fills the car and no doubt is clinging to the upholstery. I'll smell it for weeks.

'Flo ...'

She looks at me expectantly.

'About your salon ...'

As if on cue, her phone trills. It's like everything is conspiring against me.

'Hi Max, yes everything is okay for tomorrow. I just can't remember what I have to bring with me. Okay, thanks Max and you'll be gentle with me won't you. I've already got problems with the salon. See you then, bye.'

'Is everything okay?' I ask, my ears pricking up at the word *salon*.

'That was my accountant, don't even go there. What with the council tax, liability insurance, electricity, wages and ...'

'Repairs to the plumbing?' I smile, remembering the blocked sink.

'Yes, that's a point, plus I've got cracks and I thought it was substance at first, I mean subsidence, but it wasn't, but they look awful so I'll have to get those done.'

'Perhaps you would be better off selling it?' I say, grateful for the opportunity to broach the subject.

Her face colours and her eyes harden. I feel her tense beside me.

'No, I won't walk away from my salon like a loser. I'm a businesswoman after all. Would you sell your business just like that? I'm sure you didn't get where you are today by giving up.'

Ouch, she is very passionate about her salon and so sexy when she gets all fired up. Her eyes widen and she has a cute frown on her forehead.

'You're really determined aren't you?'

'I'm not giving in to Rory's. Luke wouldn't have any respect for me if I did.'

Not him again, what does she see in that plonker?

'Do you really care about that guy?' I hear myself say.

'*That guy* is going to be my husband,' she replies defensively.

'Yeah sorry, forgot about that.'

'He's a very clever man and terribly sensitive.'

Clever maybe, only in that he has Flo as a girlfriend, but sensitive ... that's arguable.

'Going back to the salon, there's something I need to ask ...' I say, trying again. This really is getting stupid.

'Oh no,' she cries, patting her hand around the seat. 'It's popped out.'

I quickly check my flies. She unclips her seat belt and feels between the seats, her hand brushing my thigh. What the hell has popped out?

'Ooh,' she says suddenly, 'take the next right,' and points ahead, blocking my view with her hand. I swerve to take the turning.

'No, the next next right. Sorry, everything looks crooked.'

'I wish you'd put your seatbelt back on,' I say, holding it out to her.

'I can't see very well, not now it's popped out. Where has it gone?'

I fumble with the seat belt and push it into her hand.

'Here it is.'

'No I don't mean the seatbelt. My eye, where has it gone? Don't go too fast I only have one eye.'

She only has one eye? This is getting too gruesome for words. I pull into a lay-by.

'It's between your legs, can I have it,' she says as I pull on the handbrake.

Now there's an offer if ever there was one. She blushes when I look at her.

'But we hardly know each other,' I smile.

She sighs good humouredly.

'My contact lens, I think that's it between your legs,' she says shyly.

I've only got one thing between my legs and it's never been called a contact lens. I look down but can't see anything, and I've got two eyes. She points but I still can't see it. She reaches tentatively towards me and I tense. This surely isn't her making a pass is it? She carefully places her hand between my legs and reaches for the lens. I tense. This is a bit too close for comfort. She leans back, fiddles with her eye and sighs.

'Sorry about that.'

'Not a problem,' I say.

Her face is open, her lips seemingly inviting and I have to grip the steering wheel to stop myself from kissing her. I'd promised myself no women. You can't trust them. As soon as they know there's money in the bank they cling like bindweed. Let's face it, this one needs money with the state that salon is in. Why she doesn't sell is beyond me. She moves in her seat so her knee touches the gear stick. Changing gear could be awkward. I start the engine and turn the car around.

'The next left,' she says, pointing ahead.

'The next left or the next next left? And putting your arm in my view means I can't see the next left or the next next left come to that.'

I hear her little cheery laugh and I smile.

'Turn here,' she says, and then, 'Oops sorry, the third building on the right,' and my heart sinks. I'd hoped it was further away than this so I could bring up the salon again. I pull up outside the apartment block.

'We're on the fourth floor,' she says without making any move to get out.

Is she going to invite me in? Her boyfriend is out but who knows when he will be back. That could be awkward as I don't imagine he would appreciate finding me in his flat, but a quick cup of coffee may be okay, ten minutes max. What am I thinking? If she knew I was Thomas Rory she would be out of the car like a bolt of lightning, I should be fair with her and tell her straight.

'Flo,' I begin.

'I want to propose to Luke,' she interrupts.

'You do?' I say, backing away from her.

Why the hell does she want to be engaged to that up his own arse plonker?

'I want to propose in Dublin; it will be my birthday you see. I'll be thirty and it just seems the right time to do it.'

'Right,' I respond in a rather deadpan tone.

She fidgets in her seat.

'I don't really like flying, I know it sounds stupid, Luke gets cross with me. I will do it but if there is any other way ...' she trails off uncertainly.

'It's not stupid, I hate being cooped up in a plane too, airports are like cattle markets, there are much better ways to travel if you have the time,' I say.

'I was wondering ...' she hesitates and fiddles with her handbag. 'I was wondering if I could buy one of your train tickets,' she finishes and looks at me hopefully, her eyes wide and her face flushed. In that moment I would have given her anything. A train journey to Dublin is a gift from heaven. It would be the perfect chance to talk. There would be time to explain everything and still be friends afterwards.

'Sure, it'll be company for me. I'm leaving on Friday to get there in time for the final.'

She stares at me.

'You don't mind?' she asks.

'Well, I have two spare seats and no one else is using them. I like to keep the seats around me free so I can work on the journey.'

She looks embarrassed.

'Oh, I don't want to disturb ...'

'You won't disturb me. If you want a seat just be there at eight Friday morning, and I refuse to take money for it. You'll need to book somewhere to stay. It gets busy when there's a tournament.'

She looks worried and bites her lip. She obviously hasn't thought this through, apart from the proposing to Luke bit. It's typical woman behaviour, forgetting the practicalities.

'If you can't find anywhere let me know. I'm booked at The Gresham. It's a two-bedroom suite ...'

Her eyes widen.

'Only if you can't get booked anywhere else,' I add quickly.

She gives me a curious look.

'A suite at The Gresham, that's really extravagant.'

I want to say it's only extravagant if you can't afford it.

'I've got some business meetings in Dublin and I needed a hotel with a good conference room.'

This seems to satisfy her and she rummages in her handbag for her keys.

'How much is the ticket?' she asks, not looking at me.

'Don't worry about paying. It's going to be wasted if you don't use it.'

And it's the least I can do considering I'm trying to get your salon.

'No, I can't possibly. I must pay you.'

'You can buy dinner on the ferry. That will be fine.'

She looks unsure.

'Well ...' she says, hesitantly.

I smile.

'That's settled then,' I say and before I can move she leans across the seat and kisses me on the cheek, her perfume intoxicating.

'Thank you Tom, I appreciate it.'

I struggle to keep my arms at my side. She opens the door and is out of the car before I have recovered from the warmth of her kiss.

'I have your email address if I change my mind,' she says, peeking back into the car.

'Goodnight.'

'Goodnight Flo.'

I watch as she walks towards the block of flats and wait until she is safely ensconced inside. This is something I won't be sharing with Grant.

Chapter Fourteen

'I can't for the life of me think why you want to get engaged anyway,' says Rosalind waddling to a table like an overweight penguin and falling into a chair. 'Engagements lead to marriage and marriage leads to this,' she says, pointing emphatically to her stomach. 'I've not slept properly in months and I've still got four weeks to go. I'm starting to think I shall never sleep again.'

'Four weeks,' exclaims Devon. 'Are you sure? You look like you're about to drop it any minute.'

'Devon, don't call the baby *it*. It's a he,' I say looking enviously at Rosalind's belly. 'And you'd better not drop any minute. I've got to get to Dublin and propose to Luke before you drop anything.'

'It feels like a bloody monster,' says Rosalind, 'and it kicks for bloody England just when I'm trying to sleep. Then it settles in that God-awful position where I have to pee all the time. I swear I'm going to give birth to a sadist, takes after his bloody father. It takes me forever to get out of sodding bed. Jeremy has to pull me up, it's pathetic. I daren't move in the bed either otherwise I wallop Jeremy with my bulge. He's had enough too. I just hope it comes on time and doesn't decide to do a Buster.'

'A Buster?' questions Devon.

'Yeah, I'm reading this God-awful book. It's the diary of this baby in the womb who decides it doesn't like the sound of his parents much so he's determined not to come out. I'm telling you this one is bloody coming out whether it damn well likes us or not. I shall push it to kingdom come. It's not staying in there past its due date. I want my sodding womb back.'

'Gross,' says Devon, pulling a face.

'What are you having?' I ask Devon.

'How do I know, I'm not even married, let alone pregnant?'

'She means for lunch you daft cow,' laughs Rosalind.

'Oh, I'll have the Caesar salad with grilled chicken.'

'Please don't mention caesareans,' says Rosalind.

Devon and I glance at each other.

'I'll have a double cheeseburger, fries, and a side dish of onion rings,' says Rosalind without looking at the menu. 'I might as well eat it while I can.'

I study the menu intently.

'We'd like to order, preferably before I go into labour,' huffs Rosalind.

'The Waldorf salad is good,' says the waitress.

'I don't fancy salad. I live on salad,' I say.

'In between chocolate,' adds Devon.

'How about the burger?' Rosalind suggests.

I laugh.

'It only needs one of Luke's work colleagues to pop in ...'

'And you want to get engaged to the guy. You don't think he's a bit controlling?' asks Rosalind, pushing herself more comfortably into her seat and shoving the table across with her bulge, squashing Devon and me into a corner.

'He won't let her eat chocolate,' chimes in Devon. 'She hides Crunchie bars in Tampax boxes.'

'Christ, as long as you don't mix them up, you don't want a Crunchie up your vagina,' exclaims Rosalind.

'Very funny. Anyway he does allow me to eat some chocolate. He just prefers I don't eat too much.'

'She's a vegetarian with Luke and eats bacon when he's not around,' says Devon. 'It's not right Flo. You should be yourself with your partner.'

'I am myself,' I say defensively.

'Sounds a bit like *Sleeping with the Enemy*,' says Rosalind, 'but without the house by the sea.'

'No it's not,' I say. 'We've never made love on the kitchen counter for a start. Luke would never consider getting it out anywhere other than the bedroom.'

'And when he does get it out, she Biofreezes it,' whispers Devon, stifling a giggle.

Rosalind gapes at me.

'Devon,' I hiss.

'Oh my God you didn't?' says Rosalind. 'Was that deliberate, you know, to curb the premature ...'

'Of course not, I thought it was K-Y. Anyway, Luke doesn't do spontaneous sex.'

'I'm surprised he's doing it at all after that,' laughs Devon.

'He's okay,' I say, looking at the menu.

'Take my advice,' Rosalind sighs, 'and avoid spontaneous fucking. That's what got me in this mess. I thought it was dead exciting doing it halfway up the stairs and now look at me. I can't even walk up them these days, let alone fuck on them.'

'Mark's adventurous,' says Devon dreamily.

I give her an envious look. Christ, is everyone doing it on the stairs? Mind you, if we did it on our stairs, Mrs Larkin from number twenty-six would have heart failure, considering our stairs are communal. Then again, the speed Luke works she could blink and miss it. Still, I wouldn't want to put a 93-year-old through that.

'Does he wear pyjamas?' I ask softly.

'God no,' cries Devon.

I lower my head.

'Christ, he doesn't, does he?' Rosalind asks.

Does she have to look so amazed? Surely wearing pyjamas isn't that odd is it?

'Well yes, but not all the time,' I lie.

'Bloody hell, that's a real turn off unless they're silk or something.'

'Marks and Spencer's,' I say.

'Jesus, no wonder you don't have spontaneous fucking,' says Rosalind. 'Sounds like your sex life needs a bit of spicing up. Perhaps you should get bejazzled down there.'

'I think it's vajazzled,' says Devon.

'Well whatever it is, maybe you just need a bit of pussy decorating to turn him on.'

'Mel had that done, do you remember? She was three hours at Gatwick after setting off all the alarms,' says Devon.

'I'm not the one who needs to vajazzle,' I say defensively. 'Anyway, it's not a case of getting turned on, more a case of keeping it turned on.'

After all, I was the one who suggested a bit of porn only to find Luke had set the parental control settings on my computer.

'What can I get you ladies?' asks the waitress.

'A cold shower at this rate,' says Devon.

'Oh I'm fine. I doubt I'll ever want sex again,' groans Rosalind.

'I'll have a tuna mayonnaise sandwich on rye bread but can you not put the mayonnaise in the sandwich because it makes the bread soggy. I'll have it in a dish on the side. I'll have the salad but without lettuce ...'

'Salad without lettuce?' says the waitress.

'Yes.'

'Jesus,' mumbles Rosalind.

I glare at her.

'What? I know what I like, that's all. I'll have a small portion of fries too please.'

'Do you know how many calories there are in fries?' says Devon.

'What can I get you ladies to drink?'

'Depends where the bloody loo is,' moans Rosalind. 'If it's downstairs forget the drink, I'd rather dehydrate. If it's on this floor, I'll have a mineral water.'

'I'll have a skinny latte,' says Devon.

I decide to go for the mineral water and the waitress finally leaves us.

'Right,' says Devon, 'so you want our opinion on you proposing to Luke?'

I nod.

'I thought I'd go to Dublin. Surprise him on my birthday, and then propose. I want you to help me choose a ring,' I say excitedly, pouring the water.

'You're choosing your own engagement ring?' says Rosalind with a scoff. 'That's not very romantic.'

'No stupid, she's choosing a ring for Luke,' says Devon.

'If he's anything like Jeremy he won't wear it. Men aren't like us. Take Jeremy for example, he hates jewellery and he doesn't even want to be at the birth of his own son. Flo has had more to do with this pregnancy than my husband.'

'I think Luke will wear a ring,' I say, while not feeling at all sure.

'It's an expensive proposal. There's the flight and somewhere to stay, and the ring. Are you sure he'll say yes?'

Surely he'll say yes, won't he? We've been together two years, if this isn't the right time there never will be a right time.

'Call me old-fashioned but I think the man should do the proposing,' says Rosalind, her eyes widening at the cheeseburger. 'Oh, this is when I love being pregnant.'

'He's obviously not the proposing kind,' I say, checking my tuna for any sign of mayonnaise.

'Mayonnaise on the side,' says the waitress, placing a dish on the table. 'And salad without lettuce.'

That's the problem isn't it? Luke is one of those men who need a little push. After all, I am the perfect girlfriend, well close to perfect. Okay, there is the closet chocoholic thing but I can deal with that and I don't mind being a vegetarian as long as I don't have to eat Quorn. It bloats me out if I am honest. Anyway, once I'm pregnant Luke will have to let me eat meat. I'll need the protein won't I?

'I worry you only want to propose so you can get married before you're thirty-one,' says Rosalind through a mouthful of burger.

I so want to be Rosalind. I envy everything, from the burger to the bump. I want to be married in my thirtieth year and Luke would make a great husband. Better the devil you know right? Let's face it, by the time I find someone new I'll be thirty-two, and even then they may turn out to be Mr Wrong. I just don't have the time, and one has to think about fertility. I need enough time should I need fertility treatment and I want to have at least three, children that is, not fertility treatments. Trust me; I have thought all this through. It has to be Luke, and I do love him and I know he loves me.

'I don't want to be thirty-one and unmarried,' I say.

'It's not the right reason to marry someone. Suppose Mr Right is just around the corner. You'll miss him.'

'Luke is Mr Wright,' laughs Devon.

'But I love Luke. We've been together two years,' I insist.

'All the same, it's a bloody expense. Can't you propose to him here in good old Notting Hill?'

'I've kind of got a free train ticket to Dublin.'

They both look at me.

'Christ, how did you manage that?' asks Rosalind, leaning forward to belch.

If that's what pregnancy does to you maybe I should think it through a bit more.

'You remember Tom, the guy who banged me in my car,' I say, looking at Devon.

'You're banging a guy called Tom?' says Rosalind, wide-eyed. 'Why do you want to get married? Sounds like you're having a great time.'

'He banged her car, not her,' says Devon. 'You should see him, if anyone is worth banging on the side, he is. I only saw him once and that was enough, he's sex on legs.'

'He's got a free seat on the train to Dublin. He's got three and he's only using one.'

Rosalind shifts her eyes to Devon and then back to me.

'Free?' repeats Devon. 'He's offering you a free seat to Dublin?'

'There's no such thing as a free lunch darling. If you ask me he's working up to banging *you*,' says Rosalind.

'Why does he need three seats, and when did you arrange this with him?' asks Devon, stealing one of my fries.

'I met him again at this charity event with Luke. He drove me home ...'

'You know, this is really not normal Flo.'

Devon gestures to the waitress.

'Can we have another portion of fries?'

'If you want my advice,' she says turning back to me, 'I'd hold back on the proposal. I've seen that Tom. No man offers you a freebie unless he's hoping for something. He's a fabulous catch and loaded with it.'

'Take the advice,' chips in Rosalind, struggling to stand up, and scattering fries everywhere. 'Believe me you want to get banged as much as possible before you get in this state. Right, where's the sodding loo. Good job I wore a Tena pad.'

I grimace. Maybe I've got a few more years before the babies.

'You're a dark horse,' whispers Devon.

'No, it's not like that. He offered to pay for the car damage and then he came round to the salon with chocolates to apologise ...'

She raises her eyebrows.

'No really, he's just one of those nice people. And I saw him at this charity event and I had a bit of an accident so he offered to drive me home and ...'

She looks at me.

'You're right; men don't buy chocolates to apologise do they?' I say.

She shakes her head.

'I think Rosalind is on the right track when she said perhaps he wants to bang you.'

I gasp.

'But he's so good looking; he'd never want to bang ... I mean look at me.'

'You must have something he wants,' says Devon.

'I'm back. God, I've got terrible wind,' groans Rosalind.

Somehow I don't feel in such a rush to have babies.

Chapter Fifteen

'If anyone comes from Rory's you know what to do don't you?'

'We'll be fine,' says Sandy. 'You have a good time. Have you got the ring?'

I point to my handbag.

'It's so exciting, isn't it Ryan?'

'Riveting, totally riveting.'

I check my BlackBerry and re-read Luke's message.

Missing you darling but enjoying the golf. Love you x.

Oh, I can't wait to see him.

'Thanks for coming in early. I appreciate it. Don't forget if that Grant Richards comes back …'

'He'll be toast,' says Ryan.

'Jethro said if we could somehow find his address he'd send someone round with a banger. How dare he steal our idea?'

'I don't think a firework up his arse is going to achieve much,' says Ryan.

Ryan has much to learn.

'Not everything is about arses,' snaps Sandy. 'It might be for you but not the rest of us.'

And I'm leaving these two in charge?

'You will be okay won't you?' I say worriedly.

'We love each other really,' smiles Ryan.

I kiss them both and dash outside to my waiting taxi. Ryan carries my suitcase and deposits it in the boot.

'Come back engaged or we'll never talk to you again.'

'Get lots of names on the petition,' I instruct.

Once inside the cab I check I have Luke's engagement band. I get butterflies in my stomach every time I think about it. I pay the driver and wheel my case into Euston station. I hope Tom hasn't forgotten. I wouldn't be surprised if he had, and I'll probably find the seats have been taken by his friends or something. I did think of buying air tickets but the flights were all booked. I probably should have emailed him to say I was coming. The station is busy with rush hour passengers and I struggle to weave my way through the crowds to see the train times. I find the platform and then realise I can't get through the barrier as I don't have a ticket. A wave of panic washes over me. How could I have been so stupid? I have a vision of the train pulling away with me standing alone and miserable. I fight down my panic and approach the guard.

'Tickets,' he says.

'I'm on that train,' I say pointing. 'I've got a free seat.'

'A free seat,' he repeats doubtfully. 'You and everyone else I imagine.'

'Well, it's not free. Obviously someone paid for it.'

'Obviously,' he replies somewhat sarcastically.

'My friend Tom paid for it. He's got three seats and I'm joining him.'

'And what would your friend's name be?' he asks, looking at the clipboard in his hand.

Oh dear.

'I don't actually know his full name …'

'I see. He's your friend but you don't know his name and he didn't give you a ticket?'

I shake my head.

'Then I'm afraid I can't help you madam. If I let everyone through who says they have a free seat courtesy of a friend whose name they don't know I'd have chaos wouldn't I?' He tips his head in the direction of the ticket office.

'Why don't you see if there are any seats left? I wouldn't ask for a free one though. I don't think there are many of those going spare.'

I sigh, turn towards the ticket office and see Tom. He is walking towards the platform. His expression changes and a smile breaks across his handsome face and I realise that I have been looking forward to this trip and not just because I'm going to propose to Luke but also because I'll be spending time with Tom. He has one hand loosely pushed into his jeans pocket and the other is carrying a small suitcase.

'You came,' he says warmly.

'Ah *Tom,* I assume,' the guard smiles.

'That's me,' grins Tom, handing over the tickets.

We walk a short way up the platform before Tom stops.

'Right here we are, first class.'

Oh my God, first class. It must have cost him a small fortune. Rosalind and Devon were right, there is no such thing as a free lunch, or a free train ride. He'll be expecting payment of some kind. What do I do now? I've got the ring and everything. I'm going to get engaged. I can't get on a train with a man who clearly wants to bang me.

'I can't possibly ...' I begin.

'It's just a seat on a train. You need a seat and I'll enjoy your company. It seems a fair exchange.'

No such thing as a free lunch Flora.

'It's fine. I can get a ticket at the ticket office,' I say primly.

'I won't demand your body if that's what you're thinking.'

I blush and fiddle with my handbag.

'You'd be disappointed if you do,' I say, without thinking.

He rolls his eyes.

'You're always underestimating yourself,' he says smiling. 'But as I don't intend to, I won't know will I? But I somehow doubt you're a disappointment. So, Flora Robson, would you give me the pleasure, of your company that is, for the next few hours.'

'Well ...' I hesitate.

'I take that as a yes.'

The guard blows a whistle. I do want to propose to Luke. It really is now or never. He opens the door and I step into the carriage. A woman can have a male friend can't she? No such thing as a free lunch Flora. Don't think about it, don't think about it but how can I not think about it? Tomorrow I'll be thirty without a wedding in sight, and I want to be with Luke on my birthday don't I? But I feel like I am being disloyal to Luke and I really shouldn't be here. If only I weren't so indecisive. I follow Tom onto the train and pass the plush seats until we come to a door.

'My suite,' he says nonchalantly.

Suite? Oh no, it's getting worse. The train is gently rolling along the track and there is no getting off now.

'Suite,' I echo in a strained voice. I can't tell Luke about this. 'But I can't possibly ...'

'I think you can,' he smiles, 'unless you're thinking of throwing yourself off the train.'

'I thought you had spare seats?' I say, trying not to sound too accusatory.

'I have. There are three seats altogether and two bunk beds. You're welcome to go on top,' he says with a wink.

I don't believe this, have I gone totally insane? My mad rush to get married has led me into dangerous waters. I don't even know this guy. He could be a sex offender or a serial killer about to commit his next crime. He may have stolen someone's identity. For all I know his name isn't even Tom. I look at him suspiciously.

'Would you like tea? I'm having breakfast. I'm sure they have something healthy for you,' he says, patting one of the plush seats and pulling out a table.

'You could be a sex maniac for all I know,' I say boldly, running my hand along the back of the soft upholstery while thinking that wouldn't really be so bad. Don't think about it, don't think about it.

'I might well be, but to be honest I don't have time, appealing as it sounds I just don't think I could fit it into my tight schedule. What would you like for breakfast?'

He hands me the menu. I glance down casually so as to give the impression that food is of little interest, but I note the full English with hash browns and my stomach rumbles.

'Toast will be fine,' I say.

'Really, are you sure? I'm having the full English. Oh, I keep forgetting, you're on the health kick with Luke aren't you? Does he dictate everything you do?'

'He doesn't dictate,' I say forcefully, while inwardly agreeing that he does. 'I can eat what I like. I just like to eat healthily.'

'When your sweet tooth doesn't dictate otherwise,' he laughs.

He looks so handsome and I am sure my heart misses a beat when he laughs. He is so easy to be with, not that Luke isn't you understand, Luke is just different that's all. I glance again at the menu and feel my stomach grumble.

'I can eat whatever I like,' I repeat.

I feel his eyes on me and become uncomfortably aware of my well-worn Gap jeans and oversize top. I pull my woollen shawl around me and pat my hair, checking it is still neatly clipped around the doughnut.

'I'll have the full English too,' I say. 'But ...'

'Here come the orders,' he says, biting his lip to stop himself from smiling.

I look at him over the menu.

'Can you ask them not to turn the eggs? I don't like the yolks fried. Can I have the mushrooms in a dish on the side, otherwise the juice makes the hash browns soggy, and I'd prefer the tomatoes uncooked.'

He scratches his chin.

'Anything else? Do you want mayonnaise on the bacon?' he asks.

'Are you mocking me?'

He shakes his head.

'No,' he stretches his hands out in denial. 'I just want to get it right.'

'I don't have mayonnaise on bacon. I only have it when I have bacon in a butty.'

He nods.

'Right, of course, is coffee okay or would you prefer tea?'

'Yes, but ...'

He laughs and flops into one of the seats.

'I love this about you.'

I wish Luke did.

'Coffee, but I don't want decaf, and with skimmed milk not full fat.'

'Got it,' he says getting up. 'I'll be ten minutes. Have a look around.'

The door closes behind him and I let out a sigh. The suite is small and compact with a corner couch and two window seats. The floor is carpeted and soft under my feet. I glance nervously at a narrow door at the back of the compartment. Feeling confident that he wouldn't come back for a while, I slowly open it to see the bunk beds, neatly made with white sheets and fluffy blankets. A small cabinet with a single clock sits beside the beds. Well, if he thinks I'm going on top, he can think again. Just the thought of it.

No, don't think about it, don't think about it but how can I not think about it? I somehow think Tom is not a tea and biscuit after sex kind of man. In fact, I imagine Tom has never eaten a *Rich Tea* biscuit in his life. Don't think about it, don't think about it. In fact why am I thinking about it at all? Let's just say there would be little chance of confusing K-Y Jelly with Biofreeze as I imagine I wouldn't need either where Tom is concerned. Step away from the bedroom Flora. I close the door carefully. The smell of bacon and sausages reaches my nostrils. What am I doing having a fry up? Luke would have a heart attack if he knew. Come to think of it I'll have a heart attack if I go on like this. There's no such thing as a free lunch or a free breakfast Flora. Don't think about it, don't think about it. My eyes stray to the briefcase sitting on the floor. I could just peek inside couldn't I? No one would blame me would they? I'd just be checking that he isn't a sex offender. Yes right Flora, like there will be a business card in there saying *Tom, Sex offender specialising in female abduction on train journeys*. I shake my head and peep inside the mini bar. I gasp. The thing is full of Moet champagne.

'Bit early for that isn't it?' Tom says as he slides open the door. A waiter bundles in after him pushing a food trolley. There are croissants, toast, bacon, eggs, hash browns, sausages, beans and mushrooms, plus a cafetière of coffee. I could get used to this. It's a bit different to the normal curled up sandwiches that are doled out in cattle class.

'Everything separate, perfect for you, I thought,' he smiles.

The aroma of the coffee is wonderful and I watch with a watering mouth as the food is put onto the table. Tom gives the waiter a tip and then gestures for me to join him. He hands me a plate.

'Bon appetit.'

We eat in silence and I glance occasionally at him. He is absorbed looking through papers. I rummage in my bag and steal a quick look at the ring I'd bought Luke and feel a tremor of excitement. I push my plate away and drink leisurely from my coffee as I watch the sights pass by. It is cosy and warm on the train and I feel my eyelids grow heavy. A sudden clatter of plates makes me jump and I look up to see him clearing the dishes and putting them back onto the trolley.

'Do you want me to order more coffee?' he asks.

I shake my head. He pushes the trolley outside and then sits opposite me.

'What's happening with your salon?'

'I really don't want to talk about the salon if you don't mind. I just want to think about nice things.'

'Like marrying Luke?' he smiles.

'Yes,' I say.

His knee presses against mine and I feel the warmth of his body on my skin. I gently move my leg. I again remember Rosalind's words, *'No such thing as a free lunch Flora. He's working up to banging you.'* The thought sends more than just a little tremble through me. One last bang before getting married, I find myself thinking and give myself a quick rebuke. I clasp my hands together nervously.

'So, you don't have a girlfriend?' I say.

He raises his eyebrows.

'What makes you think I don't have a girlfriend?' he asks, pulling a laptop from his case.

I shrug.

'You never mention anyone.'

He nods.

'This is true. We broke up about nine months ago.'

'Oh,' I say. 'I'm sorry.'

I feel a little surge of pleasure. He's available, handsome, stinking rich and according to Rosalind wanting to give me as well as my car a bang. No, don't think about it, don't think about it but how can I not think about it? I'll be engaged to Luke in a few days and that will be that. He places his laptop onto the table and looks at me.

'It was on the cards, she rather liked money too much. I prefer to be with someone who wants to be with me rather than be romantically involved with my money.'

'I wouldn't mind your money,' I say impulsively.

God, where did that come from? It just kind of flew out of my mouth.

He widens his eyes.

'That's honesty.'

Now I sound like just another money-hungry female.

105

'I didn't mean I would prefer the money to you ...' I stutter.

He continues to look at me. This is becoming uncomfortable. The only word going through my head is *bang*. Honestly I could kill Rosalind. I turn to the window to avoid his eyes and enjoy the views of green fields and countryside. The sun is shining and I feel the heat of it on my cheek.

'What I meant was, I'd like to have money but not necessarily your money. I'd obviously be happy to have you without it ...'

Oh God, what am I saying? Do shut up Flora.

'Not that I'm saying I want you, of course.'

Not much. Oh, don't think about it, don't think about it.

'It's just money from anywhere would help right now,' I say with a sigh.

He smiles and stands up. Oh no, he isn't going to make a pass at me is he? I've probably asked for it.

'Fancy a game of cards?' he asks.

'A game of cards?' I repeat.

'That's what I said.'

'As long as it's not strip poker,' I say, and bite my lip.

What's wrong with me? I'm openly flirting with him.

'I'm game if you are,' he smiles, sending shivers down my spine.

'I wasn't serious,' I laugh.

He places a pack of cards onto the table.

'Whoever loses buys dinner,' he says.

'I can cope with that,' I say.

'So how about we play gin rummy? After all you have more clothes to take off than me so I'd probably end up naked first,' he says with another wink. 'So, maybe best not to play strip poker.'

Is he flirting with me?

'Dinner it is. I never thought I'd meet anyone who thought about food as much as me,' I laugh.

It is a relief to talk about food without the threat of recrimination. Not that Luke is that bad. I don't want you to think he is. I just wish he would be a bit more relaxed when it comes to food.

'Who's talking about food?' he says, in a tone so sexual that my breath catches in my throat. I'll have to stop wearing Womanity around him if this is what it does. Or maybe I should dab a bit more on. No, don't think about it, don't think about it.

'You're wearing that perfume again aren't you?' he says, reading my mind. He has an uncanny habit of doing that.

'I might be,' I reply, aware that we are blatantly flirting.

I don't believe this. He surely must have better taste. I can't believe I am that fanciable to someone like him. He surely goes for the blonde bombshell types. You know, those women smelling of Chanel and dripping in pearls, their lips a rosy red, and glossed like no tomorrow. I've never glossed in my life. I chew it off in five seconds. They always have thick wavy locks too, don't they? Or I should say long wavy extensions? I always imagine they spend half their life in a Chanel bubble bath and the other half between silk sheets getting shagged for all they're worth. I don't think I have ever been shagged for all I'm worth, but then again I don't think I'm worth much so perhaps Luke is giving me the shag I do deserve. How depressing is that?

'We should have music while we play. What would you like?'

He turns his laptop around to show me his playlist.

'I'd like ...' I begin.

'Let me guess. You like Black Eyed Peas?'

I stare at him aghast.

'How did you know that?'

'A calculated guess.'

I shake my head.

'I don't believe that.'

'No you're right. I played a wild card. I saw it on the music player in the salon when you went to change. Anyway, we have Black Eyed Peas.'

He clicks the music player and *Tonight's gonna be a good night* belts out.

'Gin rummy, whoever wins chooses what the other has to do as a forfeit. Agreed?'

'I thought the loser bought dinner,' I say, crossing my arms.

'I just changed the rules,' he grins.

'Okay,' I agree dubiously.

'Gin rummy isn't gin rummy without gin is it?' he says searching through the mini bar.

'No mother's ruin so Moet it is I'm afraid.'

He returns with a bottle of Moet and two glasses.

'Every time I take your cards you have to drink half a glass and vice versa. I hope you're good at this game.'

'I can drink you under the table,' I say confidently.

'You think you can?' he grins.

I nod.

'Okay, let's see how you do.'

Twenty minutes into the game and I'm beginning to feel sure he has cheated. I'm already on my third glass of champagne while he's still on his first.

'Nuts,' he says jumping up.

He returns with a bag of salted peanuts.

'Or are you not allowed because of the salt?' he asks.

Oh dear. Champagne and salted peanuts, something Luke abhors.

'Never drink while eating peanuts,' he says. 'It's the quickest way to get drunk.'

'Do we have any Coke?'

His eyes widen.

'Wow, you are letting your hair down, champagne, drugs and peanuts.'

'I meant Coke the drink.'

He laughs.

'That's a relief. We do, but that's cheating isn't it?'

'Talking of cheating, I think there is a slip of the hand going on here.'

'You're getting dirty with me now,' he laughs.

He puts his cards down and I squeal with delight.

'Yes, I'm taking those.'

'Why don't you let Luke propose to you?' he asks. 'Instead of the other way around.'

I lift my head and feel it spin. I can't say because Luke may never propose. That's the truth though isn't it? I'm good enough to live with but not good enough to marry. I should never drink champagne. It always makes me maudlin and negative.

'Because I don't think he will,' I say honestly and gulp some more champagne.

'Then he's a fool,' he says.

I suppose I could have a last bang before the wedding couldn't I? Then again maybe not. I wouldn't want Luke doing it. I know I could never do something like that, not really. He knocks back half a glass of champagne and pops a handful of nuts into his mouth. Forty-five minutes later and we are on the second bottle and I'm feeling very tipsy. The passing scenery rushes by, making me even dizzier. He taps his fingers on the table in time to the music. I play my hand and he takes my cards and puts his down.

'Right, I'm laying everything out,' he says.

'You are?' I say, somewhat drunkenly.

He smiles.

'Not literally.'

'That's a shame.'

He raises his eyebrows.

'Although it could be arranged,' he says softly.

I blush furiously. Oh God, I must stop drinking. He looks at me over the rim of his glass and laughs. He totals up the scores and says triumphantly.

'I won.'

Why am I not surprised?

'Fix,' I say giggling.

He removes the glass from my hand.

'Your forfeit is to dance with me. You can choose the song. But it has to be slow. Anything too fast and I think we'll both be throwing up.'

I look at the playlist.

'*These Foolish Things*,' I say. 'It's a tempo I can just about cope with.'

'*These Foolish Things* it is,' he says, scrolling down the music.

The song begins and he puts his hand out. I take it and it feels warm in mine. He pulls me gently towards him and I lay my hand softly on his shoulder. I shudder as his arm wraps around my waist and I am pulled into his chest. His heart beats against mine as we twirl slowly around the carriage.

'Come here often?' he whispers.

'Hardly ever,' I respond.

'You should. The food and company are excellent.'

I should pull away but it feels so perfect to be in his arms. I try to think of Luke but my fuddled brain struggles to do so. He is singing the song softly into my ear and it feels like a lullaby. One hand is clasped tightly in mine and I feel his breath whisper across my neck as he moves in closer. I attempt to move back but he is holding me tightly.

'Flo, I ...' he begins.

Pull away now. Pull away now Flora. Think of Luke, think of the engagement. More importantly think of the wedding. Think of ...

'I really need to explain something to you. I ...' he continues.

At that moment the train screeches to a halt and we are thrown onto the seat. He falls on top of me, his face so close that I can now feel his breath on my cheek. Before I have time to think his lips are on mine and I'm surrendering to the warmth and passion in them. I can hear noises around us but it seems so far away. I am only aware of the deliciousness of his kiss and the saltiness of his tongue. I feel myself drift into the kiss and my arms wrap themselves around his body. There is a knock on the door and he backs away, leaving me bereft and suddenly guilty.

'Sorry sir,' says the waiter. He looks harassed and anxious.

'What's happened?' Tom asks.

I straighten my clothes with trembling hands.

'There is a tree on the track. We're getting it moved but it may be some time.'

What? He's surely joking. I've heard of leaves on the line and the wrong kind of snow, but a tree on the track, I don't believe this. Only something like this could happen to me when I'm trying to get to my boyfriend to propose. Tom turns off the music.

'Will we still get to Dublin on time?' I ask, trying not to look at Tom. How can I propose to Luke now after kissing another man? This is awful, what was I thinking of?

'I can only tell you that we're trying to get the tree moved as soon as possible, but things are out of our control I'm afraid.'

'Thank you for letting us know,' says Tom.

'There is a hotel in the village nearby and they are offering food. If you wish to stay on the train we will be serving dinner as usual. We obviously won't catch our ferry crossing but we will get going again as soon as we can.'

The door closes and I avoid looking at Tom.

'Flo ...' he begins.

'It was the champagne,' I say quickly. 'I've drunk far too much and so have you.'

Although I'm not so sure he has drunk as much as me. I lean out of the window and strain to see the fallen tree. I don't believe this. I turn to face him.

'I'm starting to wonder if you're behind this,' I say stupidly.

'You think I made a tree fall down? And how did I manage that?'

'You don't seem to want me to get to Dublin,' I say angrily, grabbing a handful of nuts.

'Luke won't like that,' he says, pointing to the nuts and collecting up the cards.

'You don't know what Luke does or doesn't like and if you think I'm sleeping in those bunk beds with you then you can think again.'

'Why are you taking this out on me?' he asks.

I feel my body flush at the memory of his kiss. How dare he kiss me? I'm on my way to Dublin. I'm as good as married aren't I? What was I thinking of? How dare he put me in such a position? He's nothing but a gigolo. He probably preys on soon-to-be-married women. I feel my legs tremble at the memory of his kiss and shake my head to push it away. He walks towards me and I struggle to get him into focus. Oh God, I've gone blind in one eye. What the hell. Did he put something strange in my drink? I knew it. He's drugged me.

'Flo ...' he begins.

'I've gone blind in one eye,' I say dramatically.

'No you haven't,' he says, leaning down.

'What are you doing?' I say nervously.

'Picking up your contact lens,' he says, dropping it into my hand. 'You're so dramatic.'

I look into his eyes and laugh.

'I need to change them,' I say, heading for the loo.

'Flo, about earlier, I'm sorry. It was the champagne.'

I feel my heart sink. I should have known. That's classic isn't it? A rich handsome man can only kiss me when he's pissed. See what I mean? I really am only meant for a *Rich Tea* biscuit man aren't I?

'That's my excuse anyway,' he says. 'And by the way, you owe me dinner,' he smiles. 'You lost.'

I rummage through my bag for my glasses and pop them on.

'They suit you,' he says.

He takes my hand and twirls me around making my head spin even more.

'Can I take *you* for dinner to apologise? We can discuss those bunk beds as it looks like we may have to use them after all.'

My phone bleeps and I turn from him to check it. It's a text from Luke.

Wish you were here. I'm doing well. You'll never guess who the reigning champion is, only your Mr Rory. Do you want me to give him a punch on the nose? ☺

I gasp.

'Mr Rory is in Dublin,' I say.

'He is?' says Tom.

'He's playing in the tournament. Would you believe the bugger is the reigning champion?'

'There's success for you,' he smiles.

'I don't know why you're so admiring of him. He preys on young women and puts people out of work.'

He groans.

'A bit below the belt Flo, from what I hear he creates jobs for people.'

I scoff.

'Huh and where did you hear that?'

'Look, about your salon ...'

'I don't want to discuss it. I don't want money-grabbing Rory to spoil my engagement.'

'Right,' he says with a sigh.

This is terrible. I have to be in Dublin before tomorrow. I need to propose to Luke while I'm still twenty-nine. That way I'll be engaged by the time I'm thirty. Somehow, I feel it is fate to propose to Luke on my birthday. I can't fail at that too. I think of the salon and push it from my mind. I'll deal with Mr Rory at the same time; kill two birds with one stone. I have to get to Dublin come what may. Luke is all that matters, reliable dependable Luke. A good-looking rich boy is not my future. I only wish he wasn't part of my present.

'Why don't we explore the area and get some dinner?' he says. 'Walk off the champagne.'

Yes, good idea. Let's get away from these bunk beds.

'I'd better change,' I say and head to the loo.

I make a firm decision not to have any wine at dinner. In fact I shall not drink anything while with Tom. Good plan.

Chapter Sixteen

'Another one Flo?' shouts Gareth from the bar.

Honestly, only I could end up in the middle of Wales in a strange pub with a group of rugby players, and Welsh ones at that. I ask you, the middle of Wales when I'm actually trying to get to bloody Dublin. It's just typical isn't it? All I'm trying to do is propose to my boyfriend before I'm thirty. It's only Dublin I'm trying to get to, not Outer Mongolia. How did a tree get on the track? It's not like we've had gale-force winds. I should have flown. I'd have been there by now and I wouldn't have had the complication of Mr Rich. It occurs to me that perhaps fate doesn't want me to propose to Luke before I'm thirty. My whole future depends on a tree. It's eight in the evening. I should be on the ferry heading towards my soon-to-be-fiancé's arms. Instead I'm sitting in The Rose and Crown with Tom and a crowd of men I met only this evening and who seem to spend their time calling each other *boyo*.

'Red wine for the lady,' says Gareth, 'and a pint for you, boyo?'

See what I mean? It seems Gareth and Tom used to play rugby together. We'd just stepped out of a taxi and were about to head into the restaurant when Gareth had called to us from across the street. After lots of back slapping we had gone with him to the Rose and Crown.

'We used to have a lot of fun until this bugger got too rich,' Gareth had laughed. 'We're here for the rugby. We're going to thrash you English.'

He'd grabbed Tom and they'd wrestled each other in what I presumed to be some kind of friendly rugby tackle. I've never understood rugby. Luke said it is far too rough a game and that golf is far more civilised. Gareth had assumed I was Tom's girlfriend and insisted we join him and his partner Rube and what felt like the whole rugby team.

'It's Rube's birthday.'

'It's mine too,' I'd said.

'When?' everyone had chorused.

'Tomorrow,' I'd said timidly.

'Another round then,' Gareth had laughed.

'You never said,' whispers Tom into my ear. 'I hadn't realised it was so soon.'

I shrug.

'Food,' shouts someone. 'Our table's ready.'

'Come on you two,' says Gareth. 'You have to join us. I've not seen Tom in years and we need to celebrate these birthdays.'

Tom looks at me.

'Is that okay?'

I nod.

'I don't mind.'

The pub is crowded and we push past the throng to reach the table at the back. Tom takes my hand and entwines his fingers in mine.

'Don't want to lose you at this stage in the game do I? Luke would never forgive me.'

An hour and a half later and I'm sitting so close to Tom that there is little chance of him losing me.

'More drinks,' yells someone and before I know it I'm on my third glass of wine and helping myself from the largest display of junk food I've ever seen.

'Good job Luke isn't here isn't it?' Tom says leaning across me to reach for some chips.

'Luke would want me to have a good time,' I say, feeling the need to defend him.

He places pieces of fried scampi onto my plate.

'Is that what you're having?' he asks, as his arm accidentally brushes my breast. I fight back a gasp. Every touch from him evokes a multitude of emotions. He is sitting so close that his hip presses against mine.

'More wine for Flo, her glass is empty,' someone laughs.

'No, really I've had too much,' I protest.

'No such thing as too much darling.'

'You can never have too much wine or too much sex,' someone yells.

'Well, you sheep-shagging Welsh should know,' laughs Tom.

'You're keeping up with us,' laughs Gareth, handing me another glass.

He must mean drinking. He can't possibly mean shagging; I'm not keeping up with anyone in that area these days. I need to keep my wits about me. I can't remember the last time I drank so much. I usually only drink white wine spritzer with Luke and even then two is the most.

'Here's to Flo and Rube, happy birthday girls,' toasts Gareth.

'Happy birthday for tomorrow,' says Tom. He lifts his glass and clinks it against mine.

Several plates of spare ribs, chips and nachos later, not to mention another bottle of wine and I find myself hand jiving with Rube while Gareth, Tom and the rugby team arm wrestle to much laughter and shouting. Gareth calls for two bottles of Captain Morgan's rum and Rube and I progress from hand jiving to re-enacting the jive scene from Grease for the patrons of the pub to loud applause and shouting. Somewhere amidst the noise I hear a phone ringing and realise too late it is mine. I fumble drunkenly through my bag, find the phone and see there are two missed calls from Luke. I sway to the exit, signing to Tom that I have to make a phone call. The cold air hits me with such force that I feel like I've been slapped. I reel slightly and hang onto a plant holder, almost pulling the thing off its hook as I slide down onto the wall.

'Hiya, it's me,' I say, in a sing-song voice when Luke answers.

'I've tried calling you all evening,' he says in an accusing tone. 'Where have you been? Didn't you have your mobile with you?'

'Yes, sorry,' I hiccup. 'I'm out with friends and I didn't hear it.'

'What friends?'

Christ, does he have to make it sound like I don't have any?

'The usual crowd, you know,' I say.

I rub my eyes to try and clear the blur.

'How's it going?' I slur drunkenly.

'What?' he snaps.

'The tourniquet, how is it going?'

That didn't sound right somehow.

'What are you talking about?'

I'm not altogether sure I know.

'The cricket, how is it going?'

Oh shit, it isn't cricket is it? What the hell is it? Christ, I can't remember. I struggle to get my befuddled brain to work. It's a car isn't it? I clap my hands as I remember. It's golf, that's it.

'Oh dear it isn't cricket is it?' I say laughing. 'Is everything cricket though, you know at the golf thingy.'

I feel myself slide off the wall and land on the ground.

'Shit,' I mumble, feeling my bum throb.

'For Christ's sake Flora, have you been drinking or taking drugs?'

Drugs? Mind you, in Luke's language that would translate into snorting a line of sugar. And let's face it, after the amount of wine I've drunk I might as well have snorted several lines.

'Well, certainly something,' I say. 'Listen Luke, I want to ask you a very impotent question.'

He sighs.

'You can be very hurtful when drunk Flora.'

Whoops, Freudian slip.

'I meant important,' I correct.

'In that case perhaps you should ask me when you're sober. You do realise that too much alcohol is bad for your liver.'

Pardon me for living.

'Don't be such a patronising git,' I say.

I must be pissed. I never ever call Luke a git and most certainly not a patronising one. I may think it but I never actually say it, and most certainly never to his face. Not that I can see his face but you know what I mean. There is an awkward silence. The only sound is me hiccupping.

'I don't believe you sometimes Flora. I phoned to see if you were okay and all you can do is insult me and swear at me.'

I didn't swear did I? He can't possibly mean *git*. That's not swearing exactly, is it? I struggle to get back onto the wall. Oh God, I've drunk and eaten far too much.

'I didn't sw … calling you a git isn't searing.'

I can't even speak properly any more. The rum has paralysed my tongue.

'Are you having a good time?' I ask and punctuate it with a burp. Oh dear. I hear a heavy sigh the other end of the phone.

'Devon is a bad influence if you ask me,' he says sternly.

Devon? What's Devon got to do with anything?

'I'll speak to you tomorrow when you've got your hangover and you can ask me the important thing then. That's if you can remember it.'

'Luke,' I begin.

'I'm going to bed and that's where you should be if you ask me,' he says sternly.

I give the phone the finger.

'I didn't ask you,' I say, but he has hung up.

Sod it. I start to walk back into the pub and then realise I am going the wrong way and am heading to the car park. I turn around and feel my head spin. I hear a train horn and a vague memory of me somehow connected to a train flashes through my mind. The train, the train to Dublin! It will go without us. I stumble into the hot crowded pub and search the throng for Tom.

'Looking for me?'

I turn at his voice and grab his arm to support myself.

'The train,' I say pointing and accidentally hitting someone in the eye. 'It will go without us.'

I tug his arm and make for the door. He pulls me back gently.

'It's okay, they have my number. They'll call us in plenty of time. They know we need to be on it.'

'There she is,' calls Gareth. 'Let the party resume.'

'So how is up his own arse Wright then?' asks Tom.

I turn and struggle to get him into focus.

'What did you say?'

'Here you go Flo,' says someone pushing a glass into my hand and jostling me even closer to Tom.

'You smell good,' he whispers, pulling me closer.

'Tequila time,' roars Gareth.

'Maybe not a good idea,' Tom says into my ear before moving his lips to land on mine.

'I don't want to be a boring old fart,' I slur, still reeling from the kiss. 'I'll leave that to the patronising git.'

The last thing I remember is betting with Gareth that I could indeed drink ten shots of tequila and stay standing and then re-enacting out the whole Grease story and everyone shouting, 'How low can you go?' Then everything went black.

Chapter Seventeen

I squint through one eye and groan. God, my head hurts. I try to remember if I was in an accident. Everything seems weirdly out of proportion and then I remember my glasses. I lean over to the bedside cabinet only to find it isn't there. I grab the side of the bed as I feel myself begin to fall. My head feels like it has a dozen builders working away inside it. I pull my knees up and groan again. Where has the bedside cabinet gone? I try to get my brain to function. Why is the flat moving? Where's Luke and why is the bed smaller? There's a ringing in my ears. Christ, I've developed tinnitus. It's like I've woken up in someone else's body. I then realise the ringing is my phone. I jump up and bang my head on a roof above me. Shit, I'm in a coffin. I've bloody died. I then remember the bunk beds and relief washes over me until I remember who may be in the top one.

'Shit.'

I lean down to the floor and grab the ringing phone.

'Hello.'

'Flora is that you? You sound different,' says Rosalind.

I let my aching body fall back onto the bed and throw the covers off, and it is then I see it. I stare in horror. I'm wearing a pissing rugby shirt and *only* a pissing rugby shirt. I hate rugby. I would never ever wear a rugby shirt willingly. I hate rugby more than I hate golf. Golf, yes, that's it golf. I'm on my way to Dublin to propose to Luke who is playing in the tournament. What happened to my great plan not to drink again?

'That's because someone stole my tongue and replaced it with a sanitary towel. God, Rosalind, I feel so ill. I don't think I'm going to make it to Dublin. I've not had a hangover like this in years.'

'You mean you haven't had a hangover like this since you met Luke and what do you mean you don't think you're going to make it to Dublin, aren't you there yet?'

'There was a tree on the track, can you believe it? It's like fate is trying to stop me from proposing to Luke. Do you think that is possible?'

'What?'

'That fate is trying to stop me. Do you think maybe I'm not meant to marry Luke?'

'I'm not altogether sure why you want to, let alone whether you're even meant to. Look, phone me when you're there. No, second thoughts, phone me when you've proposed. How's the dish by the way?'

'I think he might be on top of me,' I whisper. 'I was so shitfaced last night I don't know what happened.'

She gasps.

'You don't know? You don't know if Mr Gorgeous is on top of you. Usually one can't fail to notice these things, even with a hangover. Either you're getting banged or you're not.'

'I mean on top of me as in top bunk on top of me. He has a suite on the train.'

'Holy shit, can't be bad. Look, phone me later with the latest instalment. I've got to run I'm dying for a pee.'

I look at the time on my phone. 8 a.m. I sit up gently and look around. At least I'm alone in the bed, that's something of a comfort. I climb gently from it, giving my head as much consideration as possible but still it explodes at the slightest movement. I need aspirin. I look for my glasses, and then I see it. My bra is slung over it and there perched on the top are my glasses. How did a traffic cone get on the train, and more importantly how did it get in our suite? I struggle to focus on things around me but it's like there is a mist in the room. Shit, I've still got my contacts in. With a heavy sigh I pop them out and fall back onto the bed. I'm too scared to even try and remember what happened last night. My mouth feels like the inside of a sewer. No, that's not true. Compared to my mouth I think a sewer would be sweet. I lean over the bed and take a quick sneaky look at the top bunk and sigh with relief. The sheets are crumpled but thankfully he isn't there. I pull the blinds back and feel a thousand needles shoot through my pupils. The train is moving along at a rapid pace. Thank God. I look down at my crumpled clothes on the floor and sigh. I pull my jeans on and after putting on my glasses I open the door gingerly and see him sitting nursing a mug of coffee.

'Morning,' he says. 'You look terrible.'

I squint at him.

'Really, I rather thought I looked like Jennifer Aniston.'

'No, that's a delusion and I don't look like Tom Cruise. I know it's hard to believe but it's true. There is coffee, and the loo is all yours. I imagine you may need it. I did warn you about the tequila.'

'Tequila?' I say stupidly.

He nods.

'I don't think Luke would have been happy. You had seven, I think. I tried to keep you company but I threw the towel in after the fourth. You can drink me under the table it seems. All I know is this morning I have the mother of all hangovers.'

I groan. He looks worse for wear. His eyes are heavy lidded and he hasn't shaved. I straighten the rugby top and say,

'How did I get into the bed and more importantly, how did I get into this?'

'Search me. I don't even remember getting on the train. I've never drunk so much in my life.'

I avoid his eyes.

'Did we, you know?' I say shyly.

He shakes his head.

'I'd be absolutely amazed if we did, but you needn't worry. I have strong morals and would not take advantage of a drunken woman and you were most certainly drunk.'

There is a knock at the door and a waiter brings in breakfast. The sight of the bacon and sausages churns my stomach and I groan.

'Just leave it on the table,' says Tom, turning white.

The waiter leaves and Tom pushes the food to one side.

'It's all yours,' he says.

I shake my head and take deep breaths.

'I wish this train would stop moving.'

'You and me both,' he smiles. 'Unfortunately it's on a mission now and so are you if I remember, to get engaged to Mr Up His ...'

I glare at him.

'Mr Right,' he finishes.

He gulps his coffee.

'They were your friends if I recall,' I say, reaching for a mug and thinking how good he looks even when rough.

'It was your hand putting the tequila into your mouth if I recall,' he responds.

I pour coffee into the mug and it is then I see it. I'm wearing the ring off a lager can on my wedding finger. I stare at it for a second and then lift my eyes to him. He shrugs.

'Not guilty, Although, I've a vague memory of something, but don't ask me what. Something happened,' he says yawning. 'In fact quite a few things happened but I can't remember any of them.'

'Something happened?' I squeal.

He nods.

'What exactly happened?'

He looks thoughtful.

'No, my mind is a blank. I just have a vague memory of some kind of happening.'

'Happening?' I repeat.

I flop into the seat opposite him.

'I've got a ring pull from a lager can on my finger and you say there was a happening,' I say fearfully.

'Yes, I spotted that,' he says with a smile.

He exudes rugged masculinity even when hungover and he is deliciously so handsome that I just want to keep looking at him. Even unshaved he's appealing. He smells fresh, that *straight out of the shower* fragrance.

'I'm going to Dublin to propose to Luke,' I say removing the ring from my finger.

'I wouldn't let a Heineken can ring get in the way. I'm sure the something is nothing.'

'Did we?' I ask hesitantly.

'Not that I recall.'

'Do you recall anything?' I snap.

'Not really.'

'As long as I didn't marry some sheep-shagging Welshman,' I say.

'No, I believe you have to say I do, or I don't, or is it I will, or I won't. Anyway you weren't capable of saying much at all if I recall.'

'Fifteen minutes to the ferry,' calls a voice.

I walk to the loo.

'I'm going to freshen up,' I say.

'Happy birthday by the way, and I would have bought you something but I didn't know.'

I stop with a start. I'm thirty. Thirty and not engaged.

'Thank you,' I say, before rushing into the loo and throwing up.

A great start to my thirties. You'd think by now I could hold my drink.

I step aboard the ship.

'Welcome on board the Ulysses,' says a pretty stewardess.

I turn to Tom.

'Thanks so much for the train adventure.'

'You're welcome. Just call me next time you want a good time, and a massive hangover and I'll be there.'

'Without your Welsh friends next time,' I smile.

'I expect they'll be too busy shagging sheep,' he says with a wink and my stomach flutters.

'I'm off to find some aspirin,' I say, reluctant to part from him.

'They've got everything on the boat. Good luck with your proposal which I'm sure will be a great success. He'll be a fool to turn you down.'

'Right now I'm dying and don't believe I'll make it to Dublin. I'll die a spinster on this bloody ferry,' I moan.

'You'll be okay,' he says.

I groan.

'Did we have a good time at the pub? It would be nice to know all this was worth it.'

He rests his hand on my hip and I feel that now all too familiar surge of emotion that only he can produce. He kisses me gently on the cheek.

'Yes we did. It was fun. We were celebrating your birthday.'

I find myself wondering how Luke will want to celebrate my birthday. He'll take me to a vegetarian restaurant no doubt, and we'll have healthy juice and a sugar-free dessert. The memory of my phone call with him comes back to me.

'I called Luke a patronising git,' I say.

'That doesn't surprise me. You said a lot of things. The last thing I remember you saying was 'I can drink you bastard rugby boyos under the table.''

I groan again.

'Well, see you around, I'll probably bump into you somewhere on the ferry,' he says.

I nod and climb the stairs to the seating area. The place is packed but I find a seat at the back and gratefully flop into it. A young child bounces into the seat beside me and opens a bag of cheese and onion crisps. I fight back a gag and look on miserably as her mother and screaming sibling claim the seats opposite me. I stare at the mother's badly highlighted hair, that's a do-it-yourself job if ever I saw one. The woman gives me a tired smile before unbuttoning her blouse and popping out a monster blue veined breast. She pushes the baby's mouth onto the nipple and it proceeds to slurp away like no tomorrow.

'I wanna a drink,' yells the other child, spitting bits of cheese and onion crisps as she does so. She swings her legs, kicking me in the shin. Maybe she can have a go at the other breast. At least that way they'll both be quiet and I can get some peace. I pull my legs away from the ferocious female Damien.

'Sorry,' says the mum. 'You got kids?'

No, and when I do, they won't slurp at my nipple like that little animal on yours that's for sure, and they certainly won't kick strangers and dribble cheese and onion crisps down their front. I doubt they'll be allowed crisps anyway. I also doubt Luke will allow me to pop out my veiny breasts in public. Knowing Luke he won't even want to see my veiny breast in private, come to that.

'I'm thirsty, I wanna drink,' demands the monster.

'No, I'm actually going to Dublin to get engaged, so I guess I'll be having them soon,' I say.

'If you want my advice …'

I don't actually.

'Think long and hard. Having kids changes your life,' she says, pulling the baby off her nipple with a slurp and popping the other one out. Oh God, one was enough but the sight of two makes me feel nauseous.

'I use to buy my undies from Marks and Spencer. You know where I get them now?'

I shake my head. I've no idea. I do know that her hair hasn't been near Toni and Guys though.

'Poundstretcher. Can you believe that? Poundstretcher bloody thongs, that's sex appeal for you.'

Well, I can believe it. With your hips they must have stretched quite a few pounds.

'Breastfeeding is terrible. I've only got to hear a baby cry and I'm spurting across the room. As for childbirth, don't get me started. I screamed for bloody England I tell you.'

Oh dear. Luke hates any kind of fuss. I suppose he'll want me to have silent childbirth like Katie Holmes, and without pain relief. Christ, eyebrow threading sounds like heaven compared to that. I'll have to sneak my own painkillers into the hospital. I'll be the only pregnant woman to have an epidural dealer.

'Mum, I'm thirsty, really really thirsty.'

'It's those crisps,' I say.

She gives me a dirty look, swings her leg and aims for my ankle. I look desperately around for another seat but everywhere is taken. The baby loses the nipple and screams blue murder. My head throbs like it's about to burst and to make things worse little Damien at my side has pulled a recorder out from her *I love Kitty* bag and is squealing it into my ear. At this rate I'll be in no fit state to propose to Luke. She takes a deep breath, blows into the thing again and then chokes cheese and onion crisps over me.

'Oh shit, I'm so sorry,' says Mum, yanking the baby off her nipple and spurting breast milk towards me.

I sigh and stand up.

'If you'll excuse me I need some fresh air,' I say.

I wander down to deck four and to Café Lafayette and trust me, trying to negotiate stairs on a moving boat after a night on the lash is no mean feat. I order a latte and find a table by the window and watch the sea spray splash onto the glass. I nurse my latte and go over my proposal speech.

'Hello there,' bellows a middle-aged man, making my head vibrate. 'Is that a latte you're drinking? You know caffeine is a killer?'

It's Luke incarnate. He sits in the chair opposite me. It's not only his voice that is loud. He's wearing a bright green checked jacket over brown corduroys.

'Mind if I sit here?'

Yes I do. I shake my head politely.

'I use to drink twenty cups a day, probably more. My blood pressure was sky high. I'm lucky to be alive.'

What a shame you are. Now now Flora, just because you have a hangover there's no need to be rude, even if it is just in your head.

'I said to myself one day, I said, George if you keep this up you'll be dead before you're thirty.'

I stare at him. My God, if *he's* thirty, what must I look like? The greying hair and shiny bald patch don't help of course. His, that is, not mine. He must be forty if he's a day, surely.

'I'm George, but I just said that. Not George Clooney, easy mistake to make though, right?'

He's surely joking.

'Off to Dublin then are you?'

I bloody hope so otherwise I'm on the wrong ferry.

'Yes, hopefully not much longer.'

'At least two and half hours, why don't you and I go to the cinema? Find two seats in the back row,' he says suggestively.

I don't believe this. Someone kill me, kill me now. If this is the best I can do, then I really don't deserve to live.

'That's a nice offer,' says a familiar voice behind me. 'But I really don't like my girlfriend sitting in the back row with anyone other than me.'

I turn, relieved to see Tom.

'No offence matey, I didn't know she was taken,' says George, jumping up and backing away nervously.

'I leave you on your own for five minutes and you're pulling all the best looking men on the boat,' he smiles.

'He was hard to resist,' I laugh.

'How's the hangover?'

I grimace.

'Terrible. Everywhere is so noisy.'

'Would madam like to join me in my private cabin? I can't offer two seats in the back row of a cinema I'm afraid. He had one up on me there, but I can offer peace and quiet.'

He takes my hand.

'Come on. I know you hate luxury but I think you'll appreciate a cabin right now.'

I take his hand gratefully.

'You have a cabin on the boat too?'

'What's the point of having money if you don't enjoy it?'

I let him lead me along a corridor and into a spacious cabin with a lounge area and two beds in the corner. Not bunk beds this time I notice. I flop onto the couch and lift my legs up. He smiles and walks to the door.

'You rest. I'm going to have a walk around.'

The minute the door closes I lay my head back and relax. I know I should check my phone but all I can think about is the fact that today is my birthday and I'm all alone. Well, I'm with Tom but you know what I mean. I reach into my handbag and pull out my BlackBerry. There are missed calls and a list of text messages, the first four of which are from unknown numbers. I click into the first one.

Hey Flo thanks 4 a gr8 night and congratulations, we can't wait to cu when we're back in London. Wishing u lots of happiness 4 the future Love Rube and Gareth. Xx

That's a bit over the top for a birthday greeting. Still they are probably well and truly hungover. It is nice of them to congratulate me though and from what I can remember I did like them. I stretch out on the couch and click into the next text and the next, all from Tom's friends congratulating me and wishing me every happiness for the future. How nice is that? Finally there are two missed calls from Devon and one from my parents. I listen to their messages wishing me a happy birthday and then phone Devon.

'Hey chick, I was going to phone you but I've been in a photo shoot this morning. I thought I was never going to hear. Well, what did he say?'

I sigh.

'I haven't asked him yet. I'm still on the ferry. There was a tree on the track and we're all behind. Luckily Tom had a cabin on the train so we could sleep, and he has a cabin on the ferry too. Can you believe it? The guy is loaded Devon. We had dinner with his rugby friends last night. I got a bit pissed and ...'

'Jesus, you and Tom didn't did you?' she gasps.

'No silly, of course not, but I did call Luke a patronising git.'

'You did? Well he is, let's be honest. I mean, I think he's great and all that but just recently he has become a bit, well you know.'

The truth is that yes I do know.

'He hasn't sent me a birthday text,' I say.

'He's probably carried away with the golf. You know what they're like.'

'I suppose he's cross,' I say.

'What's Tom like?' she asks hesitantly.

'He's fun,' I say and realise that for the first time in ages that that's what I am having, fun, apart from the hangover of course.

'Mark said Luke's doing well. Apparently, that Rory guy is playing. You know the one who's after your salon?'

'Yes, I know. How strange is that?'

'Look I have to go, happy birthday. We'll go out when you get back. Celebrate your birthday and engagement.'

I hang up and at that moment the phone bleeps with a text from Luke.

Happy birthday darling, hope you're having a nice day. We'll celebrate when I get home. Missing you. I'll phone you later. Important match coming up so think of me.

I throw the phone into my handbag as Tom strolls in carrying two bags. He moves my legs and sits next to me.

'I couldn't let your thirtieth pass without a card and a little present could I? So, happy birthday and sorry they're not gift wrapped. There isn't a great deal of choice on a ferry I'm afraid.'

'Oh,' I say, taking the bags. 'Thank you.'

'You're welcome. You can open them now. It is your birthday,' he says and grins.

'You're so generous. What do you do? Your job I mean,' I ask.

He opens his mouth, hesitates, and says,

'Do you mind if we don't talk about that, at least not right now. I don't want to spoil your present opening.'

I raise my eyebrows.

'God, you're not a drugs dealer are you?'

He smiles.

'No, nothing that sordid,' he nods at the bags. 'Open your presents.'

I look into his eyes and feel a strange tingle run through me. How can he do that just by looking at me? How can I feel so much for someone I barely know? The vibration of the engine seems to run up my legs and into my stomach and I feel suddenly queasy. I lift my legs up and tuck them underneath me before opening the first bag. I pull out a bottle of Womanity perfume and body cream. This must have cost him over seventy quid.

'I can't possibly ...'

'Don't start that again. I assure you that you can. It's a big 'O' birthday.'

'Don't remind me.'

I slide my hand into the other bag and pull out a box of Belgian chocolates.

'For your sweet tooth as I'm thinking that may be curtailed once you marry Luke.'

'Thank you, it's really nice of you.'

'It's not much.'

I open the card, which simply reads: *On your biggie, all the best love Tom x.* I lean forward and kiss him tenderly on the cheek and his hand strokes my face.

'I've got some important calls to make. Why don't you rest?' He says and before I can answer he has left the cabin. It is then I know that I can't possibly take advantage of his offer of a bed at The Gresham Hotel. I'm growing too fond of him and one more night with him could ... the thought sends me into a whirl. Just his hand on my cheek had nearly driven me to an orgasm. If only Luke could produce one that speedily. In me, I mean. Luke has no trouble with speed when it comes to his own orgasms. Still, a woman can live without orgasms, can't she? Oh God, don't think about it, don't think about it but how can I not think about it? Here I am, almost at Dublin, and about to propose to the man I love so that I will be engaged on my birthday and all I can think of is Tom and orgasms. But Tom is just a good-looking rich boy. There could never be a future with him, whereas Luke is reliable, sensible as well as successful and he'll make a good father, I'm sure of it. I google *bed and breakfast* and after the fifteenth call I manage to get myself booked into one. All I have to do now is avoid Tom's gorgeous body until we disembark. How difficult can that be? I scroll into the photo of Luke and me, taken on our holiday in Italy, and feel a little tingle of excitement at the thought of being engaged in a matter of hours. I close the phone as Tom walks back into the suite.

'It's nice on the promenade deck. Fancy a stroll,' he says with a smile.

My headache has eased somewhat and the thought of fresh air is appealing. I nod and follow him. We stroll lazily around the ship. The sea is calmer now and the fresh air is invigorating.

'I love this boat,' Tom says looking out at the sea.

'Do you go to Dublin a lot?' I ask, feeling a need to know more about him.

'My parents have a house in Dublin. They spend most summers there.'

He turns to face me and seems about to speak when a woman approaches and asks if he will take a photo of her and her husband. He agrees readily and spends some time getting the photo right. The woman takes the camera and looks excitedly at the picture on her camera screen.

'Oh that's lovely, thank you so much. Do you want me to take one of you and your girlfriend?' she asks, smiling at me. I feel myself blush as Tom slides his arm around my waist.

'Well, I'm not ...' I begin.

'That would be great, wouldn't it?' he says, handing over his mobile. He takes my arm and wraps it around his waist and I feel quite faint at the touch of him.

'Smile,' he whispers in my ear.

The woman takes two photos and I feel Tom squeeze my waist before taking his phone back. He pushes it into his jeans pocket and points ahead.

'Shall we carry on,' he says and I follow like an obedient puppy.

We walk silently around the promenade and watch seagulls follow at the stern. I huddle close to him as we shelter from the wind behind the funnels.

'So, in a few hours you'll be proposing,' he says suddenly, falling into an empty deckchair and pointing to the one at the side of him. I sit down carefully. It would be just my luck to flop into a deckchair and have the thing rip wouldn't it? I mean that is just the kind of thing that would happen, especially as I'm starting to look quite good in front of Tom for a change.

'Yes,' I say, feeling stirrings of doubt. I am doing the right thing aren't I? Don't think about it, don't think about it, but how can I not think about it? This is my whole life.

A stewardess approaches us.

'Hello there, can I get you a drink before lunch?'

'Two champagne cocktails,' says Tom before I can speak.

I don't like to admit that I've never had a champagne cocktail. That's not to say I've never been offered one. It's just Luke always got in before I could say yes. I wonder what we'll have at our wedding. Surely he'll allow champagne? It will be a bit embarrassing if we have to toast with grape juice. It dawns on me that this will be the last time I drink champagne, or any alcohol come to that, unless it is a very special occasion or the next Jacksons' boring charity do. I'll also be facing life without sugar and meat. I'll have to give up everything. Christ, I sound like I'm entering a convent instead of getting married.

'To your future marriage,' says Tom, holding up his glass.

I force a smile.

'Yes, to my future marriage,' I echo.

We clink glasses and his hand brushes mine and he looks into my eyes.

'I hope you don't mind. I've arranged a little surprise for your birthday,' he says and gives me a cheeky grin.

'What?' I say excitedly.

'You might want to change,' he says, draining his glass. 'The dress code is smart casual. '

I feel my stomach flutter with excitement.

'But you bought the perfume,' I protest.

He waves a hand dismissively.

'That wasn't much,' he says checking the time on his phone.

'We've got twenty minutes. Allow me to escort you back to the suite Miss Robson.'

I laughingly take his hand. Oh, if only Luke were like this. Don't think about it, don't think about it, but how can I not think about it? This time tomorrow and I'll be engaged to Luke and I'm starting to think that proposing to Luke is a big mistake.

Chapter Eighteen

I gasp in wonder at the candlelit table. I'd guessed that Tom had arranged lunch but I never imagined it would in a sheltered spot on the promenade, under a gazebo. I feel tears prick my eyelids as I stare at a banner that hangs above the entrance.

Happy Birthday to a Lovely Lady.

Shimmering crystal blurs before my eyes. Tom pulls back a satin-draped chair and gestures for me to sit down.

'Happy birthday,' he says, his eyes twinkling. 'I hope Luke won't mind but I've got the best champagne on ice, and meat on the menu.'

He gives a mischievous smile.

I feel sure Luke would be livid if he knew but right now Luke is the last person on my mind. After all, when has Luke ever done anything like this for me?

'I don't know what to say,' is all I manage to mumble.

'You don't have to say anything, just enjoy.'

A waiter materialises out of nowhere and pours the champagne into our glasses. So much for my great plan of not drinking while with Tom.

'This is Paul, our waiter for the lunch.'

Paul nods and places the champagne back into a bucket.

'Happy birthday madam. We have a special selection for you. There is salmon mousse to start or parsnip soup. The main meal is duck in orange sauce with sauté potatoes or roasted lamb shank with roast potatoes and a selection of vegetables. Dessert is profiteroles with cream or chocolate mousse,' says Paul. 'Of course,' he adds with a smile, 'madam could enjoy both desserts.'

Madam is fully intending to.

After taking our order he leaves us. Tom looks shyly at me over his champagne glass.

'You don't mind?' he asks. 'I didn't want it to be over the top but you are thirty after all, and once you're married I doubt very much you'll be allowed champagne.'

Tell me about it.

'I'm sure I will be,' I say. I push Luke from my mind and sip the excellent champagne.

'What do you do that you have so much money?' I ask.

He looks uncomfortable and then seems to compose himself.

'I own properties. Inherited from my father. It's a large corporation ...'

'Oh, I know about those,' I say with venom.

The last person I want to think about during this lovely dinner is Mr Rory. I'll sort him out when I get to Dublin.

'About the salon ...' Tom begins.

'Please, can we not talk about the salon. This is so lovely; I don't want Mr Rory to ruin it.'

He nods and studies me for a second. He looks about to speak when Paul returns with the starter. My eyes widen in appreciation at the salmon mousse. It's no good, I can't deny it. I love my food. Don't think about it, don't think about it. Not today anyway.

I'd worn my favourite lace skater dress by Laura Scott and topped it with a black pashmina. I left my hair hanging loosely around my shoulders and popped my favourite dangling earrings in. I feel pretty and his admiring glances confirm I look it.

'Thank you so much for this,' I say as Paul removes our dishes.

'I wish I could have done more. It's not so easy on a boat,' he laughs.

I find myself wondering how much money he does have. The deck is deserted. Surely he didn't pay to have this part of the deck to ourselves. The main dish comes and I look enviously at his lamb shank. Paul places the duck in front of me and refills our glasses.

'That looks good,' says Tom.

'So does that,' I say, coveting his lamb.

We laugh and he cuts a piece and holds his fork towards me.

'Try it.'

I nearly choke on my duck. I can't remember the last time Luke and I had shared food. Well, that's not true. I can. In fact I cringe at the memory. I had offered Luke some of my aubergine salad and he had been horrified when I'd passed him my fork. *I'll take some on mine,* he'd said, pushing the fork away, *that's how germs are spread.*

I sigh at the memory. Tom gestures with his fork.

'It's only fair I try the duck,' he says.

I offer some duck on my fork and he takes it happily. I savour the lamb.

'That's excellent,' I say.

'Coming from the vegetarian that's a compliment indeed,' he laughs, cutting a large chunk from his meat and placing it on my plate. I do likewise and we eat in companionable silence, occasionally glancing at each other when we think the other isn't looking. By the time our desserts arrive I'm feeling quite light headed and thinking a second bottle of champagne is perhaps not a good idea. God, I've never eaten and drunk so much in my life. Not that I'm complaining mind you. I can barely take my eyes off Tom. He is looking so handsome and his eyes constantly meet mine until finally they lock and we just look at each other. This is so not good. Thank God I won't be spending another night in his suite. I really don't think I could trust myself.

'Thank you so much for this,' I say, feeling suddenly uncomfortable at having his eyes on me for so long.

'I'm sorry I couldn't do more,' he says sipping a cup of coffee.

Paul clears away our plates and Tom stands, offering me his arm.

'A stroll around the deck, Miss Robson.'

I take his arm and allow him to lead me onto the promenade. He carefully wraps my pashmina around my shoulders, his hand resting there longer than necessary. We walk silently for some time and then he stops. He looks pensive.

'Can I give you a birthday kiss?' he asks.

Oh yes please. I can't think of anything better. I steel myself to say no however. I can't possibly kiss him again can I? But before I can reply he has pulled me close and his warm demanding lips are once again on mine. This is becoming a habit. A multitude of emotions overtake me and I'm completely out of control. My arms slide around his neck and his arms hold me upright. He pushes me gently against the rail and his hands caress my neck. Pull away, Flora, pull away, but I'm surrendering instead and it feels so delicious to be in his arms and to drown in his kiss. His tongue gently caresses mine and I feel my legs buckle. Oh my God, this is just terrible. How can I possibly marry Luke when I'm clearly in love with Tom? He releases me gently and looks questioningly into my eyes.

'Forgive me,' he says. 'I find that perfume hard to resist.'

I go to answer when there is a crackling from the tannoy.

'Ladies and gentlemen, we advise you that we will be docking in thirty minutes.

'Saved by the tannoy,' he laughs nervously.

I'm shaking so much I can barely stand. He leads me down the steps and back to the suite. All I know is that I don't want to leave him. This is terrible; I've come to Dublin to propose to my boyfriend. I have the ring and everything; I wasn't supposed to fall in love on the way. Don't think about it, don't think about it, but this time I really do have to think about it.

Chapter Nineteen

I stand outside the B&B's tatty entrance and hesitate. I had refused Tom's offer of a lift and taken a taxi. I had, however, agreed to take his phone number and am already feeling guilty about that. What soon-to-be-engaged woman takes the phone number of another man and one she has kissed at that? I have no idea where I am or where Luke's hotel is, or where the golf course is, or even The Gresham Hotel. By the look of things I'm in Dublin's equivalent to Soho, and I've been solicited twice in as many minutes. Seriously, I could have made a small fortune in the time I have been standing outside the B&B. If I'd have known I would be so popular in Dublin I would have come here earlier. I see another man approaching and dive through the doorway. A woman looks at me tiredly from behind a desk.

'You need a key?'

'I booked a room,' I say pulling out my phone.

'Everyone books a room. How long you want it for?'

'I'm not sure. My boyfriend ...'

She laughs.

'I've heard 'em called some things but never *boyfriend*.'

'No, he's here for the tournament and ...'

Her bright pink lips open and she laughs revealing stained teeth.

'Oh be Jaysus, a tournament, that's new. You're going to be fucking busy. You gonna get some kind of medal at the end?'

I sigh.

'Do you know where The Gresham Hotel is?'

She chews on her gum.

'Go way outta that! You having this tournament at The Gresham are ya? You'll be selling tickets next,' she says and roars with laughter. She leans over the desk to give me the once over.

'You won't get into The Gresham,' she says knowingly.

'Is there a dress code?'

She laughs.

'They don't let floozies in there. Not even if you're having a tournament.'

Floozies? What a cheek. I pick my case up tiredly and walk back outside. I wave down the first cab I see and ask for The Gresham Hotel. Do I look like a bloody prostitute? I pull my phone from my bag only to see the battery has died. I lean my head back and go over what I'm going to say to Luke. All I know is I need to see Tom. Twenty minutes and fifteen euros later I am standing outside The Gresham. A doorman welcomes me and offers to take my suitcase as I enter the plush foyer. This is really a bad idea isn't it, but I can't stay at the B&B can I?

'Is it a room you be wanting?' asks the man behind the desk.

'I'm actually looking for a guest who's staying here.'

Then I remember I don't know his surname do I. How stupid is that? How can I still not know his name? How did he manage to go all this time without telling me his surname? It's a bit odd that isn't it? Now I come to think about it actually, it's very odd. The reception clerk stares intently at me and not only him but two other members of staff.

'The problem is I don't know ...'

'It's Mr Rory you'll be looking for to be sure,' says the clerk.

What? How would he know I'm looking for Mr Rory? What have Ryan and Sandy been doing since I've been away? I only said get plenty of signatures, not start a worldwide campaign. Still, it's good for the cause if people in Dublin know what kind of person Mr Rory is. By the time I get home I should have got some good publicity. Bloody hell, I'll be in the papers next. I turn to look at the clerk and my eyes fall on a display at the front of the desk. OH MY GOD, *I am in the papers.* A copy of the *Daily Mail* is displayed on a newsstand and I'm on the front page, or someone who looks frighteningly like me is on the front page, but I feel quite sure it is most certainly me. I grab the paper with trembling hands and stare at the picture of Tom and myself. I'm snuggled up to him and he is kissing me on the cheek. He has one arm around me and oh my God, is that his other hand resting on my breast? I feel my whole body grow hot. The photo is from last night and it is most certainly me because I am wearing the rugby T-shirt. I don't understand. Why would the newspapers be interested in me, and Tom and the rugby players? Did we do something really embarrassing? Please don't say we stripped off in public and did a rendition of Grease. Luke will never forgive me. No, that wouldn't make the nationals would it? What did we do? I scan the headlines bracing myself for the worst and feel my legs buckle.

Engaged
Rory's heir Thomas Rory falls for humble hairdresser after making a bid for her salon.

I stare at the bold black words. *Humble hairdresser,* what a cheek. Then it sinks in. Thomas Rory. Tom is Mr Rory ... my stomach churns and I fight the urge to throw up. What if Ryan and Sandy see it? It's the *Daily Mail*. It isn't a case of what if. Of course they have seen it. Ryan never misses his fix of the *Daily Mail*. They'll think I've had a breakdown or something. All my clients will have seen it. While Sandy and Ryan get signatures for a petition against Rory's I'm getting bloody engaged to him. Jethro will send a banger round to me, forget about Rory's. This couldn't get any direr. I step closer and stare at the tabloids. My mind reels as I struggle to remember the newspaper Luke reads but my brain is numb. I pick up another of the papers and stare at it stunned.

Rags to riches for hairdresser girl Flora Robson
Hairdresser hits the jackpot and bags multimillionaire Thomas Rory following Rory's bid for salon.

Tom is Mr Rory; I can't believe it. He is the son of John Rory, who's playing in the tournament. Tom has been lying to me this whole time. I feel my body grow hot from the humiliation. How could he?

'I'll phone through to Mr Rory's room for you,' says the clerk and dings a bell on the reception desk.

'No,' I say loudly, and thump the bell after him. I pull my case from the porter.

How could he? He lied to me. He lied barefaced. Tom, my lovely nice Tom is no other than fucking Thomas Rory. He's the

Rory who's been trying to buy my salon. It all makes sense now. He's taken the business over from his father. He said he worked for a family business. The bastard, the no good shagging creep. What a git. I stare at the headline until my mind boggles. *Hairdresser bags multimillionaire?* They make me sound like a gold-digger. This is terrible. No, more than terrible, it's catastrophic. All this time he had known how much I didn't want to sell the salon. All the nice things he did. The birthday present he bought me, all those nice gestures he made, and they were all in a bid to get my salon. The kiss, the dance, the kindness he showed me, it was all false. I feel myself cringe. Of course he didn't fancy me. I feel the tears roll down my cheeks and brush them away angrily. How dare he? Of course someone like him would never look twice at me. Stupid stupid Flora. I stamp my foot angrily and fight back the tears of humiliation. What's worse is that everyone will know what a fool I've been, and that includes Luke. I have probably lost Luke for ever now. I remember Tom's arms around me, our kiss, and his bright blue eyes. He's just one big fake and the worst thing, the really worst thing is that I'd begun to fall in love with him. I had started to fall in love with the enemy and that was exactly what he wanted, no doubt.

I read the headlines again. How dare they, how dare they? What do they mean from rags to riches? I'm not sodding Cinderella. I'll kill him, I'll kill him. I'll rip his insides out with my bare hands and then I'll ... I'll sue the newspapers, that's what I'll do.

'Hey, aren't you her, the hairdresser who's bagged a millionaire?' cries someone.

I snatch every newspaper that has me on the cover. I'm shamefaced to admit they're not the best newspapers, still, that's good in a way isn't it? It means that Luke most likely hasn't seen it. I ask the clerk to call me a cab. By the time it arrives a small group of guests have gathered to gawp at me. I dive into the cab and slide down in the seat.

'Where to?' the cab driver asks.

'Can you just drive,' I say tearfully.

No wonder the bastard wanted to talk about the salon. I'll kill him, I'll seriously kill him. How dare he make me look so ridiculous? Oh Jesus, how do I explain this to Luke? I pull my phone out of my bag with shaking fingers and then remember the battery is dead. The truth is I'm not good enough for Luke. I'm just a simple hairdresser. I always felt I wasn't good enough and Thomas Rory has just confirmed it.

'Bugger,' I say, throwing the phone back into my bag.

'Everything okay?' asks the driver.

Oh yes, everything is hunky-dory. After all I'm engaged to a multimillionaire aren't I? How did that happen, when did that happen, more importantly how did I let it happen? Don't think about it, don't think about it. What am I thinking? I've got to bloody think about it. I let my muddled brain wander back to last night and slowly bits start to click together. Didn't Jeff, one of the rugby players say he was friends with the editor of *The Sun*? I drop my head into my hands and groan. I'll hire a hit man and kill the bloody lot of them. Then I remember the ring pull and Tom sliding it drunkenly over my finger. No wonder they were texting me with congratulations. I'm never ever going to drink tequila again. I need to get my battery charged. I need a room but the only room I can think of is Tom's at The Gresham. How could he do this? Why didn't he tell me who he was?

'I need a hotel room,' I say in a shaky voice.

'Are you away in the head? Everywhere is booked. There's a golf tournament. It's the turd today. Should be a good un.'

'Turd?' I repeat. Is he referring to Luke by any chance? Let's face it all the men in my life are turds. I mean, what am I doing coming all the way to Dublin to propose to a man who tells me how much alcohol I can drink and what I can put into my mouth and who ejaculates before I've even got my shoes off?

'Who's the turd?' I ask, dabbing at my eyes.

He looks at me in his rear-view mirror.

'Turd round, it's the turd round. It's the final tomorrow.'

'Ah, the *third* round,' I say, finally understanding.

'No the turd round.'

'Whatever. It doesn't matter what it costs, just get me to a hotel.'

'Oh well, sure look it,' he laughs and takes a sharp right. 'I'll take you to The Clarence to be sure. It's owned by Bono himself.'

'I don't care if it's owned by Mr Blobby just get me there as soon as you can.'

He stares at me and then exclaims,

'Get outta that garden, aren't you that woman in the papers today who just got engaged to Rory's son?'

I sigh.

'No, I'm not.'

'Be Jaysus, you're the spitting image.'

Twenty minutes later I am booking myself into one of the most exclusive hotels in Dublin and I am determined that that bastard Tom Rory will pay for it. I'm led to my luxury room and as soon as I am alone I plug in my phone charger and run a hot bath. As soon as I plug the phone in it starts ringing. I'm almost terrified to answer it. It bleeps and trills so much that I turn the sound off. I step into the warm bath and feel the tension ease from my body. I lay there until the water grows cold, going over all the things Tom had said to me. I finally climb out reluctantly, knowing it's time to phone Luke. After all I can't put it off forever can I? I sit on the bed and rehearse what I am going to say but nothing sounds right. *Luke, hi it's me, I thought I should phone to explain about the engagement thingy in the newspapers.* No, I can't say that can I? Supposing he hasn't yet seen the papers, although that is a bit unlikely considering they are everywhere and I'm splashed all over them and, what's more, looking my absolute worst. *Luke it's me. I just wanted to say I love you and ...* yes and what exactly? Oh God, why don't I just throw myself off the top of the hotel and be done with it? As I'm trying to decide what to do my room phone rings. I pick it up and speak cautiously.

'Hello.'

'Flo,'

Just his voice makes me come over all tearful. How could I have been so stupid? I feel my hands shake so much that I can barely hold the phone.

'How dare you. How dare you phone me. You've ruined my life. How did you know where I was?'

'I've been phoning all the hotels. Look Flo, you have to listen to me ...'

'I don't have to listen to you. You're a conniving, deceitful and ...' I fumble for the worst words possible. 'The most horrible person I know. I hate you. You're trying to take my business and you've done it in the most dishonest way and ...'

'Flo, it wasn't like that ...'

'And now you've ruined my engagement. I'll never forgive you ...'

'Flo, you're too good for him ...'

'How dare you. And don't call me *Flo*. You don't know Luke. He's perfect for me.'

What am I saying? No one could be less perfect for me than Luke. I snatch a tissue from the bedside cabinet and wipe away my tears.

'Flo, I'll talk to Luke. I'll be seeing him. The tournament ball is tomorrow. I'll explain everything to him. I should never have got drunk. It was, no doubt, Gareth's stupid idea of a joke.'

'I hate them. Sheep-shagging good for nothing bloody Welsh men.'

'Flo, I'm really sorry. I promise it will be okay. It isn't what you think. I really like you ...'

'You've a funny way of showing it, and I hope Luke beats you to a pulp.'

'You don't mean that.'

'I do. Why didn't you tell me? You had so many opportunities? You have everything. All I have is my salon. I won't let you take it from me.'

He sighs heavily.

'I tried to tell you several times. I didn't want you to hate me. The more I grew to like you the harder it became.'

'Well I do hate you and you can pay for my hotel room as well, you lying git. After the perfume and chocolates didn't work you thought you'd try extreme measures did you?'

'That's not true.'

'Not much.'

'Of course I'll pay for the room. I was going to offer anyway. Anything you need Flo ...'

'Stop calling me Flo,' I say loudly.

'About your salon, why don't we meet and discuss it? I can offer you a site just say where you want it?'

'I don't believe it, you're still trying. And I have a good site and ...'

'Flo ...'

143

'Don't call me Flo, not ever again. Do you understand? I never want to see you again and I'm not letting you have the salon. This is war, do you understand. I'm going to ruin you,' I say, letting the tears flow freely.

Just hearing his voice has made me realise just how strong my feelings are for him and he has let me down so badly. How could I have been so stupid? I hate men. If I hadn't have been so desperate to get engaged in the first place I wouldn't bloody be here. Bugger Luke as well. Why didn't he just ask me like Mark asked Devon?

'You'll be isolated if you stay there. I can offer you a nice salon somewhere else we can look at sites together.'

I scoff.

'I'm not going anywhere with you, ever. You made me think you liked me and ...'

'I do like you Flo,' he says softly, 'more than you know. I thought the feeling was mutual.'

The tears fall like rain down my cheeks. Even now he is still lying to me.

'Well the feelings certainly weren't mutual. Luke is the only man for me and it looks like you've ruined that.'

There is silence at the other end and before he can speak again I say,

'This is war and there can only be one victor.'

I slam the phone down and burst into tears. I rummage through the mini bar, hiccupping and cursing. I pull out a miniature bottle of vodka and a bar of chocolate. I down the contents of the bottle before hitting Luke's number on my mobile.

'Flora, I was going to phone you in a bit. I'm in the semi-final today. If I get through this I may well be playing against your Mr Rory.'

Yes, well not quite my Mr Rory but any Rory deserves a thrashing as far as I am concerned. Just the sound of his voice makes me feel a bit better. At least he isn't sounding cross.

'I thought I'd better phone,' I say nervously.

'Are you feeling better today? Were you able to get to the salon, or were you too hungover?'

He doesn't know I'm in Dublin, oh thank God. He hasn't seen the papers. All I have to do is make sure he doesn't and then maybe, just maybe, I can salvage this mess.

'I'm not at the salon, Luke. I'm in Dublin.'

'Dublin,' he says incredulously. 'What are you doing in Dublin? I thought we agreed you were going to stay at home.'

No, you agreed I'd stay at home.

'I'm in the semis; I can't have any distractions Flora.'

Christ, let's hope he doesn't see the newspapers then.

'It's nice you're here but I just don't have the time. What about the salon ...?'

'The thing is Luke I need to see you ...'

He sighs.

'You can see me afterwards. Why on earth did you come to Dublin anyway? I don't even know if I can get you a ticket to the match ball, it's a bit last minute.'

'It's okay. You just focus on the game, but I do need to see you.'

'It's not a good time Flora I need to get psyched up for the match.'

I give up.

'Okay, I'll come and see you after the match,' I say resignedly. 'We can have dinner.'

'Where are you staying, it's nowhere expensive is it?'

'I got a special deal,' I say.

Well, that's not a lie is it?

Chapter Twenty

Tom

'I see congratulations are in order,' says Grant cynically. 'Do you want me to get our solicitors onto it?'

'No, it will only make things worse. Just let it die a natural death. If anyone asks for a comment say we were just friends celebrating a birthday. There was no engagement.'

'I know you always say do what it takes to get the contract but wasn't that a bit extreme? There was you making me feel dinner was out of order,' he says, a note of anger in his voice.

'Just soften things where you can without drawing attention to it, okay,' I snap.

'You mean smooth over your cock-up.'

I sigh.

'Whatever. Phone The Clarence and cover all her bills. I don't want her paying for anything.'

'You want us to cover everything? Are you sure that's ...'

'Just do it Grant, and send some roses, no second thoughts I'll send them.'

'I wouldn't send roses. We looked into her flowers remember and she hates roses because of the thorns and she's allergic to them apparently.'

In spite of everything I find myself smiling. Only Flo could be picky about flowers.

'Are you sure she's worth bothering with? If you ask me she's trouble,' says Grant.

'I didn't ask you.'

I hang up feeling the anger build within me. I'll murder that little bugger Gareth. I punch his number into my phone and wait.

'Hey boyo, congratulations,' he laughs.

'What the hell are you playing at?'

'I've waited ten years to pay you back for that prank you played on me in Cambridge. Come on, man, you can't dish it out and not take it.'

I sigh.

'Yeah right, the thing is she's a nice girl Gareth ...'

'It's a bit of fun, get over it. It will be tomorrow's fish and chip paper. Forget it. Great night though, you have to admit and she is a bit of awright.'

She's more than all right.

'I'll get you back.'

'I look forward to it boyo.'

I hang up and lean back on the couch. Idiot, I was a total idiot. I should have told her earlier. My phone rings again and I pick it up tiredly.

'So, when were you going to tell your father you were here, and more importantly when were you going to tell your parents about your impending wedding?'

'When there is an impending wedding. Believe me, you'll be the first to know and when did you start believing the newspapers?'

'It's not about me believing them son it's the rest of the country. A hairdresser? Is that really your type?'

'You have no idea what my type is.'

'Your mother's asking if you're free to have dinner with us this evening. It's the final tomorrow. I reckon I'll be up against a solicitor, Luke Wright. He's good.'

'So I hear. Yes, I'll see you tonight, where are you eating?'

'Patrick Guilabaud, we're booked for eight.'

'I'll see you there.'

I click off the phone and pick up the paper. She looks beautiful. Her eyes are sparkling and her cheeks are flushed. She looks happy. Why won't she talk to me? We had some good times on the train to Dublin. How can she think they weren't real? The kiss was real. I felt her breasts straining towards me, her tongue meeting mine. I push it from my mind and sigh. I was stupid, blinded by my feelings for her. Well, it's over now and just as well. A woman in my life always causes problems and this is no exception. She's right, I should have told her. I had plenty of opportunities. I behaved badly. Damn papers. *Rag to riches*, what's wrong with these people? What they don't know is that I'm the one who found the riches in her. I can't believe she wants to marry that *up his own arse prick,* Luke Wright. He obviously has a lot more to offer than I have. I'd like to know what that is. I pick up the phone and call reception.

'Can you order me a hire car please? I'll need it in the next twenty minutes. Can I also order some flowers to be sent to The Clarence? I'd like a large bouquet but make sure there are no roses in it. Thank you … no, I'll come down and write the card myself.'

I grab my jacket and check my watch. Forty-five minutes before my meeting. If Wright wins the final tomorrow that will be the ultimate kick in the teeth for me. I wonder if Flo has seen him yet. After all, that's why she came wasn't it? I could shake her. She deserves better, much better. I curse and pick up my wallet. For the first time in my life I really don't want to be Thomas Rory.

Chapter Twenty-One

I slide my BlackBerry from under the pillow and see there are twenty-seven text messages. I've never had twenty-seven text messages in my life. Well, obviously I have, but not all together. Oh dear, how do I tell my mother that I'm not engaged to one of the richest men in England? She'll be gutted. She's probably already organised the street party. I drop the phone into my handbag and check my reflection. My face is still a bit blotchy from crying. So much for Touche éclat, well overrated if you ask me. I walk to the door, throwing the bouquet into the bin as I do so. Honestly, that man, he thinks he can buy anyone. I'm totally exhausted and frankly I've had it with men. I blame myself of course. This is punishment for wanting to be engaged on my birthday. With a bit of luck I'll get blown up before I see Luke; after all, if you can't get blown up in Ireland, where can you?

'Good evening madam, your taxi is waiting.'

I step outside and yank the thong out of the crack in my arse. Trust me to put the things on back to front. I climb into the cab carefully to prevent them rising up again.

'Where to?' asks the driver.

'The best place to get blown up or shot please. I'm not bothered which as long as it's over quickly.'

'I'll just drive the cab off a bridge shall I? It'll cost you a bit more of course. Funeral expenses for the missus, and childcare for the kids, you know tat kind of ting. It will be a shite day for them, know what I mean?'

'I didn't ask you to join me,' I say stiffly. 'Just take me where it all happens.'

'Where it all happens?' he repeats.

'Yes, please.'

'You're at least a decade too late, we don't blow people up like we used to, and it will be the north of Ireland you'll be wanting.'

'That's a bit inconsiderate isn't it?'

'It's called the peace process. I guess they didn't take people like you into account. Believe it or not most of us are quite happy with the arrangements. It's the eejits that aren't.'

'Well, that's no good to me,' I say, trawling through my messages.

'You'll need to go to the States if it's a blowing up you want. Of course you could just go to Afghanistan; they do a lot of blowing up there. That's a shite place if ever there was one. You'll have to check with your travel agent. I'm sure they know the best places to get blown up. Then again you could just walk under a bus. Although why the feck you want to do it at all is beyond me. A pint or two of Gat is what you'll be needing.'

'Is that some kind of poison?'

'I've heard it called some things but poison; now there's a new one. A pint of Gat, you know, Guinness is what yourself needs.'

Not with my hangover thank you very much. I sigh and punch in Devon's number.

'You'd better take me to the Deer Park golf course then please.'

'That's plan B is it? Hoping to get whacked on the head with a golf ball are you? Is it just yourself you'll be wanting dead.'

'Why, do you know a hit man?'

'You're quite the comedienne aren't you?'

I ignore him and wait for Devon to answer.

'About bloody time, I know you're a celebrity now and all that but bloody hell Flo. You got engaged then. I hate to tell you but it's to the wrong man. And don't tell me it was mistaken identity because even I can tell them apart.'

'Please don't nag me. You've no idea what kind of a day I've had.'

'You got engaged to a multimillionaire so it sounds like your day was a hell of a lot better than mine.'

'It's not what it seems. One minute I was having a drink, well a few drinks and the next I'm engaged to a multimillionaire.'

'I can see why you want to kill yourself,' mumbles the cab driver. 'I meself would be wanting to do the same if I got engaged to a multimillionairess, to be sure I would.'

'He deceived me Devon. He's a lying no good ...'

'Where are you now?' asks Devon.

'On my way to see Luke, to explain everything, God knows how that will go down.'

'He won the semi so I imagine he is in a good mood. Good luck.'

❧

I have the ring in my bag. The proposal speech in my head and I'm wearing the sexiest dress I own. Bearing in mind the dress is sexy but whether I look sexy in it is another matter. I very much doubt it considering I have a thong disappearing up my arse and a dress that is so full of static that it feels more like the height of fashion torture. Luke opens the door and it is immediately apparent to me that he isn't the man I want to spend the rest of my life with after all.

'I can't believe you're here,' he says.

Neither can I.

'Luke ...' I begin.

He pulls me into the room and I gasp. Talk about plush. It's everything he is always telling me we don't need. To think he had the cheek to ask me if my hotel was expensive.

'Oh, it's on the business,' he says, seeing the look on my face. 'You know, I had the conference.'

I look around. I don't believe it. It's a suite. This is the man who tells me we don't need this kind of comfort on weekend breaks and holidays and yet somehow he needs it on a golfing break. Ooh I am seeing red in more ways than one. I fumble with the thong irritably.

'What's wrong?' he asks, pouring water into two glasses. Oh yes, let's get pissed on the best water the hotel can offer shall we?

'My thong is stuck,' I say.

If only a stuck thong were the worst of my problems, what a happy woman I would be.

'Shall I help unstick it,' he says huskily, stepping towards me.

Oh good grief, not now.

'God, I've missed you Flo. Why don't we have a cuddle?'

I sigh. Why does he have to call it a cuddle? We're not sodding twelve.

'I'm so high after winning. I'll thrash your Mr Rory tomorrow and ...'

Crikey for a moment I thought he was going to say he'll thrash *me*. I almost got excited.

'He's not my Mr Rory,' I say, stepping back and pulling a newspaper from my handbag. 'That's my Mr Rory. You're playing against his dad. I came with Thomas Rory to Dublin, you remember, he offered us train tickets? A tree fell on the track and we went out to eat and ...'

His eyes bulge out of their sockets.

'Cut to the chase Flora,' he says angrily.

'We went out with some friends of his and I got drunk and these pictures got taken and one of the friends gave the press the story that we were engaged. I didn't even know he was Thomas Rory. I hate the guy, he's trying to take my salon and ...'

'Everyone at the office will have seen it ...'

'I'm so sorry Luke,' I say, moving towards him.

He jumps back like he's had an electric shock. Mind you, the way my dress is giving them out he probably did.

'The conniving little creep, this is all to get your salon isn't it?'

'Well,' I begin.

'He's not interested in you that's for sure. Someone with his money and stature wouldn't bother with a poxy little hairdresser. He's gone too far. We can use this against him. I'm not having him make a fool out of me,' he says angrily, reaching for the phone.

I see. It's okay to make a fool out of me. It's okay to try and get my salon. Luke wasn't in the least interested then was he? But now he feels humiliated it's a whole other ball game. And what does he mean Thomas Rory wouldn't be interested in a *poxy little hairdresser*?

'Luke, what are you doing?'

'I'm phoning Mitchell at the office, get him to deny the story on your behalf and to say this is a ploy of Thomas Rory's to blackmail you into selling the salon ...'

'But Luke, it wasn't like that. It's best to leave it, let the story die a natural death.'

He slams the phone down.

'What was it like then? I'm not having people think my girlfriend was so drunk she didn't know what she was doing. They must have spiked your drinks.'

The thing is I *was* so drunk that I didn't know what I was doing.

'We were just having a good time,' I say and regret it immediately.

'You were having a good time with Thomas Rory?'

'I didn't know it *was* Thomas Rory,' I say.

'What you're saying is you'll have a good time with any man as long as it isn't Thomas Rory?'

I didn't say that did I?

'Of course not, and that's a silly thing to say Luke. It wasn't like that.'

'I don't know why you came here anyway,' he says angrily, rummaging through the mini bar and producing a bottle of vodka.

'To propose to you on my birthday if you must know. I thought it would be nice,' I say tearfully, pulling so hard at the thong that I hear it rip. Bugger and sod it. 'Tom offered me a way to get here but let's face it, who wants to be engaged to a poxy hairdresser right? Oh, and you can forget the ball because I won't be here. I'm going home first thing.'

I grab my bag and walk to the door.

'Flora,' he says sharply.

I turn quickly and get an electric shock from my underskirt.

'Where are you staying?'

Oh bugger.

'Don't worry Tom Rory is paying for it. It's his way of apologising.'

His face seems to turn blue. Oh no, he's not having some kind of convulsion before the final is he? I'll be in the bloody papers again at this rate: *Poxy hairdresser kills soon-to-be-fiancé after turd round* ...

'Luke are you okay?' I ask anxiously.

'No fiancée of mine stays in any other hotel but this one.'

'What?' I gasp.

How ironic is this? I come all the way to Dublin to propose to my boyfriend on my thirtieth birthday only to realise he isn't Mr Right. Okay, I know he is *Mr Wright* but you know what I mean, and then he turns around and proposes to me.

'Luke ...'

'Flora, will you marry me?'

Bloody sod's law isn't it?

Chapter Twenty-Two

'What did you say?'

'I said I'd think about it?'

'Think about it?' echoes Devon. 'You've been thinking about it for the past twelve fucking months. How much longer do you need? I thought this was what you wanted.'

'It was. I mean it is. I don't know any more. But it was the night before the final, don't forget, how could I say no?'

'He lost anyway,' she laughs.

'Yes, but at least I don't have to blame myself.'

'But I thought you really wanted to be engaged and married in your thirtieth year. Are you completely forgetting that was the reason you went to Dublin?'

She is, of course, quite right. However, it has finally occurred to me that once I am married I want to stay married.

'It's not like you and Mark, you know. I think you forget that what you have is very special. All those long intimate sex sessions with floggers and everything, I mean, your sex life is just one long workout. I don't know why you bother with kettle classes, just use the kettle for the after sex tea. My sex life is one long endurance test and believe me it's not exactly that long.'

'And Thomas Rory?' she asks quietly.

'Luke said it was all a ploy to get the salon. That someone like Thomas Rory would never look at a poxy hairdresser ...'

I break off at the memory.

'He said that? What a pig.'

'Do you believe that?'

'That Luke is a pig, yes I do.'

'No, that Tom thinks I'm a poxy hairdresser.'

'No, he sounds too nice. I think he should have told you though.'

'Told me that I'm a poxy hairdresser?'

Well, that's charming isn't it?

'No, he should have told you who he was.'

'I hate men.'

'Rosalind is planning a spa weekend when you get back. She said you need to de-stress.'

'How can she go to a spa in her condition?'

'She said if it comes to it she'll have an underwater birth in their luxury pool,' she laughs, 'and you can pant with her.'

'Kind of her to think of me. Right, I'm off to shop till I drop. I'm going to find a knockout outfit for tonight if it kills me. I'm sick of Luke always telling me to wear something nice. Do you know I only realised yesterday he is always telling me to wear *something nice,* like I would wear crap if he didn't tell me otherwise.'

'Go Flora, go girl,' she says, heartily.

'Yes I will. I'll find something stunning if it kills me.'

That's most likely what it will do too. But as Luke is the runner up I will need to look good, so armed with my Mastercard I head down to reception and ask where the best dress shops are in Dublin. I'm directed to Brown and Thomas in Grafton Street where I now marvel at the beautiful dresses on the stands.

'For yourself now would it be?' asks the assistant.

I lift one of the tags and grab the rail to support myself. £1,500 for a dress? That's criminal, so it is, as they would say here in Ireland. The assistant smiles and takes the dress from the rail. This is bad news. If I'm getting the *Pretty Woman* treatment it can mean only one thing; they've seen me in the papers.

'I'm looking for something slightly cheaper,' I say, sounding less like *Pretty Woman* by the minute.

Slightly cheaper, what am I saying? *Slightly* cheaper than £1,500 in here would be about a grand.

'I have just the dress for you, a sleek little number that would look perfect on madam.'

I'm sure anything costing a grand would look perfect on Susan Boyle, let alone me. I just don't have that kind of money, or should I say credit. She pulls a gorgeous black dress from a stand and holds it in front of me.

'Vivienne Westwood, and for you madam I think the lamé strapless feature would enhance your neck, and the oversized bow neckline is just perfect. I would say the dress was made for madam.'

I have an awful feeling that the price isn't going to be just perfect. I so need a Richard Gere right now. I stare longingly at the dress and imagine Tom seeing me wearing it and reprimand myself crossly. Thomas Rory doesn't fancy me in the least and I must stop fooling myself he ever did.

'Vivienne Westwood, that will be expensive,' I say, trying not to show my disappointment.

'Reduced madam from £905 to £250 and I tink with a gold clutch bag and satin sandals, yourself you wouldn't know.'

She's right about that. If I spend two hundred and fifty quid on a dress, myself I wouldn't know for sure. But then again, 250 quid compared to 900 is quite a deal isn't it? Blimey, even my credit can cope with that.

I tap my tummy. She looks at me over her black-rimmed glasses.

'Lycra,' she smiles.

'No, just plain old fat, but if we can do something about it that would be great.'

She laughs.

'I meant ...'

'Huge pants,' I say. 'You meant huge pants didn't you?'

'For a smooth hip line, does madam not tink it worth every moment of agony.'

'For a smooth hip line I'd consider several days of agony.'

I'll show Thomas Rory. A humble hairdresser am I? Right, Bridget Jones pants here I come. I march towards the fitting room carrying the Vivienne Westwood over my arm. Can you believe it, me, Flora Robson, humble hairdresser, carrying a Vivienne Westwood no less. Even I'm beginning to feel like *Pretty Woman*. Five minutes later I'm looking like her. I can't breathe mind you, but hey, a smooth line is worth every moment of agony. I'm not sure it's actually worth dying for though, but it does look fabulous. I don't think I've ever looked so amazing. I can't take my eyes off myself in the mirror. I'm wondering if one of those old-fashioned roll-on things would do just as well. They always seem to work on my mother until they unravel of course, leaving her with bulges in places you wouldn't expect bulges to be, but at least I would be able to breathe. At this rate I'll have to invest in smelling salts just to get me through the evening. The assistant seeming to understand my dilemma, delivers handfuls of hold-it-all-in knickers, sturdy pants and Lycra galore until we finally find one that holds everything in apart from my breath.

'Silk stockings and suspenders,' she says, assessing me.

Poor Luke will be shooting his load before he's even managed to un-pop one button, so they'll be lost on him. But, I suppose, if I should do my party piece of walking out of the loo and across the ballroom with my Vivienne Westwood stuck in my hold-it-all-in pants, at least I'll have a nice pair of suspenders to show off. There's always a silver lining isn't there.

'A lovely necklace, some sparkly earrings and madam will be the belle of the ball,' smiles the assistant, looking impressed.

Almost an hour later and I've spent five hundred and twenty pounds on a dress, bag and shoes. I stroll along the streets, humming *Pretty Woman* and swinging my bags. I'll show Thomas Rory. I'm now rather looking forward to the ball. What a shame old Mr Rory won. I check my BlackBerry and see I have time to browse more shops and now I've bashed the credit card I may as well carry on. After all, it's not every day I get to go to Dublin is it? And I do need a necklace and earrings.

Chapter Twenty-Three

'My God,' says Luke, 'you look like a, like a ...'

If he says prostitute I'll knee him in his useless groin.

'Princess,' he finishes.

'The shoes are proving to be a bit tricky,' I say.

I'd gone for the red high-heeled pumps but I'm rather thinking they'll be going for me before the evening is out. Still, Luke has plenty of Biofreeze for those aching muscles at the end of the evening.

'I'll be proud to have you on my arm,' he says.

The way he says it suggests he wouldn't be proud to have me on his arm normally but this time he is. I hide my sigh and pick up my clutch bag. Luke doesn't look so bad himself in his dinner jacket and bow tie. I find myself wondering what Tom looks like in his.

My confidence wanes as we pull up at the entrance to the Grand Hotel. It's majestic and is heaving with expensively dressed women and cigar-smoking men. The heady mixture of perfume and cigar smoke reaches my nostrils and I feel myself go from *Pretty Woman* to outcast Baby *from Dirty Dancing*, still, no one puts baby in a corner right? I scan the faces for Tom but can't see any sign of him. Luke helps me from the cab and we move through the cigar smoke haze and into the grand entrance hall where a doorman offers to take our coats. I quickly straighten my dress and grab Luke's arm. I spot myself in the grand hall mirror and marvel at how good I look. The hold-it-all-in knickers are certainly doing what they say on the tin and they're not even sticking up my arse. Hold-it-all-in pants, where have you been all my life? The sheer nylon stockings feel lovely and I actually believe that nothing Luke says tonight could make me feel anything other than sexy and gorgeous. I chose to wear my hair down after finding some fabulous conditioner, mind you, the price was pretty fabulous too but I was past caring then. It seems after you've spent a certain amount it really doesn't matter any more. Large velour rollers had given it a bounce and I now run my hands through it, feeling its silkiness.

'Let's get a drink,' says Luke leading me to the other side of the hall to the busy bar. We pass a table plan and I strain to see where the Rory's are sitting but Luke has pulled me past before I have time to study it. I again scan the faces for Tom. Maybe he isn't coming. Luke hands me a glass of champagne.

'As it is a special occasion we can let our hair down,' he says with a smile.

Oh, letting our hair down are we, I should have brought the flogger. I take a sip and then I see Tom. He looks so handsome that I choke on the champagne.

'That's because you're not used to it,' Luke says condescendingly. He follows my eyes to Tom. He is with an older gentleman and an elegant woman who is wearing a pale blue ankle-length dress. She is classically beautiful with a firm jawline, full red lips and soft gentle eyes. Her blonde hair has been expertly styled and wound smoothly into a bun so her diamond dangling earrings can be seen in their full glory. A beautiful pearl-studded comb holds her hair in place and she smiles warmly at everyone. So this is where Tom gets his good looks. I look at his father and see a strong chin and steely blue eyes. No doubt the hardness and the deceitful personality have been inherited from the father. From the moment they enter the grand hall everybody seems to gravitate towards them, congratulating Mr Rory Senior. I can't but help notice the adoring eyes of the women as they look Tom's way. He is the handsomest man in the room without doubt and I feel myself tremble with anger when I think of how he humiliated me. Using his charm and good looks to flatter me and to think I stupidly fell for it and what's worse, I fell for him. His eyes meet mine and I turn away. My heart flutters and I shake so much that drops of champagne spill from my glass. He walks towards us and my heart feels like it is going to burst from my chest. I clutch Luke's arm tightly.

'It's okay, I can handle him,' he says confidently.

Tom extends a hand to Luke.

'Congratulations. It was a great final,' he says, avoiding my eyes.

'Thanks. Unfortunately for me your father was the better player.'

'Yes, golf is all he has to do these days.'

Tom's eyes flit to me and then back to Luke.

'I'm sorry about the newspaper crap, Luke. We've minimised the damage, especially for the function tonight. It was completely my fault. My friend's crazy idea of a practical joke I'm afraid. We were simply celebrating a friend's birthday along with Flora's and the press have made a big thing out of nothing. I'm really sorry if it has caused you any embarrassment.'

Luke wraps an arm around my waist.

'We're enjoying the evening and putting it behind us. I'm grateful you had a seat to offer her on the train,' Luke smiles.

What the buggery bollocks. Surely I'm hearing things and what Luke really said was, *right, Rory, outside, let's settle this once and for all. No one makes a fool of me or my girlfriend.* Obviously not though, because we're not outside are we and Luke isn't beating the shit out of Thomas Rory. I don't believe this. Tom nods at me and walks back to his parents.

'At least he apologised,' Luke says.

Oh, that's all right then.

'I need the gents,' he says, looking around.

I wobble on my heels as he slides his arm from my waist and then I stand alone like a spare prick at a wedding. I quickly check my dress is smoothed down and that the hold-it-all-in pants are still holding it all in, and remind myself to breathe as I am seriously thinking this may be the one time I actually may forget.

'Aperitif madam?'

I turn to a waitress who is offering drinks and take a glass of Campari, knocking it back in one hit. An announcement is made for dinner and Luke reappears to take my arm and lead me into the ballroom. A live band is playing and beautifully laid tables await us. Luke checks the table plan and I follow him to a table in the corner. Tom and his parents are seated at the other side of the room. Dinner is fabulous and I overindulge, much to Luke's disgust. I'm drooling over the dessert menu when an announcement is made to honour the winning players. The chairman takes the stage and Luke lifts his chin proudly when his name is mentioned. I squeeze his knee. I'm sure we can make things work. I decide there and then to accept his proposal. Luke is the right one for me and we'll make lots of babies and live happily ever after. Well, hopefully we'll make babies. With Luke's problem it might be a little bit harder than normal but not impossible and I could try that Master's and whatsit thing couldn't I? Just a little squeeze may be all that's needed. I find myself squeezing his knee a little bit tighter at the thought. Yes, everything will be fine. Of course, I have had a glass and a half of wine at this point, not to mention the champagne, oh and of course the Campari. One should probably never accept a proposal while under the influence. Rather like driving isn't it? You wouldn't do that under the influence would you, not without expecting a policeman to pull you up.

'Excuse me madam, I'm arresting you on the grounds of saying *I do* while under the influence.'

'Flora,' Luke whispers, 'not in public darling.'

Not in public? I'm squeezing his knee, not his bloody penis. Oh God, it was his knee wasn't it? I look down at my hand just to check.

'While you deliberate your desserts, let's give a huge round of applause to Luke Wright. Come and join us on stage Luke and collect your medal. Ladies and gentlemen a big hand for this year's runner up, Mr Luke Wright.'

'Hear hear,' bellows Mr Rory Senior.

I meet Tom's eyes before leaning across to give Luke a congratulatory kiss.

'I love you,' he whispers meeting my lips with his. I wait for that explosion of feelings that I have with Tom but there is nothing. No electricity and no tingle down my spine. In fact there is absolutely nothing at all. I watch him take the stage and receive his medal. I applaud enthusiastically along with everyone else.

'Speech,' someone yells.

Luke steps towards the mike confidently.

'I'd like to congratulate John Rory, he played a brilliant game and it was an honour to play with a true champion,' he says, to loud applause. 'It's been a fabulous tournament and I will be going home not just with this medal but something even more precious. I would like to announce that I've also just got engaged to my beautiful girlfriend, Flora.'

'Well, now, isn't this a night to beat all nights,' says the chairman, 'Here's to Luke and Flora.'

What the …? Oh bloody Nora. Two engagements in as many days. My mother will be beside herself with joy. Only me, this could only happen to me. There I was, so desperate to be engaged before I hit thirty, because let's face it; an engagement seemed further away than Timbuctoo. All I wanted was a ring on my finger and a wedding date and now I've managed to get engaged, not once but twice and I still don't have a sodding ring on my finger. That's about right. Our table companions are congratulating me and all I can think about is dessert, and how there had better be chocolate on the menu. I somehow doubt they have Crunchie bars in the Tampax machines in the loos here. Now, there's an idea. Every woman needs chocolate at period times doesn't she? Every Tampax box should have one and every machine should pop one out along with a tampon. What am I thinking? I'm either in shock or I've drunk more than I thought.

'We have a tempting selection of desserts for you to choose from. The waitresses will be bringing them out in a few minutes and you can help yourself from the dessert table, but first …'

There is loud applause before he can finish.

'John Rory, please make your way to the stage.'

As they pass Luke and John Rory shake hands, and then Luke makes his way back to our table.

'I wanted the whole world to know that you're going to be my wife,' he says, before kissing me.

No you didn't, I think. You just wanted Tom to know. I empty my glass and watch John Rory receive his trophy and applaud along with the rest of the room and then thankfully it is time for dessert.

'I've got to go around the tables. It's tradition. Will you be okay?' Luke asks.

Oh yes. I have a tradition of my own, going around dessert tables, and tonight nothing is going to stop me. I nod. My face feels flushed from the alcohol and I am slightly anxious at the thought of walking to the dessert table in my heels. But hey, when has anything come between me and a dessert table, especially when Luke won't be around to see what I'm piling on my plate? I take a deep breath and pull myself up and concentrate on walking to the dessert table that is the furthest from Tom. The selection is heavenly. I stare at the chocolate-covered cream puffs and sigh with pleasure. I'm sure if there is such a thing as a chocolate orgasm then I am having one right now.

'The Italian trifle is divine,' says a woman.

'Is there jelly in that?' I ask. 'I don't like jelly.'

'Trifle without jelly isn't trifle,' says the woman.

'No madam,' smiles the waiter. 'It's tiramisu.'

'I'll have a little piece please and two chocolate-covered puffs but without the whipped cream on top and a slice of the chocolate cheesecake ...'

'But only if it has a biscuit base,' says a familiar voice.

I try to ignore him but my legs begin to tremble and my heart beats faster, and although chocolate excites me it doesn't excite me that much.

'Would madam like some lemon curd tart, it's very good.'

'I don't like lemon in desserts,' I say.

'And for you sir?' he asks Tom.

'I'll have the bittersweet chocolate tart, two slices please.'

I turn to walk past him and accidently brush his arm feeling emotions that only he can evoke.

'I'm having mine outside,' says the woman. 'It's too hot in here.'

'I'll join you,' I say, grateful for the cool air on my flushed cheeks.

We sit on a bench in the magnificent gardens and I devour the chocolate cheesecake without an ounce of guilt, grateful for my new best friend, the hold-it-all-in panties.

'You know I'm finding it genuinely bizarre that you seem to be engaged to two men at the same time,' she says, flinging off her shoes and exposing bright pink painted toenails.

'You and me both. For years I couldn't seem to get engaged to anybody and now I'm supposedly engaged to two men, and frankly I can't stand either of them. One wants my business and will go to extreme ends to get it and the other won't let me eat anything ...'

I follow her eyes to my plate.

'Yes, well, he's not looking is he? I don't mean he starves me, but God, you should see the crap he wants us to eat. And then there's the ...' I lower my voice, 'the peaking too soon problem ...'

Oh no. I've certainly drunk far too much.

'What I meant was ...'

She smiles.

'Doesn't sound like the man you should be getting engaged to if you don't mind me saying,' she says, wrapping her silk shawl around her shoulders. 'I think I'll go back in. See you later, enjoy the party.'

I look at my empty plate and dab at the crumbs, She's absolutely right of course. Luke is not my Mr Right and never has been. I hate vegetarian food, and as for his health fads, I swear my colon will never be the same after the colonic clean out diet. I love chocolate and always have. It would be so wonderful if just once I could take it from a cupboard like everyone else. I ask you, who has Crunchies in Tampax boxes? It's not natural is it?

'Tart?' says a voice.

I turn to see Tom standing behind the bench holding two plates.

'I think the word is floosie in these parts,' I say bitterly.

'You know what I meant. I thought the bittersweet tart kind of reflected us,' he says with a wry smile. 'You look beautiful by the way, and smell fabulous. I hope Luke appreciated it.'

Yes he did actually. He was actually proud to have me on his arm. I don't say that of course. I feel my mouth turn dry and my heart flutter as it always does at just the sight of him and hate him for making me feel like this. I stand up and make to walk past him but he blocks my way.

'Let me explain,' he says softly, placing the plates on the bench.

'I don't want to hear any more of your lies, please let me pass.'

A smiling waitress wanders out with a tray of champagne and he grabs two glasses.

'Have a drink with me, just one drink.'

'The last time I had a drink with you and your wanking Welsh friends I ended up in the newspapers,' I say angrily.

'I'm sorry. It was Gareth. It was suggested that we contact the papers and make some kind of statement. I said I think we should just let it die a natural death. I did what I could for tonight. I didn't want you or Luke to be embarrassed. If you want me to contact the press ...'

I shake my head. How uncanny that he said the same thing as I said to Luke, to not contact the papers and to let it die a natural death?

'Listen Flo,' he says, moving closer. 'Don't marry Luke. You're making a mistake.'

I scoff.

'I don't need your advice thank you very much.'

'Flo,' he says putting a hand on my arm.

'Don't touch me, please,' I say, struggling to fight back my tears. 'And stop calling me Flo.'

He sighs heavily.

'Just tell me what I've done wrong?'

I gape at him.

'You're a bastard,' I say, stunned he even has the cheek to ask.

'But what have I done that is so awful? I'm happy to offer more money if that is the issue. I'm happy to look at sites with you but you say no. What do you want from me?' he looks questioningly into my eyes.

What a pig and to think I feel something for this man.

'I don't want to sell my salon and all you keep doing is bullying me.'

'Flora, no one is bullying anyone. You're the one who changed your mind and for some reason it's all my fault.'

I don't believe I'm hearing this.

'What?'

'If it's about money which I think it is, just tell me how much you want. You have me in a catch-22 situation here and you know it.'

I stare at him. I have *him* in a catch-22 situation. What the hell. Before I know what I'm doing I've thrown the glass of champagne in his face. I hear gasps from some guests behind me and watch as he reels back in shock. Oh Jesus, I've never done anything like that in my life but how dare he blame me for this. I'm the innocent party here.

'You scheming bastard. You bought the two shops at the side of me before approaching me and you say I put you in the catch-22 situation. How dare you.'

He pulls a handkerchief from his jacket pocket and mops at his face.

'What did you say?' he asks, softly.

'You heard me and then you did the lowest thing of all,' I snap. 'You stole our idea about the prescriptions. You and Grant Richards are nothing but lowlife.'

I stare at him, breathing hard.

'No, in fact you're worse than a lowlife. You're just a no good scum bug.'

I see pain and confusion cross his face. I turn angrily on my heels but his hand on my arm stops me.

'Flo …'

'I never want to see you ever again,' I say, fighting back my tears.

'Take your hand off my fiancée please,' says Luke from behind me.

I feel my anger increase even more. I'm not his fiancée yet. I'm seriously wondering if Luke only wants to get engaged to me so he can have one over on Tom. How ironic all this is? I was the one desperate to get engaged and now I don't want to be engaged to anyone.

'Are you okay?' Luke asks, taking my hand.

I nod while feeling far from okay. I can see from Luke's face that he is not happy. He hates drawing attention to himself and no doubt he will blame me for this when we are alone.

'Flo …' Tom says softly.

'It's Flora to you,' says Luke. 'Now, if you'll excuse us.'

'Is everything okay Luke?'

I turn to see Tom's father. It's becoming a whole family affair now. I've seriously had it with the Rory's.

'Everything is fine,' Luke says with a smile.

'Actually it isn't,' I say, storming from the patio and into the packed ballroom where all eyes seem to follow me. I rush into the ladies and slam the cubicle door and burst into tears.

Chapter Twenty-Four

Don't you just hate pregnant women? Maybe you don't. Generally I don't either as a rule, but when they decide to go into labour just as you're going through the biggest crisis of your life it's a whole other ball game. I'd barely been home an hour when a screaming Rosalind bellows down the phone,

'Get your fucking arse over here now and for pity's sake bring a cocktail of drugs. Jeremy won't even give me a fucking paracetamol, the bastard.'

So, that's what I did, I got my arse over there, without the cocktail of drugs bit. Even I have to agree with Jeremy on that one. Well, I couldn't say, *do you mind awfully if I'm not your birthing partner after all. It's just I've had a shit few days,* could I? Although breaking up with your fiancé is more than a bit shitty isn't it? Although in theory I suppose Luke wasn't my fiancé as we never exchanged rings, all the same it's still pretty shitty to break up with anyone. Not to mention that I told the man I actually do love that I never wanted to see him again. Only I could fall in love with such a lowlife as Thomas Rory. And to make things even shittier I am now homeless or at least I soon will be. Luke has agreed to stay in a hotel for a week while I find somewhere else.

I reach Rosalind's flat and one look at her face and contorted body is enough to put me off childbirth for ever.

'Is it early?' I ask.

'I don't give a shit. I didn't book a time with the little bugger. I just want it out and ... oh Christ, here comes another one,' she yells.

'Breathe,' I say, while panting in sympathy like a mad woman.

We make a dash for the car between contractions.

'I wonder if we should get a taxi?' Jeremy asks.

'But she's in the car now,' I say.

'Are you taking me to the hospital or am I giving birth here?' Rosalind yells.

'It's just ...' he leans towards me and whispers, 'It's the company car.'

For Christ's sake.

'Oh God, bollocking Christ,' cries Rosalind, panting for all she's worth.

'Just breathe,' I say stupidly.

'Well I don't intend to stop do I?' she snaps.

Oh dear.

'We can't move her again,' I say. 'Besides it could take a while to get a cab.'

'Yes, quite right. Sorry, just being a dick.'

Yes, well you are a man. The contraction passes and Rosalind falls back onto the seat.

'Sorry,' she mumbles. 'Bad timing. I told you he was a sadistic little bugger didn't I? So, did you propose?'

Jeremy speeds through London like a crazy bank robber with a siren-wailing police car in hot pursuit. I've never been so scared. He takes two turnings at breakneck speed and shoots through a red light. I begin to worry my assed out colon won't be able to take the stress. We approach a roundabout and I close my eyes as Rosalind has another contraction.

'Jeremy, for God's sake will you slow down. At this rate I won't live to give birth.'

He swerves into the hospital car park and brings the car to an abrupt halt.

'For Christ's sake,' she snaps. 'I swear that's broken my waters.'

'Oh shit,' he mumbles. 'Not the upholstery, it's the company car.'

I shake my head. God, I'm so going off men. We bundle her out of the car and Jeremy quickly checks the seats.

'I'll get a wheelchair,' he yells.

'I didn't have to propose,' I say. 'Luke got there before me.'

'That's great,' she smiles, before grimacing as another contraction kicks in. 'Christ, here we go again.'

Jeremy gives Rosalind the white knuckle ride of her life while shouting,

'It's my wife ... she's in labour ... her water's broken.'

Rosalind rolls her eyes and I bend over to catch my breath. A nurse leans over me and taps my shoulder.

'Are you alright my love?' she asks.

'No,' says an irritable Jeremy. 'This is my wife.'

'This way,' says the nurse. 'How frequent are the contractions?'

'About every five minutes,' says Jeremy.

We all follow.

'So, did you get a ring, show me?' asks Rosalind.

'I broke it off?'

'Broke what off?' she asks.

'The engagement,' I say calmly.

The smell of antiseptic and all this sympathetic panting is making me dizzy.

'That's it,' I say. 'Just breathe, you're doing great.'

We pant together while a pale-faced Jeremy looks on.

'Let's get you into a robe shall we. Is daddy staying for the birth?' asks the nurse in a sing-song voice.

'Well ... I ... the thing ...' mumbles Jeremy,

'No he isn't,' groans Rosalind. 'Bloody coward started all this but he can't see it through to the bitter end.'

She moans and grabs my arm as another contraction starts. I wince as her grip tightens. Jesus, if she squeezes any harder my arm will turn blue.

'Shit and bollocks, why didn't someone warn me about this nine months ago?'

'Think of nice things,' chirps the nurse, helping Rosalind onto the bed and lifting the gown, exposing her vagina for all to see.

'Oh God,' says Jeremy, making a quick exit.

'Anyone would think he'd never seen it before,' grins Rosalind.

'Dilating nicely,' says the nurse.

'I want everything. Epidurals, morphine, crack, whatever you've got, inject me with it. Just give me the forms and ... oh shit.'

She grabs my hand and squeezes again. Bloody hell, I won't be able to work for a week at this rate. It's my scissor cutting hand too.

'Think of calm things, go to your happy place,' says the nurse.

I wish I could go to my happy place. It certainly isn't here.

'I don't get it?' pants Rosalind. 'How can you get engaged and then break it off in the space of forty-eight hours?'

'Less actually, I think it was more like three.'

'Jesus, three, how did you manage that? Oh God,' she says clutching her stomach. 'I swear I'm going to divorce Jeremy after this. I'll take the bastard for every penny he's got. Not that the bugger's got much.'

'Breathe, breathe,' I say, trying not to scream as her hand squeezes even tighter. Note to self, never agree to be a birthing partner again.

'And to make matters even worse,' I say, trying to take her mind off things while feeling tears prick my eyes, 'that guy, the one who banged my car ...'

'Ooh yes,' she says, wiping the perspiration from her forehead.

'He's the guy who's trying to get my salon. He's a lying, deceiving, pissing little ...'

'Oh my God, what an arse,' she exclaims. 'Oh Flo, I'm so sorry.'

I nod.

'A lying, deceiving, pissing ...'

'I get your drift. He's a fuckwit to top all fuckwits right?'

I nod.

'And you've fallen for him,' she says blandly.

'Not any more,' I say resolutely. 'From this moment on we are enemies. It's war. I'm not giving up my salon and he is now stuck with two properties both sides and no way to build a supermarket.'

She looks closely at me and releases her grip.

'So you hate him?'

'With my every fibre, I'm going to fight tooth and nail to keep my salon. I'll need as much support as I can get.'

'We're all with you chick. Just let me push this little sod out of me and I'll be there with you. We'll make sure you keep the salon, don't worry and ... oh fuck here we go.'

I give her my other hand and begin panting. The nurse looks closely at her vagina and invites me to do the same. It's a shocking sight. I never for one minute imagined I would get up close and personal to Rosalind's vagina. Still, that's what girlfriends are for isn't it? I don't mean getting up close and personal to each other's vaginas, obviously not. I mean supporting each other in moments of crisis. Thirty minutes later and Rosalind is screaming like a banshee. The air is blue and I'm privy to just a little more of her vagina than I'd like to be.

'Give me the fucking epidural you bitch,' she screams at the midwife.

'Sorry about this,' I say.

'Oh, I've heard worse,' she smiles.

I can't imagine anyone having a worse mouth than Rosalind. Two hours and an almost broken wrist later Rosalind sits contentedly holding her little sadistic sod. I kiss her on the cheek. I swear I'm more exhausted than she is.

'He's a sadistic little bugger but you've got to admit a cute one,' says Rosalind proudly.

She's changed her tune. Two hours ago she was giving it up for adoption. I smile and let him clasp my little finger in his tiny grasp.

'Right, I'll get off. I've got plans to make about dealing with my own little sadistic sod,' I say.

'Don't be too rash Flo. Give him the benefit of the doubt. Perhaps he ...'

'He had hundreds of chances to tell me,' I say angrily.

She cuddles up closer to her little sadist.

'Perhaps he liked you too much to tell you.'

I laugh. Now that is a joke.

'Have you looked at me lately?' I say. 'I'm a wreck. I'm totally unfit, fat and my hair is a mess and ...'

'I'd give anything for your gorgeous auburn hair. It's lovely and thick. And you're not fat. So what if you're not sodding fit. It's not Luke you want is it? I know I wouldn't. Christ, if Jeremy started telling me what I could and couldn't eat I'd start divorce proceedings. You're lovely, Flo. You've got a complexion to die for, beautiful eyes and a smile that lights up a whole room.'

I gape at her.

'And no I don't fancy you,' she laughs. 'I just think Luke has made you see yourself in a bad light.'

'Tom Rory is a dream catch and ...'

'Did it ever occur to you that perhaps he thinks you are too?'

'He used me Rosalind. I can't let him think that's okay. And you're right, I have let men allow me to think badly of myself but it's time to stop that now.'

I kiss her fondly on the cheek. Thomas Rory, let the war begin.

Chapter Twenty-Five

It wasn't unusual for Grant to be summoned to Thomas Rory's office. Tom would normally call him in for a catch up meeting after he'd been away for a few days. It would be the perfect opportunity for Grant to discuss the new role that had opened for a European acquisitions manager. Grant had had his sights set on this position for the last year and was expecting Tom to offer him the post sometime soon. Rory's were expanding and this would be a big step in Grant's career. It was a pity the Church Lane acquisition had gone a bit pear-shaped but Grant will have that sorted soon with a bit of persuasion. He'd found a good site for Flora Robson. Okay, it's not in the best part of Notting Hill but at least it is not the site in the East End that Grant was hoping to get rid of. Who'd have thought a little hairdresser could be so much trouble? He tapped on Tom's door and walked in. Thomas Rory was standing at the window looking at the view over the Thames. That was the great thing about having the offices at Canary Wharf, the views were spectacular.

'How was Dublin?' he asks, helping himself to coffee.

Tom turns and looks at him, his eyes hard and his shoulders tense.

'I saw your dad won. Congratulations,' smiles Grant.

The smile disappears from his face as Tom slams his hand down on the table. Coffee spills from the cup and runs over the papers on the desk.

'Did you make offers to Mr Patel and Terence Sharp before asking Flora Robson? You know what I'm talking about, divide and conquer, the quickest way to get an acquisition. Did you tell them she was happy to sell and then and only then did you approach her?' Tom asks angrily.

Grant swallows and shakes his head, feigning a look of shock.

'Christ almighty is that what the bitch told you?'

'Careful Grant, we don't talk about clients in that way. I thought you knew better than that. I'm giving you the benefit of the doubt here.'

'I told you she was trouble. What kind of games was she playing with you in Dublin?'

'Let's leave Dublin out of this.'

Grant laughs.

'She really got to you didn't she, and now you believe her lies. I told you that you can't believe a word she says. The woman is crazy. She says one thing and then changes her mind. I can't believe you're taking her word over mine. Of course I approached her first. I've been with you for six years ...'

'Yes, and I'm sincerely hoping that in that time you've always followed the rules and arranged a joint meeting with all the vendors. We don't put pressure on people Grant. We have a reputation for being fair and we're not going to lose that reputation. Now, I'm asking you again, did you approach her last?'

'I've found a nice site in Notting Hill for her. Okay it's not as nice as Church Lane ...'

Tom sighs and turns back to the window.

'I really hoped you'd be honest with me Grant. I'd honestly thought you were the right man to head up our acquisitions in Europe ...'

Grant jumps from his seat.

'Come on Tom, you know I'm the right man. You can't believe some bitter woman's lies ...'

'I do believe her. I also believe Mr Patel and Terence Sharp. They both remember when you approached them. They were not invited to a meeting and you told them that Flora Robson was selling but she wanted it kept quiet. They felt they had no option but to sell. Flora Robson never asked for a site in the East End of London because she never agreed to sell in the first place. What the hell were you playing at? If we don't get the site, we don't get the site. There are others. We give people options Grant ...'

'It's a bloody good site and you know it and that stupid hairdressers is a dump anyway. What's the fuss?'

'You're destroying Rory's reputation and I won't have that ...'

Grant laughs sardonically.

'I'm destroying Rory's reputation? She made a bloody fool of you in Dublin. Is that what this is all about? I was all set to minimise the damage but you said ...'

'Forget Dublin, Grant. It's about doing things right. It's about morals ...'

'It's one bloody site for Christ's sake.'

'Morals Grant. Do you have any concept of what I'm talking about? That prescription idea, that great idea you came to me with. It was Flora Robson's idea wasn't it?'

'So what if it was. They could never have kept up with the demand like we can.'

Tom shakes his head in exasperation.

'Flora Robson is determined to bring us to our knees. She probably won't do it. But the publicity will be bad for business. I don't know how long it will drag on for or what she plans to do and somehow I've got to smooth this over with the shareholders and ...'

'We can get an inside man in there, find out what she's up to. Beat her at her own game ...'

Tom rolls his eyes.

'You don't get it do you? We don't do things that way.'

'She's just a gold-digger. It's money she wants ...'

Tom pulls off his jacket and opens the window.

'You're off acquisitions Grant.'

Grant stares at him in shock. It feels like someone just punched him in the stomach. For a second he can't speak. That gold-digging little bitch, and to think he'd found her a good site.

'You don't mean that Tom, let me ...'

'You're out Grant,' Tom says, turning from the window and facing him, his expression grim.

'But I'm the best you've got and you know that. Let me sort this out Tom, I may have done a few things wrong but it's nothing I can't put right.'

Tom smiles.

'She hates me Grant. It's personal now. We've got a fight on our hands and I don't want you involved in it. You're being transferred to accounts ...'

'Come on Tom, we're mates aren't we?' Grant pleads.

'You're out Grant,' Tom says with finality, throwing his jacket over his arm. 'Martin in accounts is expecting you on Monday. Your salary will be the same, you're not being demoted; you're off acquisitions, that's it. I'm sorry.'

Tom walks past Grant without another word and closes the door behind him. Grant stares at the door, his heart as heavy as lead. He conjures up an image of Flora Robson in his mind. The little bitch, he'll make her pay for this if it's the last thing he does.

Chapter Twenty-Six

Tom

I take the lift to the top floor and wander out onto the roof where the view of London is spectacular. I take a deep breath and try to calm my anger. I needed to leave the office when I did. I could feel myself getting close to hitting Grant and that's the last thing I need after all that has happened. What a mess. I can't possibly let the sale of those shops in Church Lane go through now. It would be immoral. But how the hell can I back out when Grant has made them such good offers? Damn him. What the hell am I supposed to do with the shops if Flo doesn't want to sell? I thought Grant had more business sense. Why the hell didn't he stick to the rules? He's put me in an intolerable position. I rub my eyes tiredly. I can't even tell Flo the truth without painting myself as a victim. I can only hope she backs down or gets tired of fighting. Whichever way it goes I've lost her forever. At least she's not marrying that up his own arse Luke Wright. I'd like to think that had something to do with me but clearly she just saw sense in time.

My phone vibrates in my pocket and I reluctantly pull it out.

'Tom Rory,' I say.

'Tom it's Brent. I'm sorry to bring this up,' he says and I hear the embarrassment in his voice. 'I've just had the local paper on the phone, regarding Flora Robson and this protest that's planned. They're asking for our side of the story. They contacted Brian, one of the shareholders too …'

I fight back a sigh.

'It's Church Lane they're asking about, not the other …'

I find myself smiling.

'You don't have to walk on eggshells Brent. We're not engaged. Maybe we should send an email to the staff saying as much. I don't want to draw too much attention to it but an internal memo might not be a bad idea.'

'I'll get onto that right away Tom. But as I'm not too familiar with the Church Lane dispute I've asked them to hold fire on the story until we had more information for them. I hope I did the right thing?'

'That's fine Brent. I need to see you in my office say around three. I need to get you up to speed on the dispute. Meanwhile, I'm arranging a shareholder's meeting for this week. I need to clarify a few things.'

'Okay Tom, I'll let Grant know and …'

'Grant won't be at the meeting. He's off acquisitions as of today.'

'Oh, that's sudden,' Brent says, clearly shocked.

'I'll see you at three,' I say, before hanging up.

I scroll into my text messages and open the message from Flo. The only one I'd ever received from her.

I want you to know that Luke and I have broken up. I'm only telling you in case you hear from someone else and think you were responsible. I want you to know that it had nothing to do with you. You're just scum that came into my life and I'm going to wipe you clean of everything. I shan't give up my salon and I'll show the whole world the kind of man you are. You'll regret meeting me as much as I regret ever meeting you. Flora.

I save the message and push the phone back into my pocket. Hell hath no fury like a woman scorned. I have a feeling Flora Robson is going to be the biggest challenge of my professional life and most likely my emotional one too. I take one last look at the scenery that is bathed in a watery sun and then turn to the door. Let the war begin.

Chapter Twenty-Seven

'What do you think?' asks Sandy.

I think it smells like something has died in here. I only hope it wasn't the last lodger. Mind you, it's hard to smell anything over the tobacco odour that emanates from the landlord.

'It's a bit dim isn't it?' says Ryan. 'You'll never see what you're bloody eating or where you're pissing.'

'It's those new bulbs; they take a while to get going. It's called progress,' says Rick, the landlord.

'Right,' says Ryan. 'I've met a few guys who take a while to get going but I've never called it progress.'

'The kitchen is this way,' says Rick, stepping ahead of us. Ryan grabs my arm.

'Aren't there any sodding windows?'

'It's a basement flat you wally,' says Sandy with a tut. 'That's why it's cheap.'

'That's not the only reason it's cheap if you ask me,' mumbles Ryan.

'That's the beauty of a basement flat. You can walk around starkers all day if you want, and no one will see you,' says the landlord.

'In this light you'd be lucky to see yourself,' retorts Ryan.

'It's getting brighter,' says the landlord defensively.

We look stony-faced at the kitchen.

'I think I preferred it before the light bulbs progressed,' says Ryan quietly, looking at the small sink and stained drainer. He wipes a finger across the old-fashioned cooker and grimaces.

'Well, that hasn't seen a Brillo Pad for a while.'

We peer warily inside the fridge. Ryan sniffs.

'The beauty of this ...' begins the landlord.

'Frankly love, if you don't mind me saying, there is no beauty in this place even with the progressive lighting.'

'The beauty of this little place,' continues the landlord, ignoring Ryan, 'is you've got a Rory's just around the corner. If you run out of bread ...'

We all glare at him.

'Classic,' mumbles Ryan.

'It's all I can afford,' I say miserably. 'I've worked it all out. By the time I pay the mortgage and all the bills to do with the salon, and my rent. I'm barely going to have enough left to eat.'

'We'll be popping round with casseroles so often you'll be overcome,' smiles Sandy.

'Speak for yourself love,' pipes up Ryan. 'I'll pop round with the odd kebab but I'm not making no casserole.'

'Now you can see the living area. There's a two-seater couch and a bean bag. Of course you can add some stuff of your own.'

'Where exactly?' quips Ryan. 'Or is there another floor for us yet to peruse?'

Rick stifles a sigh and says,

'Shall we look at the bedroom?'

The bedroom is so small that there is just enough room for a bed and a bedside cabinet.

'The bathroom is en suite, so that's a good feature,' smiles Rick.

'Full of positivity this guy isn't he?' says Ryan.

'Well, I'll leave you to discuss it. Like I said, as Jethro is a mate I'm happy to let you have it at a reduced rate,' says Rick. 'I'll just be outside if you need me.'

The door clicks shut and Ryan groans.

'You can't be serious love,' he says, pulling some hygiene wipes from his holdall.

'Some flowers and a few pot plants and I'm sure it will look lovely,' I say.

'You could grow some lavender,' adds Sandy.

'I imagine something is already growing in this place and it most certainly isn't lavender,' Ryan groans, offering around the wipes.

'And you're getting it at a reduced rate,' says Sandy.

'That's the free rate is it?' Ryan says sarcastically.

'Hi, it's me,' shouts Devon, flinging open the front door.

She stops dead in the living room.

'Holy fuck,' she says, her eyes widening.

'The lights haven't progressed yet,' says Ryan handing her a wipe. 'It gets better apparently.'

'Shit Flo, you've got to be kidding. This is what I gave up my lunch hour for?' Devon grumbles.

'You're not seeing it in its full glory,' says Ryan.

'It's the best so far,' I say.

'And you don't know the best bit,' says Ryan. 'There's a Rory's on her doorstep, you know, should she need a pint of poison to cheer herself up,'

'I'm going to become an alcoholic aren't I?' I say depressingly.

'What are you talking about?' says Devon.

'I'll drink so I won't have to face where I'm living and then I'll drink even more to drown my other sorrows. I'll become an alcoholic.'

'No you won't,' says Ryan.

'Why not?'

'Because you won't be able to afford it, love.'

'It'll be great Flo,' says Sandy, hugging me. 'We'll have a painting party.'

'Don't you think you should have a cleaning party first?' asks Ryan.

'Ryan, can you just try and be positive for once in your life?' snaps Sandy.

'This is being positive.'

I drop onto the couch and a plume of dust fills the air.

'Well it's either this or I move in with my parents and I can't face that. Or I buy a sleeping bag and sleep at the salon ...'

'You can move in with us,' says Sandy, falling onto the couch beside me and sending more dust into the air.

In their hash-fogged flat? I don't think so. I'd be stoned just from breathing. I'd rather be an alcoholic.

'I'm going to take it,' I say resolutely.

Rick walks through the door at that moment.

'What's the decision guys?' he asks.

'I'll take it,' I say.

Well, what other choice do I have?

Chapter Twenty-Eight

A week later and my little basement flat is unrecognisable. A combined cleaning and painting party over the weekend had transformed it. Everyone had helped. Even Rosalind came with the baby. Even better, everyone bought a bottle of wine and I've tons over. The kitchen cupboards were cleaned and I've got one whole shelf devoted to Crunchies. It's amazing though how little you eat when you know you can. I'd chosen three pretty paintings with Devon's help from Portobello Market and the old bean bag has been stored in Rick's garage and been replaced by two cosy chairs which again had been purchased cheaply from the market. Sandy had given me a throw for the settee and Ryan had bought me another from John Lewis. I was extremely touched by his generosity and nearly burst into tears.

'Don't start crying you silly bitch. It was in the sale. I wouldn't have bought it otherwise, love.'

I'd hugged him gratefully. Luke had kindly given Mark a box full of crockery and cutlery with a note saying, *You bought them after all.* It's the only contact I've had with him since I broke off the engagement. Mark said he'd seemed okay. Throwing himself into work and spending more time at the gym. I'd not heard from Tom since Dublin. I had stupidly hoped he would try and contact me at the salon, but there had been nothing. Terence has a closing down sale and both shops at the side of the salon have signs on them saying, 'A new Rory's coming soon'. I must be a real thorn in Thomas Rory's side. But I can't give in. It isn't about Luke respecting me any more, it's about having respect for myself.

Tonight is our first meeting to discuss our strategy for taking on Rory's. When I say we, I mean *Team Robson*. I've tried to think of a different name as at the moment we sound like a bloody football team, and I hate football. In fact, I've decided I hate all sports and golf in particular. But Team Robson is a good start and I feel sure at the meeting we'll come up with something better. I'm the chairperson and feel like Tom Cruise heading up my undercover organisation. Not that anyone listens to me of course. I've even set up a Facebook and Twitter page to gain more followers, although at present we don't have any, but it takes time doesn't it? I'm determined to stay positive about everything, I'm even considering taking up meditation. Well, it seems all you need is a mat and a candle and at least I can sit down. Anything must be better than throwing a kettle around. It's time to try the new-age approach, I've decided. Everything is starting to look up. That's if you can call breaking up with my boyfriend, losing my business, taking on a huge corporation and moving into a tiny poxy flat as looking up. Not to mention hitting thirty and no wedding in sight. But still, things certainly seem better than they did, at least until this morning when I was awoken at five by a loud thumping from above. I'd thrown the duvet over my head, and then a pillow, but the thumping just continued. By six, I could take it no longer and drag myself from the bed. I wrap my robe around me and climb the steps where the thumping music could be clearly heard from the flat above. Oh great, just what I don't need. Rick had mentioned a neighbour but said he was holidaying in Ibiza.

'He goes there a fair bit,' Rick had said, so I had stupidly got it into my head that he was some old guy, most likely widowed. No such luck. From the rap music blaring from the open window, I don't somehow think this is a grey-haired widow unless he a very with it grey-haired widow. I tighten the robe and ring the doorbell, several times. Finally, I hear footsteps on the stairs. The door opens and I come face to face with a fair-haired man who is far from elderly. He's wearing jeans with holes in the knees and a black sweat top. He gives me the once over and smiles cockily at me. He's quite good looking but really not my type. A thick gold necklace hangs around his neck. I'm not really into that kind of man.

'You awright?' he asks in a strong East End accent.

'Not really,' I reply. 'You've had me up since five.'

I cringe the minute the words are out.

'You should be so lucky darlin',' he laughs, raising his eyebrows. 'You'd need to get in the queue.'

Cocky little bugger isn't he?

'Your music,' I stutter, avoiding his eyes. 'It's been thumping through the ceiling since five this morning. I have to work.'

Shit, now I'm implying he doesn't work but just holidays in sunny Ibiza or plays rap music all day. His eyes widen and he clicks his fingers.

'You've moved into the basement flat.'

I nod. He's quick, I'll give him that.

'Aw, I'm sorry babe. There hasn't been anyone in there for yonks. I just got back from Ibiza. I'm still on a bit of a high. I'm off work until tomorrow. That's my car there,' he says pointing proudly to a red sports car. 'Is that your Clio?'

I nod.

'I wondered whose that was. I know a bit about cars doll. If you ever have a problem just give me a knock. I'm Adam by the way.'

Why am I not surprised?

'Flora,' I say, and shiver.

'Flora, that's a bleeding odd name isn't it? I thought that's what you put on your toast,' he laughs.

Very funny. I shiver again and turn to go back downstairs.

'You wanna come in for a coffee. It's enough to freeze the bollocks off a brass monkey out 'ere'

Well, I wouldn't say it was that cold. It is April after all.

'I should be getting back,' I say.

'Tell you what, take my number. Just in case. If the old Clio plays up, just give me a bell.'

He whips out a mobile from his jeans pocket and flips open the cover.

'No really it's ...' I begin.

'Don't be one of them feminists; put it in your phone,' he drawls in what I presume is his sexy voice. Thank God, he isn't talking to Devon. He'd be walking back upstairs with a broken nose.

'I don't actually have my phone on me.'

He grabs a pad from a table by the door and jots down his number.

'I'll add it to my contacts,' I smile, thinking like hell I will.

'You got an Android?'

He makes it sound like a robot. I shake my head.

'You should get an Android. This is a Galaxy, I only get the best. You should give me your number too. Any problem with the old jalopy, just give me a bell.'

'That's very kind of you but ...'

I'm getting really cold now and have an awful feeling that my nipples might now be erect.

'You work down the markets?' he asks.

'I have my own hair salon actually, in Church Lane,' I say loftily.

His eyes widen in recognition.

'You put a leaflet through my door. You've got a protest or somethin'?'

I nod, backing away.

'I'm with you on that. I got a little shop down the market. You should drop in. I got a couple of stalls too. You like scarves. I do a lovely little wrap, what's your favourite colour?'

'That's very kind of you but ...'

'Come on, you must have a favourite colour?'

It's six in the morning. I can barely remember who I am, let alone my favourite colour.

'Blue,' I say.

'Great. I'll pop one in.'

Wonderful.

'Anything you need with this Rory business just let me know. I know people in the printing trade. You need a megaphone? I can get you one? No charge, my contribution.'

That's a point. Ryan said they had one in Screwfix but it was fifty-four quid, *screw that*, he'd said with a laugh.

'That would be great,' I say.

He nods happily.

'Brill, I'll drop one down for you,' he says with a wink.

I feel myself blush and give a little wave before heading back to my flat. A wide-boy above me, that's all I need. I open my door and pick up the post and stare mesmerised at a letter with RORY UK printed across the top. I move slowly into the lounge and drop onto the couch before opening it.

Dear Ms Robson,

We are writing to you regarding your property in Church Lane. We apologise for any misunderstandings regarding the proposed sale of your property to Rory's supermarket. As you know your shop and the adjoining premises have been selected for the site of a new Rory's supermarket as part of our community development and expansion plan. We are disappointed to hear of the misunderstandings that have developed between you and Rory's UK. We would like to amend this as soon as possible. If you would be so kind as to advise me of a good time to call on you, we can discuss this and other issues and come to a mutual understanding so both parties can move forward.

Kind Regards
Brent Galway.
Acquisitions Manager

What happened to Grant Richards, great sender of surveyors? I scrunch the letter into a ball and throw it into the kitchen bin. I'm not that easy to soft-soap if that's what Thomas Rory thinks, and if this Brent Galway comes round here with flowers and chocolates he can join the others and stick them up *his* arse.

Chapter Twenty-Nine

'I've brought wine,' says Sandy, handing me two bottles of cheap Spanish plonk. Ooh lovely. My wine collection is growing nicely.

'Not purchased from Rory's I hope darling,' says Ryan, following her in and handing me a packet of chocolate fingers and a bottle of vodka.

'Can't stand the stuff, been in the freezer like forever. I'm glad to get rid of it,' he smiles. 'Your mum's coming, she's parallel parking, or should I say trying to.'

I rush up the steps to see Mum clambering from the four by four and die from shame when she calls out,

'Is it safe to park here? I don't want the wheels stolen.'

'It's fine,' I say.

'Here,' she says, handing me a plant. 'I thought you could do with a labia to brighten up the windowsill. They make lovely window boxes.'

A labia? Jesus. I need to put her right on this one.

'It's called a lobelia,' I say.

'That's what I said wasn't it? And I've bought two bottles of wine, some cashew nuts and a bag of crisps. Rory's have got a special offer. It's called *Rory's Party Night*, the whole lot was ...'

'Mum, the whole idea is to *not* buy from Rory's. Not if you're going to be part of Team Robson.'

Ryan shakes his head.

'You're letting the side down already Mrs R.'

I knew having my mum on the team was a bad idea. The sooner I start my yoga and meditation the better. I exhale and Ryan dives his hand into his rucksack.

'I got you a little pressie love,' he says and produces *The Little Book of Calm*.

Oh no.

'It's got lots of nice little gems, like, *Lead Us Not into Temptation; just tell us where it is and we'll find it ourselves,*' he smiles. 'Something like that anyway.'

I kiss him on the cheek.

'I'm sure it will come in useful,' I say.

'Yeah, it can double up as a door jamb or loo paper when you run short.'

Devon bursts in, followed by Rosalind.

'Mark's playing squash with ... well Mark's playing squash,' Devon says quickly picking up Mum's plant.

'This is pretty,' she says. 'It will look nice on your windowsill.'

'It's a labia,' says Mum. 'It was on offer in B&Q.'

I'm losing the will to live.

'It's a what?' says a shocked Rosalind. 'Christ, are they naming plants after it now. Whatever next? They'll be a flowering purple-headed shaft in B&Q before we know it.'

'You can say his name you know,' I say, gratefully accepting a glass of wine from Ryan.

'I didn't mean Luke was a purple-headed shaft,' says Rosalind. 'Although he is a dick, you've got to admit.'

'I was talking to Devon,' I say raising my voice. 'You can say Luke's name. I don't expect Mark to stop playing squash with him just because we've broken up.'

'Right,' says Devon.

'And it's a lobelia not a labia,' I say to Mum.

'Oh right,' everyone says looking at the plant and lapsing into silence.

Jesus, this is a great start to the meeting isn't it? Mum and Rosalind are cosily ensconced on the little couch, while Devon and Sandy sit with their legs curled under them on my new chairs. Ryan and I are sitting cross-legged on the floor. Everyone looks suspiciously at the plant.

'Although,' says Ryan thoughtfully, 'I once saw a cactus that looked like a penis ...'

We all look at him.

'Although, maybe on reflection it didn't,' he finishes lamely.

'I'll pop some nuts in a dish,' says Mum jumping up.

'So who else are we waiting for?' I say.

'This is it isn't it?' says Rosalind. 'Jeremy doesn't want to get involved in case you make the papers again. Besides he's working late.'

Devon and I look at her. She shrugs.

'What? He often works late.'

I raise my eyebrows and her eyes widen in horror as the realisation hits her.

'Shit, I left Sadistic Harry in the car,' she says leaping up.

'She forgot her own baby?' says Devon.

'Should we report her?' quips Ryan.

'Don't start,' Rosalind yells from the front door. 'I just forgot. I've not had him long.'

'That's a good excuse I suppose,' says Ryan.

'Jeth says he'll come later. He's got a gig,' says Sandy. 'He's with his homeboys. They're banging. We should all go sometime and see them at the Zodiac. They really bust it.'

Mum attempts not to look confused and says,

'Sounds lovely dear, can't say I've heard of *The Homeboys* though.'

'What about Dad?' I ask.

'No, he's not into pop music, he wouldn't know them.'

'It's rap actually,' says Sandy. 'And homeboys means friends, you know it's like slang.'

I knock back some wine.

'I meant, is Dad coming to the meeting?'

'Your dad thinks it best if he doesn't get involved, just in case it makes the news,' says Mum handing round nuts and crisps.

Great, so the sum total of Team Robson is seven. I can't very well count Sadistic Harry can I? Seven against … it doesn't bear thinking about. Rosalind returns with a gurgling Sadistic Harry and we all sigh with relief.

'We need more supporters,' I say.

'We need more booze love, to soften the blow,' says Ryan.

Oh no, what blow?

'So far, the number of people defo coming to the protest is …'

We all hold our breath as he opens a notebook, glances at some figures and says.

'Twenty, and if you minus seven, that leaves thirteen.'

'And your dad can't make it. He's got a game that day,' says Mum.

'Twelve,' corrects Ryan.

I knock back my wine and Rosalind groans.

'Shit, is that all? How many Twitter followers do we have?' asks Sandy.

I down another mouthful before saying,

'Seven.'

'Well that's a start ...'

I raise my eyebrows.

'Oh, I see. The seven is actually us?' she says with a frown.

'Well, no actually, it's six of us because my mum's not on Twitter ...'

'Well, I don't see the point. You can't get a good gossip going in 140 words can you?' says Mum defensively.

'I think you could do okay with 140 words love,' says Ryan grinning.

'It's 140 characters Mum,' I say tiredly. 'And the idea is not to gossip anyway.'

'But I get your point darling,' agrees Ryan. 'They even count the hashtags. Surely they should be separate from the 140 characters.'

Sandy rolls her eyes.

'Who's the other one then?' she asks

'I don't know. But we have one follower at least.'

'We need to put on regular updates,' says Sandy.

'But it's only us. We'll just be telling each other what we already know,' says Ryan.

He's got a point.

'I had a letter from Rory's,' I say.

Mum puts down the dish of nuts.

'Oh dear, are they cross with us?' she asks.

'We haven't started yet,' says a determined Sandy. 'Don't forget Mrs R, they're doing people out of their jobs. You mustn't worry about them getting a little bit cross.'

'Yes, of course. You're quite right,' says Mum, picking up the nuts.

'And?' asks Devon.

I hand around the crumpled letter that I had fished out of the bin. It occurred to me that as we were having the meeting I really should show it to all of Team Robson. Of course, I had since chucked in several used tea bags and some leftover tuna. So it isn't looking or smelling that great.

'Perhaps you could read it out love,' says Ryan, wrinkling his nose in disgust. 'It smells like a gone-off fish finger.'

Everyone is silent as Devon dangles the letter between finger and thumb and tries to decipher the tea-stained words.

'What happened to Grant I'll-take-you-for-dinner Richards?' says Sandy.

'Ooh yes, what happened to him?' says Ryan.

'Do we just ignore it?' asks Devon.

'I think you should respond. Just in case they get legal. We need a proper solicitor's letter in response,' says Rosalind patting Sadistic Harry's back until he lets out a huge burp.

'Would Dad do that?' I ask Mum hopefully.

Mum looks horrified at Sadistic Harry.

'Well sometimes after a beer.'

I sigh. Whatever was I thinking of having my mum as part of Team Robson.

'Would he write us a legal letter to Rory's was what she meant?' asks Rosalind.

'Oh I see. I can ask him. As long as he is not on Team Robson I don't think he will mind.'

'Well we need to do something. We need more followers for a start,' says Sandy, grabbing my laptop and clicking into Twitter.

'Right the first thing we need to do is advertise the protest. We have to retweet it every day. It's only ten days away. We can't have a protest with only twenty people.'

I groan miserably.

'It'll be okay,' says Rosalind and Sadistic Harry farts in agreement.

'The first thing is to follow loads of people. That's the only way to get them to follow back,' says Sandy, 'and we should set up a web page,' she continues. 'Jethro knows this guy, he's dope.'

'Perhaps we should use someone else then dear,' says Mum while handing round chilli-flavoured crackers. 'We want someone who knows what they're doing.'

'He does,' says Sandy.

'But you just said he was a dope,' argues Mum.

I suppose I should be more assertive, like Tom Cruise, and get the mission on the road shouldn't I?

'Right, I'm officially opening the meeting. Devon, you can take the minutes?'

Rosalind waves Mum away as she heads towards her with the chilli crackers.

'No thanks darling. If I eat those the little sadistic bugger will be breathing fire tomorrow.'

I shove my mum back onto the couch.

'Right, the meeting is starting,' I say in my best assertive tone. 'We can't let Rory win. Now first on the agenda is the protest. We need more supporters. Sandy, can I delegate the web page to you?'

She nods.

'Okay, so Sandy is IT consultant and promotions manager,' I say.

'Ooh grand,' she laughs.

'We need a megaphone,' says Ryan.

'Got one, or at least I will have. The wide-boy in the flat above says he can get us one.'

'Another supporter there then?' says Rosalind.

I pull a face.

'Well, if you're going to be fussy love,' says Ryan.

'I gave him a leaflet. I think he might come.'

'See if he's on Twitter,' says Sandy.

'Lovely that you've met someone,' enthuses Mum.

'Right moving on,' I say abruptly.

'Teamrobson as a Twitter handle is a bit limp. Besides it sounds like a football team,' says Sandy.

'How about *fighting hairdresser*?' suggests Mum.

I cringe.

'Fight or dye, you know, spelt as in hair dye,' says Ryan, nodding proudly.

'Crass,' dismisses Sandy. 'I'll do a name generator. If we put in Flora fights back, we must get something.'

Mum refills glasses as we wait.

'Flopperflora, Florabomber ...'

'Well, we're not using florabomber,' I interrupt. 'I'll be arrested as a potential terrorist.'

'Floozy Flora, Flora babe ...'

'Oh come on,' I say irritably. 'There must be better ones than that.'

'I think they're cool,' says Ryan.

'How about fightwithflora or campaignflora?'

A top-up of wine and a vote later and we go for *fightwithflora*.

'I've updated the Twitter page. Made it clear on your profile what we're doing and I've tweeted the place date and time of the protest, and we now have four more followers,' says Sandy proudly.

'Wow, careful we don't go viral,' quips Ryan.

'If we could stay positive,' snaps Rosalind as Sadistic Harry farts in agreement.

'Christ, he farts for England that one, what are you feeding him on?' Ryan snaps.

'My breast, anything else you want to say?'

'Yes, I think that last one wasn't a fart, not judging by your jeans.'

'Ah Christ. The little sod, won't be a sec,' she says dashing to the loo.

I bet Tom Cruise wouldn't put up with this.

'I'll be in charge of the Twitter page and I'll update every day. We need someone to take on publicity. Ryan, can you do that? Contact the local papers and stuff like that. Posters in the library, you know the kind of thing?

He nods.

'Ryan, Publicity Manager,' says Devon scribbling in her WH Smith notebook.

'Jeth said you need strategies to make Rory's look bad,' says Sandy.

'You mean put it about that they have bad hygiene and stuff like that?' asks Ryan. 'Seems a bit underhand don't you think?'

'And stealing our prescription idea wasn't?' I say.

'I agree with Ryan. You can't do anything too extreme,' says Devon topping up our glasses. 'Nothing illegal or untrue or it will weaken our cause. You need to do little things that will cause a bit of mayhem now and then. You know, protesting outside with placards and stuff. We need lots of leaflets too.'

'That's going to be bloody expensive,' says Rosalind returning from the loo and smelling of 'Womanity'. I raise my eyebrows.

'I didn't think you'd mind. Trust me the other smell is worse.'

'She's right. The leaflets are the most expensive. And it would be good to get more stickers,' adds Sandy.

I find myself wriggling with excitement.

'Adam said he knows people in the printing trade. He may be able to get the leaflets.'

'Adam?' queries Rosalind.

'The guy upstairs.'

'That's a nice name. Very biblical,' says Mum.

'Two more followers,' squeals Sandy, holding up the laptop. 'One has tweeted us.'

We all hover around the laptop.

@fightwithflora This is awful, we'll be there. Keep up the good work.'

'Great, more people for the protest,' says Ryan. 'These Chilli crackers are nice Mrs R.'

Mum smiles.

'Yes special offer from …'

We all glare at her.

'Next rule,' I say. 'We all boycott Rory's and do our shopping elsewhere. There's an Aldi not too far away and a Tesco off Ladbroke Road.'

'Aldi,' says Mum indignantly. 'What if my friends at Health and Beauty find out, and Tesco, do I really have to?'

'Don't be a snob.'

'What if someone else gets it for me?' she asks hopefully.

'The whole point is that we don't give Rory's the custom Mum.'

'Yeah, we'll show them,' says Ryan. 'Seven people boycotting Rory's, Christ, they won't know what's hit them.'

I groan. He's quite right of course. It really doesn't matter one way or the other if my mum shops there or not. It will need more than seven of us to make a difference. Even seven hundred people wouldn't bother Rory's. It's a complete and total waste of time.

'You're right. Why are we even bothering?' I say sorrowfully. 'I might as well give them the salon and be done with it.'

'I thought you were up for a fight,' scolds Devon. 'Didn't take you long to cave in did it?'

'And what about our jobs?' says Sandy, becoming tearful.

'Yes, sweetie, what about our jobs?' echoes Ryan.

'I could take the salon in the East End of London,' I say meekly. 'Or meet Thomas Rory and discuss another site. He did say he could offer me one in a good area.'

Just saying his name conjures up his gorgeous face and I can hear his soft well-spoken voice in my head. Don't think about it, don't think about it but how can I not think about it? No one ever made me feel the way he did. It's not like the salon is in fantastic condition is it? In fact the whole place is becoming a headache in more ways than one. Luke wasn't wrong about that. There's no harm in meeting up with Tom is there, just to discuss other sites. It would be good to see him again. What if Rosalind is right and he does like me? Don't think about it, don't think about it but how can I not think about it? Surely if he really liked me he wouldn't have deceived me.

'Have you lost leave of your senses?' snaps Devon. 'The man deceived you, bought the other two properties behind your back, announces your idea at a big charity do as his own and embarrasses you in the papers and ...'

'She's in love with him,' interrupts Rosalind bluntly.

'Well, it doesn't sound like the feeling's mutual darling, if you don't mind me saying,' says Ryan.

'It might be,' says Mum hopefully. 'They did have a good time by all accounts, from the photos in the ...'

'It could be mutual. He may not have known what was going on,' says Rosalind, giving me a smile.

'He's the bloody company CEO. Of course he did,' snaps Sandy.

'You're right, it just seemed hopeless for a minute,' I say.

What am I thinking? I told Tom it was war. I can't give in this soon.

'You've got to fight,' says Devon. 'Fight for others if not for yourself because people like him don't stop at just one person.'

She's quite right of course. He's nothing but a bully who needs to be stopped.

'So our rules are,' says Sandy firmly, while eyeing my mother. 'No shopping at Rory's. We boycott them and try to get as many people as we can to boycott too. One of us needs to go round some of the smaller shops and see if they will reduce their prices so they undercut Rory's. We should follow all the local shops if they're on Twitter, get them on our side and perhaps even follow Rory's.'

There is a shocked silence broken only by a fart from Sadistic Harry.

'That's a bit crazy isn't it?' says Rosalind, popping out an engorged breast and pushing Sadistic Harry onto it. 'What if they follow back? They'll know everything we're up to.'

'Well, that's put me off the cashews,' groans Ryan, grimacing at the sight of Rosalind's breast.

'Don't you get it, they'll see how many followers we're getting?' says Sandy. 'We don't tell them all our underhand tricks obviously, just our rallies and petitions. Talking of which we should set up an online petition too.'

'Five more followers,' she announces. 'Three messages, all saying good for you @fightwithflora #downwithrory'

'I'll go round the local shops,' offers Devon.

'I'll do some too,' I add.

'I'll prepare the placards,' suggests Ryan.

'Jeremy's mate owns a joke shop. I could pop in there see what they have. You know, for props and stuff,' says Rosalind.

'Fab idea,' says Sandy excitedly.

'I'll look into jokes and research ideas,' adds Devon.

'Okay Devon, you're Projects Manager,' I say. 'I'm in charge of Social Media and Rosalind you do what you can.'

A terrible thought occurs to me.

'What if Thomas Rory follows me?'

'I'd do him for stalking love,' says Ryan seriously, uncorking another bottle.

'On Twitter I mean. What if he follows fightwithflora?'

'All the better; we'll know he's worried.'

And if he tweets me I'll have to tweet back won't I? After all it would be rude not to. I find myself hoping he does.

'I don't have a job,' pipes up Mum, raising a hand.

Just as well.

'You can be Human Resources manager,' I say. 'You're In charge of drinks, food, and entertainment for our meeting and rallies.'

'Someone has to be in charge of the PG Tips, who better than you love?' grins Ryan.

'Lovely,' smiles Mum.

'Is this meeting at an end then, because I should get Sadistic Harry home?'

'You're not going to christen him Sadistic Harry are you?' asks Devon.

'I think the vicar might have a problem with that,' grins Rosalind. 'We'll just have it as his little pet name shall we?'

'Is there any other business?' I say in an official tone.

Sadistic Harry burps. I bet Team Rory, if there is a Team Rory, doesn't have to put up with this.

Chapter Thirty

'Oh shit,' I scream. 'Did you see that, there's a mouse in the salon.'

I jump onto a chair sending it swivelling around, making me feel sick

'Where did it go?' I squeal.

'I didn't see anything,' says a calm Sandy.

'There was a mouse. I saw it. It ran right in front of me as I opened the door.'

Ryan looks around the salon.

'Must have run out,' he says nonchalantly.

I scan the floor anxiously.

'We can't have mice in here,' I say, my voice trembling and my heart hammering. 'What if the clients see it?'

'If it has run out they won't see it will they darling. I'll put the kettle on. I would pop and get some doughnuts from R ...'

Sandy glares at him. Shit, I hate mice. What is happening to my little salon? I've got cracks and now mice. I won't be able to sell to Rory's soon even if I wanted to.

'I bet it's those cracks,' I say.

'It must be a mouse on a diet to get through those,' grins Ryan.

'It's all the bloody food we have here. It's got to stop,' I say forcefully.

'Well you're the one who's always buying them, love. Frankly all those cakes are playing havoc with my figure. I can barely get into my salmon shirt these days. The other night at the club, the buttons kept popping off during the Macarena, I mean, can you imagine and I hadn't waxed. I assure you I didn't pull anything that night apart from a few muscles.'

I don't understand why he is so calm. If I had expected anyone to be jumping on a chair it would have been Ryan for sure. In fact I seriously would have expected him to have been out of the door by now.

'Have you got your contacts in?' asks Sandy.

'Yes, of course,' I say my eyes flitting into every corner.

I lower my feet slowly to the floor and gingerly wander to the kitchenette.

'I'll open up shall I?' asks Sandy. 'Now you've climbed down from the chair.'

I go to say yes when the little bugger runs straight past me and into the kitchenette.

'Shit,' I scream. 'It's in here, quick do something. Ryan, kill it,' I demand, grabbing a broom and throwing it in Ryan's direction.

Sandy rushes in and dives to the floor, skidding as she goes. God it's like a scene out of *Red*. She only needs a gun in each hand and she'd be Notting Hill's version of Helen Mirren.

'I've got it,' she shouts.

Oh Jesus, she didn't grab it with her bare hands did she?

'Throw it outside,' I say, keeping my face turned away. Or is she going to drown it in acid in the manner of Helen Mirren in the film.

'We should keep it as a pet,' says Ryan.

Have they both gone totally insane?

'Here,' says Sandy, stretching her arm out to me.

'Get back,' I scream.

'It's not a real one. It's a joke,' she laughs.

'A joke, what do you mean a joke? I could have had a heart attack,' I snap. 'What kind of joke is that?'

'I remembered what Devon said about practical jokes on Rory's Supermarkets ...'

'Yes, Rory's Supermarkets, not my salon,' I say, exhaling and trying to calm my racing heart.

'I remembered when Jeth got it to scare his landlady because ...'

'I really don't want to hear any more,' I say quickly.

It's enough I have to hear about bangers and chin checks. Heaven knows what he's used on the landlady. I'm just glad he's a friend. I would hate to have him as an enemy.

'Me neither,' agrees Ryan.

'Anyway,' continues Sandy. 'Here's the idea. One of us goes into the store and pops it in a corner ...'

'After winding it up of course,' adds Ryan.

'I'm glad you told me that,' I say, sarcasm heavy in my voice. 'I'd never have guessed that bit.'

'She's still cross,' he smiles.

'Then we scream *mouse, there's a mouse in the shop*. It's bound to cause a bit of a disruption,' finishes Sandy fidgeting about excitedly.

'And who's the one of us that is going to do this?' I ask sceptically.

They both look at me.

'Oh no, shouldn't it be Devon? That's her role.'

'You're the one fighting Thomas Rory and it is your salon,' drawls Ryan. 'Anyway, Devon's tied up with some top model. I should be so lucky.'

'So ...'

'So, you have to do the dirty work,' says Sandy.

That's just great isn't it? I look at the mouse. It's all furry and cute nosed just like a real one.

'But,' she adds, handing it to me. 'I don't mind coming and shouting as well. That way it will look better. As we get more followers of course, it will be easier to get other people to do these things.'

Oh, that's good. Otherwise I'm in danger of getting arrested.

'Talking of followers, how are we doing on Twitter today darling?' asks Ryan. 'I started following, did you see?'

'No, not unless your name is *Pinlan Wong*,' I say, 'and yes, we're doing well.'

'I must have done it wrong. I'll have another go.'

Sandy raises her eyebrows.

'It's Twitter, not rocket science. How can you get it wrong?'

This morning we had twenty-six more Twitter followers and ten messages of support. Five were in China mind you, but it's good to know our appeal is branching worldwide isn't it? If you can consider five supporters in China as worldwide, but it will sound good when we get in the papers. Although I don't imagine they even know who Rory's are, let alone Team Robson, the Chinese I mean, not the papers. I'm sure the papers know who Rory's are. I'd followed them back as instructed by Sandy and was about to close the lid when a notification came through and I had frozen at the words *RorysUK are now following you on Twitter*. I'd slammed the lid down and then realised that it wouldn't be Tom himself. I'd clicked back into Twitter and into the RorysUK page and saw they had 40,000 followers.

'And Rory's are following us. Do you know they have 40,000 followers?' I say. 'We'll never get that many.'

'Hardly anyone gets that many,' says Sandy. 'That's good, they're aware of us.'

Honestly I was on the thing for about an hour. Every time I went to leave another notification came through. I don't know how tweeters get to work.

'You should get the Twitter app for your phone,' says a knowledgeable Sandy. 'That way you can keep up.'

I'm not so sure I want to keep up. At that rate I'll not only be assed out but twittered out too.

It's bad enough I had to update my Facebook status to single last night. That was pretty depressing. I also saw that Luke had unfriended me. That was even more depressing.

'I'll open up shall I love?' asks Ryan.

I nod.

'We have a free thirty minutes at one o'clock,' says Sandy, scanning the appointment book. 'Let's do it then.'

'Synchronise watches,' grins Ryan, unlocking the door. 'Let's rock and roll'.

Chapter Thirty-One

We stare at the sign in Rory's window. I don't believe it. They've got offers on all their meat products and we haven't even spoken to the local butcher yet. We're not going to get anywhere like this. He always seems to be one step ahead of us.

'I don't believe this,' I say voicing my thoughts.

'We can't ask Jeff at the butchers to drop his price lower than these can we?' says Sandy gloomily.

'I don't understand how he is always one step ahead of us,' I say.

'Because he's in business, his mind probably works the same as ours at the moment. Or ...'

She turns and looks at me, her eyes wide.

'He's bugged my phone and my flat and most likely the hairdressers,' I finish for her. 'Shit, that means they know about the mouse and will have the police waiting for us.'

'Honestly, you're getting worse than Ryan,' says Sandy. 'They're getting their intel from Twitter. They've seen our next move. We need to use Twitter to our advantage and be careful not to give too much away.'

I'm seriously thinking selling the salon would be so much easier than all this cloak and dagger stuff. I need to watch some crime films to get a few tips. I'll pop to Terence's and see what he can recommend. After all I've got nothing else to do with my evenings these days. I can't even play solitaire without thinking of Tom and our card game and that divine kiss. It was so real. I can't believe it didn't mean anything. A man can't kiss like that unless they feel something. Maybe, just maybe ...

'Ready?' asks Sandy.

No. I'll never be ready. I'm shaking so much you'd think I was going to rob the place.

'We'll hover around the sandwiches. Make it look natural. It is lunchtime after all,' she says and grabs my arm and the next thing

I know I'm standing in Rory's and shaking so much you'd think I had a grenade rather than a toy mouse in my pocket.

'Afternoon ladies,' booms a voice behind me, making me jump out of my skin. 'Can I offer you baskets this afternoon?'

I turn to the security man and attempt to speak but find myself grunting something inaudible. 'We're just getting lunch,' smiles Sandy.

'We've a special on this week. A free bag of crisps with a sandwich pack,' he says proudly. Anyone would think he owned Rory's. Still, I suppose he's only doing his job. I hope he doesn't get into trouble for this. What if he gets the sack?

'Maybe we should go to …' I begin but Sandy pulls me towards the sandwich fridge.

'We can't do it here, he may see us,' she says. 'We'll have to buy a sandwich, make it look good …'

'But we're not supposed to buy from …'

'But if it's for the cause,' she whispers.

I finger the mouse in the pocket of my jacket. If anyone looks suspicious I certainly do, I must look like I'm about to draw a gun and hold up the checkout girl. I study the sandwiches, choose an egg mayonnaise and take my free bag of crisps.

'Best get one for Ryan,' says Sandy choosing a BLT. 'Do you want a drink? I'll get Ryan a Coke. What crisps does he like?'

I sigh. I don't believe this. We're here with intent to ruin Rory's business and instead we're giving him some.

'I don't know. I can't think straight.'

'Act natural,' says Sandy.

She's got to be kidding. I've got a wind-up mouse in my pocket. How can I act natural?

'I'll pay for these at the self-service till. Give me a minute and then let it go.'

'I … I …' I begin but the words *I can't* just don't come out.

I wind the mouse up with my thumb and all I can hear is my heart beating in my chest. I am sure the woman looking at the smoked mackerel next to me must be able to hear it too. I'm studying the mackerel like some kind of expert. I pick up one after the other and then put them back neatly.

'The peppered mackerel is lovely, have you tried that one dear? I had it last night with a bit of mashed potato. Lovely it was, here, take one and try it. You obviously like your mackerel.'

'Oh no, thank you but ...'

'Here, this looks like a nice one.'

She pushes the mackerel at me. I pull out my hand, forgetting the mouse is in it. I drop the mouse in panic and it scoots down the aisle at full speed towards the deli counter.

'Did you see that?' shrieks the woman. 'A mouse, there's a mouse. It ran right past you.'

A woman with her head in the cod fridge screams blue murder and almost throws herself in with the fishcakes. I glance at Sandy who nods at me.

'Oh where is it? I hate mice,' I squeal, trying to act terrified.

'A mouse, there's a mouse in the shop,' yells Sandy. 'Over there,' she points.

'Oh my God, where?' shrieks another woman.

Within minutes, Rory's is a pandemonium of shrieking women and macho men attempting to find the rampant mouse. Sandy walks calmly to the exit and I hurriedly follow. I'm out the door when a hand lands heavily on my arm.

'Just a minute,' says a voice.

Chapter Thirty-Two

I freeze. I don't believe it. Our first prank on Rory's and I'm getting apprehended.

'It is you. I said to myself that bum looks familiar,' says Adam grinning from ear to ear as the alarm wails.

'What are you doing buying stuff from Rory's?' he asks, nodding at the abundance of food in Sandy's arms. Christ, she could have taken a carrier bag at least.

'Oh shit,' mumbles Sandy.

I feel the tension leave my body and give Adam a smile. I'd never been so happy to see someone in my life, even if it is Adam.

'Hello Adam, can't stop, we're late back,' I say.

There is a mass exodus from the store as streams of petrified women and screaming children burst through the exit doors.

'I got your scarf. I'll drop it in later shall I?' says Adam, seemingly oblivious to the chaos around him.

'Leaflets,' says Sandy, sounding like a mad woman.

'What?' I say.

'Ask him about the leaflets,' she mumbles.

'What was that darling?' he asks.

'You said you may know someone who could do our leaflets ...'

'Yeah, of course darling. No probs, and the megaphone, I'll get you that too. Tell you what I'll get it today. Give you a knock about nine? You girls get on; don't let me hold you up.'

'But ...' I begin.

He gives a wave and crosses the street.

'I forgot to pay,' she says as soon as Adam is out of earshot.

She what? How could she forget to pay? I stare at the packs of crisps, sandwiches and drinks cradled in her arms.

'What do you mean, you didn't pay?'

'I kind of forgot when the mouse thing happened.'

And I thought I would let the side down.

'We have to go back,' I groan.

She nods. They say criminals return to the crime scene don't they? I wonder if they usually do it as quick as this. This is ridiculous.

'I don't think they know it was you,' she says.

I grab her arm.

'What do you mean *you don't think*?' I ask, trying to remain calm.

'Okay, they don't know it was you,' she corrects.

'You wouldn't say that unless you thought, that they thought, it was me,' I ramble.

'Everything's cool,' she says and knocks on the door. I feel myself tremble as the security guard opens it.

'Sorry ladies, we're closed for a while due to a minor incident. We'll be opening in a jiffy.'

Is that a funny look he's giving me? His hand moves to the radio clipped to his belt. Bollocks.

'I can check how long it will be,' he says.

'We'll come back later,' I say, turning to walk away.

'I didn't pay,' says Sandy in a rush.

He looks at the goods in her hands.

'The mouse thing ...' she mumbles.

He waves a hand dismissively.

'Oh, there were no mouse, it were just a child's toy. Dropped it I guess. You come on in. We're just getting things tidy before reopening.'

This is madness. We're the last people that should be in the store, let alone the first ones to come back. An assistant wearing a name badge with *Sally* on it comes to our aid.

'Poor you, forget to pay did you,' she says in cheerful voice. 'Those alarms scare you half to death don't they? Let me scan your things. Do you have your loyalty card?'

For some stupid reason I pull the thing out of my purse.

'Lovely. So there's the points for your goods and twenty extra points for your honesty. Not everyone would have come back, there you are ...' she squints at the card, 'Miss Grayson'.

Oh shit.

'You'd be shocked at how much went from the fish counter,' she says quietly.

I think of the little old lady with the mackerel. No, surely not.

It's six o'clock and the salon has finally closed. Our feet haven't touched the ground since getting back this afternoon. I pick up the ringing phone tiredly as Sandy sweeps around my feet.

'Flora's hair salon good evening,' I say flopping into the chair by the reception desk.

'Are you sure this is what you want Flo?' says a soft familiar voice.

His voice conjures up so many memories and emotions that I find myself spiralling into a trembling mess of mixed feelings. I can picture his bright blue eyes, the way he frowns when he concentrates and the twinkle in his eye when he teases, and the way his lips had felt when they had touched mine. In those few seconds I feel sure I can even smell him and remember the touch of his hand. His warm arms around me when we danced and his urgent body pressing into me when we kissed. Don't think about it, don't think about it. He's the enemy. He's the man who wants to take everything from you.

'We don't have to go down this route Flo. We could meet for coffee and ...'

I finally find my voice and say quietly,

'I don't consort with the enemy.'

Sandy's head snaps up and she looks wide-eyed at me.

'Thomas Rory,' I mouth.

She immediately blanches.

'I'm not your enemy. You realise if you continue like this, things will get messy and you won't win.'

Why does he always have to sound so bloody reasonable?

'I'm not in the wrong,' I say. 'And I have every intention of winning.'

'There are some things I can't control Flo. If you say anything slanderous about the company on Twitter I won't be able to stop our solicitors from taking action.'

'We are just telling the truth,' I say, feeling angry that even now he can produce such emotion in me. How can he still affect me in this way?

'Please Flo, let's talk. I'd like to see you. Give me a chance to explain. I don't want us at loggerheads like this. It's crazy.'

'I'll never give in to you. Now I have to go I'm afraid. I have clients to see to.'

I slam down the phone and realise my whole body is trembling.

'What did he say? Does he know about the mouse?' asks Sandy anxiously.

I shake my head.

'He says he can't stop his solicitors from taking action if we put anything slanderous on the Twitter page.'

Sandy smiles.

'That's a good warning. If I didn't know better I'd say that was his way of advising you. Maybe your mum and Rosalind are right. Perhaps the feeling was mutual.'

I go to answer when she begins to wave madly.

'There's Jethro. We're going over to his mates tonight to work on the web page. Good luck with Adam.'

My mind is reeling so much that I can't even think about Adam. Was Tom's phone call simply to warn me? Does he care about me? No, don't think about it, don't think about it but how can I not think about it? I fetch my shawl from the back and turn off the lights, my mind full of Thomas Rory.

Chapter Thirty-Three

Tom

'Oh Mr Rory, they never said it was yourself that was here. I thought ...' says Frank, jumping up from his seat, almost knocking over a mug of tea.

'Nothing to worry about Frank, you're the best security officer we have,' I smile. 'Those Jaffa cakes look good.'

He gives a relieved smile in return.

'You're welcome to one,' says Frank, offering the pack.

I take one and glance at the bank of CCTV displays.

'I was just curious about the mouse incident earlier and would be grateful if you'd show me the CCTV playback?'

'Oh that were nothing, Mr Rory, just some kid's toy that got dropped. Scared some of the old girls I can tell you,' he laughs.

I smile.

'I bet it did. I'm just curious to see what happened.'

'No problem. The tape is changed every hour. I'll just get the one you need, won't be a sec.'

I sit down in front of the video monitors and watch casually as I eat the Jaffa cake, and then I see her. I shake my head in disbelief. What on earth is she wearing? She looks like an accomplice for Johnny English in those shades. I can barely see her face but I'd know that walk anywhere. She dives down the sweet aisle throwing in chocolate bars as she goes. This is Flo, without doubt. I find myself laughing aloud as she looks around before throwing marshmallows into her basket. Frank strolls in and glances at the camera.

'You see some funny ones on there don't you,' he says laughing with me.

'You sure do,' I say, watching as Flo tries the sample olives before throwing a carton into her basket. I smile. I never realised how much I missed her until now. If this is war I imagine peacetime with her is fun.

'So, here's the tape from earlier. I've run it back to just before the mouse incident,' he laughs.

I pull my eyes away from Flora and watch the video, and there she is, as clear as day with another woman. They couldn't look more suspicious if they tried.

'Oh these two were clowns. I was on the door when they came back,' says Frank, looking closely at the monitor.

'Came back?' I ask, watching Flora closely. She is fiddling with something in her pocket. That's the mouse for sure.

'The whole mouse kerfuffle scared them so much they left without paying. They came back though. If only everyone was that honest, huh, Mr Rory?'

'Indeed,' I say, watching as Flora lets something fall to the floor when taking some fish from another customer.

'There you go, that's when the whole thing happened. Some kid's toy it was. But they make them look so much like the real thing these days don't they? Mayhem it was. But we made it very clear on a notice that it was a toy one. No worries there Mr Rory.'

I turn back to the camera and see that Flo is now hurrying to the exit. I debate going down and speaking to her but change my mind.

'Thanks for that Frank,' I say.

'Anything else I can help you with Mr Rory?' he asks.

'Yes, I'd like to arrange a special delivery to a very loyal customer,' I say, watching as Flo leaves the store.

'Of course, I'll send Mick up. He arranges deliveries.'

I smile as Flo disappears from view. I rather think I'm going to enjoy this war.

Chapter Thirty-Four

No matter how hard I try, I can't get Tom out of my head. It's like his phone call has had some kind of hypnotic effect on me. I open the freezer and stare into the empty drawers. The fridge isn't much better either. Ever since I stopped online shopping, I'm forever out of food. I don't have any bread. Honestly, who doesn't have bread? I open the fridge again, as though something may have miraculously appeared in the few seconds since I closed it. I don't even have a bottle of milk, bottles of wine yes, but no milk. I was in Rory's too. No, don't think about it, don't think about it but how can I not think about it? I'm starving and no one would know if I popped in there for a loaf of bread and a tin of baked beans would they? Lois will be closed now and I debate going to the little shop up the road but everything in there always looks stale. I don't want to drive to Aldi or Tesco. I open the cupboard and see I am down to my last Crunchie. Right, I can't starve, that's just ridiculous. I rummage in my tiny wardrobe and find my rain mac with the hood. I slide into it, wrap a scarf around me to cover my mouth and don my sunglasses. I'd like to think I look like Audrey Hepburn but I'm under no illusions. I look more like an extra from *The Only Way Is Essex*.

It will take five minutes to dash around the store and if anyone questions the sunglasses I'll say the fluorescent lighting gives me migraines. I pull into Rory's car park and scan the customers going in. I can't see anyone I know. I pull up the hood and walk briskly into the store. I head for the bakery aisle and throw a loaf into my basket. The smell of the freshly baked rolls makes my mouth water and I throw a couple of those in too, followed by a doughnut. I hurry down the sweet aisle and grab a pack of Crunchies and a family size bag of marshmallows; I'll have those with some wine tonight. I'm near the checkout when I remember cold meat for the rolls. I grab washing powder for the salon as they are on a two-for-one-offer, and head for the deli counter when I'm stopped by a lady standing by a snack promotion table.

'Madam, can I interest you in our range of olives?'

Oh no, not now.

'Well ...' I mumble.

God I'm so hungry I could scoff her entire display.

'Okay,' I say, lowering the scarf so I can pop one into my mouth and then another and then one more.

'Lovely aren't they?' she smiles. 'Try them with a slice of Psomi and some feta.' She rolls her eyes in ecstasy.

'Psomi?' I query.

'Greek bread.'

Oh no, that means going back to the bread counter. I grab a small carton of olives from her stand.

'Thank you.'

I continue on to the deli and then I see her, my mum, her trolley overflowing with goods. She's wearing something that looks like a rainbow coloured burka. Okay, it's a slight exaggeration, but you can't see much of her face but I'd know my mother anywhere. Good God, it gets worse. How could she? After everything that was said at the meeting.

'What are you doing here?' I say diving upon her and making her jump out of her skin.

'You scared the life out of me,' she complains. 'I thought you were one of Team Robson's people.'

'I am one of Team Robson's people. In fact I am Team Robson,' I say irritably. 'You're not supposed to shop in here.'

She looks at my basket.

'Nor are you,' she hisses. 'Why are you wearing sunglasses? You look like a spy.'

'I'm incognito,' I say.

'Well I recognised you.'

'I'm your daughter.'

'Don't remind me. You'll be arrested going on like this. Why you can't just find a nice man and ...'

'I'm out of everything. I only came for essentials,' I say, like somehow that makes everything okay.

'I never knew marshmallows and Crunchies were essentials,' she retorts.

My mother knows nothing of life.

'What are you wearing?' I ask.

'My Infinity scarf,' she says, pulling it further forward on her head.

'At least I'm not doing my monthly shop,' I say defensively. 'It looks like you're shopping for the whole of Notting Hill.'

'You can't have a go at me if you're here too.'

I suppose she has a point. Honestly, of all people it has to be my mother.

'This has to be the last time,' I whisper. 'If anyone sees us we'll lose all credibility.'

She nods seriously.

'I'll quickly get these things and then I'll get your father to take me to Waitrose. It's a bit further out and doesn't have the offers that Rory's ...'

'Mother,' I hiss.

'Sorry,' she mumbles. 'I'll phone you later.'

I nod.

'I'm off,' I say. 'I've just got to grab some baked beans.'

She rummages through her trolley.

'Here,' she hands me a pack of four tins. 'Special offer so you might ...'

I roll my eyes but take them anyway.

'Ooh there's Mrs Wallace from the off-licence,' she says pulling her scarf so low I can barely see her eyes.

'I'm off,' I say again, wrapping my scarf over my face. I'm sure the only thing on show is my sunglasses. I dash along the dairy section and remember I need milk. I see the feta cheese and chuck some in, to go with the olives and deliberate for a few seconds and dash back to the bread aisle and throw in a Psomi. I then fly along the biscuits throwing in chocolate digestives as I go. I feel like a contestant in *Supermarket Sweep*. I reach the self-service checkout, scan my goods and pay as fast as I can before heading for the exit doors. I'm in my car and on my way home before you can say *Team Robson*. If Sandy even gets a whisper of this I'll be dead.

Thirty minutes later with my beans bubbling nicely on the hob, I check the wine in the fridge. Not that I'm an expert on wine mind you. I had so little of it when with Luke that I didn't have a chance to study it, so I wouldn't know a £3.50 bottle from a £35 one. Considering they were all from my friends I doubt they cost more than a fiver to be honest. I open a Sauvignon Blanc and flop onto the couch with the glass in my hand. All I can think of is Thomas Rory. Of course it doesn't help that no sooner had I spoken to him than I was diving into his shop and now, no doubt, the Sauvignon Blanc I'm drinking is one Mum bought in his party offer. Not to mention the fact that my dinner comprises Rory's bread and Rory's special offer baked beans, with a side dish of olives and feta cheese, followed by a 'made on the premises' doughnut. I lean back and pull my laptop onto the couch beside me. At least I didn't use my loyalty card. That would have been the ultimate wouldn't it? I turn on the laptop. I'm just about to tuck in to my beans on toast when the doorbell rings. I push my eye against the peephole and see Tony, the Rory's delivery guy. What can he want? I strain to see if anyone else is with him. Perhaps he wants to defect. What am I thinking? I'm worse than Ryan. I open the door cautiously and peer through the gap.

'Miss Robson?' he asks, trying to catch my eye through the slit.

'I could be,' I say, thinking that is the best way not to incriminate myself.

'I've got your Rory's delivery. Where do you want it?'

Is he mad? I'm not long back after tearing around the supermarket looking like a poor man's Mata Hari. I'm not going to be so stupid as to order online now am I?

'I think you have the wrong flat,' I say, slowly closing the door. 'I don't shop at Rory's.'

He steps back and checks the number on my door.

'No, this is the right flat. Miss Robson, flat 6, basement. I got a box for you, where do you want it?

A box? Doesn't he mean *bag*?

'I don't know anything about this,' I say.

'You ordered it,' says Tony. 'I only deliver.'

Ever had that feeling of déjà vu?

'But a box,' I say. 'I'd have remembered ordering a box.'

'I don't make the rules,' he says. 'If you don't want it I can take it back.'

I open the door wider to see if it is some kind of joke of my mother's. Any second now she'll jump out and shout, *got you*, but

I quickly dismiss the idea as crazy. My mum doesn't get jokes let alone play them on people. Tony huffs his way from the van with the box. What the ...?

'There you go,' he says.

We give the box a puzzled look.

'I just deliver,' says Tony before I can say anything. 'That's everything, no substitutions.'

'What is it?' I ask.

He looks at me oddly.

'If you don't know I'm sure I don't. I only deliver. You've got 750 loyalty points,' he says, eyes widening.

I've never got that many loyalty points in one go ever.

'How many?'

He checks his machine, clicking a button here and another there. Finally he looks up.

'You have 750 for today's purchase. I've scanned it onto your account. We have these new little machines now. Scans your loyalty points straight on without even needing your card and it ...'

'Right, thank you. I'll just check how many gold bars are in the box,' I say, before closing the door.

Loyalty points for a delivery I haven't ordered. It's got to be a mistake. I must have someone else's order. I eat my beans on toast while studying the box. Finally, after the last bean, I stand up, place my plate in the sink and then swallow half a glass of wine for courage. I rip the lid off the box and remove a layer of tissue.

I gasp. It's a full round of Gorgonzola, and it stinks to high heaven. What the ...? Why would Rory's send me a load of cheese? It makes no sense. I pick up the glass of wine and swallow some, my thoughts on Tom Rory, when the penny drops. Oh shit. *Cheese for a mouse*. He knows I'm behind the mouse prank. He's sent me the Gorgonzola and he's given me 750 loyalty points too. The memory of my illicit desserts at the Jacksons' come back to me ...

'Yes please as long as it's not Gorgonzola. That smells like a pig farmer's bunion. I hate it.'

The little sod, he's winding me up while looking good at the same time. I can't very well complain to the papers about how Thomas Rory is playing dirty by sending me a whole cheese and rewarding me with loyalty points can I? I shove the box behind the couch and pour myself more wine. Time to show Thomas Rory two can play at this game.

I click into Twitter, and study the *fightwithflora* page. We have twenty new followers. I check who they are and see five are local shop owners in Portobello Road and two are market stall holders. I follow them all, toss back some Sauvignon Blanc, type Thomas Rory into the search box and there he is. My heart flips and I drain my glass before clicking into his profile. I stare at his profile pic for what seems like an eternity. He's smiling and there is that twinkle in his eyes that I know so well. I tear myself away to grab the wine. I quickly top up my glass and then go back to the profile. I drag my eyes from his photo and read the info.

Thomas Rory
CEO of Rory's Supermarkets

The stink of the cheese reaches my nostrils and I kick it further under the couch. I pop open the bag of marshmallows and separate the pink from the white while studying Tom's profile. My hand hovers over the follow button but I can't bring myself to do it. I shake my head irritably and wander to the loo. When I return to the living room the stink of Gorgonzola almost knocks me out. I throw back some wine and look at Tom's photo for a bit longer before I notice I have three notifications. I reluctantly pull myself away from the photo. One is an encouraging tweet from Mr Pinlan Wong in China.

@fightwithflora good luck with the revolution! We will support you. One for all and all for one.

Crikey I hope we don't have the whole of Chinatown at the protest. I retweet and click back into Tom's profile. I'm drooling over his photo when another notification pops up: *Thomas Rory is now following you on Twitter.* Oh my God. I feel like I can't breathe. It's like he knows I am watching him. I'm about to click back into his profile when another notification pops up. I hold my breath and click into it.

@fightwithflora how are you tonight Flo?

I gasp and then shake my head. Honestly how stupid is that? It's not like he is standing at the front door is it? I pop a marshmallow into my mouth and wash it down with wine, feeling myself getting heady and cosily drunk, and wishing very much that he was here with me. I pull the laptop towards me and quickly type a reply. I re-read it and hit enter.

@tomrory I never thought the big cheese would follow fightwithflora #unimpressed

I nod, feeling very proud of myself. A notification bounces straight back and I click into it eagerly.

@fightwithflora you sound a bit cheesed off tonight.#toomuchgorgonzola

Despite myself I find myself smiling. I curl up on the couch and sip the wine. I bite my lip as I think about my response, before typing.

@tomrory wonder what gave you that idea #soundsguilty

I sit back and wait, popping marshmallows into my mouth as I do so.

@fightwithflora a little bird/mouse told me #ringanybells

I nibble a marshmallow and look closely at his photo remembering his warm lips on mine.

@tomrory talking to animals now are you? Must be lonely #getalife

What am I doing talking to Thomas Rory? Team Robson would never forgive me if they knew.

@fightwithflora Yep, dinner for one, how about you? The olives are good aren't they? #whathappenedtohealthyeating

I gasp. How can he know about the olives? I look around anxiously. Have I been bugged or something? He surely isn't psychic. Oh Jesus, is my web cam on? I look such a mess too. I quickly check. This is ridiculous. Of course it's not on. He must surely be guessing.

@tomrory you tell me #peepingtom You should get out more #saddo

I wait in eager anticipation for his response but nothing comes back. I sip nervously at my wine and stare hopefully at the notification sign. Almost thirty seconds pass before it pops on the screen.

@fightwithflora good idea, what are you doing tomorrow night? #twoscompany

I stare at the tweet and feel myself tremble. It would be so good to see him again. I begin to type and then delete my tweet and start again, my heart heavy.

@tomrory I'm washing my hair #doesntconsortwithenemy

I wait nervously for his response. I realise I'm holding my breath. Finally it pops onto the screen.

@fightwithflora perhaps another time #olivebranch

I'm about to type a response when another notification comes up.

@fightwithflora night flo #sweetdreams

A knocking at the door makes me jump. I walk unsteadily towards it, my mind still full of Tom Rory. Adam stands on the doorstep, holding a megaphone and smelling of expensive aftershave.

'Awright darling? 'Ere's the scarf, beautiful ain't it? The chicks love these. I can't get them in quick enough. Sell like no tomorrow they do.'

I grasp the door tightly as my head spins. I really should eat more than beans on toast if I'm going to drink a whole bottle of Sauvignon Blanc on my own.

'You okay doll?' Adam asks concerned.

I nod.

'A little too much wine,' I say honestly, taking the scarf and wrapping its soft silkiness around my neck.

'You be careful babe. You eaten anything?'

I nod.

'Beans on toast,' I say.

He shakes his head disapprovingly.

'That's not enough to feed a sparrow. 'Ere's the megaphone. Keep it as long as you like. Me mate won't be needing it for a while. I'd ask you up for a drink, but looks like you've 'ad enough. Maybe another night?'

I nod. I seem to be agreeing to another night with everyone. I thank him for the scarf and megaphone, and ask if he likes Gorgonzola, thinking that maybe his flat can smell of pig farmer's bunions instead of mine. Sadly he doesn't.

'Stinks to high heaven that stuff babe.'

Tell me about it.

'I'm off to that new club in town later. Leaving about ten, give us a bell if you wanna come along?'

At the rate I'm going I'll be comatose by ten. I nod gratefully and close the door. I rush back to my laptop but there is nothing more from Tom. In fact there is nothing from anyone. Then again it is Saturday night and everyone is out getting pissed. Well, I am too. I'm just doing it at home. I wonder what Tom is doing now. Is he about to go out and get pissed with his mates? He surely isn't sitting at home like me, eating marshmallows and throwing back cheap Sauvignon Blanc is he? I go to refill my glass and realise the bottle is empty. I flop back onto the couch and re-read Tom's messages until my eyes grow heavy. I click follow under his name and then close my eyes.

Chapter Thirty-Five

Tom

I pull off my tie and open the kitchen door, the smell of roast chicken greeting me. Celia, in her apron is cleaning the sink. I look at my watch.

'It's well past seven,' I say. 'Don't you have a home to go to?'

She lifts her head to look at the clock on the wall.

'So it is. When are you ever home this early? I'll be off in a tick. There's a chicken in the oven with roast potatoes. You just need to do yourself some vegetables. There's a nice cabbage in the fridge.'

I smile.

'Right,' I say, knowing full well I won't bother with the cabbage.

I grab a glass and add some ice before taking it into the lounge and adding a little whisky. I sit wearily in the armchair by the fire and sip at my drink.

'You want me to light the fire?' asks Celia, following me in. 'It's a bit chilly tonight.'

I shake my head.

'I can do it. You should get on home. Frank will wonder where you are.'

'He's playing darts. They're in the final,' she says proudly.

I lift my eyebrows.

'Really, well that's brilliant. Here's to him winning,' I say lifting my glass. My eyes land on the mantelpiece clock and I find myself wondering if Flo has had her delivery yet and what her reaction is. I smile at the thought.

Celia fiddles about in front of me and I look at her over my glass.

'Something on your mind?' I ask.

She whips her apron off and stands with it held aloft like a matador, her eyes challenging me.

'I'm going to the protest,' she says. 'Flora Robson is a nice girl. I've known you since you were a lad. I'm surprised at you, harassing an innocent woman like her.'

I sigh.

'Flora Robson, innocent,' I say, remembering the CCTV playback. Innocent my backside, the woman is as innocent as O J Simpson. 'As for harassment, if anyone is harassing anyone she is harassing me.'

'Poppycock,' snaps Celia. 'The girl's got nothing, you've got all this. Now I never say anything. I never tell anyone I work for you. I respect your privacy. But from what I've been hearing, them are dirty tricks you've been playing ...'

'You've been hearing wrong, but I've got no issue with you going to the protest. Now ...' I say standing up, 'I'm going to have some of that delicious chicken of yours.'

She clicks her tongue.

'Don't forget the cabbage,' she says, walking from the room. 'I'll see you Friday.'

I hear the front door slam and walk to the kitchen to dish up the chicken and potatoes. Innocent? Flora? Yes, right. I take my plate into the lounge and sit at the table with my laptop in front of me. I spend thirty minutes answering emails and then pushing the plate away I click into Twitter and check the fightwithflora page. I scroll down to look for any updates. There is mention of the protest. I then see a retweet which was tweeted a few seconds before. She's online. I look at the time. She must have received the cheese by now. I deliberate for a few seconds and then click follow. That will no doubt throw her in a spin. I smile as I pour some more whisky into my glass, take a sip and then type,

@fightwithflora how are you tonight Flo?

I hesitate for a second and then hit enter. If I can't reach her any other way then this is surely worth a try. I scoff again at Celia's words, innocent. She's got no idea. A few seconds pass before I get a notification alert. Yes, she's online.

@tomrory I never thought the big cheese would follow fightwithflora #unimpressed

I lean back in my chair and laugh. She's got the cheese. I pick up the laptop and move with it to the armchair. It must be stinking her little flat out something awful. The urge to tease her overwhelms me.

@fightwithflora you sound a bit cheesed off tonight #toomuchgorgonzola

A reply comes back almost immediately.

@tomrory wonder what gave you that idea #soundsguilty

Ha, she's had the cheese alright. I sip my whisky and type a response.

@fightwithflora a little bird/mouse told me #ringanybells

There's a fair bit of time before a response pops up onto the screen. I've shaken her. I smile, as I picture her trying to work out how I could possibly know these things. I take the time to pop to the fridge and remove the chocolate mousse Celia had left there yesterday. If anything would make Flo jealous it's this. I hurry to the laptop to see her response.

@tomrory talking to animals now are you? Must be lonely #getalife

I picture her sitting at her computer, stuffing her face with my marshmallows. To think Celia called her Miss Innocent.

@fightwithflora Yep, dinner for one, how about you? Enjoying the olives? #whathappenedtohealthyeating

I can almost hear her gasp.

@tomrory You tell me #peepingtom You should get out more #saddo

I stare at the message, type a response and then instantly delete it. I take another sip of whisky and then type the same message. My finger hovers over the 'tweet' button. I wait a second, read it through and then hit enter

@fightwithflora good idea, what are you doing tomorrow night? #twoscompany

I sit back sipping my whisky and wait. I know the answer. But it's surely worth a try. If I can get her to come out to dinner with me maybe, just maybe, we can make some headway. I'm beginning to think she isn't going to answer at all. Still nothing and I'm about to close the laptop when a notification pops up.

@tomrory I'm washing my hair #doesntconsortwithenemy

I sigh. Well, it's what I expected. Damn woman, why won't she see reason for pity's sake? She only has to meet me.

@fightwithflora perhaps another time #olivebranch

It's stupid to push it as she clearly has a problem with me. I type quickly and send another tweet.

@fightwithflora night flo #sweetdreams

I wait patiently for a response but after several minutes it is clear she isn't going to send one. That's that then. It looks like we are clearly at war. The question is how can I fight back and maintain some kind of integrity? I close the laptop, rest my head against the back of my chair and sip the whisky. Flora's musical laugh echoes in my head and I remember Celia's words: I'm surprised at you, harassing an innocent woman like her. Harass her? I don't intend to harass Flora Robson but there's no harm in having a little fun with her.

Chapter Thirty-Six

'Gorgonzola and crackers love?' Ryan asks Ruby Smith after setting the dryer over her head. He plonks a plate on the table in front of her.

'Nothing like a bit of Gorgon with a coffee and a *Yours* magazine,' he smiles.

Sandy rolls her eyes.

'Well, I suppose ...' begins Ruby.

'I've been on one of them?' says Mrs Graham loudly.

'That's unusual love,' says Ryan washing around the basin.

'In Venice, they're everywhere you see.'

'Is that right love? No wonder bloody Venice smells.'

'I think you mean a *gondola*,' says Sandy.

'Yes, that's right,' nods Mrs Graham.

'Let's get your head in a basin shall we Barbara love? Then I can get my hands around that lovely scalp of yours sweetie.'

Barbara Graham blushes and is led like a lamb to the slaughter towards the basins. I climb up the stepladder to blue tack our poster onto the window. I haven't told Ryan and Sandy about my chat with Tom. It only lasted fifteen minutes if that, so it seems pointless to mention it. I pop outside and study the poster and step back with pride. It has a carnival look, which had been Ryan's idea, and his friend Rufus had designed it. It's so colourful you can't miss it.

Support Team Robson.
Protest on Sat 31st May outside Rory's supermarket in Ladbroke Grove.
Free Cakes and lemonade by local suppliers and a fab surprise.
Support your local stores. Buy local.
Say NO to Rory's and Save our Small Businesses.

'Looks good.'

'You don't think it's a bit crooked?' I ask, turning around and coming face to face with Grant Richards.

'Not in the least, looks perfect in fact.'

'You've a nerve coming back here,' I say, turning to walk into the salon.

'Thomas Rory fired me.'

I stop and turn to face him.

'Well, I imagine it's what you deserved,' I snap.

'He fired me because I wasn't underhand enough,' he says gently taking my arm. 'Particularly with you,' he finishes.

I meet his eyes.

'I'm supposed to believe you am I?' I ask.

He looks forlorn. I have to admit he's not the arrogant Grant Richards I remember from our last meeting.

'I came to warn you.'

The doorbell tinkles and I turn to see Ryan standing in the doorway, his flowery shirt clinging to his chest. He leans a fist on his hip and tries to appear aggressive but frankly he looks as bent as a butcher's hook and about as threatening as a Labrador puppy.

'Everything all right love?' he asks, glaring at Grant Richards.

'We've got *people* behind us now,' says Sandy, joining him, and emphasising the *people* so it sounds threatening. 'You can't intimidate us.'

No, not with *people* behind us, whoever they may be.

'I'm on your side,' says Richards. 'Thomas Rory is ruthless. He'll go to any ends to get what he wants. He's ambitious. He'll step on anyone who stands in his way. Unfortunately I did and paid with my job.'

I turn to Sandy and raise my eyebrows. She's good at seeing through people, better than I am.

'So, you don't work for Rory's any more?' she asks.

'Ooh Christ, I've left Barbara with her head in the basin,' cries Ryan, rushing back into the salon. Honestly, at this rate, Thomas Rory won't need to put me out of business. Ryan will be doing it for me.

'Brent Galway was given my job. I was thrown out on my ear. I don't approve of Tom's methods. I just wanted to apologise for the prescription cock-up ...'

He stops and takes a breath.

'You okay Flo? I should get back to my colour,' asks Sandy.

I nod.

'I shouldn't have told Tom about that. I'm really sorry. I should have realised he would have used it.'

I'm torn between believing him and telling him to sod off but it is true that I had a letter from Brent Galway isn't it? I hesitate.

'Please let me take you for dinner this evening. I can explain everything. Maybe I can even help you.'

'Help me?' I echo. 'And how can you do that?'

He looks around and leans towards me conspiratorially.

'I can maybe help with the sale of the salon,' he says.

Oh honestly, to think I nearly fell for it. I turn on my heels and begin to walk back into the salon.

'He's totally driven by ambition Flora. It's only a matter of time before he offers you a lower price for the property. It's got subsidence, you're aware of that aren't you?'

Oh, here we go. He must think I was born yesterday.

'We do not have substance,' I say and see Ryan roll his eyes.

'I can get a surveyor to you and prove that you have. All three shops have it and Tom knows it. Close to completion of the Patel's and the video shop he'll lower his price. They'll be stuck they'll have no choice ...'

'They can go to the papers with me,' I say, feeling my excitement building. This may be my chance to prove what a lying deceiving little prick Thomas Rory is.

'And say what? That Thomas Rory offered them the market price for a property with subsidence? That he also offered Mr Patel a good job and Terence Sharp money for his mother's hospital treatment. You don't think a newspaper story like that will just benefit Tom Rory?'

He grins.

'You see, he has you by the balls. This is how he conducts business.'

He looks me in the eye.

'If you don't want to have dinner with me, I understand. Just meet me for a drink. I promise I can help you ...'

I look at him suspiciously. I can't deny that Brent Galway's name was on the letter which ties in with Grant losing his job, and I've been a bit wary about the whole subsidence business since Mr

Patel said he had it. There's no harm in a coffee is there? It's not like I'll be alone with Grant Richards is it? But surely all this can't be true. Didn't I speak to Tom only last night on Twitter? Wasn't he warm, kind and funny just like I remembered him? A wolf in sheep's clothing Flora, that's what he is. But what about the kisses, and the way he held me? No, don't think about it, don't think about it but how can I not think about it?

'Four o'clock at Heroes,' I hear myself saying.

He gives me a relieved smile.

'You won't regret it,' he says as he turns the corner into Portobello Market.

'You're not going to meet him?' says Sandy, shouting above the hairdryer.

'Is that wise, love?' asks Ryan.

'I'm not sure,' I say honestly. 'He could be working for Rory's for all I know.'

'It's a pity we can't wire you,' says Ryan wrapping Barbara's hair in rollers with such speed that I'm surprised sparks don't fly from them. 'We could have listened in.'

'Great idea, if only we could bug you,' shouts Sandy.

Blanche Timms turns as white as her name.

'I've got bugs,' she shouts over the dryer.

'Of course not Blanche, love. We were talking about bugs like in the action films.'

'Maybe Adam can get us a wire?' says Ryan. 'He seems like a man that can get anything and everything, and know how to use it, just my kind of man.'

'He works down the market, not for MFI,' I say, collecting the brushes for washing.

'I think you mean MI5, love.'

'Whatever. He isn't going to stock bugging equipment is he? Anyway, this is not a covert operation. I'm just meeting him for coffee.'

How dangerous can that be, and what could possibly go wrong?

Chapter Thirty-Seven

I see Luke sitting at a corner table in Heroes. What's more, sitting opposite him is a stunning blonde. I try not to gape at them but it's impossible. They're sharing a large slab of chocolate cake. Luke catches my eye and fidgets uncomfortably. I turn away and fiddle with the tablecloth. From the corner of my eye I see him approaching me.

'Flora,' he says, looking somewhat embarrassed.

'Luke, fancy seeing you here,' I say. 'If I remember this was never your cup of tea so to speak.'

I glance at the blonde. Perhaps it just wasn't your cup of tea when with me, I think gloomily.

'It's a work thing. Have to go where the client wants to go,' he says with a forced sigh.

And eat what the client wants to eat no doubt. The truth is I was never quite good enough for Luke was I? I'm not slim enough, or blonde enough, or successful enough, but one thing I do know is that I am me and that's good enough. Maybe not good enough for Luke, but good enough for me and that's what matters. Grant approaches with two mugs of hot chocolate. A pain shoots through my heart when I remember being here with Tom and I suddenly miss him so much it hurts.

'I'll see you around then Flora,' Luke says walking back to the blonde who strokes his bottom as he passes. God, he didn't waste any time did he?

'I got you extra marshmallows,' says Grant Richards.

'Lovely,' I say picking the soggy marshmallows from the top of the hot chocolate. 'Flora,' he says, leaning towards me. I try to see if there is a wire attached to him. Ryan, being an expert on action movies had stated that the only way to see if he was wired was to get up close and personal.

'Unfortunately, it's the only way darling. Why do you think in all the movies the woman kisses the man so much? Most of the time she's feeling around for a wire, love.'

Seeing as I have no intention of kissing Grant Richards or feeling him up to see if he's bugged I'll just have to take my chances and be careful what I say.

'I know you and Tom became close ...'

I lift the mug to my lips in the hope of hiding my blush.

'I'm here to talk business,' I say firmly.

'I just feel you should know the truth about him. I've known Tom a long time. He'll use charm to get what he wants.'

I find myself recalling the Twitter conversation.

'He's a real charmer. He's also a playboy, with that kind of money who wouldn't be?'

I don't speak but feel my stomach churn and it is all I can do to drink my chocolate.

'Why do you think he has two spare seats on the train?' he laughs caustically. 'Talk about prepared.'

I feel the chocolate rise up in my diaphragm. I try to picture my lovely Tom as a playboy and it just doesn't work. But, it's true, why would someone have three seats on a train?

'You said my salon has subs ...'

I picture Ryan rolling his eyes.

'Subsidence, if that is the case why did our surveyor say it wasn't?'

He shrugs.

'Maybe he wasn't any good at his job. But I know you've got it. You see what Tom does is approach the other two shops first. He tells them that he'll pay a good price for the property. He'll do something extra too. In Patel's case, he offered him a job. Terence Sharp was offered hospital treatment for his mother. Then, near completion his surveyors find something wrong with the property and he drops his price, but by then you are in too deep and have already paid a lot in solicitor's fees. It's too late for anyone to pull out and they can't slag him off can they? He's paid a fair price and they've got great treatment. In this case the property has subsidence and he'll go to town with that. Patel's had it and so did Sharp which means you've most certainly got it. So Tom's laughing with this one.'

'I don't believe you,' I say bluntly, pushing my mug away.

'How do you think people like him make so much money Flora?'

'For all I know you're still working for him,' I snap.

'If that is the case, wouldn't that make him as underhand as I'm saying? Think about it. It makes no sense for me to be here, saying these things if I still work for him. He fired me Flora, but if I am working for him, what you're saying is he's a no good bastard because now he's trying to get your salon for even less.'

I struggle to get my head around this.

'I've got someone who will buy the salon. Sure at a lower price than Rory's but trust me, he will drop the price when you get close to completing. Besides, you don't want to sell to him do you? It's true what you're saying. He does put people out of work.'

'And why would you want to help me?' I ask, finally finding my voice and asking what I feel is a sensible question. I'm starting to wish Ryan had bugged me. We could have gone over this complicated muddle of a conversation and made some sense of it because it makes as much sense as buggery to me. It isn't helping that Luke and the blonde are now sharing an ice cream from the same spoon. It's all I can do to stop myself storming over and reminding him of how much sugar there is in ice cream.

'Won't you at least let me do that?' Grant is saying.

'What?' I ask.

'Let me get a surveyor to check it. I can get someone to take the salon off your hands for a good price ...'

'If I'm going to sell I may as well sell to Rory's,' I say, throwing my shawl around me.

'Why do you want to sell to him? He'll knock you down at the last minute. Besides, hasn't he humiliated you enough?'

I push my chair angrily under the table and turn to the door.

'Let me send a surveyor at least. I want to get back at Rory's as much as you.'

'I'm not looking to get back at anyone,' I say. 'But send your surveyors and we'll see who's right.'

'Here's my number,' he says handing me a card. I shove it into my jeans pocket and grab my handbag and stroll with my head held high from Heroes. If I have to watch Luke spoon ice cream into his mouth one more time I shall throw up.

Grant Richards turns up the volume on the car radio and whistles along to Robbie Williams. *I've got you right where I want you Flora Robson* he thinks and smiles to himself. It was easier than he thought it would be. If Tom has any designs on her he can forget it. He could see by her expression that the seeds of doubt had been planted. The train seat bit was pure genius. Thomas Rory is a fool letting him go. Brent will soon prove himself to be useless too. The wanker hasn't got an ounce of backbone in him. They'll get nothing done with him as acquisitions manager. Best thing is to sit tight, Tom will soon realise his mistake and want him back and then he can make demands of his own. His thoughts wander back to Flora Robson and he pictures her cute arse. Shame, he can't take things a bit further with her. Still, that's the way the cookie crumbles. By the time he's finished with her she'd have sold her stupid little salon for a third of what is was worth and all because of a few harmless cracks in the wall. He'd thought this through long and hard. He knows Flora Robson will have to sell her salon eventually. She can only fight for so long. He'll teach Tom to transfer him. If he wants that salon, then he'll need to buy it from him and he'll demand a hell of a price for it. He's going to make a nice little killing on this. Thomas Rory underestimated him. He knows Tom too well. The last thing he needs is three properties going to rack and ruin. He'll buy it, after all he can afford to. It's nothing to him. The fucking rich boy is getting richer and richer and much of that is thanks to Grant himself. It was Grant who got the prices down for him. You'd think Tom would be grateful instead of getting on his moral high ground all the time. Who the hell ran a business with morals these days? If he'd done things Tom's way every time, they'd have paid a fortune for some of those sites. If Flora Robson hadn't caused so much trouble, he'd still have his job and Tom would be none the wiser. What an idiot to get romantically involved with a client. A fucking hairdresser at that, honestly, you'd think Thomas Rory would have some class.

He picks up his phone and flips it open, clicking into hands-free.

'It's me,' he says, 'I've got another surveying job for you.'

Chapter Thirty-Eight

I open the door and stare at my mother. My jaw drops and I finally manage a strangled,

'Hello Mum.'

'What do you think?' she asks, handing me a tin of shortbread.

I think I need to get her into the flat as quickly as possible before she gets arrested. My mother is dressed in full combat, right down to the combat boots. She looks ready to launch a terrorist attack, all she needs is a bullet belt and a Kalashnikov and she's all set. I mean, you seriously don't dress like this in the middle of London, not even for a fancy dress party. The fact that we are having a militant group meeting to discuss our plan of action against Rory's Supermarkets doesn't help of course.

'It's for the protest. Do I look the part?'

'For a mad woman yes, you look exactly the part,' I say, pulling her in and slamming the door. 'You do realise you can get arrested walking around like that?'

'God, what's that stink?' she asks as she walks into the living room. 'It smells like something died in here.'

I shake my head in despair.

'You don't seriously intend to wear that for the protest?'

She pulls the cap off and shakes her bob free and I breathe a sigh of relief. At least she didn't get her hair cropped for the part.

'Yes, of course. I'm going braless too. That's what feminists do isn't it?'

I'm not quite sure what feminism has to do with it, but the less said the better. The doorbell rings and I push her into the kitchen.

'I'll get that, just in case it's Special Branch. You can make tea.'

Rosalind stands on the doorstep with Sadistic Harry strapped to her back.

'Good idea don't you think,' she smiles. 'This way I can't forget the little bugger can I?'

The little bugger gurgles happily. We're no sooner in the living room when she takes a sharp intake of breath.

'Jesus, what's that stink? Has something died in here? You haven't got mice have you? I don't want to risk anything with Sadistic Harry.'

Very funny.

'No I haven't and I'd prefer not to talk about mice thank you very much. It's actually Gorgonzola cheese. I've wrapped a slab for each of you, courtesy of Rory's.'

Her features contort into a grimace.

'Are you serious?' she asks, unstrapping Sadistic Harry who gurgles happily before spewing vomit down her blouse.

'I'll explain in a bit,' I say, walking to the door. 'Oh, and the woman in combat is my mother. Don't even ask.'

I open the door to Adam who smiles seductively at me.

'Awright doll, I brought some Chardonnay.'

He's wearing a tight-fitting silk shirt and smells of citrus aftershave. I open the door to let him in.

'Wow,' he says on seeing Mum.

She smiles proudly.

'This is my mother who doesn't normally look like she's about to embark on a mission with Bruce Willis. She has been known to wear regular clothes, befitting her age,' I say, giving her a harsh look.

'You look brill ma,' says Adam.

'Oh please, don't encourage her,' I groan.

'God almighty, what is that stink?' exclaims Devon, even before she steps through the doorway, with Sandy and Ryan following meekly behind her.

This is getting tedious.

'Gorgonzola,' says Sandy. 'Thomas Rory twigged it was us that set the mouse off in the store. Or at least hazarded a guess it was us and sent Flora a huge piece of Gorgonzola.'

'Which we've been working our way through for the past week,' says Ryan, eyeing up Adam.

'Well hello, you must be Adam. I love your megaphone.'

Adam shifts uncomfortably on his feet and then quickly offers to help my mum as she emerges from the kitchen with a plate of shortbread biscuits.

'Let me help you with that,' he says.

'Getting into the spirit of things I see Mrs R,' says Ryan.

Adam pours everyone a glass of Chardonnay.

'Just a little drop for me, I don't want Sadistic Harry joining AA before he can talk,' laughs Rosalind.

Devon opens a folder and claps her hands for silence.

'Right, first on the agenda is feedback from members since our last meeting,' she says in an official sounding voice.

'I saw Luke in Heroes,' I hear myself saying, 'eating chocolate cake with a blonde and sharing ice cream from the same spoon.'

There is a deathly silence and everyone looks at me.

'Shit,' says Rosalind.

'Her ex,' I hear Mum whisper to Adam. 'Her father and I were never keen.'

'Two-faced bloody hypocrite,' adds Devon.

'Hear hear,' says Sandy.

'I never did like him,' says Ryan. 'He was always too hairy for my liking.'

'I think you should take up pottery,' says my mum.

All eyes turn to her.

'Why should I take up pottery?' I ask.

There has to be a connection here. I'm obviously too stupid to see it.

'Well, just look what happened to that woman in the film *Ghost.*'

'Can you pass the Chardonnay Adam?' I say wearily.

'Well you're better off without him sweetie,' smiles Ryan.

'Okay, moving on,' says Devon. 'Any other progress reports?'

Sandy and I relay the mouse story and how we had managed to shut the store for a short time. I fill everyone in on our Twitter progress and inform them that Tom Rory is now following us. Ryan hands around the leaflets advertising the protest.

'We'll be raising money for the local hospital on the day. It's a good cause but it also shows that we care about the community, kind of shows us as better than Rory's. We'll be having a raffle and all the local shops are giving a prize. The main prize is a hamper of fruit that Geoff at the greengrocers is putting together along with a bouquet that Fenella at the florist in Portobello Road is donating.'

'That's the big surprise is it?' asks Rosalind. 'I was hoping it was a dinner date and shag with Robert Downey Junior.'

'We all have those dreams darling,' says Ryan, glancing at Adam who moves closer to me on the couch.

I throw back half a glass of Chardonnay and say,

'But there's some bad news. Grant Richards came to the salon ...'

'You're kidding, what did that creep want?'

'Apparently Thomas Rory fired him because he wasn't underhand enough in his job ...' I swallow a lump in my throat at the thought of Tom. 'Anyway, cut to the chase,' I continue hurriedly. 'It seems that the salon may well have subsidence.'

I leave out all the stuff about Tom being ruthless and ambitious.

'But I thought you said you had a surveyor look at those cracks,' says Devon, laying down her pen.

'I did but ...'

'It was Mrs Willis's cousin. He's retired and he may well have made a mistake,' says Sandy.

'Grant Richards says that all the shops have it and that Rory's will drop the price when the purchase gets close to completion. Richards says he knows someone who can give me a good price. The thing is if I'm going to sell, I don't want to sell to Rory's and if I do have subsidence then ...'

'Richards has offered to send an independent surveyor,' says Sandy.

Adam raises his hand.

'Oh, I wouldn't bother with that darling,' smiles Rosalind. 'It's a free for all here, unless it's the loo you want. Sadistic Harry is the only one allowed to shit in his pants.'

'Oh dear,' says Mum, putting down her shortbread.

'If you don't mind me saying, I'd be a bit suspicious of that,' says Adam. 'I know quite a lot of people with properties in this area and I've never heard of anyone with subsidence. You'd be one of the few people in Notting Hill that I know of who have had it.'

'Really,' I say hopefully.

'My brother is a surveyor let me send him round too, babe. Can't do any harm right?'

Everyone nods.

'At least that way we'll know if that Grant Richards is on the level,' agrees Devon. 'Hands up all those in favour.'

Blimey, we are getting official. She'll be yelling 'Everybody out' soon. Everyone raises their hand.

'I'll leave that with you Adam. If you can let Flo know when they are coming that would be great.'

He nods and gives me a cheeky grin.

'Next on the agenda is our second hoax on Rory's.'

'Well, if you ask me we should get him back for that stinking cheese. I swear I can smell it everywhere,' groans Ryan.

'You can smell it here that's for sure,' says Rosalind, wrinkling her nose in disgust.

'Any ideas how we can do that?' asks Sandy.

'You should walk around the store darling, with that gone-off fish finger letter of yours, after all two can play at the smell game right?' suggests Ryan.

Devon pulls a face.

'And then no doubt Flo will end up with a crate of cockles,' laughs Rosalind.

'Ooh, she should be so lucky,' quips Ryan.

'It's a great idea though. We can wander around the store with my waste food bin. That really stinks. They'll have to close again once someone complains. Excellent idea Ryan,' says Sandy excitedly.

I don't believe I'm hearing this. I exhale. They honestly aren't serious surely. I barely pulled off the mouse stunt. I can't possibly walk around the store with a smelly dustbin.

'Right, that's settled then. We just need Sandy's waste food bin ...'

'There's a rancid piece of fish in my rubbish, been there for a week,' says Adam, his eyes sparkling. 'Put that in your bag and the jobs a good'n.'

'I'm not walking around Rory's with a piece of stinky fish in my handbag,' I say.

'We don't expect you to carry it in your handbag,' says Sandy. 'I was thinking more along the lines of a carrier bag or a holdall.'

'A holdall,' I squeal. 'Christ, I'll look so suspicious that someone will phone the Anti-Terrorist Hotline. No, I'm not doing it.'

'Okay, a carrier bag then, not a holdall,' says Sandy.

'I'm not walking around Rory's with a stinky fish, period,' I say firmly.

There is silence. Ryan attempts to nibble noiselessly at his shortbread while everyone sips their Chardonnay. Rosalind pats Sadistic Harry's back while my mother pretends to pull the curtains closer together. Adam stands up and begins topping up everyone's glasses, his citrusy aftershave mingling with the smell of Gorgonzola.

'We're doing this for you,' Devon says finally, punctuated by a burp from Sadistic Harry.

'Sorry,' mumbles Rosalind.

'I'll walk round with you babe,' says Adam.

Mum looks warmly at him.

'That's sweet of you, isn't it sweet of him Flo?' says Sandy.

'Very sweet,' says Mum, looking at me with raised eyebrows.

For goodness' sake what is wrong with her? Adam is nice enough but far from my type. Perhaps I should take up pottery classes. I may meet someone, okay it won't be Patrick Swayze but I might meet someone nice. My thoughts turn to Tom. It seems I don't recognise a nice man when I do meet one. I certainly had him figured all wrong didn't I? That's if what Grant Richard's says is true, and why would he lie? I think back to the ferry and I just can't believe it. I really can't. I suddenly feel very tired of the whole business. The salon is starting to feel like one big hassle and although I underplayed it, I did feel hurt seeing Luke. Not with another woman you understand, but eating chocolate cake and ice cream. I bet he even farts with her. I don't mean they do it in unison, obviously, and I bet she'll never Biofreeze his cock. I smile at the memory. I find myself wondering what Tom is doing. He could be on Twitter this very moment. No, don't think about it, don't think about it.

'Sweet indeed,' gushes Ryan.

Oh for God's sake, love is carrying a stinky fish together around Rory's supermarket is it?

'Flo,' says Sandy questioningly.

I sigh inwardly. I can't very well say I don't want to do anything else that will harm Rory's Supermarkets because I love Tom Rory, no matter how rotten he might be. I know he doesn't love me. If he had felt anything for me he wouldn't have stolen my prescription idea.

'Okay,' I say meekly. 'But I'll do it alone. I really don't want anyone else getting dragged into this, but thank you Adam.'

'Smelly fish it is then,' says Sandy. 'In fact we should target two stores.'

It's getting worse.

'I can't be in two places at once,' I say.

'What about you Mrs R?' asks Ryan.

Oh no, I don't think so.

'I rather think my mother is more of a liability to our cause than an asset. Sorry Mum but you know it's true.'

'I'd much rather do the food,' she confesses.

'I'll do it,' sighs Rosalind, twisting her long blonde highlights and securing them with a scrunch at the top of her head. 'After all I've done bugger all so far and let's face it no one will suspect the mum with the baby on her back will they?'

'Yey,' exclaims Sandy. 'Two targets at the same time. That will throw them.'

The meeting moves onto the protest and Mum shares her catering arrangements. Ryan offers to get the raffle tickets and Adam surprises us all by saying he can get goldfish for the children while I find myself wondering where it all went wrong. There I was happy as Larry, well as happy as one could be, and then Devon dropped her bombshell and Tom Rory banged me up the backside in a manner of speaking. Life hasn't been the same since and I imagine it never will be after I've strolled through Rory's with a stinky fish in my bag.

Chapter Thirty-Nine

Tom

'I'm sure you won't be surprised Tom, but the first thing we'd all like to discuss is the Church Lane business,' Brian says, studying me closely. 'It seems the whole thing has got a bit out of hand if you don't mind me saying.'

I loosen my tie and stand up to open a window.

'I know all publicity is good in the long run but there's been some negative stuff about Rory's in the papers,' agrees Martin Chambers. 'Underhand dealings, that kind of thing ...'

There are murmurs of assent.

'It doesn't sit comfortably with me Tom, to be honest,' nods Brian. 'I think we all agree on that.'

I sit down and lean back in my chair.

'It's the first thing on the agenda. I'm just as unhappy as you are about it,' I say calmly.

I only need one shareholder to panic and we're in trouble.

'There is a good chance the press may approach some of you ...' Brent begins.

'They already have,' says Brian sternly. 'And I wasn't at all happy about it ...'

'Yes, I'm sorry about that Brian. You must refer all press people back to us,' I break in quickly and gesture to Brent to refill the coffee cups.

'We have had a problem. I'm not going to deny that. I've had to let someone go from acquisitions; let's just say he handled things incorrectly and against company procedures. We are working to put things right but we're not there yet.'

There is a murmur from the directors.

'We've got two empty shops and we're getting a reputation for putting local businesses out of work, it doesn't look good, and now we have a protest looming,' says Martin. 'Obviously something we thought would go away, isn't doing that is it?'

'I'm presuming by the *something* you mean Flora Robson,' I say, hearing an edge to my voice.

'I think …' begins Brian

'Flora Robson has a beef against us,' interrupts Martin, 'and …'

'Flora Robson has every right to have a beef against us. She was treated unfairly and the deal that was made on those three shops most certainly did not follow the ethos of this company. Now, that's done, nothing we can do to change it.'

I swipe my hand across the table, hoping to clearly indicate that it's behind us.

'But the good news …'

'There's some good news is there? That's music to my ears,' says Martin, his voice heavy with sarcasm.

I ignore his tone.

'Very good news, in fact,' reiterates Brent.

'We've had an offer for the two properties either side of Flora Robson's salon.'

There is a bemused silence.

'Who is it?' asks Martin sharply.

I look at Brent, who slides some papers from a folder.

'The only thing we know about this buyer is that it will be a cash sale. They want to remain anonymous. The purchaser is using a nominee …'

'What does that all mean?' asks Brian.

'It simply means that whoever is buying these properties would prefer we don't know who he or she is. The nominee purchases the properties, in this case it's their solicitor, and at a later date the solicitor will sign over the property to them. It's most likely a property developer who is hoping to get the salon, but the point is we get rid of two troublesome plots and …'

'And Flora Robson?' asks Martin.

Just the mention of her name conjures up the beautiful image of her face and her infectious laugh. I don't think anyone has hated me as much as her. I've gone over and over in my head how to explain it all to her but nothing I say now is going to make any difference. She is right. I did humiliate her. I should have told her earlier who I was. If I now tell her Grant was behind the prescriptions and the underhand sales she'll never believe me. It will seem like I'm using him as a scapegoat and I'll look like a victim and I'm damned if I'll ever become that, not for any woman.

'That's the next item on the agenda,' breaks in Brian. 'Do we counteract this protest or do we let it happen, what's the feeling on that?'

'We feel,' says Brent, glancing at me, 'that we should let this whole thing take its natural course. We will of course do all we can to minimise damage but if you put it into perspective it is just a small protest which at the most will make the local paper. Meanwhile we are approaching Flora Robson to attempt to smooth over what damage has been done. Unfortunately she has been unresponsive to our efforts so far. Tom and I feel the less contact with her the better. We just seem to incense her even more.'

I sip my coffee and wait for their reaction.

'So, we sit tight and hope it blows over,' mumbles Jeffrey Miles.

I'm about to answer him when Beth gestures to me through the glass doors and holds up a phone. I stand up, relieved at an excuse to leave the meeting.

'If you'll excuse me, I have an important call. I'll leave you in Brent's capable hands.'

I take the phone from Beth.

'It's Michael for you, he said it was important.'

My heart sinks. Why is Michael phoning me? The only time I get a call from the head of our maintenance department is either when there is excellent news or really bad news. Why do I get the feeling this is the latter?

'Michael,' I say pleasantly into the mouthpiece.

'Sorry to bother you Tom. I did try to get hold of Grant but I was told he was in finance now and …'

'What's the issue?' I say bluntly, not wishing to get into a conversation about Grant.

'We've had to close two stores in close proximity, the one in Holland Park and the other in Ladbroke Grove. I thought you should know that we're checking all the freezers are working properly. But it seems a bit of a coincidence that there is a distinct odour of gone-off fish in both stores and ...'

'Let me know the outcome. Open up again as soon as possible and obviously put notices on the window giving a reasonable explanation. What time was it reported?'

'I'll check that out Tom and ...'

'Find out ASAP for me and get the CCTV tapes for around those times sent to me. By cab if you have to ...'

'I doubt there'll be anything on the CCTV ...'

'Oh, I think there will be. I'd appreciate that Michael.'

'Will do,' he says before hanging up.

I hand the phone back to Beth, check through the glass doors that Brent has the meeting under control and walk to my office. I close the door and punch in the number for the Ladbroke Grove store.

'This is Thomas Rory. I'd like to arrange a special delivery. It's a local address.'

Chapter Forty

I first thought I would walk to Rory's but I was worried that trailing the smell of a stinking rotting fish in a carrier bag just might draw attention. It's bad enough I've had it in the flat for a few minutes. It now smells like I've got dead bodies under the floorboards. Thank God I'm in the basement or the neighbours would have me down as a serial killer. So, I reluctantly drive myself and the rotting fish to Rory's in Ladbroke Grove maintaining phone contact with Rosalind throughout. Her piece of fish is wrapped in a nappy, apparently.

'That and the smell of Sadistic Harry's own nappy should clear the joint,' she'd laughed.

My fish is wrapped neatly in a *Hello* magazine in between Charles and Camilla. The smell is so putrid that I have to open all the car windows. I pull into the car park, spot a space and zoom into it. I close the windows and pull my phone from my handbag and am about to text Rosalind when a tapping on the glass makes me jump out of my skin. I turn to see an old lady wearing a polka dot headscarf, tapping on the window with her stick. I wind it down just a tiny bit and she pushes her head in. I somehow think she is going to regret that. I swear my eyes are watering from the stink.

'Is there a problem,' I say.

'This is a disabled space ...' she begins, before reeling back and choking.

Shit. I'm going to kill a pensioner before I even make it to the store. I can just see the headlines. *Humble hairdresser murders OAP in prank on Rory's heir.* I wipe my eyes with a tissue, not because of the sadness of the situation you understand, but because this goddamn fish is killing me.

'I'll move,' I shout.

Bloody disabled parking spaces. I've got nothing against them you understand, but does there need to be so many of them? How many disabled people do you see in the supermarket? The gym is even worse, they have loads and I can honestly say with hand on heart that I have yet to see a kettle-swinging OAP, or one on the treadmill come to that. I drive around for five minutes trying to find another space. I finally squeeze my little Clio between two four by fours, both of whom have baby seats in the back and clearly should be parked in the Mother and Child bay if you ask me. I bet Rosalind got parked right away. There's probably a bay marked *mum with baby on tit* somewhere. I wish there was one for *lifelong spinsters*, that way I'll always get a space. What a depressing thought. Don't think about it, don't think about. I text Rosalind that I am about to go in and then fling open the door with the urgency of an airplane passenger about to jump on the evacuation slide. I could certainly do with the oxygen mask. I gulp in the fresh air and reach back in for the carrier bag just as my phone bleeps. It's Rosalind.

'I'm going in.'

It sounds like we're about to rob a bank, mind you, with the state of my finances that may well be the next plan of action.

'Roger that,' I respond. I consider adding *over and out* but decide against it. Just as well.

'Who's Roger?' responds Rosalind.

I sigh. Just as well we're not robbing a bank. The car is getting hotter and smellier by the second. I don my sunglasses and tie on a head scarf. I glance at myself in the car mirror and nod approvingly. Yes, I'm looking more like Audrey Hepburn by the minute, sadly not smelling as good. I snatch the carrier from the back seat and try to walk confidently into the store. A man in a Rory's shirt smiles at me as I enter.

'Basket madam,' he asks offering me one. He immediately wrinkles his nose.

I shake my head.

'I only need a few things,' I say.

He glances at the carrier bag suspiciously.

'Oh,' I mumble, waving a hand dismissively and walking on. I'm so nervous that my legs are wobbling beneath me. *Just walk through the store and then leave. Don't rush. Drop the fish into a rubbish bin when you get outside,* Sandy had instructed. I notice Sandy is good at giving instructions, but I don't see her walking through the store with rotting fish. I stroll along the freezer aisle and make my way back along the sweet aisle. Oh, fabulous they've got a three for two on chocolate bars. I scoop up three Crunchie bars and continue on down the chilled aisle, the smell drifting through the store as I go.

'What's that horrid smell?' says a child as I pass her. 'Mummy it's making me want to be sick.'

The lady in front coughs uncontrollably. I scoot past her, grabbing two packs of Hobnobs as I go. We're totally out of biscuits in the salon and I've got to buy them somewhere haven't I?

'Excuse me madam.'

I jump so much that I almost drop the carrier. I whip round and slap the elderly gentleman behind me with my handbag. My hand is gripping the carrier so tightly that my knuckles are white.

'It's coming from over here,' I hear a woman say.

'God, it's terrible,' says someone else.

I see an assistant pull out a radio and feel my heart flutter with panic.

'Spreading like wild fire,' he says. 'Customers overcome by it.'

Does he have to make it sound like bloody nerve gas? It's a fish for goodness sake.

'I think you dropped this,' says the elderly man grimacing.

Oh Jesus. He's holding my *Hello* magazine. How can that be? I look at the carrier I had been gripping so tightly and see the hole at the bottom of it. Bugger, bugger.

'Thank you,' I say, grabbing it and wrapping it in the carrier before rushing towards the exit. I skirt the flowers and am about to make my way to the self-service till when a Rory's assistant materialises in front of me. I skid to a halt, and try to catch my breath.

'Daffs, three bunches for the price of two. Spring is certainly here,' he smiles.

The fragrance of the flowers is obviously covering the terrible stink of my fish.

'Or roses. Treat yourself madam. Or if you're like my wife, get your husband to hand over the dosh later,' he laughs heartily.

He shoves the roses under my nose.

'Three bunches for ten pounds today, our special offer for the ladies.'

I shake my head forcefully.

'I don't like roses,' I say.

'You don't?' he says, surprised.

'The thorns,' I explain, edging away from him.

'Daffs,' he says again. 'Cheaper and of course there are no thorns.'

I take three bunches from him.

'That's the thing with Rory's,' he smiles. 'Everything is so hard to resist.'

Even the boss, I find myself thinking. No, don't think about it, don't think about it but how can I not think about it? I'm trying to destroy the business of the man I love. Yes, but don't forget Flora, whispers a voice in my head, 'he's destroying people's jobs every day of the week'. I turn to the assistant.

'Not that hard to resist. There are other shops you know. Besides do you realise Thomas Rory is putting good honest hard-working people out of work?'

What am I saying, have I gone insane?

'Well ...' begins the assistant.

'And he is dishonest in business.'

Shut up Flora.

'He gave me a job,' he says nervously.

Typical, bloody typical.

'Huh,' I say.

'Hyacinth,' he says shakily, holding up a plant. 'We have an offer on these and on our lavender. Very calming is lavender, my wife swears by it ...' he trails off and looks around.

Is he trying to say I need to calm down?

'He's a playboy too,' I add, feeling tears smart my eyes. It's this bloody fish, that's what it is.

'I, erm ...' stutters the assistant, while juggling the hyacinth and lavender.

'For God's sake,' I snap, taking the hyacinth and storm to the checkout.

I rush outside as assistants begin to evacuate the store. I dispose of the fish and hurry to my car. I don't believe it. I've got a carrier bag full of stuff and a bunch of daffs, not to mention a bloody hyacinth. This is getting ridiculous. My phone bleeps and I scroll in to a message from Rosalind.

'They had a special offer on nappies, I couldn't not. Don't tell Sandy.'

I look at the hyacinth and sigh. Why is it whenever we try to sabotage Thomas Rory's business, we end up giving him some?

Chapter Forty-One

'Not again,' I say.

Tony stands on my doorstep and opens his mouth to speak.

'I know, you only deliver but I haven't ordered, and even if I had I wouldn't book a delivery for six in the morning.'

I yawn and pull my wrap tighter.

'Can you hang on? I don't have my contacts in.'

'I'll make a start,' he says.

Make a start? What the hell does that mean? I fish my contacts out of the glass and wander sleepily back to the front door. How dare Thomas Rory presume I'm behind the pranks in his shop? Okay, I know I am but it's a bit of a presumption on his part isn't it? He can't possibly know it's me for sure. I'll make an official complaint. I'll ask Tony how to do it. He trudges down the steps carrying two boxes.

'Right, that's your cos lettuce. Three crates as ordered. Having a party are you?'

I stare at the lettuces. There must be about thirty.

'I hate lettuce,' I say.

'I can tell,' he says and shakes his head as he pants up the steps.

'Excuse me, I didn't order these,' I call up to him.

'I only deliver. I don't make the rules,' he calls back.

I kick the boxes to one side and am about to close the door when Tony returns with two more crates.

'Tinned fish, and there's a note with these. I've stuck it on the top ...'

Sodding Tom Rory, it has to be him. Who else would send me fish?

'You can take it all back and tell ...'

'I can't do that I'm afraid,' says Tony firmly.

'What? But you always say if I don't want them you'll take them back.'

He nods confirmation.

'Ah, now you're right there. But in this case I can't, this is an exception. I've a note saying non-returnable goods. That's the way with special deals and bulk buying. No returns. I'll get the rest.'

'The rest?' I mumble, feeling my head spin.

I yank open the crate to find an assortment of tinned fish. I fumble in my bag for my phone when Tony returns, this time carrying a bouquet of flowers so huge that they dwarf him.

'A hundred and twenty red roses,' says Tony nonchalantly, like he delivers a hundred and twenty red roses every day.

'Mind the thorns,' he warns, handing them over.

I could scream. I throw them onto the floor and begin to punch in Devon's number when Tony returns carrying a freezer bag.

'Now what?' I say exasperated.

'These are your freezer items. Twenty-four packs of prawns. Go nice with that cos lettuce,' he quips.

Twenty-four packs? I'll never get all this in my little fridge.

I rip open the envelope on top of the tinned fish and pull the card out with trembling hands.

'The best fish come in tins don't you think? Less chance of them going off.'

There is no signature. Tony returns with a white box, two carrier bags and two envelopes.

'Final one,' he says handing me the carrier bags and box.

'Chocolate cheesecake with a pastry base,' he says checking over his list.

I close my eyes and sigh.

'I hate cheesecake with pastry base,' I mumble.

'And twenty bags of marshmallows. Pink only.'

I don't believe this.

'That's your lot,' he says. 'No substitutions and ...'

He fiddles with the little machine and I peek into the carrier bag and see a prettily wrapped parcel inside.

'You've 700 loyalty points,' he says giving an impressed nod. 'You're a real loyal customer aren't you?'

I sure am.

'I want to complain about these goods. How do ...?'

'Complain,' says Tony in a bemused tone. 'Complain about what? I delivered on time ...'

'Not about you. About all this stuff you've delivered. I didn't order it. I haven't paid for it. Someone else paid for it ...'

'You want to complain that someone else paid for your goods ...'

'No, I want to complain that Thomas Rory is sending me things I don't want and ...'

He looks at the roses and the cheesecake and I see everything through his eyes. Of course I can't complain, and Tom Rory knows that. Who complains about getting free food and a hundred and twenty red roses, not to mention a free gift? I peek into the carrier bag again and pull out the wrapped parcel. I dread to think what this is.

'You're absolutely right. No one would complain would they?' I say wearily.

'I only deliver,' says Tony and I find myself wondering if he says that in his sleep.

I close the door, drop onto the floor and open the second envelope.

'On behalf of Rory's Supermarkets, please enjoy your prawns and cos lettuce. For just £1.99 our seafood sauce will make your prawn cocktail perfect.'

I throw the card across the room. Sod their seafood sauce.

I rip open the third envelope

'Enjoy the roses. Oh, and mind those thorns. Then again, what's a little prick between friends? Careful with those prawns. Gone-off fish can be awfully smelly, but I don't have to tell you that do I?' Kind Regards Tom.

I feel myself shaking with rage and can barely open the carrier bag to pull out the wrapped gift. I tear at it like a woman demented and stare at the *Womanity* gift set. I pull the small card from the top.

'I could smell you a mile off. Let me know when you want to surrender.'

Surrender? Surrender my arse. I chuck my phone onto the couch and throw myself beside it. What am I thinking? I'm no match for Thomas Rory. He has pots of money where I have ... well frankly I don't have much at all now Luke and I have split. The rent on the flat alone is killing me and although I want to shop at the local shops the truth is they are just more expensive than the supermarkets. By the time I've bought food and put money to one side for the utility bills, frankly there isn't anything left. I couldn't have a night out if I wanted one. I look at the boxes on the floor. What the hell am I going to do with all that lettuce? I can't eat the other food on principle, although I suppose I could keep a few tins of pilchards and a couple of bags of prawns. My phone trills and I pick it up tiredly.

'It's me,' says Sandy. 'Yesterday's little prank closed the stores for a bit and it looks like we're going to get a bit of publicity. The local rag emailed the webpage and asked if we'd like to do an interview ahead of the protest. What do you think?'

I pick up Tom's note and re-read it. How could I have fallen for him? I'm thirty years old. You'd think I'd have more sense.

'Flo, did you hear me?'

'Yes,' I say absently. 'That sounds great. By the way, how many vases do we have at the salon?'

'You what?'

'Thomas Rory sent me a hundred and twenty roses, oh and tons of lettuce as well as prawns and a cheesecake. I hope you and Ryan are hungry because I can't send it back. If we continue with these pranks I'm going to drown in an abundance of thank you gifts,' I groan.

'You're kidding, best not to mention that to the local paper. I'll see you later. Oh, and bring me a dozen roses will you. I'll love you forever.'

I hang up before letting out a sneeze.

Chapter Forty-Two

'Jesus Christ, did we change the salon into a florist and someone forgot to tell me,' says a startled Ryan.

'Courtesy of Thomas Rory,' I say sneezing.

'Blimey, what did you do to deserve this?'

'Walked through his store with a stinky fish,' answers Sandy from behind a vase.

I sniff noisily.

'Makes sense,' he says. 'I hate to think what you'd get if you're nice to him.'

'There's even more in the sink. We've run out of vases. Jethro is bringing some over. We're going to feature in the local paper. Isn't that fab?'

'Fab,' I say, noisily blowing my nose. 'I hope they don't want photos.'

'You'll be fine, take an antihistamine and we're giving a red rose to every client today, but don't say it's courtesy of Tom Rory,' orders Sandy.

'Yes Führer,' says Ryan, clicking his heels.

'And there are four tins of pilchards and three tins of anchovies for you,' she continues, 'as well as three lettuces.'

'And some prawns,' I add.

'Courtesy of Rory's,' smiles Sandy.

'All this and it's not even fish Friday. When's the next prank? I'm running out of loo roll.'

I shoot him a dirty look and dive for another tissue before firing off a round of sneezes. I check the diary to see I have three clients before one o'clock.

'Oh no,' I groan.

'I'll pop to the chemist and get you something,' says Sandy sympathetically as my first client walks through the door.

'Well, who's got an admirer then?' says Mrs Peterson.

'Me, kind of,' I say, sneezing so loudly that the slide holding my hair in place flies out. 'Allergic,' I mumble blowing furiously into a tissue, 'to roses.'

'You should maybe tell him.'

I have an uncanny feeling that he already knows. Although I can't work out how he knew it was me in the store. One thing I do know for sure is that he always seems to have the upper hand and it is seriously starting to piss me off. I lead Mrs Peterson to the basin fighting back a sneeze as I go.

'Mr Peterson and I thought we'd come to the protest on Friday. It's going to be a lovely day by all accounts. Mr Peterson checked the weather forecast.'

'Lovely,' I say. 'The more the merrier.'

'Well, we'll see. If it's really nice we may go to the coast.'

I sigh. Nice to know my clients are loyal to me. I finish washing her hair and take her to a seat.

'Sandy will be with you in a tic. She's just popped to the chemist.'

I sneeze again and dab at my eyes. It's no good; this allergy is playing havoc with my contacts. I sniffle my way out the back and remove them. I've just popped on my glasses when Ryan flies into the kitchenette.

'Grant Richard's surveyor is here. He's an Arnold Schwarzenegger lookalike without the Hitler accent.'

I wipe my nose and follow Ryan into the salon where Mr Schwarzenegger is tapping walls. Ryan and I watch him silently until the dryer under Marsha Smith bleeps.

'Right Marsha darling, let's make you look glam for tonight,' says Ryan stepping around Mr Schwarzenegger and guiding Marsha to the basin. Sandy flies through the door, throwing antihistamines as she goes.

'I could only get the drowsy ones,' she says, stopping in front of the surveyor.

I push her to one side and point to Mrs Peterson while Mr Schwarzenegger continues tapping the wall and sucking in air as if each tap is causing him pain. He taps again and waits.

'Waiting for a reply are you?' quips Ryan. 'We think it's subsidence, not a poltergeist.'

'Subsidence?' squeals Mrs Peterson. 'The walls aren't going to collapse are they?'

'This is Notting Hill, love, not Pompeii,' says Ryan.

'It most certainly is. In fact, I can say, without doubt that you have subsidence,' says the surveyor in a deep cockney accent.

'I told you he didn't have a Hitler accent,' whispers Ryan.

'Can you tell by just tapping?' Sandy asks. 'Don't you need special equipment?'

'Trust you to encourage him,' smiles Ryan. 'Right Marsha sweetie, are you up or under today.'

'Brian likes it on top for special functions.'

Ryan's eyes widen.

'Does he indeed?'

'Not for cases such as these,' says the surveyor. 'I can tell from a few taps.'

'It is substance then?' says Sandy.

'Subsidence,' corrects Ryan. 'I seriously give up.'

'It is indeed.'

'And you can tell that just from tapping walls,' she says again.

I pop an antihistamine into my mouth and wait while he fills in a report. Sandy begins blow drying Mrs Peterson's hair, watching the surveyor suspiciously out of the corner of her eye. I take the report from him and he zips up his briefcase.

'I'd sell if you have the chance. This place will be hard to shift otherwise.'

Ryan gives me a sad look.

'Never mind love, best to know.'

I nod miserably and see the surveyor out. I watch him walk to his car and then see Jethro approach him. They chat for a few minutes and slap each other on the back like old mates before Jethro enters the salon.

'Yo cats, what's poppin?'

He stops and stares at the roses.

'Wow,' he says, placing two vases on the reception desk.

'How do you know the surveyor?' I ask.

'I don't know no surveyor dude,' he says looking confused.

'Him,' I say pointing to Schwarzenegger as he drives off.

'Alan? He ain't no surveyor,' Jethro laughs. 'He's a painter. He did the club for us. Looks dope now.'

'Talking of dopes,' says Ryan nodding at me. 'Seems like you've been taken for one.'

I sneeze in response. Four hours later and a few less roses we stuff our faces with doughnuts in celebration of the salon being subsidence free.

'Although we won't know for sure,' I say. 'Not until Adam's brother has been.'

'But it seems likely that Grant Richards was trying it on,' says Sandy, 'which means he is still working for Thomas Rory.'

'Undercover no doubt,' adds Ryan through sugar-dusted lips.

'You really should stop watching those crime programmes,' I say, while silently agreeing with him.

It seems Tom Rory will do anything to get my salon. I suppose I have to accept he is nothing but a ruthless business man. Well, I'm not selling.

'I'm not selling,' I say in a weary resigned tone

'Of course not,' agrees Sandy.

'We'll have more support after the protest, love,' says Ryan.

That's true, unless everyone decides to go to the coast because the weather is nice. That's just about my luck isn't it? At five I close up and stand outside looking at the poster for the protest. I feel like crap. My nose is red and sore from being wiped too much and my throat feels scratchy. I pop another antihistamine and wipe my watery eyes. The two shops at the side of me are boarded up and the salon somehow looks dreary stuck in the middle, even with the carnival designed poster. I remember the day I bought the salon. I was so excited. I'd seen a whole future ahead and hoped to expand as time went on. Maybe even buy one of the shops next door. After all, Terence was always talking of selling. Sandy and I had made all kinds of plans. Giggling at what fun it would be to have an adjoining door to Sandy's clinic.

'I'll send you clients and vice versa,' she'd laughed. 'We'll be run off our feet.'

The thing is, I have no idea what I'll do without the salon. The thought of working for someone else is unbearable. Luke will know I failed. Worse of all, I'll know I failed.

'Fancy a hot chocolate,' says a voice behind me.

I'm rooted to the spot. I can't even turn around. Why is it whenever I see him I always look like Kerry Katona without a make-up team? My face turns hot and I tremble. I will myself to turn and face him and have to fight back a gasp when I do. He's wearing a short-sleeved blue-striped shirt, tucked into jeans. His hair looks freshly washed. His eyes are sparkling and he's smiling but he's looking at me uncertainly.

'Just one drink?' he asks, wrinkling his forehead as he studies me.

His voice is soft but clear. I meet his eyes and sneeze.

'Bless you,' he says with a smile.

I have to force myself to believe that this man will do anything and go to any lengths to get my salon. I'll be left with nothing if he does. He must know that. He's putting Sandy and Ryan out of jobs and he doesn't give a damn. I feel anger rise up in me and I clench my teeth and say,

'I wouldn't have a hot chocolate with you if you were the last man on earth.'

I'm annoyed to hear my voice shake. He nods.

'Fair enough, but I want you to know that I don't want the salon. It's much too high a price ...'

He breaks off and looks into my eyes. I lower mine.

'Call off the protest Flo; you don't need to have it.'

'How dare you presume to tell me what I ought to do,' I say shaking with rage. I barge past him towards my car, remembering right at that moment that my petrol gauge is on the red. Bugger it. I knew there was something I meant to do on the way to the salon. It will be just the end if I break down in front of him, well my car that is. *I've* no intention of breaking down in front of Tom Rory, ever.

'I'm pleased you didn't get engaged to that up his own arse Luke Wright,' he says softly, stopping me as I reach the kerb. 'You deserve better.'

I turn sharply.

'Too right I do. I deserve the best.'

He nods.

'You do.'

I turn again towards my Clio and stop.

'What you've done to me is unforgivable, and you still don't give up do you?' I say with my back to him.

'I've come to make peace Flo ...'

'Don't call me Flo,' I say reeling round to face him again.

A middle-aged couple pass us reluctantly. A lover's tiff, they are no doubt thinking and just the thought of Tom as a lover turns my legs to jelly. I open the door of the Clio and am about to get in when he strides across the road and lays his hand on my arm, the touch sending a multitude of emotions exploding inside me.

'Just one drink,' he asks.

I brush his hand off my arm.

'I'd rather poke hot needles in my eyes,' I say and before he has time to reply I am in the Clio and starting the engine. He makes no effort to open the car door or stop me. I pull away from the kerb and look in my mirror to see him standing on the pavement. I turn the corner and he is gone. It is only then I realise I am crying.

Chapter Forty-Three

'I don't believe it,' I say, trying to keep up with Sandy as she marches to Rory's. I can barely keep up. Ryan hurries behind me. We finally reach the store and I stand panting as Sandy points at the supermarket window. I gasp, how can that be? A big poster hangs in the shop window and I read it with a sinking heart.

Join us today in supporting our local suppliers.
All local produce sold at Rory's at discount prices.
To show your support for your community take part in our raffle.
All proceeds to go to St Mark's Hospital. Win a hamper worth £100
and vouchers worth £25.
Shop at Rory's and be part of your community.

'I ... I mean how?' I splutter.

'They stole our idea. It makes us look stupid as usual,' says Sandy, angrily sticking her nose in the air. 'They've deliberately done it on the day of our protest.'

'Bloody hell,' says Ryan.

How did they know we were going to have a raffle for St Mark's? It doesn't make sense. Unless, oh my God, unless we've got a mole. Someone in our organisation is betraying us to Rory's. There is no other answer is there? I look at Ryan suspiciously, my eyes narrowing.

'What?' he says questioningly. 'Why am I getting the stare?'

'We'll just have to make the best of a bad job that's all,' says Sandy, waving to my mum who approaches with Devon and Rosalind.

I look for Adam. Is he the mole? When did it start happening? Was it after he joined us? Did Thomas Rory plant him in the flat above me? Oh, that's ridiculous. I'm not that much of a threat surely.

'I don't get it,' says Rosalind rocking Sadistic Harry in his pram. No it can't have been Rosalind. She'd never have found the time. She's so busy changing, washing and buying nappies that I'm surprised she has time for anything else. Devon looks mildly shocked but not as shocked as I would have imagined. Surely not, Devon and I have been friends for years. How did Tom Rory get to her?

'You don't seem very surprised,' I snap at her. 'Someone must have told Rory's what we were doing. We've got a mole,' I say bluntly.

Ryan gasps.

'A traitor in the ranks, but that's awful.'

'Are you saying it's me?' asks Devon.

Mum shakes a tablecloth and spreads it neatly onto a table.

'Well, it wasn't me,' she says, before I have even accused her.

'The Royal Opera House, a box, remember?' I say sharply.

She sighs.

'Are you going to be throwing that in my face forever?'

'Probably.'

'Hiya,' calls Adam as he swaggers towards us. 'I've got the poster done. It looks good I think.'

He hands one end to Ryan and they unroll it.

Say NO to Rory's and Save our Small Businesses
Buy a raffle ticket and win a hamper of fruit or bouquet of
flowers.
All proceeds to St Mark's Hospital.
Support our local businesses and boycott Rory's
Honk if you support us

'You've obviously not seen that then,' says Sandy caustically, pointing to the shop window.

Of course it could be Sandy. They say it is the one you're least likely to suspect don't they? Isn't it a fact that most victims knew their murderer? I know we're not talking about a killer as such here, but you get my drift don't you?

'How did they find out then?' I say scrutinising each of them.

'What are we talking about doll?' Adam asks.

'Rory's stole our idea,' I say, feeling myself getting tearful. Of all the times to be premenstrual it would have to be on the day of the protest wouldn't it?

'We've got a mole,' I say dramatically.

Adam looks shocked. No, it isn't him. Besides his brother came and confirmed once and for all that we didn't have subsidence. That wouldn't fit in with Adam being the traitor would it? I have to face the fact that Tom is not the man I thought he was. His words ring through my ears: *You realise if you continue like this, things will get messy and you won't win.*

'They must have seen it on Twitter or something,' says Sandy.

'I didn't mention it on Twitter,' I say sharply.

'Well, who did tell them then?' asks Ryan. 'We've kept the whole raffle thing a secret until today.'

It is then I remember. I feel my body turn hot. It was me. I'd gone home after seeing Tom and knocked back half the bottle of vodka that Ryan had given me on an empty stomach and with only the antihistamine for company. I was wasted after the second glass. I had then gone onto Twitter and fired about a dozen tweets to @tomrory. None of them received a reply, but then again they were pretty insulting. I vaguely remember mentioning our raffle. I scroll into my phone and check Twitter. Oh my God. Yes, there it is.

@tomrory and up yours Rory. After our protest we'll have tons of followers. You never give to the local hospital do you?

I was so incensed that he had ignored them that I had finished with,

We support the local hospital, unlike @tomrory. Everyone support our raffle for St Mark's. Support our local businesses and boycott Rory's

Of course, the date of the protest is in capital letters at the top of the page. I roll my eyes. I'd totally forgotten about it. I'd fallen asleep after the third glass and by the morning I could barely remember a thing.

'Oh my God, it was me,' I say with a groan.

'You?' they all echo.

'You're the mole?' says Ryan.

'Oh dear,' says Mum, flapping about with muffins and doughnuts.

'I was drunk and I just fired these insulting tweets to Tom Rory and ...'

'Bloody great,' mumbles Sandy. 'We'll have to make the best of a bad job won't we?'

I lower my head in shame. Honestly, only me, it really could only be me.

'We should put it behind us and make the best of things,' agrees Devon, putting an arm around me.

'I'm sorry,' I say, fighting back tears.

'It's all getting to you. Let's enjoy the day.'

'Hear hear,' says Adam.

Mum gives me a wink and I take a plate of muffins from her.

'On with the show,' I say.

Two hours later and things are in full swing. We have tons of people. More than I could have dreamt of. Yvonne came with about five friends. Most of our clients turned up as well as many of the locals. Several are waving their own handmade banners. The cheesecake Tom Rory had sent me has been demolished and we're starting to run out of muffins. There is a wonderful atmosphere and even if I do lose the salon I couldn't have asked for a better turn out. I've managed to give out loads of business cards and cars have been hooting like crazy as they pass.

'We have a lot of support,' smiles Rosalind, juggling Sadistic Harry on one hip and a tray of drinks on the other.

'What do we want?' shouts Sandy.

'Keep small shops in business,' everyone shouts back.

'When do want it?' yells Sandy.

'Now,' they scream.

I'm on the fifth book of raffle tickets and Devon's home-made lemonade is running out. Ryan dashes to the off-licence and comes back with a crate of soft drinks.

'Molly said it is on them. They can't get here so this is their way of supporting us,' he chirps, pouring it into paper cups. The sound of shouts and laughter distracts us and we turn to see a rowdy group of yobs coming to join the demonstration.

'Down with fucking corporations,' they shout holding coarse placards that read *Fucking bourgeois rich. We don't need them.*

'We don't need people like these either,' quips Adam.

'I guess it's support,' says Devon uncertainly.

A blond lad approaches my mum and I watch nervously. He has piercings just about everywhere you can have piercings.

'Awright ma?' he says. 'I like the gear.'

He flaps a hand at her outfit and tips her cap. To my horror she slaps his hand.

'You can keep your hands to yourself young man,' she snaps.

He laughs and the others join him.

'I'll 'ave a muffin, 'ow much?'

'A donation in the charity box,' says Sandy.

'Don't give them attention,' says Jethro. 'They're hammered.'

'Oi, shirt lifter, you got some lagers?' one asks Ryan.

I step in front of him. That's it. No one calls Ryan a shirt lifter, at least not when I'm around.

'We're not doing alcohol,' I say. 'It's a peaceful protest.'

'Ooh is that right four eyes,' he says with a smirk.

I knew there was a reason I wore contacts. I straighten my glasses self-consciously. It is then I see the black Porsche cruise slowly past us. The driver looks vaguely familiar.

'Was that Grant Richards?' I ask Sandy. 'What is he doing here?'

'Oh no, what's this?' she groans looking ahead.

I follow her eyes and see with horror that more yobs are walking towards us and they have an effigy of Thomas Rory. They're all shouting, *down with the bourgeois rich.*

'This isn't good,' says Rosalind, 'do you think we should call the police? We don't want this to be a reflection on us.'

They grab what's left of the muffins, and thankfully continue on, shouting and swearing as they do so. We watch them turn the corner and I sigh with relief. The last thing we hear are their shouts of,

'Down with fucking Rory's.'

Chapter Forty-Four

It is Yvonne who sees the smoke first. We look to where she points and hear sirens screaming in the distance. It sounds more like downtown New York than Ladbroke Grove. The sounds of loud raucous shouts make my blood curdle. I just know the smoke is from the Thomas Rory effigy.

'What the ...?' cries Jethro.

We all look at each other as Jethro begins to run in the direction of the smoke. My heart thumps and I watch helplessly as Adam follows him. They tear down the road like two athletes while I feel my body freeze and my feet root themselves to the spot.

'Do you think it's those yobs?' asks Devon

'Christ, what morons,' says Rosalind.

I remember the effigy and feel myself tremble. My banner slips from my trembling hands.

'You don't think they'll come back do you?' says Ryan uncertainly.

Our crowd of protesters have stopped their yelling and the silence is unnerving. All that can be heard is the wailing of sirens. I watch as Jethro works his way back through the crowd.

'It's the Thomas Rory effigy,' Jethro pants. 'They've set it alight in the road around the corner. I think they're heading back here.'

'Ryan, you go and look after the salon,' I yell my heart thumping so loudly that I barely hear my own voice.

'Call the police if you have any trouble,' adds Sandy.

'We'll stay with him,' says Mrs Peterson, clasping her husband's hand.

'Thanks, you're a love,' says Ryan, his face troubled.

'I'll come with you too. I'd love to stay. In fact the way I'm spurting milk, I'd probably be a great asset. But I really don't want to scar Sadistic Harry too early in his life,' says Rosalind.

'I'll stay,' says Yvonne, grasping my hand. 'We're a community aren't we?'

I smile at her.

'Don't you mad bitches do anything daft will you,' Ryan says, forcing a laugh.

'Famous last words,' mumbles Rosalind.

I give Ryan the keys to my car and tell him where I had parked. As I do so I see the Porsche again. It's parked across the road. I strain to see the driver but he doesn't seem to be in it. I look around but can't see him anywhere.

Yvonne and Mum link arms. My heart is hammering so fast in my chest that I feel sure it will burst. The smoke makes my chest feel tight. I watch two of Rory's security men usher out the last of the shoppers and they seem to be trying to lock the doors but it is too late as a crowd of hooligans rush towards them. The next I know there are shouts and screams and people are fighting. Bricks are being thrown at the shop windows. I recognise the leader of the crowd as the one of the yobs who took the muffins. The partly burnt effigy of Thomas Rory is now being tied to a lamp post and set on fire again. I can barely look at its grotesque form. The flames rise up in front of Rory's. I can hardly breathe. Several more yobs have formed a human chain and are holding up banners which read *Bring an end to the bourgeoisie rich*. I can't believe it's actually happening.

'Support Flora Robson,' they chorus.

I don't understand, why are they shouting my name? I look around in confusion and see one of the yobs talking into what appears to be his mobile phone but on looking closer I see it is a walkie-talkie. I gasp.

'Are you okay Flo?' Sandy asks anxiously.

'It's a proper organised protest,' I say in a stunned voice.

'I know,' she says looking at me curiously. 'We arranged it.'

'No, not us,' I yell above the noise. 'These yobs, it's all been planned. They're using two-way radios. Why would they do that unless they're taking orders from someone?'

Glass shatters behind us and I feel my nerves jangle.

'My goodness,' pants Mum excitedly. 'This takes me back to my youth, although we were peaceful then, but all the same. It was *Ban the Bomb* in those days.'

I cough as smoke tickles my throat. I see the blond yob and watch as he throws a brick at a window and hear screams as the glass smashes. It's a riot. The security men at the front of the shop are pushed to one side as looters surge into the store. Sandy screams at Jethro to stop as he struggles with one of the looters. I stare mesmerised at the burning effigy and feel myself shake from head to foot. Is this the outcome of our protest? It was never meant to end like this. I turn to see my mother slapping a youth around the head with her cap, her hair flying everywhere. Jesus, my dad is going to kill me. I try to pull her off but she's having none of it.

'I'm not letting some little whippersnapper tell me to bugger off, the nerve of it.'

Like I've not got enough on my hands with a riot erupting around me, now my mother decides she wants to be bloody Vanessa Redgrave. Why can't I have a normal mother? You know, one who sits at home and does crosswords and has pen pals? Rather than one who has outlandish ideas of becoming a middle-aged Lady Gaga and part-time activist? Then again, I don't really think I want my mum any other way. I kick the yob in the shin.

'Leave my mother alone you bully or I'll cut off your balls.'

Did I really say that? I then look down and see I'm holding the knife we used to cut the cheesecake. The yob looks petrified and backs away.

'That told him,' says Mum excitedly.

I search the faces around me for Grant Richards but there is no sign of him. At that moment I see Jethro stumble bleeding from the store. Sandy and Devon run towards him. God, this is getting worse. I watch as the locals battle with the protesters. Then I see Richards. He is standing on the street corner, hiding his face behind a thick woollen scarf and sunglasses. I tear across the road, tripping as I go and almost falling at his feet.

'You know what to do and make sure you wreck the place and ...' He stops on seeing me and turns to run but I grab his arm and scream for Adam. Grant lashes out at me and I feel his hand connect with my cheek and reel back. My face stings from his slap and I watch helplessly as he turns to run.

'Hey, what do you think you're doing?' shouts Adam lunging forward and throwing Richards to the ground. I rush towards them and pull off the scarf with shaking hands. The two-way radio screeches from where it has fallen to the ground.

'*Tom Rory is on his way. You might want to get out Grant,*' yells the voice.

Grant pulls himself from Adam's grip and faces me.

'You little bitch. You didn't think you'd get away with this did you?'

Adam lifts his fist but I stop him. Grant Richards stares at me his eyes wide and his mouth curling into a sneer.

'Did Tom send you?' I ask. 'Did he tell you to behave like this?' I grab his arm as he turns to move away.

'Good old Tom with his wonderful morals, yeah what do you think?' he says scathingly.

'Why?' I ask.

'You ruined everything you stupid bitch. I had everything in hand. It was all going so well but you just had to be stubborn didn't you?'

Two yobs fly along the street crashing into Adam and knocking him to the ground. Grant yanks himself from my grip and runs as fast as he can to his car. I watch him speed off and try to get my fuzzy brain to understand what he was saying.

'You okay?' Adam asks.

'I'm so sorry,' I say.

'This is your fault,' says Terence, who seems to appear out of nowhere. 'If you'd never sold your salon and then changed your mind we wouldn't be having this carnage.'

I hardly call it *carnage*, at least not yet. What does he mean changed my mind? How could I change my mind when I never agreed to anything in the first place?

'I never changed my mind. I never ever agreed to sell.'

He doesn't seem to hear me.

'It's greed, that's what it is. We were happy with our offer. Why couldn't you be too? Rory's made us all excellent offers. You put us in this terrible situation and then you pull out and cause all this trouble. We don't need people like you in the community. We really don't.'

Adam grabs my arm.

'Flo, it's not safe for you to be here.'

'What do you mean?' I yell over the shouting. 'I didn't pull out of anything.'

Terence says nothing and just shakes his head. The smoke is giving me a headache. I allow Adam to pull me away and I ~~see~~ Sandy leaning over Jethro.

'This is terrible,' says Devon crying. 'Is this all our fault Flo?'

She looks up at me with wide watery eyes, while I still try to take in what Terence said to me. Cars screech around the corner and policemen burst from them. I watch as they come charging towards us with batons.

'Ooh do you think they have phasers?' yells Mum.

I presume she means Tasers but don't have the time or the inclination to correct her. Bags of flour are being thrown at the police and everywhere has a layer of white. I clasp Devon's hand and link my other arm into my mother's as police surge towards us. My hands are roughly wrenched from them and pulled behind my back.

'Ooh are we getting arrested?' asks Mum. 'Just wait till your aunt Maud hears about this.'

More worrying is when my dad hears about this. I look up and see Tom Rory emerging from his black Audi, his face deathly pale. He looks at the store and then at the burning effigy. Finally his eyes land on me and he shakes his head. He can't surely think I'm behind this? I see Sandy being handcuffed and taken screaming to a police car. Why are they arresting us, what about the troublemakers?

The flour irritates my eyes and I feel them sting.

'It wasn't us,' I yell to Tom.

He turns his face from me and begins to walk towards the store when he is stopped by a policeman.

'My husband is a solicitor,' Mum says to the police officer as she is handcuffed.

'Is that right?' he replies. 'You'd think he'd keep you under control.'

I cringe, ooh that was a big mistake if ever there was one. A slip of a lad telling my mother she should be kept under control.

'That will be the day my lad, when a man tries to keep me under control. You cheeky little bugger. You're young enough to be my son.'

She's not wrong. He looks so young that he could be my son. Are they recruiting them at fourteen now? I remind myself I am now thirty and anyone under twenty looks young to me. She struggles against him. That's all we need.

'It's not us,' I protest. 'It was Grant Richards, he organised this.'

'And who might he be?' asks the policeman.

'Ask Thomas Rory, he knows.'

'So, now Thomas Rory is looting his own store is he?' says the officer with raised eyebrows.

'Get off me you arrogant little bugger. I'm not going anywhere,' struggles Mum.

Wonderful, now my mother is resisting arrest. It couldn't get any worse. Another policeman, even younger if that's possible, helps to restrain her and she is taken kicking and screaming to the police car. I watch helplessly as Jethro is helped into an ambulance. Adam mouths *he's okay* and gives me the thumbs up. I smile weakly and am then pushed into the police car. I look through the window and see Adam and Devon being handcuffed. This is bloody ridiculous. We're not the looters. There is white flour everywhere and in a strange way it looks surreal and rather pretty, like snow. Suddenly out of nowhere the police turn on hoses and begin rounding up the protesters. Terence's words run round and round in my brain. What did he mean changed my mind? Then I remember Tom's question over hot chocolate.

So, why aren't you selling to Rory's? I imagine they made you a good offer. It's a good location for a supermarket. What made you change your mind?

But I never changed my mind. Why would anyone think I had?

Chapter Forty-Five

I never thought the sight of Ryan would get me so excited. Devon and I jump up almost bumping into each other in our eagerness to speak to him. I like spending time with Devon but preferably not behind bars.

'Well,' he says, hand on hip, 'I never thought I'd see you in a cell. I need to get a photo for the record. You're one mad bitch Flora Robson, and I can see where you get it from, your mother's even madder.'

He pulls out his iPhone and Devon groans. Through the door I see Rosalind waving madly, Sadistic Harry perched on her hip.

'Thought I'd give Harry his first taste of the clink, it might just put the bugger off.

'How is Jethro?' Devon asks.

Ryan waves a hand airily.

'He's okay. Sandy is with him now. Just a few stitches and a tetanus jab, the hospital has discharged him. I've got to get this pic. Do you two jail birds want to pose?'

Devon and I look at each other and then both give him the finger.

'Classic,' he smiles, clicking away. 'I got a fab one of your mum in her gear. They'll let you out in a sec. Your dad is sorting things out.'

I put my head in my hands.

'I was hoping he wouldn't find out.'

'Apparently your mum assaulted the arresting officer and then another when they arrived at the station. She's now got a record as long as your arm, darling.'

'I hope I make Sadistic Harry as proud one day,' grins Rosalind.

I groan. The officer opens the cell door.

'You can go. Your friends are waiting. Rory's aren't pressing charges. Think yourself lucky this time.'

'What a relief,' says Devon.

I rush out to find Mum and Adam waiting for us. Dad looks at me disapprovingly.

'I knew this would end in tears,' he scolds.

'Oh, do shut up Roger. This is the most fun I've had in years, I've never been *busted* before,' Mum says proudly. 'I'm to be charged with resisting arrest,' she whispers in my ear.

'Fabulous,' I say.

We all trudge outside looking the worse for wear.

'Is the salon okay?' I ask.

'Fine love, although the same can't be said for Rory's. That's a right mess.'

We head to the nearest pub and file inside.

'We're certainly giving Sadistic Harry an education,' laughs Ryan.

'Huh, like he needs one with me as his mother.'

We order shots all round and water for Rosalind and then Ryan fills us in on what happened after we were arrested.

'All this is second hand of course darlings. Yvonne rushed back and reported everything. After you were arrested, the police went in pretty heavy-handed apparently. She got out in time. They rounded up the whole bunch of protesters who were banging on about bourgeois rich or whatever, and the store has been closed. It looks bloody awful.'

'What about Grant Richards?' I ask. 'What happened to him?'

'I never saw him,' says Ryan.

'He was coordinating the riot,' I say.

There is a hush and they look at me.

'But why?' asks Ryan.

'I'm not sure but I'm starting to think maybe he was fired and he was out for revenge.'

I sigh. I so want to phone Tom and tell him it wasn't our doing. I want to tell him that we were having a peaceful protest but I don't imagine he will believe me now. I feel utterly exhausted and I wouldn't care if I never saw my salon again. Terence's words are still going round and round in my head.

'Terence asked why I changed my mind,' I say voicing my thoughts.

'Changed your mind about what darling?' asks Ryan.

'About selling the salon,' I say. 'But I didn't change my mind did I?'

'Well, we certainly made headlines today,' says Devon. 'I just hope that everyone will soon realise that Rory's are underhand.'

'Perhaps I should offer the local rag my photos for when the story goes to press,' says Ryan.

'You'd better not,' warns Devon.

He stands to get another round but Adam stops him.

'I'll get this mate.'

'Shame he's straight,' winks Ryan, watching Adam walk to the bar. I find myself watching him too but my mind is elsewhere.

'But what if they're not?' I say.

'Not what?' asks Rosalind.

I'm about to say, *what if Rory's aren't underhand* when my mum looks at me anxiously.

'Are you all right dear? You seem to be talking in riddles. You didn't bang your head did you?'

'She always talks in riddles,' says Devon, throwing back her shot.

I take my drink and throw it back too. She's quite right of course, Devon that is, not my mum. I do always talk in riddles and I didn't bang my head or if I did I don't remember doing it. I'm just being stupid. Tom Rory stole my prescription idea didn't he? He had a raffle the same day as we did. He lied to me when he had plenty of opportunities to tell me who he was and worst of all he humiliated me. No one has ever made me look as stupid as he has. I'm tired and emotionally drained that's all, and feeling a bit sorry for myself and everyone else come to that.

'Excuse me you lot. I'm not having that,' says the landlord pulling me out of my reverie. I look up to see that Rosalind has popped out one of her veiny breasts and plonked Sadistic Harry onto it who is slurping away happily.

'This little bugger is entitled to his own little dram too isn't he?' says Rosalind.

'Not in here he ain't,' snaps the landlord. 'You'll put everyone off their beer.'

'I would have thought your ugly mush was enough to do that,' quips Adam.

We stifle our laughter.

'Right, out troublemakers, before I call the police.'

'Now, that is funny love,' says Ryan standing up. 'If you think we're trouble you should see the other geezers. Come on lovelies.'

'We'll get a bottle on the way back,' says Adam.

'And some fish and chips. Celebrate your release from prison in style,' adds Ryan.

I push Tom Rory and Terence from my mind, although during the evening I do find myself wondering what Terence meant.

Chapter Forty-Six

I type *Tom Rory* into the Twitter search box and scroll through the list. There is every Tom Rory except the one I want. I reboot my laptop and try again but still no Tom Rory, at least not *my* Tom Rory. I stare bemused at the computer and then click into RorysUK and read the latest update.

@RorysUK We would like to apologise for the disruption to our Ladbroke Grove store. We will be opening again very soon.

Is that it? I try Tom Rory again but still nothing. He's closed his account. I check my BlackBerry and view my text messages but there is nothing new. I re-read the last one from Sandy,

Hiya, just to let you know Jeth is feeling fine today. We're going to the club tonight if you want to come along. Cheer yourself up a bit. Have a quiet Sunday. Let us know. If not see you at work tomorrow.

I make myself a coffee and sit on the basement steps and watch life in Notting Hill. It's the first of June. The birds are singing and the sun is shining and I've never felt so sad in my life. I think back to how it had all started. Mark and Devon getting engaged, that was it wasn't it? I had so badly wanted to be engaged before I reached thirty. I can't help wondering if supposing, just supposing I hadn't been so preoccupied with thoughts of engagements. Would I have reversed out of the gym car park a little slower? If my mind had not been so muddled would I have seen Tom's car and not reversed into it? He would have driven off without seeing me, we wouldn't have shared lunch, I wouldn't have taken his email address and I most certainly would not have had a hot chocolate with him. Now here I am, thirty years old and still without an engagement ring and not even a boyfriend on the horizon. My little salon looks drab and is now stuck in the middle of two boarded up shops. I stretch my legs out and feel the warm sun on my feet. I gaze up at the sky and let the sun warm my face. I know I can't keep the salon. What's the point? Even with the publicity, and let's face it, it's not going to be good publicity, nothing will change. I feel such a fool the way everything has gone. It would have been better if I had accepted Rory's proposal at the start and none of this would have happened. There wouldn't have been looting and riot police, it's just terrible. It wouldn't surprise me if Tom staged the whole thing to make the protest turn nasty. I stop with my coffee cup to my lips. My God, what if he did? What if he staged the riot to make me look bad? No doubt everyone is sympathising with Rory's today. Even Terence turned on me didn't he? I remember Grant Richards face, contorted with anger and bitterness. Am I such a threat? I stand up, feeling determined. I shan't give in, no matter what Thomas Rory does. I'm keeping my salon and that's the end of it

Ten minutes later and I'm at the salon pulling down the protest poster and cleaning the windows. I need to clean up the salon ready for Monday. I quickly clear out the roses before my nose begins to stream. I then clean the basins and tables and am just mopping the floor when I realise the basin is blocked again and water is starting to overflow. I curse and grab a jug to scoop out the water. I struggle with the stopcock, breaking two nails in the process. Sod it, sod it. Tim won't come out today will he? I sigh when I realise I have wet towels in the washing machine. I throw them into the tumble dryer and switch it on and there is a spark, a bang and the red light goes off. Oh no, this can't be happening. Not the tumble dryer too. I click the switch back and forth but nothing happens. At this rate I'll have to close the salon tomorrow. A day's lost income is all I need. It was bad enough being closed yesterday for the protest. I open the drawer in the reception desk where I keep the sales ledger and total up the figures. By the time I've paid Ryan and Sandy this month I won't have enough to take a salary myself. I try not to think of the rent or the almost empty fridge. Thankfully I have plenty of tinned fish in the cupboards. I'll be living on tinned pilchards and anchovies for the next month. I don't suppose Tom Rory plans to send any more deliveries does he? I push the book back and finish mopping the floor. I then see the hairdryer Sandy had left out with a note stuck on it saying *faulty*. I close my eyes and feel tears run down my cheeks. How can I keep a salon like this? I need a new tumble dryer, a new basin and now it seems another hair dryer, and the whole place could do with a lick of paint. I can't possibly close tomorrow. I hiccup back my tears and through blurry eyes scroll into my phone for Tim's number. Please let him come. I suppose I'll have to pay over the odds for a Sunday. It just never ends does it? The phone is flashing with a text message. I scroll into it. It's from Sandy.

I need to see you. Are you at home? Xx

I text back that I'm at the salon and then click into my contacts for Tim's number and listen to the ringing at the other end. I sniff, preparing myself to leave a message when he answers.

'Oh Tim, you're there,' I say, holding back my tears. Yesterday's awful happenings are still reeling around in my head and now everything seems to be getting too much. 'Please come, I'll pay the extra. My basin is leaking again and now the tumble dryer has packed up and to top it all, I've got wet towels in the washing machine and ... oh God,' I say and burst into tears.

There is silence at the other end. Well, you can't blame him can you? I don't imagine he gets many customers blubbering at the end of the phone. I wish my period would come. I must not do anything hasty. This is the worst time to make any kind of decision regarding the future of my salon.

'It's Flo,' I add stupidly.

'I'll be there in ten minutes,' he says.

'You will,' I say, wiping my nose. 'Oh, thanks ...'

I hear the click as he hangs up. He must think I'm a total wreck. I fill a glass with water, take two painkillers and wash my tear-streaked face before dragging my hair up and securing it roughly with a hairband. I then fumble around in the cutlery drawer until I find a screwdriver. I've no intention of stabbing myself if that's what you're thinking. I can think of better ways to end it than death by screwdriver, just in case you're wondering. I unscrew the tumble dryer plug and look at it thoughtfully. I've got no idea what

I'm looking for mind you. Everything looks fine. I fiddle with it a bit and plug it back in, while trying to keep one finger in my ear. Although I suppose the chances of it blowing up twice are pretty unlikely aren't they. I click the switch but nothing happens. I kick it but still nothing.

'That doesn't usually work in my experience,' says a voice behind me.

I hold my breath. Oh my God. I turn and stare at Tom who stands in the doorway. He is holding a toolbox. Why is it every time I see him I look like something that should be stuck in a field to scare the birds?

'I know I'm not Tim but I don't somehow think he's coming,' he says, his expression serious, but I'm sure that's a twinkle in his eyes.

'How do you know about …?'

'I think you got your contacts mixed up. You phoned me instead of Tim.'

Oh no. The whole time I had been blubbering down the phone it had been Tom at the other end. I blush at the memory. How stupid. I could kick myself. Note to self, when phoning plumber in tears make sure you are actually phoning the buggery plumber and not someone with a similar name.

'I know what you did,' I say.

He looks at me and lowers his eyes to my hand and I realise I'm still brandishing the screwdriver.

'You know what I did? That sounds like a good start to a horror movie. You're not thinking of slashing me with that are you?' he nods at the screwdriver.

I lower it and place it on a table.

'I'm premenstrual,' I say in a threatening tone.

'Thanks for warning me. And what is it that I've done exactly that you know about, or think you know about?'

'Are you patronising me?'

'I wouldn't dream of it,' he says casually.

'You'll do anything to get this salon won't you?'

He shakes his head.

'No.'

I grit my teeth.

'Do you want me to look at that tumble dryer? It may just need a fuse.'

My head wobbles between a nod and a shake and I end up shrugging.

'I'll take that as a yes,' he says walking to the dryer.

He smells and looks gorgeous. There is a wonderful fresh soap fragrance emanating from him. He's wearing a thin black top tucked into khaki trousers. He bends to the dryer and I try not to look at his firm thighs.

'You sent Grant Richards here to tell me I had subsidence,' I say accusingly.

'I did no such thing,' he says replacing the fuse. 'In fact Grant is no longer on acquisitions, so he shouldn't have been here at all. He certainly didn't come on my orders.'

'Did you send him to the protest?' I say, fumbling with my hair in an attempt to make it look at least a bit tidy.

He plugs the dryer in and turns it on.

'There, it was the fuse,' he says turning to me. 'Why would you believe Grant Richards over me?'

'Because you've lied to me in the past, that's why.'

He pulls a face and mumbles a long 'Mmm'.

'Not really. I've never lied to you. If I've committed any crime it's not telling you who I was and I admit I should have done that. Instead you found out in the worst way. I regret that, I really do. But Flo…'

'You've played dirty …'

'I haven't. I've been really careful how I handled this whole feud with you. Okay, I sent the flowers, knowing you had an allergy but I knew they wouldn't kill you. Generally, I sent you nice things and gave you loyalty points. Although I'm quite sure Rory's loyalty points were the last thing you wanted. I was trying to wind you up but you were deliberately trying to lose me business.'

I laugh. I cannot believe I'm hearing this. I tried to lose him business. Is he forgetting he's trying to take my salon from me and put both Ryan and Sandy out of work, not to mention me of course?

'You stole my prescription idea,' I say accusingly, feeling my face getting hot.

He nods.

'Yes, I did, but I didn't know it was your idea. Grant suggested it. He never said he got the idea from you. If I'm guilty of anything it was misguidance in who I hired. So, at the end of the day you're right, I stole your idea but it wasn't intentional.'

We stand facing each other and I feel an overwhelming urge to touch him. I cross my arms. I'm barely able to control my emotions.

'Why was Grant at the protest with a two-way radio?'

He lowers his eyes.

'Grant has been arrested for inciting the riot. I think he wanted to get back at me after I took him off acquisitions. I have to admit I wasn't aware of what Grant was doing when he was handling the Church Lane purchase.'

'So everything is Grant Richards fault is it?' I say hotly.

'Flo ...'

'Don't call me Flo,' I say softly, while loving the way he does.

He steps back.

'Have a hot chocolate with me,' he says gently.

'You think a hot chocolate is the answer to everything.'

He grins.

'It does help, especially when you're ...'

'When I'm what?' I snap.

He grimaces.

'You *are* premenstrual,' he says.

Right, that's it. There's nothing worse than a man telling you you're premenstrual when you already sodding know it, is there?

'I'd like you to leave,' I say.

What am I doing? The last thing I want is for him to leave. I'm so muddled. What if he is telling the truth?

'Did you arrange for Grant Richards to come and see me? Was it you behind that shady surveyor?'

He shakes his head.

'I don't work that way, Flo.'

'I don't know what to believe any more,' I say, struggling to hold back tears but feeling them running down my cheeks.

'Please leave,' I say quietly, wanting to be alone where I can let out my emotions and think things through.

'Flo, Rory's don't own the two shops at the side of you. Someone made us a good offer and I accepted it. I don't want the salon, I don't need it. I don't want to make things worse ...'

I point to the door.

'I really can't hear anything else you have to say. You lied to me in the past, how do I know you're not lying now? I can only see you as a two-faced lying bastard.'

He winces. There is a short silence and then he sighs before walking to the door.

'If you change your mind about the hot chocolate I'll be at Heroes. I'll wait an hour.'

The next thing I know there is a tinkle and the door has closed behind him. I rush out the back and burst into tears, which then become hiccupping sobs. I don't know how long I'd been like it when I hear the bell tinkle again. I jump up hoping it is him.

Sandy stands in the salon and stares at me dumbstruck.

'Jesus Flo, what the hell happened? You look bloody awful.'

I feel my whole body shake and allow her to lead me to a chair. She disappears into the kitchenette and I hear the kettle being filled. My head is thumping and I feel sick and to top it all my stomach is cramping. I hear the clatter of crockery and then Sandy returns with two mugs of camomile tea.

'Here, drink this. Christ alive, what the hell ...?' she begins. 'Let me put some geranium oil in the burner. That should calm you.'

I grab a tissue and blow my nose furiously.

'The basin is leaking again and the tumble dryer blew up and I just cracked up. I phoned Tim, at least I thought I was phoning Tim but instead I phoned Tom and ...'

She nods.

'Ah, I see. Drink your tea.'

I watch as she tips two drops of oil into the burner, adds some water and lights a candle.

'He came here, bold as brass, claiming everything was Grant Richard's fault. He'll say anything rather than take the blame. In fact ...'

'Flo, hang on a minute ...'

'I'm beginning to think he was behind those rioters yesterday. It's going to make us look bad in the papers isn't it? We're going to lose all support and then he can get my salon. Although he's still insisting he doesn't want it and that Grant Richards is bitter and ...'

'Flora, stop a minute,' she says, placing her hand over mine.

I exhale heavily. She tells me to take a deep breath and exhale slowly before pulling a letter from her handbag.

'I think you should read this,' she says pushing it into my hand. 'It was delivered this morning by special courier. It could be that you've been wrong about Tom Rory.'

Chapter Forty-Seven

I re-read the letter, trying to make sense of everything.

'I don't understand,' I say finally.

Oh dear God, please don't tell me I've lost the one man I've truly loved and all because of my big mouth.

'He's sold the two shops either side. He obviously didn't want to take the salon from you.'

'It was Grant Richards all along?' I say.

She shrugs.

'I don't know. It points to some kind of misunderstanding doesn't it? The fact is people like Tom don't do everything themselves do they? He'd never sleep. So, perhaps it was all Grant Richards. That would explain why suddenly that other guy is head of acquisitions wouldn't it?'

I look at the letter again and read the offer.

'But whoever now owns the shop is practically giving it away. Terence's shop must be worth at least twice that amount,' I say. 'Who's offering it to you?'

'I've no idea. The solicitors are the nominees for someone who wants to stay anonymous. I'm not going to argue the price. You know what Jeth thinks? He thinks Tom has bought it and this is his way of putting things right. He is offering to sell the shop to me at a knocked down price.'

I stare wide-eyed at her.

'But how would he know you wanted the shop ...?'

I break off at the memory.

'I told him,' I say simply.

'I wondered,' she smiles.

'Over hot chocolate, I said how you'd wanted to buy the video shop and that we had been so excited about working together and ...'

I lower my head into my hands.

'What have I done?' I moan. 'I was so rude to him. Oh Sandy, what do I do?'

She puts an arm around me.

'Why don't you phone him? Ask if you can meet for a chat. Surely it's never too late ...'

'What's the time?' I say jumping up.

'What?'

'He said he would wait an hour for me at Heroes if I wanted to have a hot chocolate with him.'

'Go,' she shouts.

I put a hand to my hair.

'But look at me,' I say, feeling suddenly deflated.

'You look the same as when I arrived. So if he invited you for a hot chocolate then, I don't think he is going to mind very much now. Just go before you run out of time. Brush your hair on the way and put some lippy on.'

I kiss her on the cheek, grab my bag and fly out of the door.

Ten minutes later and I'm sitting in a horrendous traffic jam. I don't believe this. Everything is conspiring against me. I'm destined not to put things right with Tom. I look at the clock on my dashboard. Ten more minutes and the hour will be up. I open the car door and strain to see what's causing the hold up.

'Has there been an accident?' I ask.

'A peaceful demonstration,' says the man in front of me. 'Let's hope it stays that way. Something to do with pensions. A load of OAPs probably.'

Well, that's great isn't it? A protest stops me getting to Tom. Now isn't that ironic. I look at my car and ahead to the gridlock. Right, I've got no choice.

'I've got to run,' I say, 'it's an emergency.'

'But your car,' he shouts after me.

'They can tow it away,' I shout back and start running like my life depends on it. I fumble for my BlackBerry and check the time. I've only got five minutes. I'll never do it. I skirt around the OAPs and their zimmer frames, darting in and out of the crowd with their banners held high. Honestly, I've seen it all now. I pound the pavement like a professional runner, Luke would be proud of me and I find myself smiling at the thought. Then I remember why I'm running and feel my stomach lurch. Please be there, please. My throat burns and my heart is pumping madly. I've no idea what I'm going to say when I see him. I'll most likely collapse at his feet. This is the most exercise I've had in months. I fly around the corner into Portobello Market and stop to catch my breath. What I wouldn't do for Devon's inhaler. I check the BlackBerry again. I'm five minutes past the hour now. Oh God, please make him wait. Finally I'm opposite Heroes. I'm sweating buckets and panting like an asthmatic. I grasp my knees and wait for the stitch in my side to pass. I then check my reflection in my handbag mirror and groan. I look awful. I'm red faced and sweaty. Bits of hair stick to my neck. He'll take one look at me and regret ever inviting me. I run a comb through my hair, wipe some lipstick across my lips and walk towards the entrance. I open the door and look around. I can't see him. I walk further into the coffee shop and scan the back. There is no sign of him. My shoulders slump and I fight back the tears. It serves me right. I should have trusted him. Perhaps he changed his mind. I wouldn't blame him. I check my BlackBerry. I'm ten minutes over the hour. I don't believe it. He didn't wait one extra minute for me. I walk tiredly to the door and step aside for a couple as they squeeze through the door all arm in arm and over each other. As I do so, I turn and see him coming out of the loo. He sees me and raises his eyebrows and sits at the same table we had sat at only a few weeks ago. He meets my eyes. His face is serious. He's probably regretting asking me already. He lifts a hand to the waitress.

'Two more hot chocolates,' he says. 'One with just white marshmallows, and can we have them on the side and not on the cream?'

She writes down the order and as she moves away he nods at the chair opposite him. I sit down gingerly, feeling my head thump.

'I'm glad you came,' he says softly.

'You are?' I say, relief flooding my body. I almost sway off my seat.

'Of course.'

I take a deep breath.

'I'm sorry I swore at you,' I say quietly.

'You yelled at me too.'

'Yes, I'm sorry about that. I'm a bit ...'

'Premenstrual?' he smiles.

I nod.

'As long as you left the screwdriver at the salon,' he says with a grin.

I feel myself relax. The waitress returns with the hot chocolate and I sip it, grateful for some time to form my thoughts.

'Sandy came by just after you left.'

He doesn't speak.

'She's been given first refusal on the video shop. What you said about selling the shops was true.'

'Everything I've said is true.'

I bite my lip.

'Did you buy the shops? Anonymously?'

He looks thoughtful. I wait patiently. He sips his hot chocolate before nodding.

'It was the only way I could put things right Flo. I knew I'd lost you but I wanted you to be happy. There's a letter, probably at your flat right now, offering you the newsagents, so you can extend the salon. I had hoped that was why you phoned me ...'

His knee touches mine and my whole body jerks with the force of my emotions. I don't move my knee and neither does he.

'Why didn't you tell me the truth?' I ask.

'I tried to, so many times. I didn't want you to think badly of me. It's funny that isn't it? Considering how much you hate me now. I don't play the victim very well, I'm afraid.'

'I don't hate you,' I say gently.

I so don't hate you, I think, wanting so much to touch him.

'I'd never have guessed,' he smiles.

I lower my head and fiddle with a marshmallow.

'It wasn't me, you know, the riot...'

'I know that. That's why you were arrested before the others. I didn't want you to get hurt.'

'I've been stupid ...' I begin.

'I can't argue with that,' he says, deliberately brushing his knee against mine and looking into my eyes.

'The protest ... I'm so sorry. It was meant to be peaceful.'

,He nods solemnly.

'Sounds like your mum needs tighter control.'

I look seriously at him.

'No, she ...'

He grins and I sigh with relief.

I reach my hand out across the table and he covers it with his. I feel the warmth of him and shiver.

'Are you cold?' he asks.

I shake my head.

Me with a millionaire, who'd have thought it? My mum will be over the moon when I tell her. Someone clicks on the jukebox and suddenly *Tonight's gonna be a good night* begins to play. His eyes light up.

'They're playing our song,' he says, helping himself to one of my marshmallows. 'Fancy a game of cards?'

'What here?' I smile.

'I've never shown you my house have I?' he says, lifting my hand to his lips. 'How about a game of gin rummy? The loser buys dinner.'

'As long as your sheep-shagging rugby boyos aren't there,' I laugh.

'Does this mean you're surrendering?' he asks huskily.

It's all I can do not to rip my clothes off there and then. I wonder if I have time to go back and get the flogger.

'Absolutely' I say softly.

'Wonderful,' he says.

He then rubs his foot up my thigh.

'Let's go home then,' he says taking my hand.

I take it gratefully, thinking still time to be engaged before I'm thirty-one.